THE REDMADAFA

THE REDMADAFA

(The River of Life)

Pronounced Red-maw-da-faw

To understand this book, and follow along with
its meaning,
read Ezekiel chapter 17.

Dr. Gary Warren Foshee

ELM HILL

A Division of
HarperCollins Christian Publishing

www.elmhillbooks.com

THE REDMADAFA

Published in Nashville, Tennessee, by Elm Hill, an imprint of Thomas Nelson. Elm Hill and Thomas Nelson are registered trademarks of HarperCollins Christian Publishing, Inc.

Elm Hill titles may be purchased in bulk for educational, business, fund-raising, or sales promotional use. For information, please e-mail SpecialMarkets@ThomasNelson.com.

Publisher's Note: This novel is a work of fiction. Names, characters, places, and incidents are either products of the author's imagination or used fictitiously. All characters are fictional, and any similarity to people living or dead is purely coincidental.

All Scripture quotations, unless otherwise indicated, are taken from the King James Version. Public domain.

All Biblical quotations and references are taken from the King James Bible.

Library of Congress Cataloging-in-Publication Data

Library of Congress Control Number: 2018948424

ISBN 978-1-595558619 (Paperback)
ISBN 978-1-595558749 (Hardbound)
ISBN 978-1-595558848 (eBook)

This book is dedicated to:

The Royal Rangers

(Kids who are—Alert, Clean, Honest, Courageous, Loyal, Courteous, Obedient, and Spiritual)

and

The Sheppard family: The God inside you set me free.

CONTENTS

There was a time when people rose up,
Against the darkness they feared so much;
To bring light again and restore the earth
And break the power of the evil curse.
That time is now, the person is you;
As you read this book, you'll be told what
to do.

INTRODUCTION

The heavens had changed ever since the fall of the garden serpent and the first humans. Disobedience on earth led some to question His Majesty's authority throughout the universe. If mankind could disobey his orders, what was stopping the angels? Enticed by the daughters of men, the smoothness of their dark skin and the gentle caress of their smile, multitudes of angels partook of a forbidden fruit called—lust. Under the cover of darkness, they secretly mixed heavenly bloodlines with human bringing forth giants on earth that, unknowingly, sparked a rebellion in the heavens and on earth, which ended up corrupting every thought of angel, man, and beast. Mageddon was the first to fall. His lust to control trade on earth and his desire for love and supreme power finally brought about his demise.

CHAPTER 1

MOUNT VIPER

That which stands between you and Him

The giant hunchbacked troll moved into the rocky path laden with snow. Glaring into its three eyes along the length of a dark-ribbed arrow, Caboose drew a long deep breath. His arm, throbbing with pain from being grazed by its club, strained to hold the arrow steady. Concentrating on the middle eye and not his bloodied, frostbitten fingers, he launched the vile rod with dingy yellow feathers and a pointy flint, through the trees. Jostled slightly by the wind, the arrow hummed through the forest, threaded a narrow gap, and plunged into the troll's left eye causing the hairy brute to rear back with a thunderous roar. Caboose cringed. He cupped his hands over his ears as the deafening blast pulsed by him. The wanton creature pulled the arrow from its gooey socket—the eye still attached to the tip of the arrowhead—and scanned the forest for him. Furious and in pain, the troll swung its club, shattering everything in its path before giving several loud nostril snorts.

Caboose jumped over a log and crashed through the top layer of ice concealed by a layer of snow, giving away his position. Hearing the crunch, the beast turned and batted a boulder lying on the ground in front of it toward him. Caboose harnessed the bow around his neck, spun it to his back and dropped to all fours as a barrage of wooden shanks hounded after him; he ran through the forest leaping and bounding. The boulder blasted through several trees, flew over his head, and crashed into the trunk of a Titan tree. Large seams raced up its sides all the way to its top far above the forest canopy. Its base cracked. Its middle buckled. The tree swayed back and then toppled forward bringing half the forest down with it. With nowhere to run, Caboose dove against the boulder and curled into a tight ball as chunks of bark, branches, and timber showered down upon him from above.

Caboose lie motionless wondering if he was still alive. A sallow cloud swirled above the shattered remains, which looked more like a ravaged battlefield than a forest. Muffled cracks and pops drummed a steady beat around him. Off in the distance, a large mound rose from the debris as the troll stood to its feet and shook its self off. A chunk of wood, approximately the size of a small thunder beast tail, splintered the hunch in its back. Unable to dislodge it with its stubby arms, it sniffed the air and started toward him.

Caboose opened his eyes. He moved his shoulder and groaned. Feeling the tremors of the troll drawing close, he dare not move. The beast stopped a few yards from him and sniffed again. With the stench of rotten flesh and sweat permeating the air, Caboose gagged. He looked up through the shattered pieces and remained still as he watched its frosty breath crystallize mid-air over him. He reached for the sword strapped to his side and pulled it from it scabbard. Catching its sheen, the troll swung its club and shattered the pile missing Caboose by inches. It raised the club high above its head again and smashed it down imprinting a deep crater in the ground.

Caboose froze. He watched the club take aim for his head and then rolled inward scuffing up against the troll's foot, causing it to miss again. He scurried to his feet and chopped a gash into its ankle, triggering the beast to teeter left, missing him again. Caboose ran behind a tree trying to avoid its baleful rage. Enraged and bleeding, the beast reached down and grabbed his tail. Lifting him high off the ground, it whisked him back and forth like a crocodile, ripping flesh from a five-day-old carcass.

"Help! Help!" shouted Caboose, wedged in its powerful grasp. He swung trying to cut himself free but lost his grip causing his crude sword to flip repeatedly before plunging tip-first into its hairy foot. The troll roared before launching Caboose high into the sky. With a torrent of wind beating against his face and the clouds drawing close, Caboose screamed.

"Caboose, wake up," whispered Pepper, shaking him softly. "Get up or you're gonna be late for school again."

Caboose, still mumbling in his sleep and tossing about in bed, opened his eyes with a gasp. He raised straight up placing his hands at his side as if to brace from falling.

"Help!" he shouted.

"Help you?" responded Pepper, with an odd look on her face.

"I'm not going to be late because you couldn't get your lazy tail out of bed again," she replied, walking out the door.

Caboose wobbled down the street with a vacant gaze sprawled across his face. Small leather-bound books jostled in sea-green hands as he hurried to beat the ram's horn. He skidded around the corner almost wiping out a caravan on its way to market and then weaved through several carts and wagons. With his mind focused on not being late again, he forgot about the enormous log (he called a tail), swinging behind him; it collided into several wagons sending mushy marts, apple fritters and fig cakes toppling into the air—they soared high into the air before splattering all over the people. Oblivious to his clumsiness and the shrieks being cast at him, he raced across the street to school.

The schoolyard was empty. Soft crimson leaves with frayed edges and lightened apricot centers scampered across velvety blades-of-green standing on end. Driven by the wind, they assembled in small mounds on the steps before running from the wind whistler who was marching to his own tune across town. High above the backdrop of the mountains to the North, lightening flashed against the horizon. The scent of rain filled the valley approaching town and the smell of threshed grain from the mill carried in the branches above.

Caboose hurried to the door and jerked it open. The large bronze door, its hinges recently lubricated with jojoba, swung wide toward him, hitting him in the face. His head bounced backwards hitting the wall and was followed by a loud "thud," which quickly changed his casual expression. He nodded at Brook and the other girls walking by acting as if nothing had happened, but it was too late. Faint chuckles escaped from their mouths as they looked at each other with widened-eyes. Embarrassed, he watched them disappear into the herd of students shuffling down the hallway. Caboose shook his head and followed—the door closed on his tail.

This is going to be a long day, he thought.

Koby Puller, a.k.a. Caboose, was your typical teenage Unidor. He had a long tail, medium-sized arms and hands, green leathery skin, two huge legs, and a single horn protruding from his forehead. Everyone called him Caboose because he poked around and was typically late. He was tall for his age and overweight, which made him an easy target for bullies. But he wasn't afraid of them. He just didn't want to hurt anyone, or at least that's what he told himself.

Caboose had multiple ambitions in life, ambitions that drove him hard to be the best, better than everyone else. He had one that topped them all—but he dare not talk about it with his Papa. Like most boys his age, his Papa expected him to follow in his footsteps and carry on the family business. He, on the other hand, had no such plans. He had secret ambitions of being a racer, and not just any racer. His dreamed of racing in *The Little Round About,* the biggest race on the circle. To win brought fame, fortune, and recognition, things all boys desire. Caboose spent hours in the valleys and hills outside of town training. He ran small alpine trails. He swung from vines hanging from the trees. He jumped over logs, boulders and creeks. He even practiced running on all fours—unidors can drop down and use their hands like creatures with four legs. But no matter how hard he trained, he wasn't fast enough.

Caboose wobbled when he ran, making his stride off-balance and unable to obtain the speed needed to qualify. Some said he had a hip problem. Others said that he had been punished by the gods for the sins of his family. His mother told him His Majesty had touched him for a special purpose. But Caboose just told everyone he had a short leg. He used it as an excuse to feel sorry for himself and to blame others if things didn't go his way.

Caboose lived in Thunder Juice Town, a large town filled with merchants and traders. Life in "Old Juicy," as everyone liked to call her, was fast paced. Anyone and everyone could be found there; unidors, moogles (large hairy creatures that lived on land and in trees), thunder beasts (giant reptilian creatures), and humans—all kinds of beasts and creatures. There was no better place to buy and sell than Old Juicy.

In the middle of town, near the square, was an enormous outdoor market. Every day hundreds of vendors and travelers packed into bustling streets to buy and sell fresh goods from local and distant lands. Caboose loved walking through the markets. It was exciting to see so much activity—the smell of fresh baked breads and pies was an added bonus. He liked the thrill of discovering new things and he was always up for an adventure. Each journey into the markets was like a voyage on the high seas. There was always something new, something unfamiliar, something exotic that he hadn't seen before waiting to be discovered. His favorite thing to do after school was to sit around the fountain. He sat there for hours watching travelers from all over the circle barter and trade, or gamble bones and knuckle fight.

Hand-hewn idols, sparkling trinkets, clay pottery, silk garments made from raspy crickets, and other exotic cargo was sold in shops along the outskirts of the market. Spices, grains, baked delicacies, and mouth-puckering tart treats were all available for sale off the backs of carts near the interior—spices including: cumin; fennel; cinnamon; apple mint; paradise grain; orrisroot and spikenard. Grains such as: buckwheat; rye; flaxseed; millet and sorghum were among the favorites. Since this was his last year of school, Caboose used the markets as a crossroad for future job prospects. As most teenagers, he was still searching for his purpose and mission in life.

A perimeter defensive wall seven cubic's wide and made of rough stones quarried from the mountains, encompassed the town. The different-sized stones lined with battlements on top, contained several secret passageways and caches. Positioned at each entrance were gatehouse towers with keyhole arrow slits cut into the front and sides. The towers stood guard over eight gates spread out evenly around the wall. Engraved high on each side of the gates was the head of an eagle—each head slanted toward the gate as if keeping watch upon all who entered. Smaller drum towers fortified the mid-sections of the wall while taller turrets adorned the corners; each tower quartered guards, sculleries, and an armory stockpiled with weapons and armor.

Outside the walls, meadows of mantled flowers rolled gently up the base of the mountains. Honeysuckle vines draped over bushes and thickets in the foothills filling the air with a sweet fresh aroma; the delightful smell coddled travels and soothed the soul. Attracted by the colorful blooms filled with sugary nectar, swarms of honey-buzzers (bees) and hummers (humming birds) waltzed from bloom to bloom drinking their fill of the delicious bounty.

Tributaries, formed by deep bubbling underground springs, flowed in the valleys between rows of shady knolls. Fresh water streams and lakes teaming with life nourished fields crowned with wheat, barley, and rye. Rows of olive trees covered the hill outside the eastern gate and large groves of fruit trees lined the river and streams like plagues of desert locust moving across the plains. Tribal villages spread out across the countryside and smaller towns and clans rested across the river, mountains, and plains, each one a haven for travelers on their way to Thunder Juice Town.

Thunder Juice Town was located by a majestic river called *The Redmadafa*. It was the source of life for all living things and the treasure of Thunder Juice Town and its residents. Its headwaters miraculously started from a split rock under the threshold of *The Gallery*, the temple where people worshipped a Mighty Warrior Eagle. People traveled great distances to see the split rock from which it flowed—it truly was a miracle. At the temple, the water was ankle deep; a little further it was knee-deep; then waist high, until finally becoming a mighty river that no one could cross.

Caboose walked over to his locker and opened it. The small cubby hole, which bore into the wall, looked more like a storefront in the market than it did a place for books. Small trinkets and several of his favorite snacks cluttered the tiny space. He reached in, grabbed a mushy mart and took a bite. He made space for a book, took a couple out, and then slammed the door shut without locking it; there was no need, a fist-sized hole caved through the middle.

Caboose walked down the hallway on his way to class and was struck in the shoulder by a large moogle. He looked back expecting an 'excuse me' or any gesture that would acknowledge his existence but the moogle never broke pace. Caboose was more of a people watcher than a people talker but that didn't mean you could treat him as if he wasn't there. He rounded the corner on his way to Herbs and Plants, and glimpsed Mack and Oka standing by the stairs, which were in need of repair. The old weathered boards split in the middle and sunk low when stepped on.

Mack looked at Oka, a young lad with a thick head of thatched red hair, and nodded his head toward Rammer, the new kid from Junction Point. Oka stepped in front of him and slapped his books out of his hands. The books slid across the hallway and slammed against the wall. Oka wacked his head and moved it side to side trying to get a reaction, but Rammer wasn't impressed.

Rammer looked Oka over and sighed. He noticed Mack, the leader of the lixoar gang, which consisted of himself and four others, waiting for him to make a move—lixoars are meat-eating thunder beasts that stick to their own kind. He knew now was not the time or place to deal with them.

Caboose walked over by the books.

"Hey Caboose, you been drinking Thunder Juice again? You sure are walking funny," said Mack.

Caboose didn't say anything. He reached down to pick up the books but Oka stepped on top of them and slid them down the hall.

"Hey boys, I heard Caboose and Patches are going to the dance together," laughed Mack, leaning against the wall.

"Patches wouldn't be caught with a dead beat like Caboo-boo. Her locking rocks aren't that thick," rattled Oka.

Caboose couldn't pass on that one. He turned around and wisecracked, "You're real funny, Oka. You know, I was going to take her but she said she was already going with you."

Mack looked at the others standing by him, "Now that's funny."

"Is th-th-th-that right," stuttered Oka. "We'll see how fa-fa-fa-funny you are at lunch. Meet me behind the wood shop and da-da-don't be late."

Oka stuttered when nervous. His self-confidence couldn't take the embarrassment of being challenged by Caboose.

Rammer, a medium-sized unidor, strolled over and picked up his books. Everyone laughed at Oka and then headed for class.

The ram's horn sounded marshaling everyone into class. Caboose toddled into the room with his head held low. He passed the teacher's desk and sat down.

Whispers resounded chair to chair.

Heads turned aside.

Caboose pulled out his writing pad and scribbled a drawing of a tree. His heart raced with the thought of fighting Oka at lunch.

Why didn't I just keep my big mouth shut? he thought. Caboose had a temper, that when triggered, would put him in awkward situations. And he didn't like to fight. He was big and strong, although he had yet to truly discover his inner strength, and he was afraid if he hit someone he would hurt him.

The windows in the classroom faced the tree line leading down to the banks of The Redmadafa. Class projects lined the walls and herb experiments filled transparent jars along the windowsill. A cool gentle breeze blew across the room ruffling writing pads and pushing dust clouds along the floor—they slammed against the wall and crashed back down, brown-washing the floor.

"Hey," echoed a whisper behind Caboose. "Are you really going to fight Oka at lunch?" asked Zoan. Zoan had known Caboose since the sixth grade. He was real smart but not very athletic.

"I'm not fighting anyone. Besides, without Mack and the others, Oka wouldn't be as boastful as he is."

The teacher, a medium-sized herbivore with maroon strips on his body, glanced their way. He hesitated while Zoan slid back in his chair, and then continued his lecture on which plants were eatable and which ones have natural healing properties good for cuts, wounds, and digestion.

Zoan leaned forward again. "You better pay close attention to this. You're gonna need it."

Caboose didn't respond. He didn't even want to think about it. He just wanted to be left alone. Caboose, for the most part, was quiet. He minded his own business and tried to get along with everyone. He helped others when he could and was an over-all nice guy. He loved doing things with his Papa and, to his little sister, he was the greatest.

The horn sounded signaling lunch. Zoan jumped out of his seat, slapped Caboose on the back and sarcastically gave an encouraging word; "Don't worry Caboose. It only takes five days for a black eye to heal; I'm not sure though about a cracked rib."

Caboose rolled his eyes and proceeded outside wondering how he was going to avoid Mack and Oka. He paced around the schoolyard, too nervous to eat his lunch. He stayed as far away as he could from the wood shack. He saw several people gathered around the back of it so he stayed by the water hole.

After several minutes of waiting, Mack, Oka, and the rest of the gang funneled out from behind the wood shack and searched the grounds. They circled several of the trees towering over the schoolyard before Mack spotted him by the water hole—the others quickly closed in.

"I knew you weren't much of a unidor Caboose, but I didn't realize you were a squealer too," said Oka. "You know what. I bet you're not even full-blooded. I bet you were adopted and your real Papa was a lopsided bush squealer."

Everyone laughed. Bush squealers were unclean brutes unable to speak.

"Don't you have better things to do than make fun of people?"

"Make fun of people," gestured Oka. "I don't make fun of people. I just make fun of you Ca-boo-boo."

"You wouldn't be so eager to fight if Mack wasn't standing behind you."

Mack stepped out from behind him and laughed.

Oka smiled, "Is that better."

Oka stepped forward.

Their eyes locked.

A crowd gathered around and waited. Mr. Sunka looked up from his desk and then proceeded outside.

Rammer pushed his way through the crowd and watched from a distance.

"You're never gonna amount to anything. In a few years we'll see you hobbling around begging at the gates."

"You don't want to do this," said Caboose balling his fists.

Oka lunged forward pushing Caboose back. Caboose surprisingly remained calm but within his anger boiled.

"Oh yeah. And what are you gonna do about it?"

Oka jabbed with his left.

Caboose caught it with his right, twisted it 'round, and planted his elbow on the left side of his nose. Blood splattered through the air landing on those closest to the fight.

Oka couldn't see. Water from the impact glossed his eyes causing him to panic and swing aimlessly.

Caboose dodged the shadow boxing and came in low gut-shoting him three times. Oka sank down into a half crouch, huffing in pain, just as Caboose finished him off with an upper cut knocking him into the crowd.

Mack, not wanting his gang to look foolish, nodded.

A lixoar ambushed Caboose from behind with a blow to the back of his head crashing him into a human girl holding her lunch, knocking her back into the crowd.

His anger spiked.

He spun around wind-milling his knuckles up against the jaw of the lixoar. When he did, his tail knocked Mack off his feet, plunging him face first into the mud.

The crowd gasped.

Oka and the others froze.

Furious and humiliated, Mack sprung from the mud and grabbed Caboose by the throat.

Caboose drew back to swing but was bombarded by Oka and the rest of the gang. They hit and kicked him several times before Mr. Sunka emerged through the crowd and broke up the fight sending them all to the principal's office.

Rammer un-balled his fists and breathed a sigh of relief. He was inches from Oka just about to cave-in the back of his mangled head.

* * * * * * *

"Hey Brook," said Rachael, sliding on the lunch bench slamming her in the side. Rachael peeked over her shoulder at the few nibbles missing from her sandwich.

"Hi, Rachael," responded Brook, looking up with heavy eyes burrowed into a pale gaunt face fair as the moon. Choppy cherry-brown hair with curled split ends drooped past her ears; a small strand curved down over her eye and rested upon cracked lips entrenched with thin lines. Brook was sick but not in the usual way. She is bulimic. After she eats, she goes to the bathroom and throws up.

Why?

She thought she was fat and ugly. Over the past year, she's lost 35 pounds and was losing strength. Her cheekbones protrude through her face and her body was slowly wasting away from malnutrition. Brook's father left the family several years ago and now her mom had to work two jobs just to keep food on the table.

Brook was a daddy's girl growing up. She painted his fingernails, brushed his hair, and entertained him with cinnamon tea parties. Every Saturday, he carried her on his shoulders to the market and bought her the most beautiful dolls with colorful woven cotton dresses embroidered with white lace. She spent hours in her bedroom fixing their hair, rocking them to sleep, and pushing them around the house in a little red carriage telling them how pretty they were.

Everything was different now that her parents were divorced. She use to love being around friends at school and always had sleep-overs. Not anymore. Now she stuck to herself and was consoled by writing in her diary.

"Are you going to temple tonight?"

"Temple? Tonight? No, I…need to clean my room and…get caught up on homework."

"That's too bad. We're going to have a special youth service tonight at temple. Traeger the howler is going to be speaking."

How many times do I have to tell her 'no' before she stops bugging me about temple? thought Brook. "Oh yeah, I've heard of him," she said, trying to be polite.

"Brad is going to be there." Brook liked Brad—she had had a crush on him since the 5th grade. "I will be by at six to pick you up," zipped Rachael, polishing off her lunch in record time.

"But, I already told you—"

"It's Friday. Nobody does homework on Friday. See you at six."

"But—"

Rachael whizzed outside and out of site. Rachael was no ordinary girl. She had been created by His Majesty to do Great

Things. Her family were shepherds, temple servants; servants that had served sacrificially for years, never expecting anything in return. At times, many in the community and the temple had even mistreated them, but their hearts were not of this circle. They never lost focus of what they knew they had been created for. It was because of them, that many had called out his name.

* * * * * * *

Caboose sat nervously outside Mr. Hammer's office—who had a reputation of living up to his name. Caboose studied the floor trying to think of the best way to explain his current situation. His ears twitched toward the door, listening to the intense scolding Mr. Hammer gave Mack and Oka. Caboose wiped his mouth and looked at his finger.

Blood traced the edge.

He licked it off.

Silence retreated as the thick oak door with a black cast iron handle opened. Heavy trodden footsteps marked Mack and Oka's brutish departure—scowled eyes telegraphed retribution.

Caboose looked up and then down again. He breathed deeply, exhaled, and then stood up. How was he going to explain this to his Papa? Being the son of a Temple Elder, he was expected to set the example and stay out of trouble.

Caboose plodded into the office and shut the door.

Mr. Hammer's office was a collection of exotic arts and crafts from all over the circle. He loved trading in the market and he had a weakness for shiny silver things; he loved showing off his collection to everyone that visited his office—under favorable conditions of course.

Mr. Hammer looked through Cabooses file, closed it, and then looked up.

"Koby, why are you here?"

Caboose looked puzzled and didn't know how to respond. He folded his hands, "Mr. Sunka said I had—"

"I know that," interrupted Mr. Hammer. "I'm asking you. 'Why are *you* here?' You are better than this."

Caboose dropped his head and looked at the floor.

"You must learn to control your anger, even when you have every right to be angry. If you are overcome by the simple, you will never stand against the great."

Caboose thought for a moment. Unsure about a response, he shrugged his shoulders. "I expect more from you. Next time, I want you to think before you act. Pride brings about shame but with humility comes wisdom."

"Am I supposed to stand there and be the brunt of their jokes every day Mr. Hammer?" he said with a smug look. "I'm sorry, but I can only take so much. I know I'm different. But I'm tired of everyone always expecting me to be someone that I'm not."

"I'm not expecting you to be anyone but yourself. But I do expect you to follow the rules and to treat others the way you would like to be treated. Koby, I'm sorry but I am going to have to suspend you for three days. I want you to wait outside my office until your Dad comes to pick you up."

Caboose stormed out of the office, down the hallway and out the front doors. He ran across the schoolyard and through the woods all the way to The Redmadafa. Down by the river he sat venting his anger. He didn't want to go home and tell his parents, but he didn't know what else to do.

Caboose lived a good life. His parents loved him very much and his father was always there for him. He enjoyed going down to the river with his family and swinging on the twisted vines hanging from the trees—he could swing way out and soak everyone on the bank with his enormous splash—his swimming abilities, on the other hand, were questionable.

Hearing the commotion, Toby and Tyku swam over and looked up through the water. "Hello Caboose," bubbled voices from the water.

"Hi Toby, Tyku," answered Caboose in a gruff tone.

Toby and Tyku were Bugler fish that lived in The Redmadafa. They're called bugler fish because their mouths are shaped like bugles. Every morning down on the river at dawn, you can hear them and thousands of others playing wonderful musical ensembles. Bugler fish talk through bubbles. They speak underwater and words rise in the bubbles. When their bubbles reach the surface "Pop, pop, pop," out come the words.

"Caboose, why are you so upset, did something happen at school?"

"It's not me, Toby, its Mack and Oka…and my leg. They're always running their mouths. They said I was adopted and my real Papa was a lopsided bush squealer," said Caboose, looking for an answer that would shift the blame and bring him sympathy.

"Mack is nothing but a flibbertigibbet," said Toby. "You can't believe a word coming out of his slimy mouth."

"Caboose, why do you let that bother you? You know that's not true," replied Tyku.

"It doesn't matter. I'm not like them. I'm different."

"Of course you are. There is only one Caboose in this great big circle and he is wonderfully and fearfully made."

"Fearfully made, you see, I told you I was different."

"No Caboose. Fearfully made means, *when* you were created,

The Augur created you for a special purpose and designed you to do great things," bubbled Toby.

"I don't believe that and I don't believe in The Augur. Besides, even if he was real, he obviously doesn't know what he's doing," grumbled Caboose referring to his short leg. "Great Things, I can't even run in the Little Round About. How can I do, *Great Things*?"

Tyku remained silent. Those words had once echoed from his own past. He remembered when times were tough and he blamed The Augur for all the troubles he had endured. "Things don't always happen the way you want, Caboose," responded Tyku finally gathering his thoughts.

"They sure don't. For me, they don't ever happen the way I want them too," snapped Caboose.

"I waited patiently for him to lift me out of the muddy dried-up pool of water I was in," replied Tyku. "He came for me and brought me to The Redmadafa. He placed a new song in my mouth, and ever since that day, I have played a new melody."

Toby swam around and jumped out of the water. "Caboose, you have a great family that loves you very much. I know many people that wished they had a Dad like yours."

"Great things...you know; I think you may be right."

"Good, I'm glad you are feeling better," answered Toby feeling good that his words of wisdom had helped.

"Yes, I'll show everyone. I'm gonna find the gate everyone talks about. That will be something great."

Stunned, Toby stuttered, "Caboose, I don't think that's a good idea."

"Good idea? That's a *great* idea," voiced Caboose, feeling confident about his decision. "My mind is made up. I'm going to find that gate if it is the last thing I do."

"Caboose, don't go. Come back!" yelled Tyku. "It may very well be the last thing you ever do." It was too late. Caboose faded from the bank and out of site.

Caboose set off in search of a gate that the younglings sang about at school. At recess, the younglings played hop-addy-hop on rocks and sang:

"Over the mountains, over the hills,
through the valley, better watch your heels;
Diamonds and pearls, gold and fate,
there you will find a magical gate.
Listen to the air, listen for the click,
better beware, or you'll be tricked."

He didn't know where the gate was but he didn't care, he was tired of Mack and the lixoars and he really wanted to do something great. Trying to find the gate sounded like an adventure too good to pass up.

Caboose was in no hurry to embark on his spontaneous quest. He dawdled through town using back alleys and deserted streets to remain unseen. He avoided the markets not wanting to run into anyone from the temple that might recognize him. He skirted the shaded arches of the central square and took to the tree line behind the university. He followed a narrow dirt path that sloped underneath an aqueduct around to a canal and came out not far from the gatehouse on the north side of town.

Trudging up the stairs he noticed the afternoon sky rapidly changing. Herds of clumped blueberries tiptoed across the sky crowning the mountains in a dark veneer; the drowsy canal underneath him reflected raspberry as blue mixed with red and dimly rippled downstream.

"I cut off your hand," shouted a brittle voice bounding down the steps.

"No you didn't. I already chopped off your arms," argued another youngling whizzing pass him dueling valiantly with a stubby wooden sword.

Caboose stepped to the side and smiled. He envied their joyful enthusiasm. A light drizzle squelched the moment as the pitter-patter of raindrops cadenced the anger still throbbing inside his chest.

At the top of the steps, sitting on a small stool underneath a ramshackle roof held up by two flimsy poles that looked like they would collapse at the slightest touch, was a plum-cheeked old woman with bushy grey eyebrows and crow's feet furrowed deep beside her eyes.

She looked up.

Stacked in bundles at her side and feet, were thin amber stalks of wheat—she ground them slowly on a small quern into flour. The stone quern had a notch on the bottom edge of the upper handstone that "clicked" every pass as she turned the wooden handle. Little creep tails scurried beneath the bundles as if they were listening to the tune she hummed quietly to herself.

For a brief moment, their eyes locked. It was like he could hear her speaking to him—"*Don't do it…Stop…Turn around before it's too late…*" He paid the voices no heed.

Caboose blended in with a large caravan of vagabonds leaving town after a brutal day of trading in the markets. He passed under the gate with his head low making sure not to make eye contact with the guards posted above. He knew this was his last chance to turn around. Exiting the gate, he looked back at the eagle's head mounted high on the wall. He thought for sure it had twisted toward him.

That's strange he thought. He shrugged it off and disappeared down the road drifting out of sight.

* * * * * * *

The ram's horn sounded ending another long day of school. Pepper, Caboose's little sister, collected her things, straightened up her writing tablets, and pushed her chair under the table, then waited in line as everyone bustled about, scrambling to get their leaf packs.

Pepper bounded outside in her own, little world. She knew Caboose was in big trouble but was surprised to see her Papa still waiting outside. She said goodbye to a couple of friends and ran over to greet him.

"How was school today princess?"

"Fine Papa, how is Caboose? I heard it really wasn't his fault that he got in a fight with Mack and Oka, and he got suspended."

"What! He got suspended?"

"Ah…oh, I thought you already knew," she hesitantly replied, confused about the matter.

"No, I haven't seen him."

"That's strange he left school after lunch. Didn't Mr. Hammer send you a wing message?"

"I did receive a message that he needed to speak with me, but I was delayed at work. Why don't you walk home with Helio and Splint? I need to have a talk with Mr. Hammer."

Disturbed and concerned about his son, Chesty plodded up the stairs and proceeded down the hallway to the principal's office. Vague memories flooded his mind of times past. He remembered walking the long hallways, which echoed softly with each step, when he was young. He also remembered visiting the principal's office on more than one occasion himself.

Chesty spotted Mr. Hammer coming out of a classroom.

"Mr. Hammer, do you have a second?"

Mr. Hammer slowed his pace. "Chesty, good to see you again. I sent you a message, did you get?"

"Yes, I got it. Sorry I took so long. I was detained at work."

"Don't be too hard on him—I know it wasn't his fault. Mack and the lixoars are always getting into trouble. I hated to suspend Caboose, but school policy is no fighting."

"I understand. I will talk with him when he gets home. Do you know where he is?"

"No. I told him to wait outside my office until you arrived. I assumed you had already picked him up."

"He probably went home. I'm sure he's already there."

"Please let me know when you find him."

"I'll let you know."

Splint's belly churned at the smell of fresh baked bread wafting down the old cobble-stoned street. He searched his pockets for a few spare coins only to find a secret tunnel leading covertly to his leg. His finger slipped through the hole igniting the attack. Hunger bugs, salivating intensely in his belly from the intoxicating aroma of fresh bread, launched three-pronged grappling hooks, which attached to the upper cavity of his stomach. In protest, they kamikazed through the protective layer of mucus and splattered themselves against his inner stomach lining.

Splint buckled over in pain and grabbed his side.

"Hey, can I borrow two tachmas?" he asked Helio.

Helio, completely ignoring Splint, seemed to be on another

circle as he observed the town's people busy with their daily excursions. The outdoor market was filled with carpenters, builders, masons, stonecutters, miners and lots of foreigners buying and trading goods. Old wooden hoof-drawn carts lined the streets and alleys; fresh herbs, vegetables, greens, spices, and all kinds of baked pies and breads lined the bottoms of carts, crates, and storefronts.

"I don't have any coins," responded Helio quietly, not wanting to alert his hunger bugs to their own misfortunes.

Splint, realizing his hopes of fresh baked bread would have to wait until he got home jabbed Pepper in her side and asked, "Did you see your brother take out Mack today?"

"I'm so glad someone finally stood up to Mack," piggy-backed Helio.

Pepper, with a fiendish look on her face from the unexpected jab, replied, "No. I can't believe he actually fought him. That's not like my brother to get into a fight." Pepper searched her thoughts. She wondered what could possibly have driven Caboose to fight Mack and Oka. Then again, she had witnessed his anger first hand.

"I don't think he meant too," said Splint. "Mack and Oka were bullying Caboose at lunch after he failed to meet Oka behind the wood shop. Oka pushed him and took a swing. Caboose blocked it and made his nose match the color of his hair. Then one of the lixoars bashed him from behind causing Caboose to crash into a girl holding her lunch—it splattered all over the crowd, it was great. Caboose turned as red as an apple-stick on the fire…I've never seen him so mad before.

When he reeled around his tail accidently knocked Mack right off his feet, flinging him face first right into the mud."

"It was the funniest thing I've ever seen," said Helio.

Splint smiled and looked up toward the sky. "He's my hero. Anyway, Mack got up and they all beat the tar out of him after that."

Pepper didn't respond. Her eyes told the story of a little sister that loved her brother and the concern she had for him. Like most little sisters, she blew everything way out of proportion when it came to her big brother and his mischievous ways. She placed her thumbs underneath her pack straps. "That's not like my brother."

CHAPTER 2

THE TEMPLE

Better is the end than the beginning.

Chesty hurried home. A hundred different things raced through his mind as he walked down the road past *Feathered Friends Gatehouse* and then around the square. He cut through the alley behind the markets and came out across from the stables. The thoroughfare was crowded with people and creatures strolling with small bundles tucked under arm or carried on head or back. Others stood bartering with shopkeepers as small groups, watched close by learning the tricks of the trade. He crossed the street and, without realizing it, was halted by a loud clanging.

Deep in the shadows, illuminated by a small ray of sunlight gleaming upon a broad sweaty brow, stood the gruff silhouette of the town smithy. Draped around his thick muscular neck, rippled two blue veins, with a leather bib covered in black soot. Standing at the edge of a pile of charcoal, he reached over with his tongs and pulled out a short iron rod from the fire. The rod glowed yellow at the end and then tapered to red. He laid it on a stone anvil and raised his hammer.

Chesty hesitated outside his door which was latched back by a small frayed rope hooked onto a wooden peg; it was as if the whole circle had stopped for a moment and he was stuck somewhere between dimensions. He watched the smithy strike the rod with his short stubby hammer into a curved sickle. Each strike sent small fireballs crackling into the air. The tiny sparks faded black mid-air and ricocheted off his bib before dancing around his feet.

The smithy raised his head and spit a dark sappy stream of tobacco onto the ground; it splattered at the feet of his young apprentice wearing a green dappled long-sleeve shirt.

He nodded at Chesty and continued.

Chesty drifted back from his hypnotic trance. He glanced at the apprentice blowing a long-drawn breath through a hollow copper tube into the base of the hearth.

Unsure why he had stopped, he continued.

He bypassed the mill, where he worked with his older brother, and climbed old, worn-out steps under a stone archway that wound up to a gatehouse. At the top, the guardsman stood arguing with four travelers dressed in strange attire. As he walked by, Chesty overheard something about water and a well.

Chesty lived around the corner from the gatehouse. He opened the gate outside his house and walked up the dirt path lined with orange and yellow mums. Mrs. Puller heard the squeak from the gate and met him at the door; her face bore the worry piercing her heart. She looked over his shoulder and asked, "Is everything ok? Where's Caboose?"

"I was hoping he was here. Have any of the neighbors seen him?" he responded, his suspicions gradually becoming reality.

Mrs. Puller wiped the back of her hand across her forehead and held it there for a moment as if she was hot or going to faint. "No, Pepper already asked. I think you should gather the elders and ask them to pray. Something isn't right; I can sense it."

Chesty, trying to block the memories from his troubled past, trudged over and sat down. He searched his thoughts and replied, "This is not like Caboose. Mr. Hammer said he told him to wait outside his office until I arrived. I think you are right. I'll send a message to the elders right now."

* * * * * * *

Caboose followed the awkward looking creatures down the road into the mountains, which grew taller around each bend. They stopped at a grove of olive trees after several miles and set up camp.

He kept his distance at first.

He watched them set up camp and kindle a fire in a grassy flat under the trees. He watched younglings collect firewood. Others climbed high in the trees picking olives. He watched women dance around the fire. They twirled round and round, spinning their dresses into the crackling fire—he got dizzy just watching. The men walked across coals and held torches to their lips. Filling their mouths with thunder juice, they spewed flames high into the air.

Caboose sat under a tree listening to the sounds of laughter filter through the thick grove. He reached up through a screen of leaves and picked a couple of olives. He nibbled on them for a second, and with a sour look on his face, spit them out. Driven by hunger, and enticed by the hand of a beautiful girl that walked through the trees and invited him to dance, he joined them around the fire.

He listened to stories about adventure, danger, fame and fortune. He ate and drank and laughed so hard his stomach ached. Meeting new people and exploring relationships turned out to be exciting—an adventure in itself he thought. For the first time in his life he finally felt like an adult. His confidence swelled making his decision to leave feeling better.

* * * * * *

After school, Brook went straight home and locked herself in her bedroom. She sat in the corner of her bed writing in her diary—she didn't have any homework.

> "He didn't look at me again. I walked right pass him in the hallway and he didn't even see me, it's as if I'm not even there—it would probably be better if I weren't. I'm so fat he must be embarrassed to be seen around me. I need to lose more weight and fast. Rachael came over again. I get so nervous every time she hugs me and looks at me; I wonder if she knows? I like her. There is something different about her, something inside—she's different, but in a good way. Oh no, I hope she doesn't come by, surely she will forget. Why would anyone want to be seen with me?"

Rachael came by at six-o'clock and let herself in. Brook was dressed and ready to go, although she acted like she didn't want to. Brook's bedroom door cracked opened. A small red tongue flashed and retreated, then a leg, an arm, until finally a head peeked back and forth.

"What are you doing?" sighed Brook. "You are so crazy."

Rachael's head popped back out from the door, smiling wide and laughing. She jumped out, clapped her hands together and cheered, "Ready, ok!" Jumping around like a cheerleader she sang, "Two, four, six, eight, you need to hurry, or we'll be late."

She sprung over and jumped on the bed, almost bouncing Brook onto the floor. "Are you ready, or are we going to be late?"

"I don't think I better—"

"Oh come on. You spend too much time in this room day dreaming."

"I'm not day dreaming," said Brook. "I'm working."

"Working? On what?" asked Rachael, rummaging through her shelves.

Brook thought fast. All she did was daydream, write in her diary, and find excuses to not do things. "On things, you know; this and that…nothing special."

"Do you remember in seventh grade when I first moved here? The girls were so mean to me. They spread all those rumors about me that weren't true."

Brook nodded her head wondering where this was going. Rachael paraded over and searched through her flower fragrance bottles and berry lotions and creams. She put some on her nose and then blended it in. "Well, it was you who first sat by me at lunch and invited me to your house for a sleep over."

"Yeah, those were fun. I remember your hair. It was all big and poofy and stood straight up in the middle."

"Hey, I liked that," said Rachael, spinning around with a surprised look on her face.

"That was the best summer, we were inseparable; conjoined twins at the hip. We went shopping in the market. We swam in The Redmadafa—remember that time Brad and his friends came down and we stole their lunch and hid their shoes? They were so mad—they never did find out it was us. We explored the university campus and spied on the girls with their boyfriends at night. Remember how we talked for hours at night, never going to sleep. I miss my old friend. Is something wrong?"

"No," replied Brook. "It's just different now."

"You can say that again. You know those delicious red mushy-mart tarts we used to get at the market. They taste funny now. I think they're using imitation mushy-marts instead of the real thing."

Brook looked at Rachael kind of funny and thought that strange.

"Look, I know it must be hard now that your Dad is gone, but life goes on. You are a beautiful girl with lots to live for. You can't just lock yourself in this room and push everyone away. There are a lot of people that miss having you around."

Rachael grabbed her arm and pulled her off the bed, "Let's go. I think a night out will do you some good."

Brook reluctantly stumbled out of the house. Down deep she was excited to have a friend that wanted to spend time with her.

They walked up the street and past the mill. They cut through the park, to save time, and entered through the winnower's door of the temple wall.

They were late. The service had already started.

They tip-toed through the crowd and sat on a cotton blanket, weaved with strands of grey and green, with some of Rachael's friends outside in one of the outer courts. Traeger, a large howler with scars on his back and neck was in the middle of his story:

"I tracked her for several miles and knew she was close, I could smell her. I climbed up the rocks to get a better look and when I did, I saw her parched face blackened by the sun coming right down the trail towards me; somehow, I had gotten ahead of her. I snuck down the ledge and perched above her waiting for her to pass. Clueless, she walked right underneath me. I dropped down on her, knocking her to the ground. She got up and tried to run but when she did, she ran right into a dead-end canyon.

Cornered, I slowly approached; my body crouched low; terror dripped from my fangs; the spikes on my back stood up like thorns. She was a nice-looking girl. Her hair was brown and eyes blue. She was skinny, very skinny and scared to death. I dug my claws into the dirt to thrust myself at her and just as I went to eat her, she called out HIS name. I jumped, opened my mouth, and that's when it happened—something hit me. Something hit me so hard my bones rattled from my head all the way down to the tip of my tail.

I stood up to attack, but when I saw it, I couldn't believe my eyes. It was an eagle—His feathers, so colorful, his wings, so powerful. In his presence, I felt something I hadn't felt in a long time—Guilt…Shame…Disgust. But then it was strange. Peace…Hope…and…Love."

Traegor made his way through the crowd making sure to look everyone in their eyes. Hearts, gripped with fear, skipped a beat as he retold his story about life in the dark valley filled with death.

"I'm not proud of the things I used to do. I hurt a lot of people from this town, but ever since that day, my life," he hesitated, almost crying, "It's never been the same. When I saw him, it was strange? Even though I saw him, I couldn't see him. I mean, when I saw him, I realized the wickedness in my heart and I saw the bad things I had done. It was at that moment, the moment I heard his voice that something changed in me. I don't know what to compare it to. His voice was like the sound of…rushing water. As he spoke, a peace flooded over me, lifting a burden I didn't even know was there. And, you want to know something else? The girl, it was the first time she had seen him too. Do you know why she was there?" He lowered his head and with great sadness in his voice said, "She thought she was fat and ugly."

Brook's eyes just about popped out of her head. She melted in place and thought for sure everyone was looking at her. Rachael must have told him something about me, she thought. Did she read my diary?

"That day changed my life. It wasn't long after that, that a member of the pack jumped me from behind when we were on patrol and left me for dead. He had been wounded by a young grunter and was demoted by Rukbat our leader. There was no reason why he did what he did to me. He was filled with so much hate and anger he didn't trust anyone.

He left me for dead that day and as I lie in the dirt, in my own puddle of blood, I remembered how that scared helpless girl had called out His Name. For a while I was too proud to call it out. But as my eyes started to close, I called out to him. I cried out, 'Great Augur, I made my pact with death long ago and evil has consumed every ounce of good that ever existed in me. My conscience is scarred with the mangled blood of all those I mercilessly killed. I know I don't deserve to be in your presence, but please, have mercy on me now.'

As the light faded, I felt the vibrations from his landing go through my body. Do you know, with everything that I had done, he came and rescued me? He picked me up and brought me to The Redmadafa."

Traegor started to cry. He lowered his head for a moment and then looked straight at Brook.

"Look. I don't know what is going on in your life, but he does. He's waiting for you to call out His Name and believe in him. There's no other way. He doesn't force himself on anyone; he's waiting for you. Will you call out to him now? I did and my life has never been the same."

Brook couldn't move. Way down deep she was crying, screaming! She wanted to yell out, "That's me…That's me…Somebody help me!" But she didn't. When it was over, she went home and cried through the night. When the moon stood straight in the sky, she decided to leave. Gathering a few things, she snuck out of the house, crept pass the guards sleeping at the gate, and drifted down the road into the mountains.

* * * * * * *

Shadows flickered under the door and crawled across blue-gum planks rubbed and polished with honey buzzer wax. Pepper listened in her bed, soaking up every syllable, every sound, her eyes staring off into the darkness. Beyond the door, her mother and father searched for answers as to why Caboose hadn't talked to them about being bullied at school?

Pepper slipped out from under the covers and softly pressed her ear up against the door.

Silence hovered in the room.

She moved to a better spot on the wall and listened again.

Nothing, the door and wall were too thick.

After a few moments, she couldn't take it any longer. She opened the door and pretended like she had heard something.

"Papa, I heard something," she said, with her best sleepy-face disguise.

Chesty pulled her close, warming her in his massive arms, while he stared into her little green eyes.

"Are you going to look for Caboose?"

"Princess, you need to get back to bed, it's way past your bed time."

"Do you think he's lost Papa?"

"No…Caboose is fine."

"Jaxer said a ragoole snatched him up by his tail and tried to carry him away but then a mighty wind blew and it lost its grip causing Caboose to fall into the forbidden forest. Then he said a moggle grabbed him from the ground by his leg and took him high up in a tree. He said it hung him upside down and ate him… or something like that."

Mrs. Puller stopped her pacing and stood with a wry look on her face.

"Princess, I don't want to hear anymore talk like that. I

already told you that Caboose is fine. Now, get back to bed. I'll be back with Caboose soon," said Chesty.

He patted her on the bottom sending her back to bed.

Chesty Puller was Caboose's Papa. He worked for Myott his brother at the local mill as a puller—pullers pulled the rollers that crushed seeds and grain into flour, meal, and other things. Although he was a puller, he didn't do much pulling any more. He mainly helped Myott run their father's business. Myott inherited the business after their father died but Chesty had a way with people. Myott wisely let Chesty handle all deliveries leaving himself in charge of accounting.

Chesty was an elder at the Temple. He served the people of the Temple and the community for several years, looking after their needs, visiting the sick and dying. He grew up in Thunder Juice Town and had reluctantly followed in his Papa's footsteps. He hoped that Caboose would come and work at the mill when he graduated, although he dreamed of something more for his son. Caboose though, despite his challenge, had dreams of becoming a racer and running in *The Little Round About* and maybe someday the grand-daddy of all races, *The Big Round About*.

Rinox arrived at the house during the mid-watch and let himself in. Rinox was an old and experienced elder with a portly countenance. His bowed shoulders were broad and thick, and two scared horns rose like blackthorns from his long grey snout.

"Chesty, any word yet?" he asked walking through the door.

"No but thanks for coming Rinox. How many do we have?"

"Five. Syma and Adromus are on their way from the market right now. Geon and Paumga were finishing up at work and shouldn't be far behind."

"What about Henry and Zung?" asked Chesty.

"They said they couldn't afford to miss another day of work."

"Then this will have to do. Rinox, you take Syma and Adromus with you and head south. I'll have Geon and Paumga go West and see if they can pick up any tracks."

"What about you Chesty?"

"I'm going to check in the mountains to the North. I know that country pretty well and if he went that way, I should be able to find him," said Chesty, not realizing what he had just admitted.

Rinox hesitated. The mountains to the North, that's dangerous country. Most people that travel there never return, he thought. "You think Caboose would have gone that way? Surely not," said Rinox. "I don't think you should go there alone. Why don't you take Adromus or Paumga with you?"

"No, if he did go that way, I know where he's going."

Mrs. Puller and Rinox looked up at each other—neither dared to ask. Mrs. Puller walked over and placed her hand on Chesty's shoulder. "Why don't you take Adromus with you? You know I don't like you going out alone."

"No. This is…this is something I need to do alone," he responded, rubbing his hand over hers while looking at the floor in a self-induced hypnotic trance. "There comes a time in every boy's life when he needs to break away from his mother and father, and become a man. Often, it's a quest for thrill and adventure; alternatively, it's in pursuit of purpose and love. Sometimes it is out of necessity or rebellion, but regardless, a boy must become a man. He must accept the calling of the divine that created him. He must leave his father and mother and figure out life for himself. It's during this time, and this time alone, that he makes the transition. He's no longer a momma's boy or a shadow following aimlessly in his father's footsteps. He now steps out of that shadow and makes his own path. He rises up to find his name, his true name, the name that will follow him for all eternity."

Chesty stood up and faced his wife. "Our son is gone. He will never return. Whether we find him dead or alive he will never be the same. He will have made the transition. He will have a new name—I pray it good."

The others arrived one-by-one and greeted Mrs. Puller. Mrs. Puller packed a few snacks for each of them and poured them all a cup of hot thunder leaf tea with a hint of honey buzzer.

Chesty grabbed his lightning bug lantern and a few other things. Everyone stood in the middle of the room.

"Rinox would you pray before we split up?"

"Of course," he said, honored that Chesty asked. They bowed their heads and closed their eyes.

Rinox looked around the circle and reverently said:

"Great Augur, we know you never sleep or grow tried.
We know you search the furthest and most desolate places,
for those who are lost, hurt and dying. Guide us now as
we search
for Caboose. Protect him from harm and speed us to
him we pray. Amen."

* * * * * * *

Early the next morning Caboose woke to an empty camp. The fire was out, the wagons were gone and he was alone. Dew covered the grass and sparkled in the sun as it rose over the trees. Thinking he could catch up, he scrambled down the road looking for them. After several hours, he arrived at a fork in the road.

He stopped and looked both ways.

Wind whistled down the canyon as if warning him once again to turn around and stop this hopeless quest.

He studied the ground and then looked up.

Which way, he thought?

He looked to the left.

The trail looked narrow and not well-traveled. Leaves blew across a broken overgrown path beckoning him to follow. The lonesome road offered more shade and green grass but the trail to the right was much wider and looked suitably traveled. Grooves cut into the winding road revealing a well-worn path easy to follow.

For a brief moment, he contemplated turning around and going home. But against his better judgment, he decided to take the broad path—a decision he all-too-soon would come to regret.

He slumbered down the trail for several miles thinking about what he would do if he found the gate. Dreams of riches danced in his mind, like the undulations of a ship, thoughts about what he would do with his riches once he found them.

At a switchback, prickly low-budding bushes sparsely covered the lower edges of the walls. They had velvety-green leaves with small red berries—Caboose learned in class that small red berries usually mean danger and major stomach issues if eaten.

He wandered down the switchback and into a vaulted gorge that spilled into a draw and fingered off in hundreds of different directions.

"I'm never gonna find this stupid gate. It probably doesn't even exist," he muttered in frustration.

He picked up a rock and threw it down one of the fingers; it tumbled down the path and smashed to pieces against a boulder.

Determined to find the gate and not return home a fool, he ventured on. After a few more hours of aimless wandering, Caboose realized he was lost. He didn't know which way to go, nor did he know how to get back home. Just when he thought things couldn't get any worse, and with night falling, a strange fog crept over the ridge. Dark as a dragon's claw, the fog slithered up the path, as if stalking prey, and twisted around him like the sinuous coils of a snake. The fog was so thick he couldn't see five feet in front of him. Faint voices keened in the fog startling him, calling to him:

"*I am happy, I am free.*"

Singing—someone or something was singing. The voice had a sharp accent that sounded funny and it didn't sound like anyone he knew. He took a few steps and then stopped again:

"*I'm in charge of my destiny.*"

"Help, help me!" shouted Caboose, but no one answered. "Can anybody hear me?" he shouted again.

The voice seemed to move further away from him as he ran deeper into the fog.

"This way," whispered voices.

After a few minutes, the voice faded:

"*I am happy, I am free.*"

Then it was gone.

"No!" cried Caboose as he fell to the ground, exhausted.

"If I didn't have this stupid short leg, I would be able to run faster, jump higher, and I could have caught whoever that was singing. As a matter of fact, I wouldn't even be here. If I didn't have this bad leg I would be able to keep up, I would have friends, and I could race in *The Little Round About.*"

Caboose was mad and tired, but most of all, scared. With his face in the dirt and tears in his eyes, Caboose knew he was in big trouble. As he lay on the ground, bewildered and confused, the fog cleared. Caboose lifted his head, rubbed his eyes and to his amazement, there it was—The Scorpion Pass Gate.

CHAPTER 3

SCORPION PASS GATE

The lust of man: The greed of the heart:
Dreams of the dreamer.

The elders searched everywhere for Caboose. Geon and Paumga crossed The Redmadafa and split up to cover more ground. They looked up and down the banks but didn't pick up any signs. Rinox, Syma, and Adromus went south all the way to Jasmine Crossing. They stopped at all the outer villages talking to town leaders, but no one had seen Caboose. They even traveled through the land of the Sand Pipers looking for tracks, but luckily for them, they didn't find any and they went unnoticed.

Chesty headed north. He followed the trail out of town and into the mountains until it came to a fork. He noticed a small trail to the left but it was covered with grass and leaves. There were a few tracks leading that way but not many and not any that looked familiar. It also didn't look like it had been traveled in the last few days. He pulled open his skin of water and took a sip. He popped the cork back in the top, adjusted the string around his neck and examined the ground again. He then followed tracks leading down the trail to the right and followed it until he came to a switchback several hours later. At the switchback, he saw a set of tracks that looked familiar—it was hard to tell though if it was Caboose's. Numerous tracks paved the dirt up and down the broad trail.

Wind ricocheted off the canyon walls softly mumbling in his ears. Chesty looked around, spooked by the harsh sounds. He thought he heard his name but knew he was being paranoid and hearing voices.

His hand started to shake.

He tried not to think about what he was trying not to think about—his secret—but was losing the battle as memories flickered over times past. He closed his hand and opened it again, and then shook it out. Although the temperature had dropped considerably, sweat seeped down his face forming short creek beds in their course. He took another drink, wiped his face and kept going.

The stars were extra bright as night fell in the canyon. They were so numerous and close that Chesty felt like he could reach out and grab a whole handful. Brown teeth blew around the corner jumping over boulders along the edge. Others piled high, trapped by gaps and crannies. Concealed under the cover of darkness, crickets rhythmically sang love songs to one another from the bushes. Chesty wandered for hours through the dark calling out his son's name, desperate to hear his voice.

* * * * * * *

Caboose thought he was dreaming. Sparkles danced off his pupils as he focused on the enormous gate poised before him. Caboose felt strange but good. He forgot he was lost and all his energy returned. Enticed, he walked over to the gate and stroked his hand across thousands of tiny crystals, all reflecting a wide spectrum of colors. Caboose observed his reflection staring back at him as lights skipped upon its smooth, yet jagged surface.

To the touch, it felt cold and wet, but amazingly it was dry. The two doors were attached to two columns on each side, which stood over 80 feet tall and were made from Red Poppy Jasper set in a fiery base. Above the gate was a black onyx headstone adorned with a variety of jewels and precious stones. It had an inscription on it that when translated read:

PASS THROUGH THIS GATE AND BECOME LIKE GOD

On each side of the gate, stood two magnificent stone scorpions with their bellies touching the ground; scorpions that Caboose did not recognize. He walked over and peered through a crack in the gate. He glimpsed a faint garden with lots of grass, flowers and lush vegetation. Trees were so tall they reached up and touched the sky. They stretched out across the garden, waving at Caboose, beckoning him to enter. Beyond the trees was a sea so vast and large, it converged with the horizon and had no end. He reached for the handle to open the gate, but couldn't find one. He looked all over but couldn't find a way in. He tried pushing on the door, hitting it, yelling at it:

"Open Sesame; Abracadabra; Ali Baba; Simon says open," but no matter what he tried, he couldn't open it.

From out of the sky, or so it seemed, a thick accented voice laughed cunningly:

"*Ha, Ha, Ha,*
Ho, Ho, Ho,
open me door,
No, No, No."

Startled, Caboose joggled his head, mystified yet perplexed, and grunted, "Who's there?" He stumbled back from the gate and looked around while his eyes scanned the area. He noticed many other footprints on the ground leading up to the gate but then they disappeared.

"*Ask me once,*
ask me twice,
only if you dare
ask me thrice."

Caboose looked up at the large headstone atop the gate. Sitting on top of it was an eccentric little man staring down at him. The man mindfully sized Caboose up.

"Where am I," gasped Caboose, taken back by his callow appearance.

The little man pondered the question with a candid smile and rattled, in a droll voice, "Silly grunter, you are at The Scorpion Pass Gate and you can't open it that way."

"Who...who are you," mumbled Caboose, scared but intrigued?

"I," said the little man heaving his chest out like a warrior from ancient old, "Am the Keeper of the Gate. Asssss for my name," he began to sing:

"My name is Lucy but people call me Lucky
Lucky Lucy is my name,
I like to run and jump, I like to sing and play
I like to lie around and play charades.

Lucky, Lucy is all you have to say
For me to come around and take your troubles away
So if you forget my name, just sing this melody
And we will be together, in perfect harmony."

Lucky was not exactly a man. Choppy lava-red hair brushed his shoulders and tickled his back. His skin changed color with the background as he moved about—rather like a chameleon. He had four legs and six arms which rested on his paunch belly. Long pointy green ears peeped out from under his hat that stretched high upon his elongated head. A crown encompassed his hat, with a large ruby at bottom center and a dragon wrapped around and draped over the top. Lucky crawled down the column and strutted around Caboose looking him over from head to toe. He rubbed his chin and shook his head at Caboose's leg and gloated:

"I give visions, I give leave,
Trussssst in me and I will give you your dreams."

His eyes were yellow with a hint of red, and his pupils were long and straight. But, there was something about his voice that enticed Caboose; it was beautiful, absolutely beautiful. Caboose was mesmerized by it and the calming sense it gave him as Lucky talked. He couldn't take his eyes off of Lucky. There was something about him; something that drew him in.

Lucky jumped up on a rock and held out his hand. A long twisted staff appeared from out of nowhere that forked at the top and had a small black dragon-bat perched on top. He tapped it on the rock and immediately legs grew from underneath it. The rock twirled around Caboose as Lucky once again began to sing:

> *"Grunter, you look like a very smart lad.*
> *But, you walk with a limp and you seem so sad.*
> *So put away your past and stand up you cad,*
> *Come away with me and I'll make you glad."*

The rock twirled Lucky around stopping him directly in front of Caboose. He leaned close—real close—then whispered, "Grunter, what if I told you I could fix your leg, and make you as fast as the wind. I could give you your every dream, your heart's desire."

"You can do that," said Caboose with a look of disbelief in his eyes.

> *"Do that! Do that!*
> *Well of course I can me boy.*
> *I can do that or my name's not coy,*
> *I can make you fast, I can make you dream*
> *I can make you king of all that you see."*

Eyes peeked out from the crevasses above the gate watching the spectacle unfold. Light glided back and forth across the gate as if the gate itself were alive and watching.

Coy, I thought his name was Lucy, Lucky Lucy, thought Caboose. Confused, yet liking the sound of it, Caboose pulsed, "King, of all I that I see?"

Lucky unfolded a pair of his hands and brushed the skyline with his staff.

"Of all that you see,
Of all that you see;
Just bow down to me,
and it becomes...r-e-a-l-i-t-y."

"You see, inside the gate I am king of all the land. Go through and I will share it with you."

"Wow, I could go home and race in *The Little Round About.* No, I could go home and win *The Little Round About.*" Caboose stopped for a moment and thought about what Lucky was offering. This all seemed too good to be true. Besides, he might have been born at night but it wasn't last night. Caboose had a good heart and others often took advantage of it if they thought they had something to gain—or if they were out right mean and no good.

"But why?" asked Caboose. "Why would you do this for me? I am nothing, a nobody; I am slow, clumsy and no one ever wants to do anything for me."

"Grunter, don't you dare
Say that I don't care,
I'll treat you like a son
You'll be me number one;"

riddled Lucky, nervous that he was about to lose this one.

Changing his tactics, Lucky stopped the rhymes and jumped down from the rock. The rock walked back over to its spot and returned to the ground.

"Grunter, I just want you to be happy. I want you to come away with me and live a life of indulgence; a life with no worries, where you can run fast and win every race: The life of a king with people at your service day and night awaiting your every command."

At that Lucky turned and started to walk away. "Or you can go home and continue to live the miserable life of servitude that you've been living back home."

Caboose liked the sound of being a king. Besides, at home, no one treated him with any respect and they certainly never treated him as a king. This was his chance to finally be somebody. Mack and the lixoars would never bully him again, nor would anyone ever laugh or make fun of him.

"Happy, fast, and a king, that sounds great," affirmed Caboose. "What must I do?"

"What do you have to do?" japed Lucky twirling back around. "You just have to open the gate, grunter," said Lucky holding all arms and hands out:

"Just bow down
and open the gate,
never be a clown
or show up late."

Caboose thought for a moment—never show up late. Yes! "But, I don't know how." Gumshoeing for more time to think he said, "I already tried. I looked all over and tried everything, but I couldn't open it."

"Well boy," Lucky said lifting his chest and tilting his head toward the sky, like he was a statue of great fame, ever so slowly lowering it before he sung:

"You just need to have the golden key,
the golden key, is the song, that you sing.
The song that you sing, is the golden key,
so listen to me and I'll sing it for a fee."

"A fee? But I don't have any coins," said Caboose, digging through his pockets aimlessly.

"Don't brow beat me-boy," said Lucky. "Didn't I tell you to trust in me?

"Trusssssst in me and be filled with glee."

"Once you open the gate you will find a treasure chest waiting for you on the other side. When you find it," he began to dance around his staff and wave his hand in the air by his ear:

"Silver, silver, ringing in my ears,
Silver, silver, brings me happy jeers,
30 pieces, is all I ask,
30 pieces, such a small task."

"That's it," said Caboose. "Just bring you 30 pieces and that's it."

"That's it me boy. Thirty pieces and you can keep the rest all to yourself. Just sing the song and it will all be done; and remember. Don't forget to bow," said Lucky leaning in on his staff. The dragon bat smiled and nodded its head.

The song, thought Caboose. "But I can't sing and I don't know any songs."

"Are you sure you want to go
through me gate, through me gate.
Go through me gate and never be late."

"Yes sir, of course I do; I mean, I think so," bumbled Caboose.

Lucky slammed his staff on the ground knocking the dragon bat off. It flew over and rested on one of the scorpion statues.

"Well then, stop bumbling lad. Sing the song and open the door."

"But I don't know *what* song you're talking about," said Caboose in frustration?

"Grunter," sighed Lucky, "The song that brought you here." Lucky cleared his throat, looked at Caboose, and with a devilish smile on his face, sang:

"I am happy, I am free,
I'm in charge of my destiny.
No more hurting, no more sob,
pass through me gate and become like God."

"Ha, ha, ha, ha, ha. Ha, ha, ha, ha, ha. Ss, ss, ss, ss, ss, ss." And with that, he was gone.

"Lucky? Lucky Lucy?" Caboose stood puzzled and uncertain. That is all I have to do, sing a song. Walk through the gate and give him 30 pieces of silver, he thought. Caboose didn't know what to do. He didn't know how to get back home and even if he did, everyone would laugh at him for getting lost. And besides, no one would ever believe that he actually found the gate anyway.

Caboose sensed something wasn't right, but it was getting late and he really wanted to see what was on the other side of the gate.

Why not, he thought? I'll just go through for a few hours, look around for a while and after that, I can head home. When I show up back home with my pockets full of jewels, I will be a king. Caboose looked around and then walked over and stood in front of the gate. He bowed down on one knee and sang:

"I am happy, I am free,
I'm in charge of my destiny.
No more hurting, no more sob,
pass through me gate and become like God."

A thunderous crack echoed through the canyon walls as the gate opened. Seduced with excitement, Caboose walked over and stood in the middle of the gate. The fresh smell of adventure garbled his mind. The garden was enchanting and beyond imagination. It was just as he had seen through the crack and even better. Lush tropical spurs funneled hundreds of waterfalls over tall mountain ridges on every side. Crimson, auburn, indigo, emerald, jade, burgundy, scarlet, and violet colored gems lined the granite walls. Yellow and red mushy marts—mushy marts that explode in your mouth as you eat them—lined an elaborate mosaic path which wound through the garden toward the sea. Blue tongue sickles glittered in his eyes making his mouth salivate. Caboose tried to see what they were connected to, but they weren't connected to anything; they magically floated in the air.

An enormous garden full of Blossom Berry trees, Caboose's favorite, beckoned his lustful desire for greed and indulgence. Down the middle of the garden flowed a purple mountain majesty stream. It sparkled with a luminous glow and waved at him before uniting with a crystal sea. Its water was cold, ice cold and sweet like brumpel juice—Caboose's grandmother made him brumpel melon juice all the time back home. Caboose drank so much that his stomach rumbled and sloshed about as he walked down the alluring path.

He ran around the garden and stuffed his belly will all kinds of magical delights—even his hunger bugs had had their fill and agonized in pain from gluttony. He swung from vines and cannonballed into the middle of the stream, over and over, splashing water way-up in the sky, soaking much of the garden in delightful drops of purple mountain majesty. He tumbled down hills woven thick with tall green grass.

I must be in heaven, he thought to himself, lying on his back staring up into the sky. I can live here forever and never need anything again. There is food, water, and Blossom Berry trees. I've done it. I've found paradise…and it's all mine.

From the other side of the stream hundreds of little voices echoed, "Pay the fee and you'll be free."

Caboose, half asleep and sure that he was dreaming, raised his head slightly off the ground.

"30 pieces is all I ask, 30 pieces such a small task," said the voices again.

He remembered. Lucky said there was a fee for going through the gate. "A treasure chest! Yes. I'm supposed to find a treasure chest."

Caboose got up and strolled back down to the path. He peered down toward the sea. At the end was a golden chest carved with open flowers and an image of a serpent in-between two palm trees. He wobbled down the path and approached the chest. All kinds of colors glinted from the chest, radiating sparkles from the box-of-dreams.

He reached down and opened it.

He couldn't believe his eyes. He ran his fingers through gold and silver coins, diamonds, sapphires, and all types of priceless jewels.

"It's all mine. Lucky said I could keep all of it except for thirty pieces of silver. But where?" he thought. "Where do I pay the fee?"

His eyes surveyed the garden. He noticed a whirlwind circling on the other side of the stream right in front a Titan tree—Titan trees are the oldest and wisest trees in the entire world. Caboose knew of only one other; the one that lived by The Redmadafa.

In the whirl, thousands of little white bogies fluttered. As he watched, the bogies formed into a face and whispered, "This way Caboose. Hurry, don't be late."

He picked out 30 silver coins and started for the stream. He slid down the bank and scouted for a way to cross. Up stream, rocks from the bottom rose forming a bridge. He crossed over and approached the bogies, and as he did, they broke apart and hid throughout the garden. Grim silver eyes peaked at him through the leaves.

Rising high into the sky was a Titan tree. Its gnarled branches festooned out across the top of the garden flaunting an interwoven chain of brightly colored leaves rustling in the wind. Its roots were a massive system of interlocking tubes that twined out and connected with every tree and plant in the garden. Wrapped around the base of the Titan where decorative doors of varied size; some large, some small, some wide, and others narrow. The doors shuffled as Caboose roamed by them, reshaping once past. There was a door for the size of any creature or beast that wanted to enter.

Caboose toured around the girth of the titan, which stretched the length of ten large thunder beast head to tail, looking for a door his size. Above him, and without him noticing, the bark peeled, murmuring and laughing, silently heckling Caboose.

He stopped and reached for a knob.

A face formed on the knob and sighed, "Too small."

Startled, he snatched his hand back and stared at the knob. He tried another one, "To big" it said. He stopped in front of another one and grabbed the knob. It twisted in his hand and opened.

Caboose entered cautiously observing his surroundings and footsteps—the door closed on his tail. Riddles and rhymes etched into the walls and stretched higher than he could read. Stacks of books lined the ledge and shelves: *Fairytales, Dream Maker, Magic Potions, Disguises, Amusement Games, Tricks and Treats, False Religions, and Thunder Beast Deception,* were just a few.

Caboose meandered over and opened a bronze door that revealed a small closet. Hanging on three pegs was a black cloak sparkling of silver, a suit of gold armor, and some other funny looking red garment with a big black belt. In the middle of the room, stood a black stone chiseled by a skilled mason. On top of the stone was a slot the same size of the silver coins. Engraved beside the hole was a message. It read:

The wisdom of man is within your hand. Deposit the dross and betray the cross.

Caboose walked over and read the message. "Betray the cross...what does that mean?" he said to himself with a weird look on his face. "Oh well, it doesn't matter. When I deposit the coins, it will all be mine."

Caboose counted each coin as he put them in, "One, two, three...twenty-eight, twenty-nine, thirty."

Click!

BATTLE FOR THE FIERY STONES

You are a man not a god!

3500 years earlier:

THE HOLY MOUNT

Mageddon stood atop the fiery stones; his beastly eyes fixated in a red pulsating trance, obsessed with her every move. "Master," Legion whispered, "Crimson moon, black sun; it's an omen. Victory is within your grasp. The scroll foretells a woman will give birth to a son who will rule the nations with an iron scepter. If we move now and kill the child, fear will run rampant throughout the southern forces and you will possess the power to overthrow His Majesty."

Mageddon, the Supreme Commander of His Majesty's Imperial Guard, brushed his hand across the seer portal and strutted across the room. He stared into the stones until a grim smile swept across his face.

"His Majesty; yes, his deception has failed. Alert the generals and await my command. We must strike before the southern army arrives. There can be no mistakes, no retreats."

He turned and peered across the stones straight into Legion's eyes. "We cannot fail. I don't care if we have to sacrifice them all. We must kill her and the child."

Legion, fearing Mageddon's wrath replied, "Yes, my master. Everything is ready, everyone's in place."

Mageddon took to the sky, and with his guards flying in formation close behind, he flew over the battlefield surveying its final preparations. The battlefield, which was once filled with lush gardens and vibrant courtyards, had been transformed into a maze of trenches with a barricade of jagged crystal beams, encircling the outer perimeter. Mageddon landed on top of the south tower. He drew a deep breath before addressing his forces.

"This is the moment we have all been waiting for. Stay here and keep control of the Holy Mount and the fiery stones. Once I kill the child we will possess the power to overthrow His Majesty. Then, together we will rush the throne room and kill His Majesty."

His army raised their swords and shields, and roared in unison.

Mageddon closed his eyes, raised his arms, and summoned the power of the stones. Fire rushed up the tower exploding in a beam of fire, high into the galaxy. He spread his wings and shouted, "I will rule the universe as the god I was created to be!"

MOUNT ZION

Miaphas marched through the door. He approached His Majesty's throne and bowed low in reference, his heart beating zealously within. "Your Majesty, the reports are true. He has proclaimed himself a god and the entire northern army is worshipping him."

"Blasphemy!" jolted His Majesty. "A god he is not; there is no wisdom in a fool." His Majesty rose from his seat and walked down the steps placing his hand on Miaphas' shoulder.

Miaphas rose, but remained silent. He candidly took note of the others in the room as His Majesty glided by.

"Pride has filled his heart and folly has replaced the wisdom I anointed him with," said His Majesty.

Miaphas handed him a small rolled parchment with writing on both sides and sealed with seven seals. "Your Majesty, he has been involved with dishonest trade and," with hesitation in his voice, "He has desecrated the Holy Sanctuaries and the fiery stones."

"Then, it is true." His Majesty took the scroll and opened the folds of his robe. Skin, unlike any substance in heaven or on earth, peeled back between his ribs opening a small hole; a fluorescent light burst out of the opening, blinding all present. He placed the scroll inside his body and withdrew his hand. The hole closed as he released his grip on the long white robe.

"Miaphas take charge of the Southern army and remove him from the Holy Mount. He can no longer be allowed to keep his place of authority."

An angel stepped out from behind a column; his body was covered with a labyrinth of smooth rocks of different shapes and colors. "Your Majesty, what about those who follow him?" he asked.

With tears in his eyes, His Majesty walked back up the steps, sat in his seat and dropped his head. "Cast them to earth."

Celestial beings stretched as far as the eye could see. Light flashed throughout the galaxy as others reported from their posts all over the universe. Column after column formed in ranks and drew weapons from the armory. Others secured the outer perimeters of Mount Zion, His Majesty's throne, and raised the shields.

Galamus arrived from the outer realm. He reported to Miaphas (who was organizing the army) and drawing up battle plans. He stomped down the ancient hallways and past the Fountain of Light. He cut through the gardens and around The Great Hall, which was filled with activity and crowded with angels. He ascended the spiral staircase of the East tower and past the guards posted outside Miaphas' door.

Inside, Miaphas sat quietly writing with a long, white quill pen. Atop the table stood a black oblong inkbottle and a red wick candle, sparkling bright. He laid the quill down, rolled up the parchment and grasped the candle in his left hand. He tilted the candle over the parchment allowing three drops of wax to pool on top of the outer edge; allowing the drops to cool for a few seconds, he pressed his signet ring into the wax sealing it with his mark—an Eagles Head.

"Miaphas, the northern armies are intoxicated with his lies and have sworn allegiance to him," said Galamus entering the room.

Miaphas looked up from the table and handed the scroll to Frost, the angel of clime. "Where is he?" exclaimed Miaphas, calculating Mageddon's next move.

Galamus moved next to Frost and embraced her. They were old friends and had embarked on numerous adventures together.

"He and the Northern army are imbedded at the Holy Mount. Mageddon plans to attack her in the outer realm, the moment the child arrives; I fear he plans to kill her and the child."

He nodded at the scroll in Frost's hand. She smiled and shrugged her shoulders enticing his curiosity.

Miaphas walked over to a globe rotating above the floor in the middle of the room. Twelve crystal columns surrounded the atlas, which contained every planet and star in the universe. He paced inside studying the Holy Mount and its fortified positions. Locating his troops posted throughout the galaxies, he reached up with his finger and touched several spots. With each touch, the brightly colored light-balls opened, allowing Miaphas to see the outposts and its regiments. He double-touched key outposts sending a burst of light racing out the window—the light carried orders to report immediately.

He turned toward Galamus. "We don't have much time. Take the first and fourth divisions with you and launch a frontal attack clearing the Holy Mount sweeping East. I will take the rest with me, then ambush Mageddon in the outer realm. Sound the alarm and assemble the forces; we must leave at once."

THE HOLY MOUNT

Galamus and his forces scaled the cliffs from the West hoping to catch the Northern army off guard; they covered the cliffs like ivy, anticipating that Legion would be expecting an aerial assault. Galamus wanted to clear the Holy Mount before taking the battle to the heavily fortified positions below.

Legion, Mageddon's Imperial Commander, stood on the Holy Mount looking into the clairvoyant portal.

His face grimaced.

He looked up and shouted to the guard on the Eastern wall. "The cliffs—are they clear?"

The guard looked over the wall. He looked back up and shouted, "All clear."

Legion cocked his head toward the Western wall and shouted, "Is all clear?"

The guard walked over to the ledge and looked over. Before he could say a word, a sharp, double-edged sword pierced his chin and exited his helmet. His body toppled over the wall and out of sight as Legion drew his sword and raised it high and shouted, "It's an ambush—attack!"

The sky exploded as light ignited by thousands of celestial beings filled the sky.

Hydro flew over the wall, cupped his hands, and slowly moved them apart. With a beam of water streaming hand-to-hand, he turned his palms toward Legion and pushed. A tidal wave rippled across the sky, soaking the fiery stones, covering the Holy Mount in a dense mist that crept down and hovered over the battlefield. The fog sent the Northern army into a frenzy, as Legion, drenched and disoriented, ran into the gardens on the upper courtyard into an arched alcove overlooking the battlefield.

Galamus cleared the Southern wall and jumped into a trench. Several celestial guards jumped on top of him, pinning him to the ground. He kicked them off and slashed through the narrow gauntlet. He rounded the corner, slipped past several battles, and flew out of the trench and back onto the battlefield. Behind him, a large demonic figure with a silver shield engraved with the head of a serpent, jumped out of the trench. The beast had one large eye and five tails covered with serpent heads. Bronze greaves adorned its legs, tightly knit mesh protected its body and red armor covered the mesh.

An angel, whose body burned like an ember, spun around and threw a flaming yellow spear of fire through the air, right past the left ear of Galamus; it knocked the beast off its feet inches behind him.

Galamus grabbed his ear and looked at his hand. "Hey, whose side are you on?" he exclaimed across the battlefield.

The angel smiled and replied, "Yours. And you can thank me later." He turned, raised his sword and struck several more guards.

Galamus flew over and plunged his sword into the lumpy brute that had broken off the spear lodged in its shoulder and was rising back to its feet. He pulled his sword from its belly, and with one stroke, severed all five heads. He surveyed the battlefield and then pointed up the mountain.

"Secure the Holy Mount and take possession of the fiery stones. They must all be driven out and cast to earth. None can stay."

Frost, standing in the middle of one of the trenches, held out her hands and blasted a wall of ice. The frosty indigo crystals snaked through the trench entombing hundreds of dark figures. She flew out of the trench, looked at Galamus and asked, "What about Legion?"

Legion stood in the middle of the yards battling several Southern guards with a bright red sword. She started toward him, however Galamus, with fleeting shadows glittering against his pupils, stuck out his arm and held her back. "I'll take care of him."

Galamus zigzagged through the battles raging around him and cautiously made his way to Legion. Now just a few yards from him, he shouted, "Legion!"

Legion whirled around and threw a scorpion-tipped spear at him.

Galamus cart-wheeled backwards, blocking it with his sword.

"How quick you are to betray your maker, Legion. Only a fool would make his alliance with a dreamer. Now you will suffer the wrath of His Majesty."

"You are the fool Galamus," spit Legion, drawing his sword from his side. "Mageddon is on his way to destroy the woman and her child. When he does, we will possess the power to overthrow His Majesty. Join us now before it's too late. Perhaps Mageddon will show you mercy."

"Overthrow His Majesty; and then what? Mageddon will never posses the full power of the fiery stones and he will never share power with you."

He stepped closer.

"Join you? I don't think so," remarked Galamus. "Mageddon will pay with his life for this and so will all who follow him… including you." He jumped in the air and kicked Legion back into the Holy Mount leaving a large indention in the footings. Legion picked himself up and shook off his wings. He scrapped his sword across the ground then ran up the wall, flipping backwards as he attacked Galamus. The clash of swords sent silver sparks blazing high into the air. Galamus blocked his feeble attack, and with his left hand, hit Legion with a force-field that launched him up and over the Holy Mount tumbling end-over-end through the air. Legion crash-landed next to the fiery stones and rolled across the courtyard up against an enormous statue of an Almighty Eagle.

Legion crawled over and stood up on the fiery stones. He raised his hands in front of him and shouted, "I, Legion, keeper of the Holy Mount, call upon the power of the fiery stones. Give me your power that I may defeat those who have come to destroy thy sacred command."

The stones trembled causing Legion to stumble. The rumbles thundered throughout the battlefield, momentarily paralyzing everyone while power surged from the stones and raced up his legs, igniting his hands in bright-red flames.

Galamus cleared the East wall and landed at the opposite end of the stones and instantly became engulfed with an atomic blast of fire. Struggling to keep his footing, he raised his hands and blocked the fire, only to be met with a power far greater than his own.

"You cannot defeat me. Surrender your forces now or I will destroy you."

Galamus strained to hold Legion back, his hands glowing brighter as he slid backwards. "I'm not afraid of death and I would never save myself at the expense of my brothers."

Legion's eyes seered with scorn. "Then you will die…fool! And to think, you could have shared power with us and ruled the universe. What a waste."

Several angels landed beside Galamus and rushed inside the flame to help hold it back. Several others landed all around Legion and raised their swords to cut him down. Greatly out-numbered and alone, he sprayed the courtyard with fire and lowered his hands.

"This is not over, Galamus. You will bow before Mageddon and call him master. You *will* succumb." He pointed at all the others and bent down to the ground as if picking something up, "You *all* will bow." He broke from the fight and took to the air. With casualties mounting and against Mageddon's orders, Legion sounded the retreat. They were defeated. Not only had they lost the battle, they had lost their stations of authority. Rightful passage to the Holy Mount and the fiery stones would forever be blocked. The universe glowed red as battles dwindled and stars were hurled across the universe by Legion and his army, protesting their retreat. Massive boulders of broken stars and meteors peppered the planets and moon, leaving large craters scattered across their surface.

MABGONIAN SYSTEM

The solar system stood on edge. Bolts of energy stretched from star to star. Above her head was a crown imbedded with the twelve stars of Andorra. She stood in an expanse above the moon; her body clothed with the sun. About to give birth, she cried out in pain as a great and wondrous sign appeared; globular clusters exploded with a spectacular display of colors resulting in a majestic rainbow across the universe.

Mageddon, hiding in the orbs of Mabgonian, had seen enough. It was time! With his army in place, he spread his wings, lowered his head and shouted a thunderous blood-curdling shriek initiating the attack. His colorful wings ruffled in the wind and were highlighted by small pockets of air, white-capping underneath, as he descended through a black hole concealing his approach. He had one goal; to devour the child and kill his mother.

Aware of his presence, the stars from her crown blinded him with an immense mother-of-pearl light. As the woman made her escape, she raced through the galaxy and navigated through a massive star cluster camouflaging her with millions of lights. She weaved through a dust field then back out into open space, and paused. Up ahead, hiding behind ranks of black shields stacked together, a battalion of Mageddon's army blended into the darkness waiting to ambush.

Sensing their presence and looking for an escape, her eyes roamed the galaxy. Beneath her a wormhole opened. Scared, and uncertain what to do, she dropped headlong into its median as the army broke rank and followed close behind spinning into the funnel after her. Deep inside the blackness, she felt them nipping and slashing at her feet, but one by one, they ripped into the mainstream of its gravitational pull and, to their surprise, emerged in different constellations.

She spiraled out of the hole and shot wide-around the two moons of Cadiamorsus—Mageddon emerged from the hole just as it closed and followed her. She twisted through an asteroid field and then out into space, but with every second, he drew closer. With the child tucked under her wing, she sang to the comets for help. Reporting from across the galaxy, they attacked from every direction launching at him.

Mageddon, full of surprises himself, felt their vibrations locking onto him and he transformed into an enormous seven-headed red dragon. Each head had ten horns and seven crowns, from which fire erupted, turning the comets into ash. His voice, majestic yet deadly, sent shock waves disintegrating the rest, crushing them into tiny pieces. The small fragments ricocheted off his body and floated away becoming trapped in the rings of several nearby planets.

The woman turned and sped toward earth. As she approached its upper atmosphere, she sang to the clouds for protection. The sky turned red and the barometric pressure in the air dropped, creating a large vortex in the sky. Lightning flashed against Mageddon's body. Hundreds of tornadoes raged all around, twisting and flipping him over and over. Rain and hail slammed against him trying to slow him down, but he was too powerful and his armor of thick scales—impenetrable.

He folded his wings to pick up speed causing fire to spark off his body. Preparing his final approach, in unison, all seven heads screamed a venomous shriek, paralyzing her mid-air. With victory now in reach, he stretched out his claws to clutch-kill the child, but was struck by Miaphas emerged from the clouds directly above him. Mageddon pummeled round and round in an unrecoverable spiral-of-death. Struggling to pull out, his tail swept a third of the stars out of the sky, raining giant fireballs on the earth, torching the ancient old-growth forests of Guma. Mageddon struck the earth with such an enormous force that he cracked its crust, shifting it off its orbital rotation. A plume of dust mushroomed into the atmosphere, covering the earth in darkness, killing, burying, and suffocating millions.

Mageddon listlessly picked himself up off the ground. Shell-shocked eyes scanned the sky and valley for any sign of her. Exhausted from the relentless pursuit, the woman landed on the back of Behemoth—the chief of all His Majesty had made. With bronze bones, limbs of iron, and a tail like a cedar tree, he was ready to sacrifice his body to protect both her and the child. The woman's frail, tattered body was draped over Behemoth's neck as she rested in the rhythm of his gallop, fondly soothing her beating heart. As they ran through the forest, she sang to the trees to conceal her. Hearing her voice, Miaphas emerged from the clouds and landed on a mountain plateau high above the forest. He spread his hands far apart and then slapped them together, pulsating a gust of wind through the trees awakening them from their ancient slumber.

Leaves soared into the sky.

Branches snapped.

Cracks and rumbles echoed throughout the forest.

The trees sprang to life. They spread their burly branches high into the air, confusing Mageddon with an array of colors.

Others formed in ranks and marched against him, while others flanked him.

Mageddon tried to pursue her, but he was wounded and his left wing broken. In one last desperate attempt to achieve victory, he turned toward her, inhaled deeply, and spewed a torrent of water into the air. The water raged across the valley and through the forest, uprooting the trees, breaking their ranks and washing them away. The torrent picked up other trees and rocks, and showered them down all around her. Although the waters raged, Behemoth could not be stopped. His colossal body stormed through the forest unscathed by the terror chasing them.

With the small amount of energy that remained, she sang out, this time to the earth.

The earth trembled and quaked.

Boulders smashed into the creek.

A canyon opened into the horizon and cut the water off, wrestling it down its colossal walls. The water, furious at the canyon, surged and scratched into its sides, scaring it with deep ravines. The canyon sucked the water down then channeled it away.

Mageddon watched the canyon open and race toward him. Unable to fly, he rolled out of its path. Devastated that his plan had failed, he pondered his next move. Legion circled the earth and landed beside Mageddon, falling face-down.

"Forgive me Mageddon, I have failed you, we have all failed you. Galamus and the others ambushed us and kept us from carrying out your plans. He knows about us; His Majesty suspects you. He has taken your place of authority and given it to Miaphas."

"Miaphas; Coward! Next time we shall meet face-to-face."

Mageddon walked to the edge of the canyon and looked down, his eyes following layer upon layer of finely cut lines. The lines, many of different colors, ran horizontally to form a new river, approximately a mile below.

"Get up, we have work to do."

Legion rose and discreetly observed Mageddon's wounds. "But, they have blocked the way; we have lost our places too. All is lost."

"Fool!" shouted Mageddon in a bestial rage. "All is not lost. No," he said staring out across the war torn and ravished landscape, "This may work to our advantage yet."

"How?" asked Legion, trying to hide his skepticism.

"I will destroy her offspring and turn his people against him. When he returns, I will have amassed a force as numerous as the sand of the sea. I will have my revenge."

"What about the woman and her child?" he asked, his voice trailing off feebly.

Mageddon's eyes glowed red. "Once I've healed," he moved his broken wing slightly and grabbed Legion by the throat lifting him off the ground, "I'll find them and crush them myself."

He threw Legion off into the canyon.

"Victory will be mine!"

THE BALAMARA DESERT

Miaphas took the woman to the Balamara desert and placed her in a cave high above the desert plateau. The cave was hidden deep in the maze of an area called "The Land of a Thousand Canyons." Inside the cave was a tropical paradise. Rotating just below the ceiling was a star cluster that provided light to the fertile plants growing below. Fiddlehead ferns, rainbow chards, and longed-nose pokeberries grew amongst the floor. Fluted pumpkins, drumhead cabbage, and big-eared sugar beets grew along the walls. A fresh-water spring overflowed into a sparkling steel-blue lake. Its shoreline was speckled with fruit trees and edible red, blue, yellow, purple, and green polka dotted toadstools; the toadstools tasted sweet, like a dessert—especially their white spots.

Miaphas took the child in his arms and covered him in bobo balm.

"What will become of my child?" she asked, still traumatized by the separation. A small white tear fell from her left eye and rolled down her cheek, chapped from the wind.

Miaphas cradled the child in his arms and smiled. Without looking up, he responded, "Your child will be safe. We will take care of him and hide him from the great dragon until it is time."

"But what about me? The dragon will not sleep until he finds me."

"Guards have been placed throughout the land to protect you. Stay here until I return. When the time is right and the earth is ready, His Majesty will return on the wings of justice. He will destroy the dragon and all who follow him."

Miaphas exited the cave and laid the child, which was wrapped in a swaddling of coney fur, next to a rock. He looked around and then knelt down and scooped up a handful of dirt. He raised his hands to his mouth and whispered before inhaling the dusty granules. With the dirt dancing around inside his mouth, he breathed over the cave opening. Dirt tendrils wisped out of his mouth and crystallized, forming a secret door concealing the entrance to the cave.

* * * * * * *

Many years passed. The earth lie in waste, its landscape forever changed from Mageddon's devastating impact. Tall mountain ranges and deep ravines rose up and splintered out around the earth. A dust cloud blocked the sun for hundreds of years allowing great ice formations to lay siege upon earth's surface. Millions died, and Mageddon and his followers enslaved those that did survive. But not all; there was a remnant, a chosen people that had been protected. Mageddon dispatched his servants to kill, steal and destroy all that remained. The war against earth had begun.

CHAPTER 4

BONE VALLEY

The Valley of the Shadow of Death.

"Mogi, crawl through the weeds and get in front of him. When you see me climb up the ledge, stand up and let him see you. Then I will jump," whispered Rammer, crouching in the weeds next to a large overhanging cliff face. Mogi nodded his head and low-crawled through the weeds smiling and laughing, thinking about what was going to happen. Rammer climbed the rocky ledge and shuffled across. Scurrying across the ledge, his foot slipped on moldy bird droppings, freeing a few small pebbles, tumbling them down upon the ground and into the water below.

The large croaker popped its head up and looked around. Rammer froze and became one with the cliff, remarkably blending in with his surroundings. Large sweat beads dripped down his face into his eyes. A small butterfly floated by and landed on his nose. Straining to hang on with both hands, he blew upward trying to dislodge the pesky creature from its perch. The butterfly opened beautifully patterned wings blocking Rammer's view— Rammer looked like he was wearing fancy-looking rocks.

Mogi edged closer to the croaker. His tail whisked around in the air almost blowing his cover. The croaker lifted its head and spotted his furry tail bobbing with excitement. It also noticed numerous other fuzzy tails blowing in the wind and returned its head to the water's surface. Mogi crawled a little further and looked up searching the cliff face. He spotted Rammer on the ledge directly over the croaker. Rammer shook his head, silently giving the signal.

Adrenalin flushed through Mogi's body. He sprang from his hiding place spooking the croaker.

It jumped backwards and froze in place.

It slowly backed up and prepared to make its escape—just what Rammer had been waiting for.

"Yee Haw!" shouted Rammer, releasing from the cliff ledge.

Rammer landed on the croaker's slimy back and struggled to find a grip. Almost falling off, he quickly wrapped his legs around its body and his arms tightly around its neck and hung on.

The croaker jumped trying to buck him off. It twisted to the right and then to the left, bucking its back legs high into the air.

"You've got him Rammer. Hang on! Hang on!" shouted Mogi, laughing hysterically, running around trying to stay out of the croaker's path.

Rammer's head and tail jostled back and forth, whipping him around like fuzzy tails in the wind. The croaker crashed against trees and bushes. It jumped higher and higher, twisting in all directions. Finally, it spun back around and kicked, toppling

Rammer over its head, landing him face first in the muddy bottom of the pond.

Mogi waited in shock as bubbles, filled with laughter, surfaced.

Rammer's head peaked up through the giant water lilies with bright red flowers in their middle.

"That was awesome!" he said, spitting out a mouth full of water.

Mogi laughed and ran over to pull him out of the mud. "You should have seen his face when you landed on his back. He thought you were a Magondrea about to eat him."

Rammer rolled over onto the bank laughing. "That was great. You know we should build a large ring with holding pins and saddle them. I bet people would come for miles to watch us ride them."

"Yeah, until my Dad found out, then I'd be dead," responded Mogi. They looked at each other and busted up laughing again. "Come on, we'd better start heading home."

"Hey, do you think your parents will let me spent the night again?" asked Rammer.

"Sure, if it's ok with yours."

"They don't care what I do. As long as I stay out of trouble, I can do whatever I want."

Rammer slanted his eyes at Mogi. "I'll race you home."

"Last one home has to ask patches out on a date," said Mogi.

"Looks like you'll have a hot date for the weekend, Mogi," wisecracked Rammer, as he pushed Mogi into the muddy water getting a head start.

* * * * * * *

Morning dawned over the mountains. Golden rays crept up the dark dismal canyon shedding light on the wet, lonely-trodden trail. Chesty rubbed his sleep-deprived eyes and yawned. He had pressed through the night and continued to follow tracks down the gorge and into a draw. He followed the draw for several more miles until a thick fog moved in on him. He held out his lantern again trying to find his way through the fog—he knew he was close.

In the distance, he heard singing:

"No more hurting, no more sob,
pass through me gate and become like God."

His heart sank.

He dropped the lantern to the ground—it shattered against a rock, freeing the lightning bugs inside.

"No!" he shouted running through the fog.

"Caboose, don't say it, don't say it." As he rounded the corner the gate closed.

"No! No! No!"

He ran over to the door and hit it with his fists. Frantic, he fell to his knees and looked to the sky, "Not my boy, not my boy!"

From atop the gate Lucky gazed with a strange look on his face. He paced atop the gate observing Chesty from both sides. "Well, well, well, look who we have here—Pauper," he said, his lips making a sharp "popping" sound.

"I didn't expect to see you here again."

"Did he pass? Did he pass?"

"Now just hold your horses. Did who pass?"

"Don't play games with me Lucky. I know your tricks and you can spare me the riddles and rhymes."

"Yes, I suppose I can. Well, let me see…I guess you must be looking for…Me boy." Lucky laughed loudly.

"You better not lay a finger on him, or I'll, I'll—"

"Now Pauper, what makes you think I would lay a finger—"

"I know who you really are," interrupted Chesty. "You are nothing but—"

"And I know who you are Pauper," Lucky spewed back.

He climbed down the gate and transformed into a serpent. He coiled around Chesty and squeezed him tightly, bulging out his eyes, protruding his tongue from his mouth.

"Yesssss, you know who I am. And don't forget, I know who you are *Mr. Hypocrite*. I ought to kill you right here, right now."

"You have to let me pass," gasped Chesty.

Lucky, puzzled, loosened his grip and moved his head back. "What did you sssssay?"

"You have to let me pass. I have to save my boy," he responded, trying to regain his breath.

Lucky released his grip and dropped Chesty back to the ground. "Ha, Ha, Ha, Ha, Ha. You can't sssave your boy, fool." You escaped me once. You will not escape me again. He won't be there for you this time, 'Elder.'"

"Just let me pass, Lucky."

Lucky transformed back and motioned his hands toward the gate, "Be my guest. You know the key, go ahead and open the door—Caboose just passed. Maybe you can catch him before, Ha, Ha, Ha, Ha, Ha." Lucky disappeared.

Chills crawled up and down his spine hearing Lucky say Caboose's name. Chesty ran to the gate, bowed low and sang the song:

"I am happy, I am free,
I'm in charge of my destiny.
No more hurting, no more sob,
pass through me gate and become like God."

A crack thundered down the canyon walls as the door opened. Chesty ran through the door down the path. He didn't see Caboose at the chest so he forded the stream and ran to the Titan.

Boogies scattered from tree to tree watching him with excitement. The bark rippled around the Titan tree gossiping as Chesty emerged from the water, his body growing larger on the trail with his approach.

Inside he heard, "Twenty-two, twenty-three."

"No Caboose! Stop! Stop!" he yelled, banging on the thick outside trunk. He ran around the tree, grabbing knobs looking for one his size.

"Twenty-seven, twenty-eight, twenty-nine."

He jiggled another one and slid to a stop. The knob formed around his hand and opened. He slung the door open and bellowed, "Stop!"

His eyes focused on the last coin falling through the air. It hit the side of the stone, rolled along its topside and then fell to the ground. Standing at the stone was a young human girl shaking with tears in her eyes.

"You scared me," said the girl.

Chesty didn't know what to say. He looked around the room and asked, "Where's Caboose?"

"Who?"

"My boy, have you seen him?"

"No sir," she answered, bending down to grab the last silver coin lying in the dirt.

"Don't touch that coin!" shouted Chesty. He ran over and kicked it into the corner. "It's a trick," he said, gasping for air. "Lucky is not who you think he is."

She scurried over by the wall and searched in the dirt forming small mounds on the floor. "No, you don't understand," she said, her heart now beating rapidly, confused about what was happening. "When I put this coin in the hole it will all be mine. Lucky promised to make me beautiful and give me all the gold and jewels in the chest."

"It's a lie," grunted Chesty, disappointed she wasn't Caboose.

The girl, suspicious of Chesty and his intentions shouted back, "No, you are a liar! You just want it for yourself. I got here first; it's mine!"

The girl found the coin, scooped it up in her hand and stared at the stone.

"Please stop and listen to me for a second. You can't deposit that coin," said Chesty. He lowered his body and walked sideways around the stone preparing for her charge.

Her eyes focused on the hole as she matched his footsteps. Chesty knew she was going to go for it. She bent down, jerked to the left, jumped right, and then dove for the stone. Chesty jumped to block her but she slid under his belly and stood up over the stone. With her heart pounding, she reached out to deposit the coin.

Distressed, Chesty froze with his eyes staring at the ground— "Don't move." These tracks; do you see these tracks? These are the tracks of my boy. Chesty followed them around the room. "He must have come in right before you."

Although curiosity sent covert messages to her brain to

listen to him—she thought to herself, he may be right—skeptically she stood with her hand over the hole hesitant to trust him. Regardless, he had said enough to hold her attention.

Chesty walked over to a door the size of Caboose. "Look, he entered through this door. He went over to the closet. He looked at some of the books and then he stood here and read the wall. He then walked and stood there." Chesty's finger pointed to tracks right beside her left leg.

Chesty stood on the other side of the stone. "That is where he must have deposited the coins. You see? It's a trick. You can't deposit that coin."

"How do I know that your son didn't get what he was promised from Lucky? He is probably enjoying something great right now."

"Because," responded Chesty, "there are no tracks leading out of here. There are tracks coming in and walking around. And, there are tracks walking up to the stone, but that's it. All tracks stop here; it's a trick. As soon as you deposit that coin, a trap door will open sending you to a place of great sadness and death."

"Why should I believe anything you say? How do you know what will happen? You just want to deposit the coin and take the treasure all for yourself."

"There is no treasure. It's dross. Didn't you read the sign? It's not real." He looked around and waved his hands into the air, "It is…this is…all of this…it's not real."

She moved her hand closer to the hole.

"I've already deposited 30 coins," said Chesty, his secret now revealed.

She looked at him with disbelief in her eyes. All of her hopes and dreams where one coin away from becoming reality. Her hand quivered slightly.

"I already deposited 30 coins," said Chesty. "That's how I know what will happen. It was a long time ago, ok; this is not easy for me. But you have to believe me. I was here. I deposited the coins. And when I did, well...bad things happened. Things I've never told anyone."

Chesty buried his face in his hands. "And now my boy is lost and he may already be dead."

She lowered her hand but stayed by the stone. "But Lucky said I would be very pretty, like all the other girls."

Chesty looked over at her and asked, "What's your name?"

"Brook," she responded.

"I'm Chesty, Chesty Puller. Brook, putting coins into a stone in the middle of a hollow tree will not make you or anyone else pretty. It will not bring you wealth, nor will it make your father come back."

Brooks' belly turned upside down at the mention of her father. Was this man a seer, she wondered? How could he know such things? "But Lucky said—"

"Brook, Lucky is a liar. He lied to you, he lied to me, and now he's lied to my son. He is the father of lies."

* * * * * * *

"*Caboose is a goose and he smells like a moose. Caboose is a goose and he smells like moose.*"

"No...No...Stop calling me names."

"*Caboose is a goose...*"

"Stop calling me names;"

"*Caboose is a goose and he smells...*"

"Stop calling me names!"

"Where am I? What's going on?" Caboose was dreaming.

When the last coin dropped in the hole, it opened a trap door plunging him down into a cold, dark, muddy tunnel. He had tumbled for miles sliding down the slimy tube, finally washing out in a valley of bones. Exiting the tunnel, he hit his head on a rock knocking him unconscious.

Caboose was in the middle of nowhere. Dust covered the cloudless horizon as dirt funnels chased each other across the valley floor tossing brown teeth high into the sky—they drifted back to the ground, bouncing several times before being launched over and over again. Caboose watched as the last rays of hope were dragged into the catawampus peaks of Mount Viper. Every day, the sun tried to pass Viper's steep and jagged peaks to bring hope and rest to those deceived by Slithler; but each day Slithler laid a trap, and just when it looked like the sun would triumph, he would wake Viper, his beastly fire-of-death, and Viper would shake the earth, darken the sky, and swallow the sun whole. All that was left was the eerie sound of his ghostly laughter as Viper vomited the suns mangled remnants back into the sky. Dark crimson lava, the last remains of the sun, drooled down the sides of Viper's mouth, over ridges and boulders, moving ever so slowly between a maze of crooked fingers—or at least that's what those trapped in the valley thought.

Viper's shadow of death rained destruction over the valley. Under this shadow of darkness, Slithler's evil servants dispersed from a labyrinth of caves, tunnels and secret passageways, burrowed deep within Viper. Others stretched for miles across the open plateau, bringing havoc and death to all trapped in the valley.

The mountains were a death trap. Deep caves and crevasses in the canyon walls were infested with crawlers. They lived in bottomless caverns with quick access to the valley floor. They are crafty, eight-legged creatures with toxic fangs filled with venom. Concealed by the shadows, they creep out of their dens and check traps of smelly grass, which are long webs of string that look like grass, but are covered in a sticky mucus that only crawlers can make. Smelly grass lets off a tang aroma that's intoxicating and alluring. When some curious unsuspecting creature comes to savor the succulent blades-of-death, it entangles them making escape virtually impossible.

Fire-breathing ragooles (mutant dragons) traverse the skies at full moon, raining death and destruction from above. They cover vast domains in a single night and patrol the outermost boundaries of the valley. Their eyes are toxic blood-shot green that glow in the dark and they can detect the slightest movements from miles away. Their skin is coarse and dry. It clumps around the sinews of their necks as they search the ravines and plains. Their claws are saw-tooth black and curl at the ends, and their breath is a liquid inferno flame-of-death that turns everything to ash and stubble.

Patrolling the valley canyons and dry creek beds are thunder beasts, also called "grunters" because of the grunting sounds they make when fighting. Some thunder beasts are so large that when they walk it sounds like thunder thus the name "Thunder Beast." Not all thunder beasts are bad. In fact, most are friendly, but not the Magondreas. Magondreas are fierce beasts that walk on their two hind legs—they kill anything and everything in their path. They are unruly giants with a great sense of smell.

Lurking among the shadows are howlers, the most cunning killers of the valley. They move in packs twenty to thirty-strong, patrolling the flat lands and mountain ridges. They are soul-thirsty cannibals with six-inch carnivores, claws that can scale rocks and trees, and black red-tipped spikes for fur. They ambush their prey and capture more souls than all the other servants combined.

Slithler, the most feared beast of the land, rules the valley of bones, which is located at the base of Mount Viper and covers thousands of square miles. Slithler, which means "The Fallen One," is prince of the valley and ruler of the air. He is a long, black scaly serpent that slides on his belly and travels on top and under the valley through tunnels. He has a long, red line that curves down his spine all the way to his stinger-forked tail.

Slithler is not bound to the original form of his body. His knowledge of the dark arts allows him to transform into any beast or creature regardless of shape or size. His voice is deceptively mesmerizing and his beauty is unequaled. He is always on the hunt looking for someone to devour. He comes forth with the darkness and with one bite from his razor-sharp fangs or one attack from his stinger he traps souls forever in his kingdom. Once souls are sucked from the body, the body wastes away, littering the valley floor with bones—bones by the millions.

The day was hot, extremely hot. A spellbinding heat-haze rose from the parched terrain blurring his vision. Looming high in the skyline, Mount Viper stood like a fortress of doom. There wasn't a hole in the valley deep enough to hide its jagged peaks that clawed the smoke billowing from the center of its crater. Caboose watched streams of lava creep down its fluted spines into the ravines below. The lava scorched every brown tooth and green spike in its path before accumulating in large rivers that split across the valley and spilled into a dead sea.

Scattered across the land, russet sandstone pinnacles soared high against towering mesas; they painted a rusty horizontal backdrop across the landscape creating an optical allusion confusing those trapped in the land of tragedy. Small mounds of bones spread across the loathsome surface. Sallow piles of them were stacked deep in low-lying waterless basins and depressions, while others gathered in wide rows. The hollow rods-of-death rattled in the wind as he walked by causing his stomach to retch. Faint wheel impressions, which were wider than normal cart tracks, cut into the ground. They curved up and over the plateau following a path toward Mount Viper.

Shrill howls pierced the wind. Caboose stopped and listened but couldn't tell which direction they were coming from. The vibrations from the wind and the constant pounding of dust and pebbles disoriented him. He was covered from head to toe with it; he looked more like a water-grazer than a unidor. It was in his teeth and his mouth, which was making him cough up brown slimy slobber; it was even in his ears making him scratch them until they bled, impairing his hearing.

"Water, if I only had some water, I could—I could make apple fritters," uttered Caboose, not making any sense; his stomach was as dry as a summer drought. He was not going to make it much farther if he didn't get some help, and fast.

The valley of bones was not the lush green garden filled with all kinds of spectacular delights Caboose had seen through the gate. No, he had been tricked. It was a harsh land buckled with steep mountains and scarred with deep ravines—a death trap licking up any ounce of moisture that managed to gather in low areas. It lacked lakes and rivers teeming with cold, fresh purple mountain majesty. There were no Mushy Marts and Blossom Berry trees as far as the eye could see. The crystal sea was a dead sea. It offered no water; it gave no life. It was full of salt and poison with terrible creatures lurking beneath its surface.

A constant east wind blew over the barren wasteland making

it difficult for anything but green spikes and brown teeth to grow. When a storm blew through, it broke off brown teeth and cast them across the valley floor like sand pipers marching into battle. Their short stubby teeth tore through flesh and bone, and injected painful venom into anything they scraped.

Darkness covered everything in the valley. The Shadow of Death laid siege to the sky; it was so thick and powerful that only a few rays of sunshine ever made it through. The valley floor was littered with bones, thousands and thousands of bones covered in a thin layer of ashy-soot from Mount Viper. The bones were from all those who had been tricked by Lucky and who had never found their way out of the valley.

The only way out was back through The Scorpion Pass Gate; but that was the problem. Scorpion Pass from the North side was easy to enter. It had a broad, wide trail that was flat and easy to navigate. But once through the gate—and the trick—it dropped 15,000 feet into the valley of bones. No one in all the earth could climb its steep face, and even if they could, a battalion of monstrous trolls guarded the cliff face.

Slithler's servants patrolled the valley in front of them and could feel the vibrations of anyone approaching. It was impossible for anyone to make it through the guarded fortress; impossible at least for anyone of this world. There was one—and only one that was not bound by time or space. Legend spoke of a warrior, mighty in battle that would come and deliver those trapped in the valley.

A dust storm blew across the valley disorienting Caboose and causing him to walk in circles. The dust was so thick he could barely see his hand in front of his face. After several hours the storm finally cleared, revealing a mountain silhouette in the distance. He followed a dirt path to a dry creek bed adjacent a ridgeline. He followed the ridge along the valley continuing south for what seemed like an eternity.

He walked along the rocky trail, still confused about everything that had happened. Something felt wrong and it wasn't just the hunger bugs revolting in his stomach. How did all these bones get here?

Caboose stopped and looked over his shoulder. He felt like someone or something was watching him, following him, closing in on him.

Exhausted and besieged with stomach pains, he stopped and took shelter in a cave under a large craggy cliff face several days South of Viper. The heat from the valley floor had charred his dusty-black feet making them throb and tender to the touch. The cave looked like a safe, cool place to rest, so Caboose ventured in and found a place to relax. Not realizing how exhausted and dehydrated he was, he dozed off.

Outside, the wind picked up accumulating brown teeth at the entrance to the cave. Banis (tiny cave creatures with winged ears and three small horns flowing single-file down the back of their head) crawled across the cave floor. Wind funneled through the cave howling and whistling. It filtered pass Caboose cooling large sweat beads on his body and making him wake with shivers. Awake and cold, he continued to lie on the ground, not wanting to stand on his charred feet. His ears twitched to sounds of howlers off in the distance. Caboose still had no idea how he ended up so far away from Mount Viper and the Scorpion Pass Gate, but finding his way back was proving more difficult by the hour. Viper, by his estimates, was at least a four-day journey. So, he decided to stay the night in the cave; it would protect him from the wind and would keep him warm through the cold, dark night.

Caboose trekked deep into the cave fascinated by its unique rock formations. He noticed strange strings of grass all over the walls covered in slimy brown mucus that had a faint tang smell. Under each cluster of grass was a collection of various types of bones—bones from all types of animals and creatures. What he had failed to realize was he had taken shelter in the den of a crawler, who, at any moment, would be waking to start its nightly hunt.

Caboose saw something flicker out of the corner of his eye. Then he saw it again.

His heart raced, causing his chest to heave.

He hid behind a stalagmite, but it was too late. Whatever it was had seen him. He ran further into the cave trying to get away, but because of his short leg, he could only go so fast.

The beast matched his footsteps stride-for-stride. He could hear it drawing closer as sounds ricocheted from all directions, confusing him. Caboose was scared. He rounded a corner and entered a large cavern. Straight in front of him, barely visible by a dim light, tunnels splintered off in different directions. He took the third one to the right and ran down it and then took another one to the left. He squeezed into a crack behind a rock and waited.

Silence; there was complete silence. All he could hear was the pounding of his heart as he listened, turning his ears ever so slightly. After a few minutes, he peeked his head out. He waited a few more minutes and, thinking it was clear, squeezed out of his hiding place and backtracked to the entrance. Caboose walked around the corner and ran right into the beast. He bellowed, knocked it up against the wall, and turned to run, but it grabbed his neck causing all of his muscles to freeze instantly—a death freeze, collapsing him to the ground in shock.

The beast closed over him, and just when he thought he was going to die, a strong masculine voice whispered, "Caboose, be quiet, you don't want to wake the crawler."

Still in shock and with both eyes closed, he peeped one open and gaped, "Who are you? Please don't eat me."

"My name is Urium. And who I am, is not important right now. I have to get you out of here."

"Why? It's cold and dark outside and I have nowhere to go. And how do you know my name?"

"Caboose, this cave is a crawler's den. If he awakes and smells you in his cave," Urium stopped and reconsidered what he almost said, "It won't be good."

Deep within the cave, a low-jackaled voice reverberated:

"*Sticky fingers, sticky toes,*
My nose is a great hunter
And it smells a grunter."

"Hurry Caboose, you have to hurry." Urium helped Caboose to his feet and then ran for the entrance.

"What's a crawler?" he asked, running briskly.

"Quick, I don't have time to explain. You have to get out of this cave, *now!*"

Urium tried to lead Caboose out of the cave but Caboose struggled to keep up.

"Caboose, you must run faster. He's coming. I can hear him coming."

"I'm going as fast as I can. I have a short leg and I—"

"Hurry Caboose, you must hurry." Urium realizing he wasn't going to make it stopped and spun around. "It's too late, he's going to catch you, here, take this."

Urium tossed a small red engraved bottle through the air. Caboose reached up, barely catching it before it fell into a pool of water.

"What is it?"

"It's crushed dragon bones."

Caboose grimaced and looked at the bottle confused.

"Blinding dust," shouted Urium. "Throw it in his eyes. It will blind him for a few minutes and give you time to escape."

They ran out of the tunnel and back into the cavern. Caboose rounded the corner and slammed into the cave wall. With panic setting in, Caboose yelled, "Which way?"

"This way, hurry."

Caboose dropped to all fours and fell into a gallop. Urium ran so effortlessly through the dark Caboose thought for sure he must be a humanoid like himself.

Caboose felt a cold rush of wind dart over him but he dare not break pace to venture a look. Along the ceiling the crawler pricked. Silently getting ahead of him, it dropped on top of him knocking him to the ground. Caboose rolled across the ground and smashed against a stalagmite toppling it over—he rolled out of the way right before impact and jumped back to his feet. The crash reverberated off the walls causing everyone to pause and cringe.

"Go back Caboose, you have to stay alive," yelled Urium.

The crawler laughed hideously:

"You can run, and you can hide,
but come morn, I'll be eating your insides."

Caboose knew he couldn't out-run the beast so he scooped up a hand full of rocks and threw them at it. Unscathed, it hopped around and swung one of its legs knocking Caboose into the wall.

Dazed and confused, he pounced back to his feet driven solely by adrenaline and pulled the cork from the bottle of blinding dust. Inexperienced in combat, he threw it without so much as a fake or any type of diversion. The crawler, cunning and alert, dunked right before impact, but luckily for Caboose, the bottle broke on the ceiling, spraying dust back into its eyes. Blind, the crawler swung furiously, shattering everything in its reckless attempt to locate Caboose. Up ahead, Caboose saw small rays illuminating the cave entrance. Caboose dropped to all fours and plowed into the crawler knocking it upside down as he made a mad-dash for the entrance.

The smell of damp mildew and limestone slowly changed to a faint, hot sulfur dioxide as Caboose approached the entrance. With the opening in sight, Caboose yelled, "I can make it, I can make it." The crawler flipped over and hurried to cut him off as its dark-yellow, blood-shot eyes tried to focus.

Behind him the crawler spewed a ball of webbing from its mouth. The webbing clawed through the air closing the entrance as Caboose raced out of the cave. Once out of the cave, he ran for several yards and then wandered off the trail and stepped right onto a patch of smelly grass. It grabbed his foot, wrapped up his leg and around his body, pulling him tightly into its clutch. Caboose struggled, thrashing his body back and forth to get out, but the more he struggled, the tighter its strings lynched him in.

The crawler crashed through the webbing and started toward Caboose. This was it. He would never see home again. Caboose was going to die and there was nothing he could do about it. He pulled and jerked at the strings but couldn't break their grasp. The beast, with its eyes still hurting and blood-shot from the blinding dust, walked over to Caboose and gloated, *"Fool! No one escapes me. I told you, come morn, I will be eating your insides."*

Caboose shook with fear. He closed his eyes and waited for the kiss of death. The crawler's legs, prickly and hairy, crept eerily over him. Slimy mucus dripped from its mouth, covering Caboose in murky brown saliva.

"Please don't eat me. I'm not supposed to be here," pleaded Caboose, shaking uncontrollably with the rush of adrenaline still flushing through his veins.

The crawler opened its mouth. Venom-dripping fangs unsheathed and sparkled in the moonlight as it lowered its head.

From the darkness, faint tremors resounded. With the earthly sounds growing louder, from the twilight, a large Magondrea appeared with its jaws wide open. It grabbed the crawler and flung it against the cliff wall. The Magondrea raised its head and roared.

Caboose, with his eyes still closed, screamed.

Urium ran over and poured water from the dead sea on the smelly grass, drying it up, freeing Caboose. Caboose opened his eyes, bewildered. He reached down and broke off the remaining dried-up strings and jumped to the ground.

"Run for the hills Caboose." The Magondrea is deadlier than the crawler."

The crawler scrambled up the side of the cliff and spewed webbing all over the Magondrea. It jumped on its back and bit the large beast repeatedly with its fangs. The Magondrea, immune to the venom, shook the crawler off and knocked it back with its tail.

The crawler flipped over and lunged back and forth, snapping its upper fangs against its lower fangs, making a loud chopping sound. It then made a mad dash back to the cave trying to escape. The Magondrea chased it down from behind pinning the crawler to the ground. The Magondrea bit it on the back of its head, and with its front arms, tore it apart.

Caboose ran back to the trail and continuing to follow the ridgeline. His tender, charred feet seemed to be working just fine—it's amazing how much pain the body can endure when the stakes are high. Behind him he could hear and feel the vibrations from the Magondrea tracking him. Caboose was not sure where the beast was and couldn't see very well in the darkness. He rounded a bend and followed a cross cut up into a small draw. The Magondrea closed in and somehow managed to get ahead of him.

"Caboose, come this way," said Urium.

Caboose turned and just as he did, he found himself standing right under the beast.

"Don't move," whispered Urium.

Caboose froze. The beast hadn't seen him yet. It sniffed the air but couldn't smell him either.

"Caboose—stay still; the mucus from the crawler has affected his ability to smell you."

Brown slobber mixed with prickly crawler hair oozed from the beast, once again covering Caboose. The Magondrea looked around, sniffed the air and then moved on, disappearing into the night.

Caboose collapsed to the ground and sighed.

"Follow me," said Urium. He took Caboose by the arm and lifted him up. "You can't stay here. Howlers will have heard and won't be far behind."

Urium led Caboose up a shallow gully to an over-hang up in the foothills. He ducked his head in and out and then proceeded inside. Caboose, exhausted from the terrifying experience, followed closely. He walked to the back and laid down beside some small stones protruding from the ground. He could go no farther. His eyes closed and his mind raced with fear.

CHAPTER 5

THE AUGUR

The owner: The big boss. The one to whom all things belong.

Brook sat down beside Chesty. "I trust you, Mr. Puller. I guess I've known all along that this was a lie. I just wanted to be pretty, to be…noticed. To have a man…or my father, take me into his arms and tell me how pretty I am. Look." Brook handed Chesty a small trophy with a beautiful girl mounted in the hand of a dragon. "Lucky gave me this trophy. When I arrived at the gate, he was holding a beauty contest. He said I could enter if I helped him open the gate. I entered the contest and…I won."

Brook cried.

Chesty looked away and tried hard, but he too, began to cry.

He looked back at her with tears trickling down his face.

"Brook—silver coins, trophies, awards, clothes, and jewelry are not the things that make a girl beautiful."

She raised her eyes at him quickly, letting them fall.

"Beauty, real beauty, comes from the deep inner chambers of the heart. It counsels the mind, which inspires the tongue with a poetic melody. When that happens in you, you will sing a song that will fill the air with great rejoicing. Then, and only then, will your beauty illuminate the sky in a spectacular rainbow of a thousand colors."

Brook wiped her face. "Mr. Puller, I can see that rainbow now. I see it in your heart. I don't think mine can ever look like that."

"Why do you say that?"

Brook slogged over and pulled a book off the shelf. "I'm a bad person. I have bad thoughts and I've done bad things."

"You're not a bad person, Brook. You may have made some bad choices, we've all done that, but you're not a bad person. With some help and good choices, I believe you will see that rainbow sooner than you think."

She placed the book back on the shelf and picked up a charm from the table. She looked at both sides and then held it up to the light. "How does someone like you end up here, Mr. Puller? I mean, you are the nicest person I've ever met. How did you ever come to deposit 30 coins?"

"Well that's funny," he replied contemplating what he was about to disclose.

"What's funny?"

"You, asking me that question: You see—I've never shared this with anyone before. I knew this day would come, but I never dreamed I would be telling it to a 15-year-old girl—human girl at that—no offense."

"None taken, this is 'kind of weird.'"

She walked back over by him and sat down.

"Well, here goes. It was...let me see...about 35 years ago. My Papa owned a large mill, the mill I work at today. He was a wealthy man and loved my older brother and me very much, although I didn't realize it at the time. When I turned 17, I was tired of being told what to do and couldn't wait to move out of the house and away from my Papa and brother. One day I went to Papa and asked him for my inheritance.

My Papa was a humble and kind man. But, he didn't think I was responsible enough to manage that amount of money, especially at such a young age. I became very angry and didn't speak to him for several weeks. Finally, he came to me and gave me the money. I will never forget what he said to me. He said:

'*Son, my heart is old. It has embraced love and been scorned by hate. It has laughed with joy and wept with sorrow. It has nurtured life and stared death right in the face. I don't know how many more years it has, but I know one thing it can't overcome, and that is the loss of my beloved son.*

This inheritance is yours, take it. I pray you use it to find wisdom, not folly: Humility, not pride; compassion, not contempt. But, no matter what you find, I want you to know, you... are always welcome home."

Brook's stomach churned. Chills crawled up and down her body exploding small mountain ridges all over her, giving her clucker skin. "Wow, your father must have loved you very much."

"Yes...very much," reminisced Chesty, fighting back the tears, his heart jumping inside.

"So, what happened?"

"Well, I took the money and traveled all over the world. It was wonderful. I had lots of friends and the girls thought I was so handsome."

He laughed, shook his head, and continued.

"I bought my friends nice clothes. We ate the best food money could buy. I had the best of everything, but soon my money ran out and so did my friends. When the delusions of grandeur ended, I didn't even have enough money to make it home. I looked for work, but times were hard. I finally got a job feeding bush squealers from a mean, stingy old man. I was so poor and hungry I longed to fill my belly with the slop I fed them.

After several months, I finally came to my senses and decided to go home and beg for my father's forgiveness. After a long journey, and to this day I'm still not sure how I found it, I rounded a corner and there it was—*The Scorpion Pass Gate*. As I approached, I met *Lucky Lucy*; he saw me coming a mile away. He told me he would restore my lost inheritance and make everything the way it was before. So, I went through the gate and deposited the coins."

Brook sat calmly for a second and thought, Lucky sure does have a way of knowing what our weaknesses are. She waited a few more seconds and then asked, "And?"

"It was like I told you, a door opened up and I ended up in a valley of bones. I was scared, really scared. There were all kinds of evil creatures and bones...Shhh."

Chesty turned his ears and listened.

Footsteps beat in the dirt outside the tree.

"I think someone is coming," whispered Chesty.

"Who?"

"I don't know. Hurry, hide."

"Where?"

Chesty and Brook scrambled around the room looking for

a place to hide. Chesty spotted the closet. "Over there, in the closet."

No sooner had they closed the door, when three of Slithler's tunnel guards came walking in. Each guard carried a hand-carved staff in his hand—tunnel guards have a mushroom head, eyes that stick out of their sockets and swivel around, and their bodies look like plants of various kinds.

"It must be broken," said one of the guards.

"It can't be broken. It's never been broken," said another.

"Well it must be broken now. Lucky said two came in here and the sensors never went off in the hole signaling they had dropped through."

"Maybe they didn't deposit the coins," said the other guard.

They looked at each other dumbfounded and then smacked him upside the head with their staff. "Everyone deposits the coins, stupid."

He rubbed his head and moved away from their reach, "Then maybe they're still in here."

Chesty and Brook peeked through the crack in the door. They moved to the back of the closet but there was no place to hide.

The guards looked at each other, "Yeah, maybe they're still in here. Search the place from top to bottom," yelled the leader.

They spread out and searched behind the bookshelves and around the corners. Then they looked at the closet and raised their staffs. The guard took hold of the door knob, yanked it open, and plunged his staff inside yelling, "Gotcha!"

The closet was small with nowhere to hide. But it was empty. There wasn't anyone in there. He poked his staff around and then closed the door and walked over to the stone.

"You see, I told you. It's broken."

"Oh yeah," said the leader. He reached over and pulled a secret lever, plummeting his friend down the dark muddy tunnel. "Nope, it works." With that, he turned and exited. The other guard looked at him and asked, "What are we going to tell Lucky?"

The leader looked at him with a drawn face. "We? You're going to tell him it's broken."

"But…," said the other guard scratching his head with his staff.

In the closet, Chesty removed the cloak from them. The cloak was an invisible cloak that, when draped over something, made the object completely disappear.

"That was close," said Chesty. He snuck out of the closet and made sure they were all alone.

"It's all true. It's all true," said Brook following close behind. She walked out of the closet and dusted off her shirt. She walked over to the stone and ran her hand over the engraving and wondered how she could have been so foolish. It looked like her dreams would have to be put on hold a while longer. There would have to be another way, a better way, to heal her mind from the sickness it suffered. What Brook didn't realize though, was that healing—a spiritual healing—was already taking place, as she would soon discover.

"Sorry for ever doubting you Mr. Puller."

"That's okay Brook. I believed it too. Everybody believes it," said Chesty. Everybody wants to be somebody—somebody important, beautiful, talented—somebody that others look up too and respect. It's what gets us all—The Lie: The lie that we can be like God."

"What are we going to do Mr. Puller?"

Chesty walked over and stood right in front of Brook. He grabbed both of her shoulders gently and in his best 'Fatherly' voice replied, "You are going to go back the way you came and never come here again."

"But what about you? You can't stay here," responded Brook, not realizing that she was actually concerned about someone else other than herself.

Chesty stuck out his hand.

"Brook, give me the coin. I have to save my boy."

Brook, still holding the coin, pulled her hand back.

"Mr. Puller you can't go down there again."

"I'm not afraid anymore, Brook. I do not fear Lucky and his servants any longer."

Brook didn't say another word. She could see the love, the love of a father longing to be with his son. She reached up and wrapped her arms around Chesty's neck and squeezed tightly.

"Thank you. Thank you for telling me the truth," she whispered.

Chesty grinned and hugged her back. He took the coin from her frail little hand and walked over to the stone and deposited it. He was ready. He was ready to face the challenge of uncertainty in a valley of death to save his son, even if it cost him his life.

"Wait!" yelled Brook. "You never told me how you got out of the valley."

Click!

Chesty smiled, "The Augur," and he was gone.

Brook stood in the middle of the Titan motionless. She stared at the trap door and repeated The Name in her mind. The Augur; he's been with me all along. He led me to the temple that night. He knew what I was going through. Even in my darkest times, when my friends were gone, he was there. Brook fell to her knees, looked up and cried, "Great Augur, if you can hear me now, please help me get out of here. I believe in you. I believe in you now."

She looked around for a way out of the Titan but there were no doorknobs on the inside. She went from door-to-door finally finding the one she had entered through. When she touched it, it sprang open. She ran outside and headed for the stream.

Behind her, small dust clouds rose from her tracks and briefly gave chase as she followed the trail back to the stream, but to her surprise, the rock bridge was gone. Behind her, bogies formed into a long black face and shouted, "Traitor!" The sound waves from their voice blew over all the vegetation along the path and knocked her to the ground; her chin bounced off the dirt knocking her senseless for a moment.

Scared and lying on the ground, she glared through sharp blades of grass. Hundreds of Gogs (human slaves of Slithler that had become the evil found in their hearts) infiltrated the garden searching for her. She crawled upstream through the tall grass searching for a safe place to cross. The grass cut into her arms and legs causing them to bleed sending a pungent aroma of blood floating up into the air, which then permeated through the garden.

"There she is. Get her!" yelled a gog from across the stream, whiffing the smell of fresh delicious young blood.

She whirled around and disappeared through a grove of trees. She ran in-between the roots and hid in a large patch of mushy marts. She lay down flat under a cluster of them and tried to control her breathing. Panic rushed through her muscles and fear seized her mind, momentarily disorienting her. Unfamiliar with the garden she listened for the slightest sound, not wanting to feel the cold steal of a gog's blade piercing her side. Gogs crept around the trees looking in every interlocking root, crevice, and bush.

Brook froze and stopped breathing.

A gog passed within inches of her and stabbed his blade into the patch. He slashed the heads off of several mushy marts and then moved on to the next patch.

Brook sighed and breathed calmly. With vague apprehensions, she started to stand up. From above, a long skinny crooked branch reached down and grabbed her leg. It whisked her high into the air as if taking her to the gallows.

"She's here! She's here!" shouted bogies, circling in and out of the branches.

The gogs turned around and surrounded her.

"Kill her! Kill her!" chanted the bogies over and over.

The tree released its grip, dropping her to the ground. The gogs drew their swords and charged.

Brook hunkered down and closed her eyes. Her life flashed before her as the circle stopped. Life what a wonderful gift, a precious gift, often taken for granted. For many years she had abused her body and denied it the attention and nutrition it so desperately needed. Now, on the brink of death, everything inside her wanted to live. She wanted to experience life without shame and guilt. She wanted to experience life to its fullest, in the open, with no secrets, no purging in the bathroom; a life of trust, living in confidence, with purpose and hope.

From out of nowhere, gogs flew backwards through the air. Others were cut down and flung across the garden—what Brook couldn't see were the celestial guards fighting for her, protecting her from harm.

She did not understand what was happening, but glimpsing the opportunity, she ran. She darted back into the trees and down a path of stones. The narrow path weaved casually through the trees and came out at a shrine of statues. She stopped and spun around and then squeezed through the statues searching for a way out.

The statues grabbed and hissed at her. Others moved and boxed her in. She spun around and around dazed and confused, but it was only fear that made her hallucinate. She ran out of the statues and across a field of blue tongue sickles down to a set of stone stairs. The stairs curved under an arch of branches, back down to the stream. Brook ran down and stopped on a stone pad near the bank. She entered the shallow water and started to cross.

Slithler, The Great Serpent, slithered around the gate and made his way down to the stream, blocking her escape. He raised his dark hideous form from the ground and hissed, "And where do you think you're going, *Little Girl*. There was a fee for passssing through my gate and you failed to pay it. Now you will pay with your life."

He struck at her several times and then heaved with his chest as he opened his mouth. Exhaling her doom, Slithler called out, "Eckelbesh!"

The garden vibrated, tumbling rocks down the mountainside. Statues crashed into each other and blue tongue sickles fell from the sky. Large boulders crashed into the rapidly rising stream. Brook, still standing in the middle, heard a roar coming from upstream. Small water drops pelted her face causing her to blink repeatedly.

Petrified, she turned and ran for the bank.

Around the bend a tidal wave ripped toward her. With the face of a dragon, it swallowed her, sweeping her downstream in its murky waters.

Brook fought to keep her head above the rapids, but the

current was strong and arrogant; it quickened it pace and tossed her up and over the waves like a cat playing with its food.

Marconeon fought his way through the gogs and stood on the edge of the tree line overlooking the garden when he heard Brook's scream. He took flight and saw Slithler sliding down the stream after her. He scanned the water for Brook and caught a small glimpse of her before she disappeared behind a rapid.

Banakamus was some 300 yards upstream from Marconeon. Three gogs circled and jabbed their swords at him but they were no match for the experienced and skilled swordsman. He blocked every feeble attempt and sent two of them hurtling back into the trees.

"Banakamus, quick, she's headed for the falls," shouted Marconeon, who had left the tree line and was making his way to Slithler.

Banakamus jumped in the air and kicked the other gog into the bushes before he broke from the fight and took to the sky. He soared down the winding stream and caught sight of her in the current.

Brook could barely keep her head above water. She screamed for a savior as she plunged over a small waterfall and got caught in the undertow. The current acted like a large chain. It pulled her to the bottom and reached down her throat, trying to wrench her soul from her body.

Banakamus tucked his multi-colored wings behind his back and dove into the cloudy white-capped water, churning with vengeance. He swam around and searched the bottom, but visibility was poor and bubbles blurred his vision. He surfaced and then dove again. After several seconds, he surfaced, this time with her in hand. He spread his wings, ruffled the water off of them, and started to lift from the water.

From a peak on the mountain overlooking the stream, a ragoole launched and locked in on him. It dropped long and hard and pulled up inches from the top of the trees. It flew over the mosaic path and crashed into Banakamus knocking all of them back into the water.

Brook splashed and disappeared under the water only to emerge several yards down-stream. Banakamus and the ragoole thrashed back and forth, slashing each other with their claws, both trying to stay afloat in the turbulent water.

Brook, barely conscious, bobbed up and down in the rapids. In the distance, a thunderous roar filled the air and drew close with every doomed second. She snaked down the treacherous stream, unable to free herself from the rapids. She rolled over several rocks and boulders headed for the fall. The waterfall was a 5400-foot drop straight down into a black abyss that crashed into the rocky shoreline of the Dead Sea far below.

Brook, battered by the waves, fought to swim to the side but the current clutched her feet, spoiling her escape. Spotting a stick lodged between two large rocks, she paddled, barely grabbing it before she was swept by. The stick strained to hold her. It swayed back-and-forth several times before finally breaking.

Brook held on hoping someone would save her. Banakamus heard her cry but couldn't break free from the battle. As he watched from the distance, he heard the stick snap. Just feet from the fall, the rapids vaulted Brook over the edge and out of sight. She faded into the darkness—her screams growing faint as she plummeted to her death.

A gush of wind penetrated the garden, toppling trees, bouncing their heads on the ground in holy reference. Over the gate and down the stream he flew, powerful and majestic, splitting the water in his wake. Disappearing over the falls and into the darkness, he grabbed Brook in his talons seconds before impact. He burst back over the top of the falls gliding down the mosaic path. The light from his body blinded the garden as he rose over the gate and the jagged peaks of Mount Viper. The garden grew dim and vanished from sight while Brook, overcome with fear, rested in his arms.

He flew through the canyon and switchbacks. He navigated up the draws and past the fork. He followed the trail back to the mountain pass and landed at the bank of The Redmadafa just outside of Thunder Juice Town. He waded out into the water and gently washed the blood from her. He clothed her with an embroidered dress and put leather sandals on her feet. He adorned her with jewelry; a bracelet for her arm, a necklace for her neck, a ring for her nose, earrings for her ears and a beautiful crown for her head. He summoned the temple elders and took back to the air to start the search for the next lost soul.

Back at the gate, Slithler rose off the ground. "Master, he has spoiled your plans again," squelched a gog standing beside him.

Slithler swung his stinger-forked tail behind the gog running him through. He raised his lifeless body into the air and tossed it into the stream and writhed, "Yes, it would appear he has."

Slithler turned and gawked at the remaining gogs and beasts. "Strange. I feel strange. I feel...Good."

"Good? Master, what can be good about losing another one, rattled a voice from way in the back?"

He gazed at the gate and pondered for a moment. "He has swoggled me for the last time. Two can play this game," he hissed. "I will show him what a true Horn Swoggler can do."

"Master, what do you plan to do?"

"Beat him at his own game. Remove the bodies from the garden. Clean it up and open the gate."

"Open the gate? What do you mean master?" asked another gog.

"I've been going about this the wrong way. I'll open the gate and let them in by the droves."

"But master, what about the fee?" asked a tunnel guard.

"Fee?" he answered, with a devilish smile on his face. "If he loves them so much, he can pay their fee."

* * * * * *

"*Repent!*"

Caboose opened his eyes, stretched his arms and yawned. Still under the ledge, he looked out across the valley.

A voice echoed in the desert, "*Kingdom at hand!*" It was broken and faint, and then it was gone.

A new day dawned across the valley. Caboose spent the night under an overhang that stuck out from the mountain face and curved around the corner. Howler tracks imprinted the ground outside. They had crept in on him during the night but Urium covered Caboose in bobo balm, masking his scent and disorienting the howlers.

Urium looked at Caboose pointing his finger upward and motioned for him to be quiet.

"What is it?" mumbled Caboose.

"Howlers, they're still looking for you. They picked up your scent during the night and know you are close."

"Howlers? You mean the little ones like we have in Thunder Juice Town?"

"No. They are the creatures you heard in the desert when you first arrived. They are one of the most cunning and deadly creatures in the valley. They are fast and can climb rocks and trees. They capture more souls for Slithler than anyone else."

"Who is Slithler?"

"Shhh, I think they are on the ledge above us."

An ominous looking howler with a large scar across his face climbed down the overhang and sniffed the air. He looked out across the valley and then ascended the cliff face.

"What?"

"Just stay still. I covered you in bobo balm last night. It has confused them."

"Ok," said Caboose, with doubt in his voice, each answer only mounting more questions.

"Don't worry, in a few minutes it will be time for them to head back for their morning report."

"Who are you?" asked Caboose, "And how did you get here?"

"Sorry for scaring you in the cave yesterday. I am Urium, a member of the celestial guard. I was assigned to watch over you."

Urium was dressed in silver armor trimmed in gold with an eagle imprinted on the chest. He was white with purple stripes and his eyes sparkled of diamonds. Long wavy purple hair flowed over his shoulder and wings, which folded in layers tucked behind his back.

"Watch over me, since when?" asked Caboose

"Since you were conceived."

"Conceived?" he replied with a clouded look on his face. "Then why haven't I seen you before?"

"I've always been with you Caboose. You just chose not to see me."

Chose not to see you? He sat motionless for a moment. That doesn't make any sense. How can I choose not to see him if I didn't know he was there, he thought? Slowly drifting back he asked, "How can I choose not to see you when I didn't even know you were here?"

"It's complicated," responded Urium. "The best way to explain it is that most people don't choose to see us until they are in great danger."

"Oh," replied Caboose looking at the ground and gathering his thoughts. "But you were in the cave. I saw you following me," he uttered, with a shriveled face.

"Caboose, I am always following you; before you, beside you, over you."

"I don't understand. I saw you in the cave and—"

"You were scared and chose to see me. When you did, it finally allowed me to show myself to you and talk to you," said Urium.

Caboose flashed back to the cave and everything that happened inside. He was not used to being scared and alone, especially in an unfamiliar and dangerous land. His Papa made most of the important decisions in his life and was someone he understood and could turn to for help or answers. Urium spoke differently with him, like he was an adult. And even though it was hard to understand, down deep, Caboose liked it. He momentarily tensed up thinking about the cave and the crawler, but then relaxed.

"You almost gave me a heart attack. I was so scared I couldn't move. My muscles froze. I mean it. I couldn't move," he said gesturing with his hands.

"Sorry, you were going fast and almost lost me. When you fell asleep, I patrolled outside making sure your tracks couldn't be followed. When I came back you were gone. I didn't mean to sneak up on you like that."

"Who sent you to watch over me? I mean, what is a terrestrial guard?"

Urium leaned back and laughed. He took a small rock and tossed it up against the wall. It bounced off and rolled out from under the overhang. "Not terrestrial, *celestial* guard."

"Whatever," grunted Caboose, shrugging his shoulders.

"He assigned me to you the day you were conceived. His name is—" Urium put his hand over Caboose's mouth and nodded to the right. Caboose looked away afraid of what he might see. A door opened from the ground a few yards from him. His body tensed again frozen with fear. A shadow from the overhang hid them as two gogs crawled from the hole and started out across the valley.

"Master said he should be close to Graver's cave," said one of the gogs.

"I bet Graver ate him," responded the other.

"He will be mad and punish him again. The master wants this one for the games. He said we're not to lay a finger on him."

"How about a fist and a kick to the face?" replied the other gog with a smirk stretched across his mangled face. They looked at each other and busted-up laughing.

"The master didn't say anything about that," laughed the gog, prodding the other in the side.

Urium waited for them to fade out of sight. He stood up and looked down the hole. "That was close. Come on, these tunnels run for miles under the valley."

Caboose leaned over and looked down the dark hole. Panic churned in his stomach and his body shivered with the thought of going into a cramped dark tunnel again, especially after what happened in the Titan Tree.

"I don't want to go down there," shivered Caboose.

"It will be safer in the tunnels than out here," said Urium crawling down the hole. "Besides, the howlers know you are here. I don't know how much longer I can keep fooling them."

As they entered the tunnel, Caboose was still not sure they were making the right decision. The tunnel was formed by lava flowing from Mount Viper. Slithler and his servants used the tunnels to navigate the valley undetected. Torches resting in dragon claws mirrored up and down the tunnels lighting the ceiling more than they did the floor. Tunnels split off in every direction forming a large, interwoven network of mazes.

"I've never seen a tunnel like this before," said Caboose with strong implications that maybe they should turn around and leave. "Where are we going?"

"To find Seven," said Urium ruffling his wings.

"Seven. What's that?"

"It's not a what, he's a *who*," implied Urium with reverence for his friend. "Seven is a celestial guard whose been assigned to keep watch over the valley. For some reason my message hasn't gotten through, and he will be able to help us."

"What message?" asked Caboose.

"Your message…for help."

Caboose hesitated. Had he really been in the valley for so long that he was losing his memory? "I don't remember sending a message for help," he replied, with concern on his face.

"Of course you do. Remember the cave and the crawler, you cried out for help."

"Oh yeah, I guess I do," he replied, not sure that he really remembered anything from the cave and anything that he did remember about the cave, he wanted to forget.

"Who are you sending the message to?" asked Caboose

reaching back trying to scratch his side which painfully reminded him of the crawler and how close he came to being dinner.

"The Augur of course," responded Urium, surprised at the question from the son of a temple elder.

"The Augur, you mean, he's real." Caboose reached up and touched the handle of one of the torches. The flame raged wildly jetting sparks up on the ceiling. He pulled his hand back and pointed, "Did you see you that?"

"Of course he's real," replied Urium, focused on Caboose's knowledge of The Augur.

"Oh," answered Caboose, embarrassed that he had asked.

Urium stopped at a cross section and raised his star torch. "This way," he mumbled. "It's this way."

They continued for days, only stopping to rest under large lava falls from underground spill ways—large lava-rivers snaked through the tunnels and spilled over crags. On the sixth day, they came to a "V" shaped column with a dragon face carved into it. Urium studied it closely. They turned and walked down several small steps that led to a doorway which opened into a large cavern of honeycombed structures that where neatly attached to the ceiling and upper walls. Below them, hundreds of narrow stairs and bridges crisscrossed each other disappearing into a pitch-black bottomless void.

Caboose looked down and then took a few steps back. "I can't see the bottom."

Urium pulled out a star flare, cracked it, held it out and then let it fall. It glowed a dazzling white with a bright yellow center, vividly revealing the cave sides before being swallowed by the blackness.

"It's not that deep," said Urium, trying to reassure Caboose. "It's not much further. Just a few more miles and we should be there. What do you know about The Augur? What did you learn about him at the temple?"

"Not much," said Caboose trying hard not to look down. "Papa forced me to go the temple but I never paid attention. My Aunt Nanny talked about him a lot too, but I thought it was just a bunch of stories. I also heard some kids at school making fun of people who went to the temple. They said The Augur was just a mythological creature the temple servants made up to scare everyone into following their rules…Oh no…"

"What is it?"

"I just remembered. Those same people said the gate didn't exist either."

"Caboose, The Augur is real. He is the one that assigned me to you. And I wouldn't say that your Papa forced you to go to temple."

Caboose looked at him with a peculiar look but didn't say anything. He was afraid of heights and his knuckles were turning white from gripping the railings. And of course his Papa had forced him to go—they never missed a service, he thought.

"Your parents have a responsibility to teach you about The Augur. They are responsible for setting an example for you to observe and learn from both at home and at the temple. By taking you to the temple, it allowed you to observe worship, worship of the One and Only true, living God. It is at the temple that he speaks to his people through his priests and seers. The priests and seers teach from the ancient scrolls about how he saves from the valley and about the power of The Redmadafa. This is the responsibility of everyone that decides to follow The Augur. When you grow up, it then becomes your responsibility to decide whether or not you will believe what you have observed and learned, or whether you will reject it and go your own way. The Augur does not force himself on anyone. But he does charge those who believe, with teaching the next generation about him, especially their own children."

Convicted, Caboose asked, "What is he? Who is he? And what does he do?"

"Take a look around."

Caboose looked at the tunnel and shrugged his shoulders. This doesn't seem so great, he thought.

Urium, realizing the tunnel wasn't a good example said, "Well there isn't much to see in here. But everything you have ever seen, heard, touched, or smelled was made by him."

With a puzzled look on his face, Caboose asked, "He made the Valley of Bones?"

Urium realized he was getting nowhere fast. They stopped and took a rest next to a bridge made from the saliva of dragon bats. The bridge stretched across a bottomless cavern and ended at two stone statues of trolls wearing helmets and holding swords.

"The Valley of Bones didn't use to be like that," said Urium. He reached into a leather pouch and handed Caboose a square grain-cake wrapped in mint leaves. Caboose looked at both sides, smelled it and then took a bite.

"This is pretty good. What else do you have in there?"

Urium reached in and pulled out a few more treats and handed them to Caboose. "In the beginning, everything The Augur made was good. But then a serpent told the first man and woman that they could be like God, and they believed him.

"That sounds like a person I know," said Caboose. "Serpent... what is a serpent?"

"A serpent used to walk upright like humans. He had arms and legs and could even talk. He was the smartest of all the animals that the Augur made, but that ended up being his downfall.

A member of the Celestial Guard came and deceived him and had him sing a song. The serpent then taught it to the first man and woman. When the Augur found out, he cursed the serpent, turning him into a slider and said to him, 'You are cursed above all the beasts. Upon your belly you will crawl and eat dust all the days of your life. I will make you an enemy of the humans; they will crush your head and you will bruise their heel.'"

Caboose thought for a moment. He remembered the song the younglings at school sang about the gate. So excited to disclose his apparent knowledge of the subject, he choked trying to get the words out. "The kids at school sing a song about that I think," said Caboose. "The first part of it goes like this:

> 'Over the mountains, over the hills,
> Through the valley, better watch your heels.'

That's what that means. Now I get it:

> 'Listen to the air, listen for the click,
> better beware, or you'll be tricked.'

I've never seen a serpent, but I think I met one, and his name is Lucky—'Lucky Lucy.' He's a no good, double crossing liar, worse than a three-legged lizard." Caboose moved his head back and forth and, in a sarcastic tone, sang:

> "Lucky Lucy is all you have to say,
> for me to come around and take your troubles away.

Why, if he were here right now I'd show him what real trouble was all about. I'd—"

"Caboose, you must not let anger determine your actions."

Caboose kicked a large stone over the side of the ledge. "I wouldn't let anger determine my actions. I'd let my fist determine what size of a big fat nose I would give him right after I beat his face into the ground. Anger, I'm not angry. I am mad—completely, stark-raving mad."

The stone smashed against a rock bridge, which broke apart a small section, which then smashed into several others below it toppling them down and out of sight. The sounds echoed through the caverns and rushed down the tunnels. Two red eyes opened far above them and then quickly disappeared.

"Caboose, calm down, your face is turning red and your ears are going crazy. It's okay to be angry. Anger is an emotion that The Augur gave us to alert us that something is wrong, but you must learn to control anger and never let it control you. In your anger, you must not do wrong. You must overcome evil with good."

"But, I don't know how. That all sounds good, but I really want to hurt him."

"His wrongdoings will find him out. You said he made you sing a song."

"Yeah, that's how I ended up here."

"Do you remember it?"

"Yeah, I don't think I'll ever forget it. Let me see, I think it went like this:

I am happy, I am free,
I'm in charge of my destiny.
No more hurting, no more sob,
pass through me gate and become like God."

"So, is that what he is going by now, Lucky Lucy."

"Do you know him?" asked Caboose, his eyes growing with wonder.

"If it is who I think it is, I do."

"Well, who do you think it is?"

Urium stared off into the distance—that day at the Holy Mount and the fiery stones had changed his life and the course of history forever. "I was there when he fell," said Urium.

"You were where when who fell?" asked Caboose, confused.

"Sit down Caboose. I want to tell you about a celestial being that use to be the Supreme Commander of His Majesty's Imperial Guard. The song that he made you sing was the original lie. He tricked the first man and woman into singing it too and this was the song that ended up getting him cast from the Holy Mountain. It's the same lie that continues to deceive many today.

In the beginning, when His Majesty created the heavens and the earth, he created us, the celestial guards; we were created right before the humans and the beasts. We were assigned duties throughout the heavens and the earth. Our main duty was to watch over humans and creatures like you. Mageddon, the Supreme Commander, was assigned duties in a beautiful garden, the same garden that the first man and woman lived in.

Mageddon was not like the rest of us. He was the most beautiful and wise Celestial Guard His Majesty created. His setting and mountings were made of gold. His eyes slanted sharply and glistened of rubies. His skin was silky smooth to the touch and was overlaid with blue topaz. Emeralds traced the contours of his wings, which stretched high above his head and sparkled brightly when in flight. His finger and toe nails were painted with jasper—they were extra long and pointed at the ends. Red sapphires streaked with white beryl were woven into his hair and flowed down his back. Onyx and turquoise pierced his ears and nose. And his tongue…

oh, it was so stunning. It was made from chrysolite and spoke wonderful poetic symmetries. His songs filled the universe and were synchronized to spectacular displays of light, which shot across the galaxies illuminating the solar system with showers of cosmic explosions. I remember how all the starry hosts use to sit and watch, listening for hours, captivated by his rhythmic melodies."

Caboose watched Urium's facial expressions as he talked about Mageddon.

"Wow, he must have been, beautiful," said Caboose.

"Very," answered Urium. "On the day he was created, The Augur anointed him a Guardian Cherub and put him on The Holy Mount. He was even allowed to walk among the fiery stones. But his beauty and special authority soon became his downfall. His heart filled with pride and he proclaimed himself to be a god. So, there was war in the heavens and Mageddon, and the whole Northern army, lost their place of authority and were cast to earth. That is why the Valley of Bones is the way it is; that is why there is a gate, and Mageddon, I bet you, is behind all of this."

Small red eyes glared as dark shadows stirred within each honeycomb. Footsteps clobbered down the tunnels toward them. Urium turned around, squinted his eyes, and looked through the walls into the tunnels. With his back turned to Caboose, and in a calm voice he said, "Run."

Caboose didn't hesitate. He didn't ask why or which way. He didn't wait to see what Urium was looking at. He turned and made a mad dash for the bridge. He ran across the bridge tightly knit together with bat saliva and slipped on its slimy surface—he crashed face-first into a side railing and landed on his left shoulder, about midway across. Tunnel trolls emerged from the archway on the other side but didn't see him lying on the bridge.

Blood ran from his nose, down his lip and into his mouth. He spit it out and wiped his nose with his hand. He then lowered his head and tried to crawl back to Urium without being noticed.

Tunnel trolls erupted through the doorway from the other side stopping his escape. They spotted him in the middle of the bridge and closed-in from both sides. Unable to see Urium, they ebbed closer and closer with swords drawn. Urium flew over and grabbed Caboose. "Hang on."

"Hang on, to what? What are you going to do?" asked Caboose looking around for something to hang on to.

"Grab onto the corners of my armor, quickly."

Caboose looked at the trolls and then at Urium. Urium drew his sword, raised it high and struck the bridge. Caboose grabbed onto the corners of his armor and yelled, "What are you doing? You're gonna kill us!"

Urium struck the bridge again opening a crack down its foundations that splintered out across its base. Trolls pushed backwards as others tumbled over the side, disappearing into the darkness: others hung from the sides pleading for help. The bridge broke apart and collapsed underneath Caboose. He fell into the darkness but then rose from the dark carried by Urium. Black dragon bats with red eyes dropped from the honeycombs above and flew past them, ripping and tearing at Caboose with their long vampire fangs and claws, as spears and arrows took to the air and joined the fight.

Urium ducked and twirled, flipping Caboose over and under the fiery onslaught as he ascended toward the opening behind the two stone trolls—Caboose's face turned blue with airsickness. His eyes rolled back in his head and his stomach grumbled.

Urium plowed through the trolls and down the tunnel knocking trolls off the cliff while smashing others against the statues and wall face. Behind them, the tunnel filled with dragon bats, screeching and hissing. They nipped at Caboose's tail causing him to swing it vigorously, smashing several of them against the wall and knocking others senseless. Urium darted down the tunnels, zigzagging in and out of cross sections. He dropped low over a lava river and shot up an airshaft back into a large cavern. He dropped down another deep airshaft.

Caboose's eyes focused on the bottom quickly approaching and yelled, "Pull up! Pull up!" At the last second Urium darted into the bottom tunnel and dropped Caboose on the ground. He reached into his armor, pulled out a dragon's eye and tossed it to Caboose. Caboose juggled it several times before finally gaining control.

"Rub it hard and throw it," said Urium.

Caboose looked down and rubbed it energetically in his hands. He threw it back toward the opening and waited. Urium jumped over Caboose and spread his wings. The mauve/black-slit eye rolled into the corner, vibrated and exploded. The shaft entrance caved in, sealing the dragon bats and tunnel trolls on the other side.

CHAPTER 6

THE LITTLE ROUND ABOUT

The race does not belong to the swift, nor the battle to the strong.

"It's another great day here in Thunder Juice Canyon," said Mike, an announcer for 'The Little Round About' race. The Little Round About was the biggest race of the year. Creatures and beasts from all over the circle came for miles to test their skill and strength against the best in the land: Humans were not allowed to race—they were slow and would get stepped on.

"It sure is Mike," said Johnny, another announcer. "Conditions are perfect. We might see some records broken today."

"There's been a lot of talk about the new kid. Trax better not underestimate him."

"I couldn't agree more. You know, his father was quite the

prodigy in his day. Many still believe he would've broken Old Pete's record if it hadn't been for the accident," said Johnny.

"In practice the other day, I saw Rammer run three seconds behind Trax's best time this season."

"His coach said he is already jumping higher than Trax and his form is better."

"Johnny, I think we're in for the race of the season."

Coach walked over to Rammer who was swinging his leg from left to right loosening up. "Now remember, in Crooked Creek Pass there's a lot of loose gravel. As you approach the turn, bear to the left inside corner. It will keep you in line coming out of the turn and prevent you from going over the edge. Watch the loose gravel in the turns and…"

"Coach, I know, we've been over this a hundred times," said Rammer, now jumping up and down and moving his shoulders in a rowing motion. Rammer had worked hard, extremely hard to race in 'The Little Round About.' He knew a win today would make his Dad proud and perhaps persuade him to spend more time with him.

Coach flipped-open his map holder. "I'm just making sure," said coach, re-evaluating the course map looking for anything he might have overlooked. "Rammer, you can beat him, but you must believe that you can beat him. If he starts to pull in front of you close to the end, don't give up. That is the most important time of the race. Reach down deep, let him think he has the edge and then, accelerate by him and don't look back."

Rammer looked around the crowd. He knew he would need more than his own strength to beat Trax and the others. He needed the strength of his father. He needed that extra boost of energy that every athlete gets when they know their father is in the crowd shouting their name. He needed confidence, confidence that only a father can give to a son—male to male. Mothers may try but they just don't understand. It's a male thing. Sons need their father's support. They need his recognition. They need his time. They need his encouragement. Love is the ultimate compliment of achievement. They even need his discipline. And above all else, they need his love. The masculine love of a father taking his son, whether in triumph or failure, into his arms and saying, "Son, I am so proud of you…You did good today…Son, I love you."

"Do you see my Dad?" asked Rammer, hoping coach would give him a boost of confidence.

Coach, with hesitation in his voice, knew the answer to that question without having to look around. "Your Dad? I'm sure he'll be here."

"Yeah, this time. He's been really busy coach, but he'll be here this time. He's going to be so proud of me when I beat Trax and win 'The Little Round About.'"

"He sure will. Hey, do some more lunges and tail kicks. You need to stay loose and ready."

Creatures, beasts and humans lined up and down the starting line. Others climbed trees and hillsides to get a good view of this year's race. Rocks formed a wall along the trail-head to keep the people back while race officials scouted-out the route for any last minute hazards or obstacles—competitors were known to place things on the trail from time-to-time to gain advantage for themselves or disadvantage others.

Johnny, suspended high above the crowd in a leaf hut with four grass-weaved ropes carried by four flying trelaby hummers, spoke into the sea shell:

"I want to welcome everyone to the 49th 'Little Round About.' You folks are in for a real treat today."

The crowd erupted with excitement.

"They sure are, Johnny. We have people all the way from Jasmine Crossing and beyond. Everyone's come out to see if Rammer "The Rambam" Cooper can beat the three-time defending champion Trax "The Cat" Louise."

"Mike, we have some great competitors from all over. I hear Wally could be the long- shot today. And Tank is always in the mix of things."

"Johnny, I believe I see them lining up. The race is about to start."

Rammer's tongue was super-glued to the top of his mouth. He swallowed but couldn't make enough spit to knock a fly off a yellow belly if he tried. Rammer had trained for months for this moment, but he didn't expect to be so nervous. Trax looked fast, real fast. Rammer tried to remember what his coach said…something about rocks, but all he could think about was his father. He kept looking in the crowd to see if he was there, but Rammer knew he wasn't coming, he never came. Why would today be any different?

"Ok, whippersnappers; shut your yappers, and open your flappers," said an old, crusty shellback with the thickest spectacles you ever did see.

"You're standing on the start and the finish line. This is a one-lap event. You must go over or under every obstacle on the course. If you get off the trail or go around any part of the race you will be disqualified. There'll be no tripping, kicking, and under no circumstances, 'Tail Whipping!' Any questions?"

A funny looking creature raised his paw and said, "I have—"

"Good, then," said the old shellback paying him no attention:

"Let's get ready to thunder! Ca, ca, ca, ca, ca, he coughed; just line up and get ready."

'The Little Round About' was the biggest race of the year for Thunder Beasts and other funny- looking creatures. It was only one lap, but that lap consisted of a five-mile loop over some of the toughest and most rugged terrain outside of Thunder Juice Town. The first mile consisted of several jumps with the biggest jump being over Meteor Rock. In the second mile, athletes had to go through Skull Tunnel, which was a maze of turns, overhangs and darkness—a place where a lot of cheating took place.

Next was an agility test across Shifting Sand Bridge, where one misplaced step could bury competitors up to their waists. The final couple of miles started with a rope swing over Lava Pit, a balancing act over Rolling Timber Jam, then a treacherous decent down Crooked Creek Pass—which had a sharp hairpin turn with a dangerous cliff ledge, and then an all-out sprint finishing back at Junction Point.

The old shellback stretched his head out of his shell and raised it high into the air. He signaled a small dragonfly and pointed at Mack. The dragonfly flew over with a small stick in his hand and smacked Mack's slimy feet, instructing him to move back across the starting line. Mack, mad and embarrassed shot his tongue out and gobbled up the fly.

"I saw that," yakked the shellback. "Let him go, croaker, I'm warning you."

Mack spit him out and nodded to his gang. Their eyes gleamed at each other—they knew what to do with him when no one was looking.

"On your mark, get set," Aurrrrrr, the ram's horn sounded.

"There they go Mike. Woe, did you see Tank cut off Trax and Wally."

"Johnny, it looks like Rammer is having a little trouble finding a spot on the trail."

Mack spit slime in the eyes of Rammer and kicked him in the chest as the mob jostled for position. Rammer wiped his eyes and fell in behind Trax who had been blocked in by the howler twins. Trax faked right and then jumped left easily passing the twins—he looked more like a ragoole than a saber tooth as he went up and over the first jumps like they were twigs on a trail.

Rammer kept him in sight. He rounded the second turn and closed in on Meteor Rock. Tank ran by Holz and whipped him in the face with his tail knocking him off the trail.

"Mike, did you see that. Holz just got a tail to the face and went flying off the track right into a patch of green spikes."

Mike winced. "He's gonna feel that in the morning!"

Rammer cleared Meteor Rock but hit his tail hard coming down. Mack, also from Jasmine Crossing, took the lead and was first to approach Skull Tunnel. As he approached the tunnel, he slid on his belly and kicked, pelting Trax and Rammer in the face with rocks and dirt.

In the tunnel, Wally grabbed Rammer's tail and climbed over him slamming him against the tunnel wall. The howler twins returned the favor and knocked Wally into a column, which exploded and toppled down across the trail causing several competitors to dive for cover. Rammer jumped on top of the column at the last second and rode it down the tunnel, before jumping off and rejoining the race. Tank ran by, just as the others were standing back up. He taunted them with his tongue and smacked them back into the wall with his tail.

The lixoar gang, waited in the darkness with a rope. Trax and several others rounded the corner and tripped over the rope, toppling them end over end, piling them up in a large heap. Mack leaped over the pile and slimed them with a barrage of green-mutated mockery.

Once out of the tunnel, Rammer began to catch the lead pack. As he arrived at Shifting Sand Bridge, Tank was climbing out of a hole and cut back in front of him. Trax regained the lead and pulled away from the rest of the pack, who were having trouble with the sandy bridge.

Rammer approached the bridge and jumped to the right and then leapt forward. With a roll to the left and a huge spin, he jumped over the last sinkhole and back onto the trail. Free of obstacles and back in the open, he focused on Trax.

Trax miscalculated Lava Pit and landed with two feet out and two feet in, covering his back legs and tail in thick, red mud. Wally hurdled in the air and grabbed for the rope. It burned as it slipped through his hands, planting him face-first in the sticky red clay. Tank, not missing a beat, spit on his head and ran him over clearing Lava Pit with ease.

Rammer soared through the air and grabbed the rope. He swung across the pit and started to close in on Trax and Mack. The howler twins appeared out of nowhere. They closed- in from behind, hitting him from both sides. After several collisions, Rammer cleverly threw on the brakes, causing the twins to crash into each other, knocking them off the track and down the side of the mountain into a gully.

Rammer rounded the turn and closed-in on Rolling Timber Jam.

At the jam, Mack was having trouble keeping his balance causing all the logs to vibrate and roll out of control. He fell hard and rolled off the logs. Rammer never broke pace. He lowered his head, crouched down, and with a move that had never been seen before, jumped into the air, turned to his side, and rolled all the way across, jumping off Mack's head—almost catching Trax in a single move.

The lead pack ran down the trail and over several small hills toward Crooked Creek Pass. They entered the tall, narrow straights of the mountain leading up to what many competitors had dubbed Hangman's Noose turn; they called it that because after the turn on the right-side of the trail was a cliff ledge that dropped several thousand feet into a shallow creek bed below. Any athlete that fell from those heights would never be seen again.

Trax and several others hugged the left inside wall, squeezing Rammer up against the mountain face wedging him in. As he approached the turn (and forgetting the advice of his coach), Rammer swung outside the pack and tried to pass. Exiting the turn, the loose gravel gave way under the speed and force of his body and thrust him out against the edge. Unbalanced and skipping along the side, he tried to shift his body weight to keep from going over, but his momentum carried him off the path and over the side.

Trax and the rest of the pack, ran by Rammer with jaws wide-open and eyes bulging. Rammer, who was well off the path, was now running on top of the air. He mysteriously glided back onto the trail and continued into the straightaway and the final leg of the race—something strange had just happened—something "Celestial" of course.

Trax sensed Rammer's approach. With the finish line in sight, Rammer caught the pack and pulled in front of Trax—he was going to win. As they entered the last stretch, a crowd had lined up on both sides and was cheering them on; heads bobbed up and down, and arms waved at the competitors.

With Rammer in the lead and less than a hundred yards to go, he could hear from the crowd, "Come on Son you can beat him!" His heart raced, pumping adrenaline through his body.

Dad is here! He is going to see me win! In front of everyone, he is going to see me win the Little Round About. Where is he? Is that him? Rammer thought while scanning the crowd.

He looked over to see his Dad, and there he was, wearing the red shirt he had bought him for his birthday. But that's weird, it doesn't look like him, thought Rammer. Did he color his hair? Wait a minute…that's not my Dad. That's a Saber Tooth!

Trax heard his father's voice. When he did, a burst of atomic energy surged through his body. It picked him up, and like a cyclone force wind, it propelled him past Rammer as if he were standing still. Rammer felt powerless, weak, and alone.

It was over. Trax's nose cut the string claiming his fourth title in a row. Rammer fell across the finish line in shock. He couldn't believe what had just happened. With his dad's face imprinted in his mind, exhaustion turned to anger and hate burned within.

* * * * * * *

Thump, thump. Thump, thump, thump! "Wakey, wakey, Mr. Shaky," said a howler holding a long stick in his paw striking Chesty several times in the side. Thump, thump, thump, thump! "Wake up grunter."

Chesty, dazed and confused awoke slowly. He heard muffled voices echoing in the wind, but thought he was dreaming.

"Are you sure we can't eat this one, he's a big one? He could feed us for weeks."

Thump, thump, thump, thump. Kuta struck him again and several other howlers pelted him with rocks. Chesty opened his eyes struggling to focus as he swung from the rope. He looked around and then straight down. He was hanging upside down over a ledge.

"Hey, look who decided to join us," said Zakok, just about to launch another rock.

"Yeah, look who decided to join us," repeated another howler.

Zakok shifted his gaze around the pack and shook his head. "There must be an echo in the canyon." The rest of the pack lowered and shook their heads too.

Chesty was surrounded by a pack of howlers. He had traveled in the valley for days cleverly going unnoticed but had accidently stepped into a gog trap that wrapped around his leg and catapulted him up and over a ledge. Kob walked out of the twilight and approached the cliff ledge. Ever so serious, he sniffed the air. The marred blood vessels in his scar pulsed, causing him to twitch.

"I've smelt this one before."

"Where, where would you have smelt him before Kob?" asked Kuta.

He sniffed the air again and tilted his head. Kob rummaged through the vast stockpile of his scent memory and turned toward Kuta. "Impossible."

Kob, the leader of the howlers, hated grunters more than any other beast or creature. Several years ago, a young grunter's horn slashed across his face leaving him with a scar that ran across his eye all the way down to his lower jaw.

"Kob, is that you," said Chesty, still dangling from the rope?

Kob's eyes glowed fiery red as he pinpointed the identity of the grunter. Kob stared back at Chesty. Hatred raged within him, as black red-tipped spikes rippled across his body. The other howlers looked at each other and backed away fearing his anger.

"Pauper!" spit Kob, in a blind rage. "Look who we have here boys. Pauper, or should I say, 'Prodigal,' The Prodigal has returned."

Chesty hated being called that. It was a part of his past that had haunted him for years. "I found forgiveness for my past long ago Kob," said Chesty, trying to twist his leg in the rope to help blood circulate to his foot. "I see you're still a slave of Slithler. I hear you're still jumping people from behind," said Chesty, referencing Kob's ravage attack on Traegor.

Zakok walked beside Kuta who had finally put two-and-two together and asked, "Who is that?"

"That's the grunter that gave Kob the scar."

Zakok swallowed and moved back to his latter position.

"I don't know how you ended up back here Pauper but I can assure you, no one will save you this time," vented Kob. Just the sight of Chesty galled him. He paced back and forth, searching his thoughts.

"But why? Why have you returned?" he said, standing on the ledge next to Chesty. He glanced at him and thought for a moment.

"Maybe he squandered his wealth again and wanted Lucky to bail him out," replied Kuta.

"No. Not this time," said Kob. "Money alone would never be enough to bring someone back here." Kob searched his thoughts again. Why would he come back? It must be something really important, or something, he paused—seconds later a slumbered smile revealed two fouled ivory fangs… "Dear to his heart," he spoke out loud.

"There's only one thing that would ever bring someone back

to this god-forsaken place," responded Kob. "Love: Only love would dare bring someone back. But who?" he pondered. "A wife? A child?"

Chesty listened but the words were muffled. Blood flooded his brain making it throb. He tried to disguise his emotions and hide the truth from Kob, but Kob leaned over the ledge and stared into his eyes. It was there, on a ledge, in the middle of a Valley of Bones, a valley of death and suffering, that hatred met love face-to-face; vengeance met mercy eye-to-eye.

Kob turned toward the pack. "It's a child. It's...his son. Decided to follow in dad's footsteps, did he?" gloated Kob, realizing he had sniffed out the truth. Have any grunters been captured or killed in the last few weeks?" he asked the pack.

"Several have been captured but Slithler ordered that none be killed," spoke a howler standing behind him.

"I heard a magondrea killed a large one just a few days ago. He was punished and cast into Dead Man's Despair," answered another.

"We tracked one the other night but lost his scent, you know, the one from Gravers cave," answered Kuta.

"Cut him down and get out of my way."

"Kob, what's going on? You can't kill him. Slithler wants all grunters alive."

Kob knocked Zakok back, grabbed him by the throat and threw him over the ledge.

"Don't tell me what I can or can't do. This grunter dies today!"

"I don't want to fight you Kob. I just want to find my boy; then you can have my life."

Kob grabbed Chesty's face with his claws and pulled it close. "Your life! Your life! Your life and soul will rot in this spot for the rest of eternity." He thrust his face away and stepped back. Kob's body shook rabidly from the endorphins pumping through it. Mucus salivated from his mouth as the red-tipped spikes on his back reached for the sky, ready for battle.

Chesty remembered the last time they met. He was 17; he had squandered his inheritance and had been trapped in the valley by Kob and several others. Kob, who was second in command at that time, cornered Chesty, whom he called 'Pauper' because he had lost all his money and was a poor, restless wanderer trapped in the valley, and had wounded him severely. In front of the pack, he tried to attack Chesty by himself instead of using the strength of the pack. When he did, Chesty swung around, trying to protect himself and accidentally slashed Kob across the face with his horn. Embarrassed, Rukbat, the leader of the pack, demoted Kob making him subject to the others and last to feed.

Two howlers walked over to the thick lodge pole holding Chesty and swung him over land and cut the rope. Chesty dropped to the ground and sprang to his feet. Thinking only of his son, he puffed-up his body making his appearance even larger. He lowered his head and matched Kob's footsteps.

They circled each other.

"Come on Kob, rip his throat out," growled one of the howlers.

"I'm going to kill you Pauper, and once I tear out your throat and the ground licks up your life-blood, I will personally take your soul to the pit and cast it in myself. Then I'm going to find your boy and unleash the hounds of hell. When I find him," Kob stopped and savored the thought, "I'm going to kill him slow—real slow. I'll gorge myself on his flesh and drink his blood until my stomach burst from gluttony. Vengeance is finally mine."

Chesty fought hard to control the rage building inside, but couldn't stop his heart from beating mad. He knew he could not allow Kob and his pack to harm Caboose, and to kill him; that wasn't an option. He must protect his son no matter what the cost or pain to himself.

"Vengeance is The Augur's and his alone. You have mocked and terrorized his children for far too long. The first time we met, I was young and afraid of you. I'm not afraid anymore."

"Good, your pride has blinded you; I will use that to my advantage."

"Pride? I don't come against you today with pride. I come against you in the name of The Augur. The battle belongs to him."

Chesty flinched back and then leapt forward, catching Kob off balance. He rammed him in the side and spun him around. Kob's jagged claws dug into the ground and grabbed his back leg, ripping flesh high into the air—it splattered on the pack causing them to wince. Chesty bellowed and charged Kob, tossing him into the pack like a rag doll.

Kob recovered and climbed up the cliff directly over him and ran across its face. He jumped backwards, spinning in mid-air, and tore a large gash down Chesty's side. He then landed on his feet and raked dirt into Chesty's eyes, temporarily blinding him. Chesty reeled around trying to protect his flank, and advanced right into Kob's trap. Kob jumped on his back and sunk his six-inch fangs into the back of his neck. Chesty swung, trying to knock Kob off, but his fangs were long and deeply embedded. With blood running down his back and nothing else to do, he ran backwards into the cliff face, crushing Kob with his massive weight.

The pack watched in panic. Their leader's brutal reign had finally come to an end. It was the second time Chesty had altered Kob's life.

Chesty stood up. He was wounded from the battle and took no pride in Kob's misfortune. In victory he walked over him, but surprisingly, Chesty felt nothing but defeat.

Kob's battered body lay motionless on the ground. The blood in his heart coagulated, slowing it with every beat. Kob peered down his vile, spiked nose frothing with tiny red bubbles.

"I hate you! I hate you!" he scorned, gasping for air. Little red bubbles fell from his nose soaking into the dirt beneath.

"I wish things could have been different between us Kob. Anger has consumed you and hate has clouded your judgment. I forgave you a long time ago."

"Forgave me?" roared Kob coughing up blood. "Who do you think you are? Don't dare coddle me with your pathetic self-righteousness."

Kob lifted his head slightly from the ground. "You will die in this valley Pauper and when you do...Ca, Ca, Ca," he coughed again, "Your soul will belong to Slithler. We will meet again; in the pit...meet...again."

His eyes closed. His heart stopped. All that remained was the gargling sound of death leaving his dark bloodstained body.

* * * * * * *

The crowd thinned and walked back to town. The long uneven clay road bustled with activity as vendors and competitors packed and headed home—their pockets bulging with profit. News of the race spread throughout the marketplace and taverns. Thunder Juice mugs slid down the bar as spirits soared high and accounts of the race spread. Laughter echoed out of doors and windows as many retold the race with great excitement.

Along the trail, small creatures swept trash that littered the trail all the way up to the finish line, some blowing off into the carrot-colored sunset. The wind whistler brushed tracks away, covering them with small granules of dirt and sand. All that remained were the small indentions of another vague race where dreams ran high and disappointment low. Yellow and brown leaves shuffled across the path and accumulated into small burrows against the trees and rocks; insects scurried to claim a home and fought heartily to defend it. Younglings raced each other down the trail pretending they were racers, testing themselves, honing their skills with future dreams of grandeur.

Rammer sat on a stump behind a grass hut; a year of sweat, pain, and agony all for nothing, he thought, as self pity consumed him. Anger boiled deep within him. It constricted his heart and convinced his mind he was not as good or important as others. People told him he wouldn't amount to much, and now it seemed like they were right. He sat outside, venting, mad at himself for foolishly thinking that his Dad was in the crowd.

How could I be so foolish, he said to himself? I could've won if I hadn't looked in the crowd.

"Good race Rambam, you almost beat him," resounded a quaint accent from someone passing by.

Rammer didn't say anything. He just sat there, static, frozen in times past.

"Maybe next year Rambam. You will get him next year," said another.

Coach came around the corner and stopped. He watched Rammer for several seconds. He knew the pain he was feeling was not from a lost race that he had trained so hard for. He knew it was the pains of a son longing to have his father's support, his father's validation that he was becoming a man. Coach walked over, gracefully escorted by a presence, a Spirit, not his own.

"Rammer, I've been looking all over for you. Are you ok?"

"You almost beat him—maybe next year. That's all I've ever heard. 'Son, I'll be there this time. I will be there watching you.' I

can't stand him. He's not my father," said Rammer, without looking up.

"Rammer, don't talk about your father that way. I'm sure he's
doing the best he can. He probably got held up at work."

"Work, play, the tavern, it's always something. A new excuse:
a new opportunity. Trax' Dad was here. He was here for his son."

"Rammer, this race was not about whether your father was
here or not."

Rammer jerked from his seat. "Of course it was! It had everything to do with him being here. Don't you understand? Don't
you understand anything? Trax beat me because he heard his
father's voice."

Coach looked away. Silence crept in. Memories flooded his
mind as those same words echoed from long ago.

"What would you know about it anyway?" vented Rammer.
He walked inside the hut and jammed his things into his burlap
sack. "You have the perfect family. I bet your Dad came to all
your races."

Coach followed close behind but stood off to the side. "More
than you know Rammer, more than you know." Coach sat down
on a chair and stared off into the distance.

"I do have a great family *now*, but it wasn't always like this. I
used to feel like that about my Dad too."

Rammer didn't say anything. He finished packing his
things and then faced coach with a focused gesture. After a few
moments, coach, looking back into his past and spurred by the
divine, replied, "I grew up in a home that was filled with violence.
My Mom and Dad drank Thunder Juice and fought all the time;
so much so that my little sister and I used to hide under the bed
or in the closet, scared their anger would be taken out on us.
Sometimes we were pulled out of bed in the middle of the night

and had to go stay with our mother's friends. I cried myself to sleep many nights wondering why The Augur had given me the parents he did. My Dad never came to my races. He never did anything with me."

Rammer looked down but not at coach. Coach hesitated for a moment and wondered if he should continue. Now was probably not the best time to have this conversation, but then again, maybe it had been ordained before time began.

Coach continued.

"I stood and watched the fathers of my friends come and cheer them on at the races. I heard them talk about the fun vacations they took together; we never took a vacation as a family. Never! I didn't realize it then, but my distorted perception of reality was transforming me into an angry young man. I started to hate men because of my father and the sense of abandonment I felt from him not supporting me. It didn't take long for selfishness to lay siege to my mind and eventually consume the benevolent heart I had. My life spiraled out of control for several years after that. So, don't tell me that I don't know how you feel, because I do."

Coach stood up, walked to the door and stared outside. He placed his hands on the doorposts and continued.

"When I was old enough, I left home; I got as far away from him as I could and never looked back. I ran straight for the gate and didn't want anything else to do with Thunder Juice Town and the people of the temple. But do you know, the harder I ran, the faster The Augur pursued me."

Coach reached up and wiped his eye. A small smug of wonderful mercy traced the edge of his finger. He wiped it against his leg.

"I ran to the mountain-top and he was there. I hid in the valley and he was there. I sailed across the sea; there was nowhere I could go that he couldn't find me. Even the fallen celestial guards tried to keep him from me; they failed.

You see, during that time, the time I tried to run from him, people back at the temple were praying for me. One day, before I left to find the gate, I ran into a couple of them. They said The Augur loved me and wanted me to come back. Do you know what I said?"

Rammer shook his head no.

"If he is such a loving Augur, why would he create me if he knew I was going to reject him and go my own way? Then one day my Aunt Nanny finally answered that question. She said, 'Young man, The Augur gave you life and planted you by The Redmadafa. He gave you his love, but to receive yours, he had to let you go. That is the only thing The Augur can't do; he can't make you love him. *Because if you make someone love you, that's not love.*' Those words changed my life that day.

I can't go back and change how my parents lived and how they treated my sister and me. I can't go back and make my father love me. But, do you want to hear something really awesome?"

He walked over and stood beside Rammer and said, "I can't go back and change what happened in my family. But now The Augur has given me a family of my own. I have three sons and a daughter. Children that I take in my arms and show them the love I never had. I go to their races. I take them on vacations. We go and eat in the marketplace. We even swing on the vines, way out into The Redmadafa. But above all else, the best part is, we all go to temple together and worship him as a family."

Tears ran down both their cheeks as coach took Rammer in his arms and pulled him tight.

"Rammer, call out to him and let him take you into his arms and show you a love like no other. When you receive his love, it will change your life, and you, Rammer 'The Rambam,' will go and do Great Things."

Rammer hesitated to speak. He didn't know what to do or how to respond to the emotions flowing in his body. Coach's words…they spoke a truth he hadn't heard before. Life was in his words. Healing, but not an herbal or physical healing. It was a spiritual healing—a healing unknown and unexplainable by books or professors at the university.

"You said Trax beat you when he heard his father's voice?" inquired Coach.

"You may think I'm crazy Coach, but I could feel the energy flowing through Trax when he heard his father's voice."

"My life changed the day I heard my father's voice cheering me on."

"I thought you said he never went to your races?"

"He didn't. That's not the father I'm talking about. When my Aunt Nanny told me about The Augur and the love he had for me that was when I heard his voice. It was then that I realized he had been to every practice, every scrimmage, every race. He promised he would never leave me and that he would always be there. I foolishly thought I was alone during that time of my life. But I wasn't. I was never alone. He was always there."

CHAPTER 7

YELLOW BELLIES

Lukewarm: neither hot nor cold. Beasts:
Creatures:
And Humans afraid to choose a side.

Rocks and boulders clogged the shaft entrance. Loud rumbles echoed up the tunnel and vibrated off the walls. Caboose stood up and shook the dust off his back. He held his head and muttered, "Now I know why The Augur didn't give unidors wings." He grabbed his stomach. "I think I'm going to be sick."

Still dizzy from the wild ride, he wiped his face and inspected his tail. Bite marks pierced the skin on the right side, and on the top left side, several small chunks where missing. He reached back and pulled out a tooth that had lodged deep inside one of the bite marks.

He examined it.

The tooth was white at the tip and black near the root.

"That was close," he sighed.

"Let me see that." Urium took the tooth and held it up to the light. He touched the tip of it with his finger and then sniffed it.

"Disgusting little varmints," he replied.

He pulled out a leather pouch and dropped it in. Caboose heard a dim jingle as it landed in the bottom of the pouch. He shook his head. He didn't bother to ask what it would be used for.

Muffled shrieks permeated through the pile of rocks shifting his focus away. He thought for a moment about what had just happened. He realized once again how close he had come to death. He wondered how anyone could make it alone in the valley without help. Without Urium and those back home praying for him, he would have never made it out of Graver's cave.

"They wanted to kill me; they wanted to kill me. Urium, they wanted to kill me!"

"Death has a rightful claim on all who enter the valley."

"A rightful claim; what does that mean?"

"No one forced you to go through the gate. Death has a rightful claim to all souls that enter the valley," said Urium, cleaning off his wings and tucking them back in place.

"Oh," acknowledged Caboose, not caring to know anymore about that. "Where do these tunnels lead? They look different."

"We are getting close to Mount Viper. Many are dead ends that come out somewhere in the valley. The rest are used to transport smaller creatures and humans to Viper, or the ferry, which takes captives to the Pit."

"*The pit*," gasped Caboose. "What's that?"

"The Pit of Souls; it's in the floor of the colosseum. It's a place you never want to go. Slithler uses it for his games. Slithler is the father of lies. He moves about the circle spreading his lies and empty promises to those who are hurt, lonely, feel out of place, or lost. Outside of the valley he only has the power to trick, deceive, and kill the body. But, inside the valley, if he kills you, he owns your soul. Most of the time he lets his servants kill all who enter. But, when he wants to be…amused, he has his servants bring the captives to the colosseum.

At the colosseum, his servants gather around and haggle over who gets to fight first. Then they bring out the captives and the slaughter begins. Once all the captives are killed, their bodies are used for food and their bones are brought back here and scattered across the valley. Regardless whether you die in the colosseum or in the valley, all souls are taken to the colosseum. At the bottom of the arena, is the door to the Pit of Souls. All souls are taken to the door and cast in."

"By whom?"

"By Apollyon, the king of the Abyss."

Caboose hesitated. He was learning more than he cared to know. "What's inside?" he asked, not really wanting to hear the answer.

"A river of fire, trapping souls for all eternity."

Caboose stared off into the distance. I don't remember learning any of this at temple he thought. "Wow…that is the exact opposite of The Redmadafa. The Redmadafa is a river that brings life and healing to all who enter it. Slithler…He really is the father of lies."

"I couldn't have said it better myself, young grunter. I see wisdom starting to surge within you already."

Caboose stopped and looked at Urium. "Wisdom. Really?" With a smile touching both ears, he looked into the air, "Wisdom."

"We're here," said Urium.

Caboose stepped forward. His head followed a cracked wooden ladder held together by twisted vines. The ladder ascended into a black musky shoveled-out hole. Urium grabbed the ladder, shook it a couple of times, and then disappeared into the shadows. At the top, he opened a hatch that exited back into the valley. He climbed out and then shouted down at Caboose.

Caboose grabbed the ladder and started up. About mid-way up, he started to sway from side to side, so he plastered his tail against the back wall to steady himself and then pushed forward. At the top, while crawling out of the hole, he slipped on its slimy surface causing him to fall to the ground. He rolled up against Urium's leg.

Urium looked down and laughed. "Are you alright?"

Caboose lay on his back with all fours pointed to the sky. "I'm fine, thank you; just stretching my back…Yeah my back… Oh that's better." He stood up and shrugged his shoulders.

Urium led Caboose across a valley splayed with thick under-growth and traps of sticky grass keenly hidden across its billowed expanse. Hunger bugs beat in his stomach at the smell of tang wafting by. Caboose didn't say much. He constantly checked behind him surveying the numerous trails that traversed the valley floor. He thought about his family back home. He missed the big dinners and the family time. He wondered what the guys at school were saying about him. He was sure their stories were growing larger with every passing week he spent in the valley.

A dark haze gripped the vast wasteland scattered with bones. Huge stand-alone mountains silhouetted the plains far away. Accumulated at their base, were mounds of rocks that had broken off from the top. Caboose, tired and uncertain about being back in the valley, kicked a set of bones off the trail. The bones tumbled off the trail and rattled against others lying on the ground, catching the eye of The Wind Whistler.

The Wind Whistler, upset he had been disrespectful to the dead, hummed a tune diagonally through the valley, pelting Caboose in the face with sand, laced with green spikes and pebbles. He reached down and cupped dirt in the hollow of his hands. Lifting his hands to his mouth, he blew in-between his thumbs and then lowered his hands and threw the dirt across the valley floor—like throwing a pair of bones across the table.

Small dirt funnels emerged from his hands and chased behind Caboose. The Wind Whistler laughed hysterically as they wrapped around Caboose, causing him to cough and choke. Bones bombarded him from the sky beating him mercilessly. He dove to the ground and covered his head with his hands.

The Wind Whistler blew past him and ripped down the canyon tossing brown teeth high into the sky, raining them back down on Caboose like a meteor shower, pelting his head, back, and tail.

Urium didn't say anything. He discerned the agony churning inside. He also knew this was good. This agony was the agony of conscience; the agony of knowing one has done something wrong; the agony of realizing no matter how hard you try, no matter how smart and talented you are, you can't right the wrong by your own means. This was something Caboose needed to come to terms with on his own. He needed to realize the consequences of his decisions and how they affected others. He needed to realize it is only by the power of The Augur, living fresh and anew within his heart, that he would be able to do Great Things and help those that deserve to be thwarted, forgive those that deserve to be condemned, and love those that deserve to be hated.

The valley has that effect on man and beast. The business of life and work often keeps people from ever contemplating the meaning of life and their purpose on the circle. They never question why they were formed nor what their mission is. But once trapped in the valley, it seems like the sheer solitude and loneliness brings them a fresh perspective on those things, or at least it did for Caboose. His mind played back Urium's stories about the original garden, the first man and woman, and it especially took note of the serpent. If Urium was right, he was in serious trouble, and he wasn't quite sure what he would do if he came face to face with the slithering beast.

On the other side of the valley they entered a rolling ravine and followed it around a rock-strewn bend. The narrow path curved sharply around the bend and dipped before entering a corkscrew. Several miles in, they found themselves sandwiched in a deep gorge with steep walls laddered-up on both sides and high, overhanging bluffs.

Caboose, severally dehydrated, started to see and hear things. Muffled sounds swooped overhead casting hideous shadows on the wall. Caboose thought for sure this must be the home of The Wind Whistler. Wind blew down the deep gorge, causing Caboose to tense with fear.

"His cave is just around that corner," said Urium, breaking the silence. "Oh yeah, there is one thing I forgot to mention."

"What is that?" asked Caboose, looking high up the gorge walls scanning the ledges and overhangs.

"Around the next corner, before we get to his cave, is the Gorge of Gargoyles."

Caboose swallowed deeply.

"Gargoyles...I hate gargoyles."

"They should be asleep right now. Just be extra quiet and everything will be fine."

They rounded the corner and continued for several hundred yards. Subdued shrieks echoed off the walls and slowly floated past them. Sparsely illuminated by the twilight, dark silhouettes lined the scabrous walls and rocky floor. Thousands of gargoyles twitched and shuffled, sleeping on any square inch of space they could find.

"Just watch where you step and everything will be fine," whispered Urium, trying to build his self-confidence.

Caboose rocked his head back-and-forth and sarcastically replied under his breath. "Just watch where your step." Sure, he thought to himself, that's easy for him to say, *'just watch your step.'* I survived a crawler and a mangondrea, to be eaten by *gargoyles*."

The gargoyles seemed to be on edge. They shifted around a lot and pushed each other for space. Caboose carefully stepped over and around them, being extra careful not to step on one. With the cave in sight, he anxiously pushed the limits of his patience. He stepped over a gruesome-looking small one and stepped right on the tail of a bigger one.

A screech echoed throughout the gorge.

Caboose froze and lifted his foot.

The creature smacked the little one next to it and went back to sleep. The little one rolled-over with a smile on its face, grabbed its neighbor's long floppy ear, blew its nose and mumbled something under its breath.

Caboose looked at Urium and mouthed, "That was close."

Urium mouthed back, "Keep moving."

Exiting the gargoyles, they entered the mouth of the cave. It was a labyrinth of tunnels that looked more like catacombs, rather than a place where a celestial-being lived. The tunnels stretched for miles into the mountainside. Urium had obviously been there before. He navigated in and out, and around corners like it was his backyard. Caboose stooped to drink in a small but deep cave puddle, quenching his thirst, and momentarily appeasing the hunger bugs who were at this point satisfied to receive anything. Up ahead was an impressive display of giant stalactites and stalagmites; columns of them had grown together. They stretched from wall-to-wall deep into the cave.

Caboose, a little drowsy asked, "Are we there yet?"

"As a matter of fact, we are." Urium stopped. "I'll summon him."

"He lives in here. Aren't these caves filled with gogs and crawlers? How does he go about without being detected?"

"He's a…very unique celestial being. When you see him you'll understand. He's probably standing beside us right now."

Caboose looked around. Urium pulled a small pipe from under his armor and blew three long blasts, two medium blasts, followed by one short peep.

They both looked around and waited.

Drops of mineralized water trickled down small stalactites and landed in a large pool of bluish-green water at the center of the cavern. Small rocks tumbled down the sides as if they were all lining up to take a seat. Creeping creatures scurried about through the cracks and along the floor, strutting by like they owned the place.

Unexpectedly, a voice materialized right behind Caboose. "Urium, is that you, my old friend?"

Urium and Caboose spun around but no one was there.

"Seven, I need your help. This young grunter has been trapped in the valley for weeks. I sent his message weeks ago but I haven't received a reply."

Urium raised his light and moved it right and left. Seven stood a few feet from them but they couldn't see him.

"Where is he?" whispered Caboose.

"I'm right here young grunter. And who might you be?"

Startled, Caboose peered around the cavern.

"He's standing right in front of you," whispered Urium.

Seven peeled himself off the stalactite column making himself visible to Caboose. Seven's body was a maze of contours covered with rocks and small rock formations. His ears, hands, and feet looked like a taro leaf with suction cups.

Caboose followed the light sparkling off Seven's body. "Sorry Mr. Seven, I…didn't see you standing there. I'm Koby, but everyone calls me Caboose."

"Nice to meet you Caboose; now, what may I do for you?"

"I sent his message several weeks ago but something must have happened."

Seven looked at Caboose as if he were looking right through him. He searched his thoughts and asked, "What is your last name?"

Caboose touched a small column protruding from Seven's body and accidentally broke it off. "Puller, Koby Puller," he replied, trying to put in back before he noticed. The piece fell to the ground. They all looked down and then back up.

Caboose gasped and smiled. "Sorry."

Seven put his hand to his mouth in deep thought. "Unbelievable. Unbelievable!"

"What is it?" asked Urium.

"I've never seen anything like it in all my days."

Seven walked down the cave and stopped in front of a smooth wall with thousands of coded symbols carved into its side. He ran his finger along a small crack, stopping next to a symbol with three swoggled lines running through its center and nodded his head.

"This is strange."

"What's strange?" asked Urium and Caboose at the same time. They paused, looked at each other and then back at Seven.

"Your message: It's been held up for exactly...21 days."

"Held up, by whom," asked Urium?

Seven raised his eyes and lowered his chin, "Mageddon."

Bewildered, Urium exclaimed, "Mageddon. Why would he be involved with this?"

"That's a good question." Seven searched the wall again, this time running his finger from top to bottom.

"Galamus has your reply and...is trapped by Mageddon and his forces. He is hiding in sector C9 Gamma. I will dispatch Miaphas to see what he wants to do. I remember seeing your message come through here Caboose. What's odd, is that I also saw another message...where is it?"

Seven stepped to the left and looked high on the wall. "Let me see, oh yeah, here it is. No, that's not it." He looked a little higher. "Here it is." He rubbed his finger across the symbols. "It can't be. It can't be."

Urium stood puzzled with lots of questions racing through his mind. He knew if Mageddon was involved that something of great value must be at stake. Seven turned around and looked at Caboose. "Young grunter, do you know a Chesty Puller?"

Caboose's jaw dropped and his heart stopped beating; tears the size of blossom berries lined his eyes.

"Papa. He's my Papa!"

"Ha, Ha, Ha!" laughed Seven, with his hands resting against his side. "I've just about seen everything now. This is getting good—real good."

"What's going on Seven?" asked Urium, who couldn't take the suspense any longer.

"I don't know. I don't know. But, whatever it is, it's big—real big. Caboose, your Papa is here looking for you. Your Papa, he's been here before."

Upset that Seven would dare say something so awful about his Papa, Caboose replied, "Impossible. My Papa is an elder at the temple. He's never been to the Valley of Bones. We have a great family and my Papa would never do anything that would bring him here."

Seven, impressed by his optimistic passion for his father's honor, responded, "Your Papa has been here before and he's here now."

He looked at Urium, "They've taken him to the Sea Throne."

"Sea Throne, what's that?" asked Caboose, still upset by Seven's accusations.

Urium swallowed, "Mageddon's throne. It is also the location of…" he looked back at Seven, "The Pit."

"*The Pit!*" Caboose paced, uncertain how to react to his newly acquired knowledge about his papa. "We must help him. You have to take me to him."

"Urium, go with him," asserted Seven. "It is the will of His Majesty."

"But, we've never taken anyone to the Sea Throne, it's forbidden. Are you sure?"

"Positive. It's written on the wall. You are to lead him there. The rest…" shrugged Seven, "Is yet to be told."

He turned back toward Caboose. "The Augur has plans for you. Great Things, he has planned for you."

Seven reached down and pealed a small pouch from his side. "Here take this. Use it when others need it most."

"What is it?" asked Caboose, holding it up to the light.

"Dragon claws:

Pull them out, cast them about.
Water, wind, fire, and earth,
Is all you need to give them birth.
Dragons for friends trapped by sins,
To be used by the wise,
Or it will be your demise."

"How do I get him to the Sea Throne? I can't…fly him across. Besides, even if I could, ragooles, and the Southern Celestial Guard heavily guard the air—they would see us coming. And, the route by sea is more treacherous than the sky. There are beasts lurking beneath the water that I'm afraid of."

Seven smiled and climbed back onto a column. "Beast for beast," he muttered, in a long drawn out voice. As he disappeared into the cave, his voice echoed:

"Stand aloof, at Dead Man's Drop,
Quarter 'til noon, whistle the tune;
A ripple, a wave, out of the cave,
Count to three, anchors away."

* * * * * * *

Thunder Juice Town was quiet. The marketplace was closed and streets empty. Adults and children exited through the Northern gates and made their way up to the Temple of the Sun dressed in their Sun Day attire—long red robes with black sashes. Sun Day was the day people worshipped "Ra" the Sun god. People who had grown up in Juicy, who did not know or believe in The Augur built a large temple with an ornate altar to Ra on the outskirts of town. Everyone great and small, rich and poor gathered there to engage in all kinds of revelry—except those who believed in The Augur.

Usha served as High Priestess of the pagan temple. She had served in it from a young age and assumed High Priestess nine years ago. She had a large staff of eunuchs that served her day and night. They carried out her orders with great fervor and their devotion to her was without question.

Usha meditated in her chamber waiting for everyone to assemble and take their place. Hundreds of hand-hewn idols adorned her chamber; they were stacked on desks and pedestals all around the room. Candles stood on top of smooth rock basins. Teardrops teetered down their side, forming wax waterfalls that edged off the sides of the stones. Small colorful charms and trinkets dangled from hooks in the window and ceiling, and were draped over idols, stands, and anything else that would hold them. Each one sparkled in the candlelight casting an array of colors throughout the room. Potions littered the tabletops in her back room and incantations lined the bookshelves. Long strips of colored silk hung down from the ceiling kissing the granite floors—blue shadows flickered as they waved gently off the floor, tossed about by a breeze from the window. The sweet smell of calamus filled the room.

Outside, six shaggy long trunks, in single file, raised their trunks and blew. Beside them, six moogles stood opposite each other beating drums. Six Ragooles stood at the entrance while six hundred and sixty-six human girls danced around them with tambourines streaming with long red ribbons striped with gold.

In the center of the main room was a large looking stone, round and smooth—its eye watched all who entered her chambers. Usha, levitating above the ground, heard the sound and opened her eyes. Solid black eyes slowly turned to blue. Her servants entered the room and dressed her in elaborate ceremonial garments. They ushered her down the hallway glazed with red roses and stationed her behind the thick golden curtain laced with red velvet and trimmed with red and black rubies.

The crowd chanted "Ra," over and over waiting for Usha to emerge and start the beastly ceremony. The thick curtain drew open revealing her ill-omened form standing in the middle of a large arched column. Fire erupted from the mouths of the ragooles standing opposite each other with their wings fully extended creating a tunnel of fire. Usha stood backwards with her legs and arms crossed while she floated down the fiery tunnel. She stopped at the edge of the stairs and twisted around. With her arms raised high, and in a cackled voice, she shouted, "You have fallen from heaven to give us light, Oh morning star, son of the dawn. Speak to us Ra and give us a sign that we may fear your great name."

She walked over and grabbed the offering tied to a large asherah pole and slit its throat. She filled a small golden goblet inlaid with black onyx stones with its blood and poured it out on the stone altar and waited.

Silence fell across the crowd.

Little children climbed atop their parent's shoulders to see the altar.

Rumbles oozed from the ground and crawled up every leg. Hearts grappled with fear, as minds, intoxicated with endorphins, raced with fantasies.

Fire engulfed the stone altar and spewed high into the air.

Worshippers fell to the ground and bowed over and over chanting, "Ra, Ra, Ra, Ra."

A dark demonic form appeared in the mist of the fire. It leaped into Usha causing her body to convulse at its presence. It picked her up parallel to the ground spinning her body 'round and 'round. She stopped over the altar and rested on its smoldering surface. The fire subsided as the worshippers, in a spellbinding trance, focused on the altar. Four moogles approached the altar and slipped two large bronze poles in each end. They lifted the stone and carried her back to her chamber—the curtain closed behind them.

Located in the southwest corner of town was *The Gallery*, the great temple of The Augur. Beasts, creatures and humans, all that had been rescued from the valley of bones, set aside this time to gather together and give thanks to the *One* and true God—His Majesty:

<u>HIS MAJESTY</u>

The *Gallery* was the temple where new life was birthed, a symbol, a beacon, a jewel of the earth. Fifty majestic towers dawned on high, from all directions, drawing me nigh. All in universal and cosmic display, pointing the way in spectacular array. At night, each tower illuminated the sky, a city on a hilltop, no one could deny. Piercing the darkness revealing the slope, with glorious rays of eternal hope—*and glory shone and shone, shone and shone, shone and shone.*

The temple brilliant and skillfully made, from precious stones his tender hands had made. A large central dome adorned the sanctuary, circled by 12, governed, by the son of Mary. Twelve arms flowed from each shiny dome, why, oh why, do my little ones roam. Gardens, sculptures, porticos and cisterns, were scattered throughout, their praises glistened—*and praises rejoiced and rejoiced, rejoiced and rejoiced, rejoiced and rejoiced.*

Hundreds of corridors faded away, no need to fret or be dismayed. Leading up to the doors large cobbled stones lay, inviting, they were, no fee to pay. At the end of each step large statues prayed, to The Almighty Eagle that had formed them by clay. Enormous hallways of columns and glass, filled with jubilee, all leading to mass—*and jubilee danced and danced, danced and danced, danced and danced.*

The stairs half circled around to the top, a mighty threshold he alone could cross. Beneath the crystal floor out of the cleft, healing tears, from The Augur wept. A split rock from which headwaters flowed, The Redmadafa, oh, how it glowed. Water from a rock, how could this be? Only by sovereignty—*and victory shouted and shouted, shouted and shouted, shouted and shouted.*

Purple pearl doors strong and straight, opened to those with unmovable faith. The windows and ceiling all told the story, of the countless souls that had entered His glory. Amber arches and icicle columns rippled the aisles tranquil and solemn. All the way down no need to falter, there before me was his glorious altar. The sun fled from his presences, the moon hid asunder, His Majesty, oh what a wonder—*and glory and honor rose up, kissed the sun and moon goodbye, and took their rightful place.*

The orchestra assembled and took its place, as little creatures bustled with smiles on their face. Music thundered from the outer courts as mushrooms drummed, flowers hummed and grasses strummed. Water clapped, trees snapped and rocks tapped. Bugler Fish played, Thunder Beasts swayed and little children serenade.

The melody resounded throughout the streets, as everyone stood to their feet. With angelic voices the choir sang, perfect harmony from their mouths rang:

> *Your Word formed the universe*
> *Your hand's carved out the galaxies,*
> *Lord Almighty.*
>
> *You hold the world in the palm of your hand*
> *You formed the earth and dry land,*
> *From the sea.*
>
> *Majesty, Majesty,*
> *We worship you.*
> *Your presence fills this place*
> *We are covered by grace,*
> *Your Majesty.*

A young girl stepped out of the choir and moved to the front and continued:

> *When I look to the sky*
> *I see your face,*
> *Smiling back at me.*
> *When I walk in the night*
> *I hear your voice,*
> *It comforts me.*

The choir joined back in:

Majesty, Majesty,
We worship you.
Your presence fills this place
We are covered by grace,
Your Majesty.

A young boy stepped out of the choir and moved to the front and continued:

You made every creature and man
We're all a part of your plan,
At your command.

You are the Potter I am the clay
You knew me before I was made,
Your glory on display.

The choir joined back in swaying side to side:

Majesty, Majesty,
We worship you.
Your presence fills this place
We are covered by grace,
Your Majesty.

Onuka, a moggle and high priest of the temple looked out across the crowd. He majestically rose and sauntered over to the ambo. The old silver back, well along in years, knew it was time. With wisdom he laid the ancient scroll on the ambo and opened it with his deeply contoured black hands. He walked out, cleared his throat, and in a deep, low-rumbling tone, boldly declared:

The Boiling Pot

"Last night as I lie in bed I fell into a deep sleep. A celestial being came and carried me to a place once bright and clean, but now in ruin. Before me stood a *Boiling Pot* fashioned by a skilled craftsman. The pot glowed red as fury boiled over, igniting the fire beneath—scorching my face. As I watched, smoke leached out down the sides of the pot and waged war with the fire…extinguishing it. The once bright and glowing pot froze as smoke turned to ice and became one with the ground.

A voice said to me, 'Onuka, do you see this Boiling Pot, once hot and bright, now before you cold and trite: my children are neither; they have become lukewarm. They love the things of this world and have forsaken their first love. Tell them Onuka, did I not leave the ninety-nine to find the one; I have not forsaken them. Tell them Onuka, did I not deliver them when they called my name; I still love them. Tell them Onuka, did I not forgive their debts; return to me and I will forgive them once again. *Light the fire, boil the pot!* Tell them Onuka.'"

Onuka paused.

He walked across the altar collecting his thoughts. He had served as High Priest for several years and had served many of the faces in the crowd since they were children.

"I have served this temple for many years. I've seen The Augur, day after day and night after night leave this flock to search the highways and byways, and the most desolate places to find lost souls. Like a cedar tree's topmost shoot, he breaks them off and carries them back to The Redmadafa.

He harvested where he has not planted. He gathers where he has not sown. Most of you sitting here today were despised and without love when he passed by and saw you kicking about in your blood. 'Live!' he said to you. He took you in his talons and brought you here to Thunder Juice Town. He planted you like a willow tree by abundant water. He caused you to multiply like a plant in the field; you grew and became the most beautiful jewels of the land. And, if that weren't enough, when he saw you were old enough, he covered your nakedness with his love and you became his most beloved."

He walked down the steps and slowly paced up the center aisle, his gaze piercing the heart of every individual.

"Yet, as I walk these hallowed streets my mouth is speechless with disappointment. As I attend the festivals and new moon parades, my eyes are blinded with shame. As I listen in the marketplaces, my ears are deafened with disgust. My heart is broken—Broken I say! Broken, because streets that once flowed red, as his children spread His Word, now run yellow as the cower and churn. Yellow bellies as far as the eye can see. All of us have turned and gone our own way.

'*The Boiling Pot*,' a pot that once glowed red because

his children were not ashamed, has now become stagnant as they blaspheme his name. Lukewarm people who sit around and drink thunder juice and listen to lies until their ears are intoxicated and overflowing; only to awake and lust for more."

Chains of guilt yoked necks in holy reverence.

"Has it been so long? Have you forgotten the valley, the Shadow of Death? Rekindle the fire. Fan into flame the spark. Boil the pot once again, before it is too late."

He walked back up the steps and stopped. He turned around and looked at the ceiling with his arms raised high.

"The Augur…is coming. He is coming back—"

He lowered his head.

"Soon."

* * * * * * *

A face peaked through the cracked murky window. Little green eyes followed every glimmer of light, scanning the street for any sign of him. This was Rammer's nightly routine. He often waited up at night to see his Dad. It was usually the only chance he had to talk to him. His Dad worked late most nights and the nights he didn't work late he spent at the tavern.

The door creaked opened and in trudged a distinguished looking man, late as usual and oblivious to his surroundings.

Rooter went straight to the kitchen to fill his belly before hunger bugs ate through his stomach and escaped into the night. Rammer, still awake, climbed down from the window and stumbled out into the front room. He sat for hours by the window waiting for his Dad to get home.

In the kitchen, thunder juice bottles littered the counters. Dishes and trash peaked out of the sink. Little creeptails replenished their reserves; they scurried back to their holes with cheeks full of tasty morsels and crumbs.

"Hi Dad, did you have a good day at work?"

"Where's your mother? This place looks like a squealer's den," asked Rooter in a raised voice. "Has she been drinking all day again?"

"Asleep I guess."

"Aren't you supposed to be in bed?"

Without missing a beat, Rammer walked into the kitchen. "I raced in The Little Round About today."

Rooter rummaged through the ice hole pushing multicolored jars of creatures aside looking for his favorite, hungry bug killers.

"Don't you have to qualify for that?" He pulled out a jar and closed the door with his foot.

Not surprised and fully expecting the answer he received, "I qualified weeks ago Dad, don't you remember?"

"Of course I do," mumbled Rooter with his mouth half full of honey buzzers. "How did you do?"

"I almost won. I was winning with about a hundred yards to go—"

He opened a bottle of thunder juice and sat down on the divan with the jar of honey buzzers under his left arm. He propped his legs up on a small carved stump and asked, "What happened?"

"I…tripped over a rock," 'Thanks to you,' he thought to himself.

"Again?"

"I guess I'm just clumsy," he said.

"Maybe you should try a different sport. Where is the paper? Your mother didn't throw it out again did she?"

Maybe you should keep your word and show up next time, thought Rammer, handing his father the paper. He so wanted his Dad's attention and approval but all he ever got was criticism and rejection. Shifting the blame to himself was the best way he found to cope with his father's rejection.

"Next time you can watch me win it Dad. I'll train real hard. Do you think you can come next time?" he asked.

His father looked at the paper and then, as if he had forgotten, replied, "Sure, if things slow down at work. I'll be there next time."

Rammer whirled around, and with a heavy foot, walked back to bed.

"That means no. Things never slow down at work."

CHAPTER 8

THE HORN SWOGGLER

Exquisite voice: Unequaled beauty:
Being of light: Master of deception.

Located in the mountains just outside of town was a large gold mine. It supplied a fresh supply of gold to town residents and was used to barter and trade at the market and down at the docks. It was the pride of many fathers for their sons to follow them in the mines. Generations of young men willingly lined up to follow their father's legacy and to make them proud.

Hyben had worked in the mine for twenty-two years. He proudly followed his father and his grandfather who were great miners in their days. He rose through the ranks as a mine boss and now serves as a teacher and mentor to all new aspiring young lads who dream of wealth and great fortunes.

"Hey shipwreck, did you make it to the Little Round About the other day?" asked Hyben.

"Did I? That was the closest finish in years. I thought the new kid had him for sure. Strange how he flopped at the end? It was almost like something in the crowd distracted him."

"You know…I noticed that too," said Hyben, tilting his head slightly. "Hey, some of the guys are going to Snails and Tails after work to knock down some thunder juice, 'wanna come?"

Klug, thrilled at the invitation responded, "Do I! I thought you'd never ask." Finally, he thought, after six weeks on the job I am getting in with the guys.

Klug, a young thunder beast with plates lined down his back, was new to the mines. His father had worked the mines for years and was proud to see his son follow in his footsteps. Klug worked on Hyben's shift, a clown and a bonafide jokester who was always joking and getting into trouble. Everyone loved to work with Hyben, though. After work, his stories, all in elaborate animation, were the life of the party at the local tavern.

"Hey Klug, stop for a second," said Hyben, walking over and taking off his hard hat. "See this vein right here? We call this a 'paycheck vein' because it's not the big one, but it's the sure one. It pays the bills and keeps the mine open."

"Yes sir," said Klug, eager to learn everything he could from Hyben. Klug took his pick, raised it high and swung at the vein. The pick slipped out of his hands and sailed across the room.

Laughter erupted down the tunnel.

"Hey boy, that pick too much for you to handle," rang a voice down one of the side shafts.

Hyben, a joke that was played on all new guys, had greased Klug's pick. Klug picked it up, rubbed dirt on it and started to chisel away. He knew he couldn't let their jokes affect him, or he would never last long down in the mine.

Klug, young and strong, worked tirelessly at the vein. Large chunks of rocks flung through the air and landed on the floor.

Hyben walked up and down the shafts inspecting the timber supports holding the ceiling at bay and he directed the placement of new ones as new shafts drilled deep into the side of the mine. Hyben walked back by Klug and stopped. His ears moved and his senses went on full alarm.

"Get out of the way!" yelled Hyben.

A huge crack ripped across the ceiling and raced down the walls. The floor rumbled as creature and beast scrambled for the exit. Hyben, Mack's father, pushed Klug out of the way, just before the ceiling collapsed on him.

Dust permeated throughout the tunnels. Men and beast crouched low holding their hard hats, waiting for the rumbles to cease. Klug stood up and felt his way through the dust.

"Hyben, can you hear me? Are you alright?" yelled Klug.

Hyben lay on the ground crushed under a massive support beam. Klug and several others worked fast but were unable to move it. With sweat and dirt all over his face, Klug knelt down and said, "Hyben, you saved my life; you saved my life."

Hyben knew this day would come. He knew the joke would someday be on him. Yet there was so much left undone. He thought he would have more time to do the things he dreamed of and say the things he needed to say.

But time had run out.

Death played the ultimate joke and called sooner than Hyben had planned. He gambled with life and lost. A gamble many men take and lose.

"Tell my son…I…love him. I never…told…" his eyes closed.

Klug rose and looked at the guys. "He saved my life. He put my life before his own. He's…he's a hero."

"He sure was," said Pounder. "He sure was."

Arriving on scene exhausted and out of breath, Rockbone, the mine boss, yelled, "What happened? Is everyone alright?" He noticed the debris and saw a mangled figure trapped underneath. He pushed his way forward and lowered his light. "Hyben," he exclaimed, looking at those standing by. "What happened?"

"Klug was drilling and hit a vein. It cracked and everything came down," said Pounder. "There was nothing we could do. It all came down so quick."

Rockbone was a mean surly man. He had learned to hide his emotions and drive men with a hard, unforgiving whip. "Get a mover in here and clean this up. Steady the rest of the roof with beams and secure this shaft until it can be inspected. I'll notify his family."

"Boss, can I go with you?" asked Klug. "He saved my life."

Rockbone nodded in agreement.

Rockbone and Klug arrived at Hyben's house several hours later. Rockbone collected his thoughts. He stepped onto the steps and raised the corroded paw door-knocker which was slightly lower than his chin and attached to a dilapidated faded blue door, and tapped it three times. With over 30 years of experience, Rockbone had lost numerous friends in the mines. He hated this part of the job. Seeing a family devastated by the loss of a loved one never came easy for the old timer.

Jitter bugs raced up and down his throat as he waited for the door to open. Each time he visited a house to express his condolences he couldn't help but remember the visit he got when he was a little boy. He knew the pain and sorrow first hand and had seen his mother and sisters struggle for years after the death of his father. It wasn't something he would wish on his worst enemy and being that Hyben was a friend, made it more difficult.

Hyben's house was located just outside of junction point. The family was poor, as were most of the families that worked at the mines. Clutter gathered outside and the yard overgrown with weeds. One shutter hung low on the right window and the roof was in dire need of repair.

Footsteps softly pattered behind the door.

Rockbone's hands trembled hearing the lock jiggle.

"Wait just a minute," said Mrs. Davoo, unlocking the door.

The door opened.

Mrs. Davoo took one look at Rockbone and collapsed into his arms.

"No! No! Not Hyben. Not Hyben. Tell me it's not so."

Mack heard his mother's cry from his bedroom. He stood up and listened for a second. He walked down the hallway and rounded the corner.

Klug stood in the doorway.

His mother sobbed in Rockbone's arms.

"What's wrong? What's going on?" he asked.

Rockbone had not yet officially told Mrs. Davoo. She knew why he was there, but it was his responsibility to tell her so she wouldn't try and deny it later.

"Mrs. Davoo, I'm sorry. Hyben was killed in an accident in the mine today. I'm so sorry," said Rockbone.

Mack froze in place. He didn't know what to do or say.

Stunned, he looked down at the floor devastated. His mother took him in her arms and held him tight. He didn't shed a tear; he didn't embrace her; he was numb.

Mack and his father weren't close. Hyben had worked in the mines since graduating school. After work, he frequently visited the local tavern, where he spent any extra money he managed to scrounge.

After several minutes Klug stuttered, "Mrs. Davoo, your husband saved my life today. I wanted you to know. As the ceiling collapsed, he pushed me out of the way. I'm sorry. I'm so sorry."

Tears streamed down her cheeks. She glanced up at Klug and wiped them, "Thank you. Thank you for coming."

Klug twisted around toward Mack. "Your Dad is a hero. He saved my life."

Mack continued to stare off into the distance motionless. A hero, he thought to himself, never expecting to hear those words and his Dad's name in the same sentence.

"I'll send Klug by in a few days with his things. If you need anything before then, please let me know," said Rockbone.

Klug walked off the porch. This was the first of many visits he would make if he stayed in the mines. "Boss, what will the family do now?"

Rockbone felt terrible. He knew the family couldn't make it without Hyben. They didn't have any money and would probably lose the house.

"Oh, I'm sure they'll find away," he said, not wanting the young and inexperienced thunder beast to lose faith and be discouraged.

He placed his hand on Klug's shoulder and squeezed. "Why don't you take the rest of the day off? I'll see you in the morning."

"See 'ya in the morning boss."

* * * * * * *

Thunder Juice Town was busy. Tree floaters filled the harbor loading and unloading their exotic cargo of animals, freight, food and spices. The smell of baked bread flirtatiously drifted down the street, knocking on every door, peaking in every window. Little creatures raced old wooden box crates down the street weaving in and out of legs, tails, food stands and carts loaded with straw.

A cool gentle wind blew across the water ricocheting violet rays of sunshine on the shoreline; mid morning always was the best time to view the beauty of Old Juicy. Bugler fish could still be heard off in the distance playing their wonderful ensembles at The Redmadafa: there was no other place on the circle like Thunder Juice Town.

The temple resounded with activity. People gathered in the outer courts listening to lectures on all types of subjects. Gardeners trimmed trees and shrubs. Temple servants collected delicate juicy fruit from the trees lining The Redmadafa's banks. Leaves used for healing were pruned from the topmost shoots. Placed in decorative baskets, they were taken into the inner chambers of the temple. The orchestra rehearsed as little children played hide and seek around the statues.

He followed The Redmadafa low, inches from its surface, rippling the water. Displaying his flying superiority, he followed every oxbow, flipping and barrel-rolling in spectacular splendor catching every violet ray. He entered the outskirts of town and rose high into the sky. Circling over town, he cast his majestic shadow over its inhabitants.

Heads rose upward.

Eyes glimmered.

Doors and windows flung open.

Word raced down the streets and scattered through the markets.

Everyone took to the streets and fields to get a glimpse: *The Augur had returned.*

Up at the university, campus was in an uproar. Students had long been taught that The Augur did not exist. Professors and students both stood dumbfounded as he soared over the campus and landed in the center square.

A mighty eagle with long feathers and a full plumage of varied colors stood before the people. Shouts of joy came from some; cries came from others. Some hid, afraid because of what they had done and said about him. Others rejoiced and ran to greet him.

The square filled, overflowing down the streets and into the allies. Second story windows opened and rooftops filled with adults and children all trying to get a glimpse of the long awaited return. In unison, the crowd bowed as he opened his wings and spoke. The beauty of his voice and the eloquence of his tongue mesmerized the crowd filling them with awe-struck wonder.

"My children, it is so good to finally be with you once again. I have waited for so long now to come and take you under my wings and protect you from those who would do you harm," he said, walking up the steps of the great fountain perching himself on its top step.

"My heart wept bitterly every day, longing to see your lovely faces. But now," he said changing his tone, "I have returned to save you from a deadly beast that is ravaging the land. An evil from the North has spread across this circle that is beyond imagination. Many of my children have fled their homes and are now lost and confused, wandering alone in barren wasteland. But do not be dismayed," he reassured. "I have come to take you to a new land, a land where this beast will never be able to harm you. I will not rest day or night until this Shadow of Death is destroyed. Do you believe?"

"Yes," a few people shouted from the crowd.

"Do you believe in me now?"

"Yes," the crowd cheered now gaining momentum.

"I have come to give you rest! Trusssssst in me and I will give you your dreams!"

The crowd erupted.

Dancing broke out all around the fountain filling the square with celebrations. Everyone jumped and whirled around throwing flowers, hats, and anything else they had, into the air.

Onuka pushed through the crowd trying to get a glimpse of him. Barely catching the last sentence his excitement abruptly ended. Before him stood a powerful eagle, whose appearance was captivating and majestic by all measures—*His voice, exquisite; his beauty, unequaled: a being of light.*

Onuka shouted, as the eagle embraced the crowd. "Eagle, where do you come from?"

The people, many who had visited the temple, looked at Onuka like he was crazy. "He is the High Priest and does not know where The Augur comes from," they said to each other with puzzled looks.

The eagle paid him no attention. He continued to walk about the crowd greeting the little children.

"Mighty eagle, what is your name and where do you come from," persisted Onuka, this time standing a few feet from him?

The eagle recognized him and thought carefully before responding.

"Onuka, you are High Priest and guardian of the temple and you don't know the answer to that question?"

Everyone laughed and looked at Onuka wondering the same thing.

"Eagle, it has been a long time and many in this crowd have lost their faith in you. I thought it might be wise to hear from your own lips the origin of your genesis."

All eyes rotated back captivated by the eagle.

He thought for a moment and then with a calm reassuring reply answered, "You're absolutely right, my wise and loyal priest. As a matter of fact, that is why I have come. Gather everyone at the temple tonight and I will answer that question then."

* * * * * * *

Pepper sat quietly at her desk thinking about her Papa and brother. She sketched a picture of her teacher, a heart, and a few other whimsical symbols. Pepper and her mother had been alone now for a couple months and life, as she knew it, was beginning to change. From her bedroom at night, she overheard her mother crying, praying to The Augur for help. She had many unanswered questions about what had happened and desperately needed to talk to someone, but everyone overlooked her and her needs. They concentrated on finding Chesty and Caboose, and comforting her mother's needs.

She felt all alone, something she had never felt before. The calm, secure, peaceful feeling that once filled her life was slowly replaced by restlessness, insecurity, and fear.

Her teacher, a middle-aged human with black hair salted with grey on the sides and sticking straight into the air, drew a half circle on the board and turned around. Over his shirt he wore a white lab coat that halted at the knees. Skinny spectacles rested mid way down a stout ebony-hooked nose. A thick, heavily beeswaxed mustache, curled underneath and a blue and green polka-dotted bow tie spread wide under his portly black beard that tapered at the end.

"Flat," he said to the class who were bored out of their minds, most resting with chins in hands looking out the window into the sky or at the trees down by The Redmadafa.

"The world is flat," he continued. "On page 97 in your text books, you will see that our best and brightest scientist have concluded that the world is flat. And if our brightest minds have concluded that the world is flat then we consider that to be fact. So, I can boldly proclaim that it is a fact that the world is flat. If you were to travel in a tree floater out into the vast blue ocean, you would come to a point where the suction of the gravitational force of space pulling against the water would slingshot you off into the galaxy and you would drift around forever lost in the universe."

He stroked his beard several times with his hand and walked down the aisle toward Pepper, snobbishly looking over his spectacles. She focused from her doodling, turned the page, and slid her book over her drawings.

"Now you wouldn't live very long because there is no oxygen in space," he said, looking down at her desk. He reached down and slid her parchment out. He gazed at the drawing of himself, looked her in the eyes, and continued. "And if the lack of oxygen didn't kill you first, you would probably smash into a star or some other floating object drifting around in space. Or of course you could get sucked into a large rotating vortex that would catapult you through an immense black hole sending you back in time into another dimension when aliens ruled the world and built the pyramids."

The students all perked up in their seats and looked at him.

"Really, Mr. Haggo?" said Jabin, sitting close to the front, enthralled with the extra-terrestrial account. He flipped the pages in his book looking for the elusive data.

"Well," answered Mr. Haggo, in light-hearted banter and a smile on his face. He stuck his hands in his lab coat and looked up toward the stars. "That's not in the book, but many leading minds believe it must have happened that way. People living long ago were primitive and ignorant. There is no way they could have built them. There is no other logical explanation. Aliens..." he shook his head, his beard brushing his coat. "Aliens."

Pepper shook her head. He gets paid to teach this stuff, she thought to herself.

The bell rang signaling lunch.

"Tonight, I want you to read chapter seven and be ready to discuss the origin of the platypus," he said, while everyone gathered their things and pushed in their chairs.

"The platypus," laughed a student walking out the door. "I bet he's going to tell us its mother was a quacker and its father was a water slapper."

"No" said another student laughing. "He'll probably say it came from rain...raining upon the rocks for millions and billions of years."

They both busted up laughing.

Pepper walked down the hallway with her friends. They opened the doors to the lunchroom and sat down at a long square table with wide wooden benches. Pepper took out her lunch and took a bite—a wheat bread sandwich with greens, cucumbers, and yellow squash, topped with herbs and a special blend of spices passed down to her mother by her grandmother.

"Can you believe that guy?" she said to her friend Zelophy setting next to her.

"Who?" asked Zelophy, popping a brussel sprout in her mouth.

"Mr. Haggo," said Pepper. "'The world is flat.' You know, I wonder if anything in the textbook is actually based on facts. Sun Day at the Temple, we read from the ancient scroll of the prophet Isaiah. Isaiah already told us that The Augur sits above the circle of the earth. The world is not flat, it is a circle," she said taking another bite.

"What is he going to tell us next? That the earth is not the center of the universe or rotating around the sun?"

"So, you don't think Caboose stowed away on a Tree Floater and fell off the end of the earth?" asked Zelophy, with a confused look on her face.

Pepper's face turned cherry red.

"Is that what everyone is saying now?"

Zelophy stuffed her mouth with a few more sprouts, shrugged her shoulders, and looked away wanting to change the subject.

"If I hear one more ridiculous story about my brother and what happened to him, I think I'm going to scream for three days."

She stuffed the rest of her sandwich in her mouth, stood up, and walked outside.

Zelophy looked at the other girls. "So, we probably shouldn't say anything about the little green men at the end of the rainbow holding him ransom in the clouds?"

Her friends shook their heads and quietly continued eating.

* * * * * * *

The gorge was clear of gargoyles when they exited the cave. Although the sun never rose over the valley, light from the moon lit up the horizon. The gargoyles used the light to hunt and carry out their mischievous ways—you could see the relief in Caboose's eyes that they were gone.

They didn't go back the way they came. They continued North out of the gorge and into Blindman's Despair. Blindman's Despair was where Slithler sent his servants who had disobeyed or failed to carry out his orders to satisfaction. Great agony lurked in the land. Servants walked the foothills blinded, tormented by their failures and disappointments. Gogs, creatures, and beasts, stole, ravished, and killed each other, just to stay alive. They answered to no one; the only rule: kill or be killed.

"Here take this." Urium handed Caboose a small clear bottle with diamond-cut groves encircling it.

Caboose looked at the bottle. Smoke danced around inside, enticing him to open it and let it loose.

"What is it?" he asked, squinting into it, while shaking and turning it upside down.

"Dragon's breath. Be careful, this bottle never runs dry. Open it, but not for too long or we will be lost for days. It will hide you from harm and mask your scent. You'll need it in there."

"But, isn't everyone blind?" said Caboose. "How will this help?"

"They are. But they can see up close, about twenty feet. Their sight though is not what I'm worried about."

"It's not," said Caboose, wondering what else could possibly go wrong.

"No. Their hearing and sense of smell are their greatest weapons. So, try to be quiet and watch where you step," referencing the close call back in the gorge when Caboose stepped on a gargoyle and almost got him killed.

"Do we have to go through? Why can't we go back and use the tunnels?" remarked Caboose regretting the choices he made back in town and at the Scorpion Pass Gate. He felt a familiar sensation in his stomach, like the feeling he felt when swinging on the vines down at the river.

"I know you are tired Caboose, but now is not the time to give up. The journey before you is long and hard, but you must press on and not be overcome by the evil of this land. People are counting on you. I don't know what will happen when we reach the Sea Throne, but Seven believes The Augur has something special planned for you. The majority of the souls that get trapped in here are not because of Slithler and his many servants."

"It isn't?"

"No. It's because they gave up believing in themselves and His ability to save them from the Shadow of Death. You have a lot to live for Caboose. Your Papa wouldn't be here looking for you if he didn't believe that too."

Just hearing the name 'Papa' brought renewed strength and comfort. He nodded his head and sped up his pace.

They ventured through the pass and further into Despair. They stuck to the high country determined to stay undetected. The slopes were steep, loose gravel threatened each step. They followed a small Alpine trail for days, over some of the most rugged and uncharted terrain in the land. Caboose remained quiet for the most part. He wondered what would be waiting for him at the Sea Throne and if he would have the courage to face it.

He nonchalantly studied Urium walking in front. He watched his wings jostle back and forth like a pendulum. He noticed how his head moved forward and backward, not side-to-side. His stature was tall and straight; there was no hunch in his back, no slump of timidity. He noted the confident swagger in his step. It boasted of a mighty warrior, strong and powerful, marching into battle with no fear. That was a walk Caboose had yet to discover, although he practiced it secretly from behind.

"So, what is like being an angel?"

"Do what?" replied Urium, busy watching the path and rocky plateaus ahead.

"What is it like being a celestial being? Flying back and forth in the universe and through the stars; that must be pretty awesome."

"It is. There's nothing like it. Remember when I told you that I was assigned to you when you where conceived?"

Caboose nodded his head in agreement.

"Well, once we've been assigned to someone, we never leave them or we only leave them in case of an emergency or a special assignment. But once the person we've been assigned to passes from this life, we are free for a while to explore the universe. After every seventh person, we all have to do a 250 year post somewhere in His Majesty's throne or a post in one of the outer realms."

"Explore the universe in the outer realms…Wow. I can only imagine what that must be like. So…what's out there?" inquired Caboose. "Are there big green aliens waiting to come and destroy us?"

"Well, now that you mention it, that might be one way to describe the Northern celestial guard—but no. The most wonderful things anyone could ever behold are out there waiting to be explored. I haven't explored all the galaxies, but the ones I have, are absolutely amazing—cosmical paradises, each with a beauty unseen or unknown by mortal man or beast. Each galaxy has its own unique purpose in the universe. They contain vast storehouses of wisdom about how His Majesty created all things and some even contain the plans themselves. The stars actually tell his story too, you know."

"Really, how?"

Urium stopped and searched the sky and then pointed. "Do you see that cluster of stars over there?"

Caboose searched hard. He looked back at Urium's finger and then looked again. "I guess so—he was lying, he didn't see anything.

"That's Virgo the Virgin. If you start with it and circle 'round, you end with Leo the Lion."

"Ok..." Is that supposed to mean something, thought Caboose? "So, what is the story?"

Urium lowered his hand and started walking.

"Don't know. But talk is, is that we're all about to find out. Whatever it is, it's 'gonna be a good one."

He cocked his head to the side. "No...it's gonna be a great one."

Caboose kicked the whole idea around for a few moments. What did he mean by 'storehouses of wisdom'? Are there large libraries in each galaxy filled with books and ancient scrolls? Are angels up there filing them and checking them out when needed?

"Storehouses of wisdom. I don't understand."

"Wisdom is how he made everything. It's how he laid the earth's foundations and it's how he set the heavens in place. You see, after he created the stars and the galaxies, he stretched them out with his own hands—he even gave each one a name. And no, I can't name them all. No angel can even get close, only His Majesty can. He did this to destroy the wisdom of the wise and frustrate the intelligence of the intelligent. This is why the wise can never figure out his plans, nor can they duplicate his mysteries. He made foolishness the wisdom of the world."

"But my teacher told me that the stars are billions of light years away, and that it takes billions of years for the light to reach us. She said that proves our planet is billions of years old and not thousands like my Sun Day school teacher at the temple used to teach."

"Your teacher at school is presenting '*A False Triad.*'"

"My Sun Day school teacher; a false triad…what do you mean?"

"No, not her, the other: A False Triad takes two objects that are known and then inputs an unknown which produces the false triad—Known x Known x Unknown = False Triad (K x K x UK = FT). The false triad pulls two positive elementary truths into an equation for validity. Then it inputs one unknown elementary object which causes the negative and false result—Positive x Positive x Unknown = Negative (P x P x U = N). This triad is used to deceive the pupil into believing the false triad because two elements of truth are present.

Let me explain.

Stars and light are both visible and measurable objects that no living creature can deny; as a matter of fact, in the future, man will figure out how to stop the speed of light all together. For those who do not believe in His Majesty, when they look up at the stars, all they see is the aftermath of his works. So, when they try to measure the distance of the stars by the light they generate and by their distance from the earth, they interject the known—only that which is visible and that which is visible is not relative to the original—the unknown. This gives them *A False Triad* because what is visible today does not represent the original creation before he stretched it out.

Thus, the question is not 'How does the light get from the stars to us?' The question is or should be, 'How did the stars get to where they are in the first place?' His Majesty made the stars and then stretched them out. Believe me I know. I was there when he laid the foundations of the earth—what you call 'The Circle.'" I was there when the morning stars sang for joy and all the angels shouted at the work of his hands. I was there when he set the boundaries of the sea, when he made the clouds their garments and when he ordered the dawn to take the edges of the earth and shake the wicked out of it. I was there when he made the first man and woman and placed them in the garden.

Caboose, I was there when he knit you in your mother's womb. I watched each stage of your growth as you tumbled and tossed within her belly. I saw your arms and legs stretch like mud bugs building chimneys after a midday shower. I watched your fingers and toes take sprout like lilies in spring. I watched your nose creep from your face and your lips blossom round. I even watched as His Majesty placed a soul inside your heart. That's always my favorite part—his fingerprints upon the souls of creation. He does that to everyone," laughed Urium.

Caboose stopped in the middle of the trail. A puzzled look canvassed his face as he processed the information. "But my leg? What about my leg? Why is it shorter? Why did I have to be different?"

Urium hesitated to answer. He knew Caboose wouldn't understand. He paused for a moment and then looked straight into his eyes.

"To bring you here Caboose: to bring you here."

"Here?! Here?! Why would he want to bring me here?!! Is this some kind of a sick joke? Does he enjoy watching me suffer pain and misery? Ok, I'm done; I'm ready to leave. Is the lesson over? That's what this is right? A lesson from the elder to the young 'inexperienced' apprentice? Well, you can take me home anytime you like, because I'm done. I'm really done."

"It doesn't work like that. I know this is hard to understand, but, this valley, for some, is the only way. It's the only way for them to realize they can't make it without him. It's in this valley, a valley of bones and death, that many finally solve The False Triad. Once solved, the truth rises to the surface revealing the lie. When that happens, you'll discover your real name and purpose in life."

"Well, I already know my name and my purpose in life is to get out of this place."

Small rocks jumped down the slope just above them. Small rocks turned into medium rocks right before Urium shouted, "Avalanche!"

Caboose ran by Urium like he was a croaker stuck in the mud. Rocks landed all around Caboose missing him by inches. He tried to keep his footing on the uneven barbed trail but each step proved more challenging than the next. With the slide closing fast, he lost his footing and slid down the mountainside about fifteen feet. He regained his balance and continued pace.

"Run for the boulder it will shield you from the rocks."

Up ahead, protruding from the slope, a large boulder dueled with the rocks, holding the mountainside at bay, beckoning for Caboose to hurry. He ran and, with barely a second to spare, dove behind the boulder. The bulk of the mountainside rolled over the boulder and slid past him.

That was close, thought Caboose, looking himself over for cuts and scratches.

Urium flew over and landed on top of the boulder. He looked down, "We better keep moving," said Urium, studying the top, scouting for something.

"What is it? Did you see something?"

"No, but something triggered the landslide. I'm afraid our presence is no longer a secret."

A loud crash echoed above. Someone or something landed on the rocks, then another and another. With rocks tumbling down again all around Caboose, Urium, standing on the boulder, yelled, "Run!"

Caboose turned to run and caught a quick glint of a dark leathery beast with raised veins landing on the slopes above him. He knew with his short leg he didn't stand much of a chance going in a straight line across the loose unstable gravel. But going downhill was different. He turned and jumped over and over, landing and bounding, landing and bounding—he looked like a large croaker trying to escape the jaws of a water chomper.

Banished Ragooles, fire-breathing monsters that patrolled the sky, closed in from all sides. They couldn't see Caboose but they could smell him. Large lightning rods of fire scorched the rocks turning everything to stubble and ash.

Caboose, nearing the valley below, spotted a glowing red lava creek lined with old tree stumps and bushes. He needed to reach the creek before they caught up with him. Hearing the noise and smelling the ash several gogs, howlers and a Magondrea snuck out from the tree line and positioned themselves while fighting each other, to intercept him. He spotted them and slid to a stop. Trapped, he panicked and whirled around looking for another way out.

"Dragon's breath," carried down the slope as Urium distracted the Ragooles. Caboose reached into his pocket and pulled out the bottle of dragon's breath. He struggled to open it. He finally put it in his mouth, bit down on the cork and popped it out with his teeth.

Grayish-white dragon's breath rose out of the bottle twisting and winding around every rock, tree, and beast, filling the valley with a heavy fog. Sounds of fighting could faintly be heard over by the tree line as an eerie silence descended on the creek bed. Flashes of light flickered through the breath as Ragooles spewed out fire trying to locate him.

Caboose, walking on pins and needles, made his way through the thick breath. He approached what he thought was the creek but mistakenly walked right under the jaws of the Magondrea. Once again, brown slimy slobber covered him and oozed down between his ears. His eyes followed the beast's leg, torso, and neck all the way up to its enormous teeth, inches from Caboose's nose. This time the beast saw him. Nose-to-nose, Caboose froze with fright. His legs trembled and his lips quivered. An agonizing decay crept into his heart.

He reached into the bag of dragon's teeth and dropped a few of them on the ground. The Magondrea growled and opened its mouth. Caboose, waiting for the dragon's teeth to do something, felt deathly alone. The beast drew back and attacked, scarcely hitting him. He jumped into the breath trying to hide, but ran right into a howler, knocking it backwards. They both rolled across the ground and struggled to come out on top.

The howler broke free, spun around and grabbed Caboose, embedding his claws deep into his hind leg. It chiseled its way up his petrified body, still frozen stiff with fear. With Caboose pinned to the ground, six-inch fangs sunk deep into his neck, spilling his life blood all over the ground.

The Magondrea smelled the blood and emerged from the breath. It grabbed the howler and thrust it upwards into the air. Without missing a beat, the howler jumped on the Magondrea and bit its back. They both disappeared into the breath.

Caboose lay motionless on the ground struggling to breathe. The dark red dirt licked up his lifeblood, ever so slyly trying to escape with his soul. Tears rolled down his cheeks making small puddles below. He thought of his Papa and all the wonderful times they had had playing down at the banks of The Redmadafa with his mother and sister. He could hear the kids at school singing and playing hop-addy-hop. He even saw Mack and the lixoars chasing him after school—he remembered how he use to give them the slip at *Feathered Friends Gatehouse*—the back ally had several loose boards allowing him to slip through without them noticing.

"Papa...Help me Papa. Please forgive me...Please forgive me...for bringing...you here."

* * * * * *

Humans, creatures and beasts lined the aisles and overflowed down the hallways spilling out into the outer courts. With all eyes and ears affixed to his every move, the mighty eagle rose from his seat and glided over to the ambo. He feasted his eyes on the crowd and examined the ceilings and windows. He leered out across the temple; every seat filled to capacity, every mind standing at attention. In eloquence and splendor he spoke:

"Today, my wise and faithful priest advocated that I tell you my name and explain to you the place of my abode. Far be it from me to disappoint my children, many of whom he claimed had lost faith;" numerous eyes waterfalled to the floor, while others, with pious heads held high and glassing around, bobbed their heads, shaking invisible fingers relaying the message, 'Shame on you.'

He dipped his head low, in a reverent act of humility, while slanting his eyes toward Onuka, and addressed the crowd. "I…humbly…come before you this night to declare to you my name and the origin of my genesis." He marched boldly across the altar, raised his head, spread his wings and proclaimed in a boisterous voice, "The origin of my genesis is at the fiery stones of Zion, The Holy Mountain of His Majesty!"

Goose bumps canvassed the crowd, jumping and crawling over every captive soul, tickling their awe inspired ears. "I was the model of perfection, full of wisdom and perfect in beauty. I've walked in Eden. I was adorned with every precious jewel known to man and beast. My settings and mountings were made of pure gold. But," looking back at Onuka, "For love, I left it all, to come down to this circle and dwell with my children. Gold and silver are like dross before me and could never take the place of the beauty…I see in you. This is the hour and the day you have all been waiting for. I have come to take you home.

Why now, you may wonder? An evil serpent has swept across this kingdom and has infiltrated every level of law and government. He now lies in wait to destroy this town and all whom have taken sanctuary behind its colossal gates. The Redmadafa, the river that gives life and healing, will soon run red with the blood of all who remain in this town.

Let me share with you the story of, 'The Serpent and The Seed.'

The Serpent and The Seed

One day the serpent strolled along,
Safe and secure, his home—O so strong:
When, what to his wondering eyes should appear,
But a man and a woman, filled with cheer.

O how his heart longed for love,
Not song, nor dance; not even a dove.
'You'll surely not die,' he said with tease,
Lighting the way, dawning a new Eve.

Before them lie the forbidden fruit,
As he played a dirge from his deceitful flute,
With eyes wide open and nakedness revealed,
They bruised his head, he struck their heels.

Thorns and Thistles, and pain to her young,
"What have you done?" to his belly he was flung.
Alone, he now sits, on his throne above the sea,
Plotting to destroy the woman and her seed.

On the day I was birthed, I was anointed a guardian cherub, for so I was ordained. Come, come away with me my children. I will guard you from the serpent; no need to be bloodstained. And as for my name, from this day on, *The Augur*, is no longer to be proclaimed; gifts of gold, frankincense and myrrh, *My Name is Lucifer*!"

"Horn Swoggler! The Horn Swoggler! It's a trap, he's the ser…" Lucifer opened his wings, knocking Onuka back across the altar muffling his desperate attempt to expose his evil identity.

The crowd shouted and chanted his name. The temple shook violently trying to rip him apart as several temple elders came down and bowed at his feet. Rinox and Adromus slipped through the crowd. They ran around the back and through the great hall meeting Onuka in the inner chamber that contained the ancient scrolls.

Onuka sat in a chair with his face in his hands.

"Onuka are you alright? What are we going to do?" asked Adromus.

"I have failed you," sighed Onuka. "I let him waltz right in here and desecrate this holy temple and deceive the people with his lies and poison-drenched tongue. I am no longer worthy to serve you or this temple."

Adromus walked over and placed his arm on his shoulder. "Onuka, I've never been more proud to have you as my High Priest than I am right now. We were all captivated by his beauty and lies. You defended the faith and together, we will restore the honor of this temple. The Augur will hear of this. With justice he will restore this temple. He will return. He will return."

CHAPTER 9

DEAD MAN'S DROP

All who hate me love death.

Urium's large apocalyptic body emerged from the breath. The fog haggardly elevated revealing Caboose's lifeless body lying on the ground. Urium walked over and pressed his fingers firmly against the puncture holes in his juggler—nothing; not a beat or a pulse. He looked up and searched out a safe place to move the body. Up ahead, between the remnants of what was left from an old growth forest, he noticed a dirt trail that led down to a creek flowing with glimmering hot lava.

He picked Caboose up in his arms and walked across the rocky uneven path and laid him down by creek's edge. Urium reached into his armor and pulled out a red ivory bottle with rococo carvings. He popped the cork, took out four dragon scales, dipped them in the lava—which had no effect on him—and providently placed them over Cabooses juggler holes.

The scales instantly came to life, attaching to his cadaverous neck, sealing up the wounds. Long red blood fibers grappled nimbly through his veins. They splintered out across his chest and funneled into the aorta, cascading into the subterranean chambers of his jelly clotted heart until finally reaching its apex, shocking it back to life.

Caboose lay motionless, breathless on the ground.

"Caboose, can you hear me?" said Urium, after waiting several seconds.

Slowly coming too, Caboose opened his eyes. Discombobulated he said, "Where am I? What happened?"

"Take it easy big guy, you gave me quite the scare. Are you alright? See if you can stand."

Caboose stood up and checked his body.

"Ouch," he murmured, grabbing his back leg. "The howler, where did he go?"

"Oh, I think you sent him running scared. Let me see that." Urium grabbed his leg and twisted it slightly. "Oh no," he said, with concern in his voice. "It looks like I'll have to take your leg."

"What, I can't lose a leg," responded Caboose, grabbing his leg. He sullenly pulled it away from Urium inspecting it closely.

"Ha, ha, 'gotcha,'" laughed Urium. "It doesn't look too deep. Can you walk?"

Caboose walked around and jumped up and down, "Yeah, it's ok. Sorry Urium. I used the dragon's claws but nothing happened."

"They can only be used to help others, remember. Besides, Seven said it takes all the elements to bring them to life."

"Oh yeah, I remember now. But that doesn't seem right. Why can't I use them to help myself?"

"Sometimes the greatest lessons in life come when you put others first. There is no greater love than to lay down your life for your friends."

"Wow, someone needs to write that down, that's good."

Urium laughed, patted him on the back and put his arm around him.

"Caboose, I can't wait to see what he has planned for you. Here drink this." He handed Caboose a small white skin of dragon's blood.

Caboose opened the top and sniffed it. "It smells good. What is it?"

"It will help you regain your strength."

Caboose sniffed it again and then put it to his lips.

"Umm…this tastes good. It tastes like…like, summer in a cup."

"Glad you liked it."

Caboose danced around shadow boxing the air. A fond smile rekindled across his face. "I feel good. I feel like…a mighty warrior on the front line about to engage his enemies."

"Well…*mighty warrior*, we better get going or you may find yourself there sooner than not."

Caboose didn't hear a word. He floated on air a few feet behind Urium, his body tingling with euphoric sensations.

They continued to follow the creek for several days finally coming to Dead Man's Drop. Caboose approached the entrance cautiously; he had second thoughts about going this way. Skeletons impaled posts lining the trail all the way up to the entrance of a narrow passage cut between the rocks. Large thick overhangs slumped over the horizon and faded into a dimly-lit carroty sky—the overhangs looked like large rib cages protruding into the air. The sweet aroma of tang filled the air triggering Caboose's nose. He noticed patches of sticky grass on the ground and attached to the sides of the walls. He scanned the area and looked behind him.

"Urium, that's sticky grass" he whispered. His head rubbernecked in all directions. "Crawlers must be close. Don't you think I should have a specially-designed sword that shoots out lightning bolts, knives, rocks, or something? I could slice through those who tried to harm me like," he searched his thoughts for the right analogy and then continued, "Like curd cooling on a window sill on a hot summer day?"

Urium shook his head in agreement; he had been waiting for that question.

"That would seem to solve a lot of problems and believe me, a lot of people use the sword to try and solve..." Urium tilted his head and searched for the right word... "Oh, their difficulties. But there's one problem."

"What's that?" said Caboose, he picked up a stick from the ground and started waving it in the air, skipping forward.

"All who live by the sword die by the sword."

Caboose stopped his air jousting conquest. "But you have one?"

"That's different. I'm not of this world."

"Oh."

Caboose dropped his head and the stick in disappointment. He would feel a lot safer with the feel of cold iron in his hands, especially in this place.

"Let's stop here and spend the night. We'll need to be on full alert once we enter the passage," said Urium.

Urium led them up a tall rock formation to a safe cutout overlooking the entrance located about a quarter mile up the path. They quietly ascended the teetered rocks and bedded down in the small cave.

Caboose looked in, easily seeing the back of the cave. He sat down and looked out over the landscape. He saw the entrance to Dead Man's Drop in the distance. It curved high into the air from both sides and barbed at the end like a hook waiting to catch prey.

Shivers raced up his legs causing him to shake with chills.

A small fluffy cotton-puff, with long stringy fibers blossomed wide, floated by. It whipped and twirled in the wind resting shortly on the ground beneath his feet before taking flight again and floating away. He looked at his hands and then down at his feet. Red volcanic dirt packed hard around his nails irritating him. He dug at them for a moment and then nudged Urium in his side.

"Hey. Does it really never rain here? I miss the rain. It nourishes my skin and tickles when it runs down my belly."

Urium remained quiet. He searched through the orders in his head and took out a skin of water. He took a drink and then passed it over.

"No, it never does. Not since Slithler laid claim to this land… and not since—" he looked up to the sky, "We angels aren't supposed to speak of this."

Caboose turned his head and listened with interest. "Speak of what?"

"Let me share with you a story, a story that has been kept secret amongst the angels for a long time."

Caboose adjusted himself on the ground. He loved listening to Urium's stories—except for the last one. He still didn't understand why The Augur would cause him, or anyone for that matter, to be born different knowing it would bring them to the valley. But the cold hard truth that no one wants to accept is that he does. The Augur allows trials, difficulties, misfortunes, sickness, disease, and deformities, or what others refer to as, "Divine Interventions" to take place for many reasons. Sometimes they are a result of disobedience. Sometimes they are lessons to help us to become mature and complete so we will not lack anything. Sometimes they seem to come for no good reason at all—but then pan out somewhere in the future after you've grumbled about it for years. Most of the time though, they are so the works of The Augur can be revealed. But there is one thing that is for certain. One thing that is undeniable. The Augur made everything and everyone for a purpose—this he has made clear. He made everyone to Go and Do Great Things.

Urium continued. "We are not to speak of this, especially with those here on earth, but somehow, I know I'm supposed to teach it to you—I think The Augur is about to do something new, something that has never been seen or heard of before. It's the story of The Rainmaker."

"The Rainmaker. Is that a person 'kind of like The Wind Whistler?"

"Kind of." Urium took the skin of water back from Caboose, took another swig and laid it down.

The Rainmaker

"Long ago when His Majesty created all things he created the angels; one of them was Fedila. She was an angel and used to be like the rest of us. Fedila was assigned the responsibility of circling the earth, day and night to provide nutrient-rich pellets of rain upon the land—thus we called her 'The Rainmaker.' She faithfully flew around the earth nourishing plants and trees, man and beast, and every living thing that creeps about, with her succulent vitamin enriched drops-of-life. Trees grew so tall their heads stretched into the heavens and drank directly from the clouds. Flowers bloomed by the millions and displayed spectacular assortments of colors and patterns—their sweet delicious nectar accumulated in vast amounts as honey buzzers stockpiled huge hives, hives the size of a thunder beast, of large honeycomb reserves.

Plants thrived abundantly with columns of sunlight and moist morning drops of dew bubbling on top of their leafy boughs—the drops rolled down contoured groves feeding dark red soil which incubated their roots keeping them warm, safe, and secure. The fields of man gently rolled across the plains and disappeared into the horizon. They stretched for miles and rippled of thick grain, ripe for harvest. Heavy heads of grain, loaded with little golden nuggets-of-life, bobbed repeatedly every time she flew by singing to her like baby birds singing to their mother for food. High above the prairies, you could see her footprints treading across the long, dark green sea of grass carpeting the plains; feather, spear, steppe, fescues, buffalo and rye grass was so thick and green, people thought it had been hand painted by His Majesty himself—each blade was a shade different, no two were alike."

Caboose moved his tongue around in his mouth oozing saliva down his throat. It was as if he could taste each blade. He pictured himself there, rolling in the lush green banquet, his mouth and belly stuffed with the delicious blades.

"Late one afternoon, just before sunset, she innocently strolled through the deep green grass on the open prairie. Off in the distance she heard the sound of music and felt the vibrations of drums pass through her. She followed the sound to a Tamarisk Tree, perched on a steep embankment overlooking a small stream below. At its bottom, circling a large horned fire clawing the dusky sky, the Icha Tribe danced and chanted long into the night. King Ichabod, their king, sat on a chair of bones watching the ceremony. Their faces streaked of paint and their bodies shown of nakedness, except for small bands of animal hide placed in discreet areas.

She watched quietly from her perch above, mesmerized by the enthralling ritual. Dangling brightly from their ears were shiny purple sapphires, chiseled into small arrowheads. Colorful beads of pearls circled their necks and large bands of Aztec gold, inlaid with purple and green rubies, wrapped wide around their heads, arms, and ankles.

Her lungs skipped. Her eyes sparkled. Her mind flooded with envy. And her heart… filled lustfully with desire. She flew to the other side of the earth trying to elude the dazzling temptation. She tried to suppress the feelings burning within. She even bypassed the plains for months trying to curve the lust swelling inside. But she didn't realize that, on the cliff, high above the fire that night, Mageddon was there. He studied her from a distance. He saw desire seize her heart and wonder fill her eyes. This was the opportunity he had waited for."

"Was this before he lost his place of authority?" asked

Caboose, engulfed in the story. He shifted his bottom around, leaned forward and waited for more.

"Yes," answered Urium. "Unbeknownst to anyone, Mageddon had been traveling throughout the earth for a long time. He flew back and forth from the Holy Mount trading with the kings of the earth, especially King Ichabod who owned the prairies. Mageddon became very successful in his widespread trade and his heart swelled with pride on account of his wealth and fame. It didn't take long for greed to seize control causing him to lust for more. He became so powerful and controlled such vast amounts of wealth he discovered he could control and manipulate the markets.

He first lowered prices and drove his competitors out of business. Then he raised prices and proclaimed himself a god—the people groaned in misery as inflation soared high causing many to lose the small plots of land they owned. Countless became destitute, poor, and homeless. Starvation, crime, and murder ran rampant. Man and beast struggled just to find a few scraps to feed the hunger bugs revolting madly inside. But, Mageddon had underestimated the power of the kings. They rallied together and refused to trade with him ever again. They levied an embargo against all his goods and posted port sentries at sea ports to monitor all freights inbound.

Furious, Mageddon went to The Rainmaker and enticed her to make a pact with him. He promised her if she would withhold rain from the king's fields he would share his spoils with her. Mageddon wooed her day and night with his looted riches. He lavished her with diamond rings, pearl necklaces, ruby bracelets, all kinds of precious jewels. He clothed her with silk dresses trimmed in fine gold. He colored her face with exotic paint and gave her an endless supply of oils and creams making her skin silky smooth. Baths of floral and spiced fragrance were prepared for her—she soaked for hours as young maidens washed her, causing her body to radiate with intoxicating smells of enticement.

But she still remained loyal to His Majesty and carried out her mission. So Mageddon pulled his last and greatest trick on her; he supplied her with an abundance of Thunder Juice—the very thing King Ichabod loved so much himself. Intoxicated and blinded with lust, her heart turned from His Majesty and she worshipped Mageddon alone."

Thunder juice, thought Caboose. I don't understand why everyone loves it so much. The circle would be a lot better place without it.

"First Mageddon made her withhold rain from the king's fields—fields slowly dried and withered away, scorched by the powerful rays from the sun. Then he made her opened the floodgates of the heavens—crops and land washed away, others rotted in the plot they were planted. It wasn't long until the kings of the earth bowed low to Mageddon's power. With the Rainmaker on his side, they could no longer withstand the floods nor could they stand by and watch their people waste away from drought and famine."

"What happened to her? Is she still following Mageddon?" asked Caboose. He arched his back and yawned.

Urium stood up and walked over to the ledge. He looked down through the columns methodically spread abroad.

"When His Majesty found out what had happened he stripped her of her power and cast her to the plains-people she lusted after. Mageddon abandoned her and now she is the mother of prostitutes and an abomination on the earth. The kings committed adultery with her, and the juice of her adulteries intoxicated the people of the earth. This valley, the valley of bones and all that you see here, this used to be the prairie—King Ichabod's land. He's still alive..." said Urium. "He lives inside of Lucky."

"Lucky? But wasn't that years ago? How could he still be alive?" asked Caboose.

"King Ichabod was one of the most powerful kings in the world. But, just like Mageddon, his wealth and fame corrupted him causing him to lust for more. Mageddon promised him immortality if he would sell him his soul. Fueled by thunder juice, he sold his soul and became that which he hid inside—his true identity—a weak, insecure, fearful little man, afraid to stand up for what was right."

Lucky, thought Caboose. He didn't say anything. He sat there running Urium's words over and over in his mind. This story, and the others he told, were all starting to fit together like one giant puzzle. But a few pieces still remained. And he wondered... which part of the puzzle was he?

Urium walked over and sat back down. He stretched his wings and leaned his head up against the wall. "Posers..." He said. "Many powerful men are nothing but posers. They're like white-washed tombs. They look good on the outside, but inside, they are filled with death. Countless men and women appear to do great things, and the world tells them that they have done great things, but all their achievements are meaningless. They lie, cheat, and steal their way to the top, and all for what? So, they can make the scared little child hiding inside feel better. They are evil. They have eyes full of adultery and work only to benefit themselves. They carve their names into history by the blood of workers they failed to pay a decent wage too. You see, unless The Augur builds the house, its workers labor in vain. A day is coming, when the fire will test all things; the day when the dross will be removed. Then the truth will rise. Then a man's work will be shown for what it really is. Then the secrets of the heart will be laid bare and the true man will be revealed."

Urium's eyes closed as his lips mumbled. "Wisdom…better than gold…better…" he yawned… "Than gold."

Early the next morning, Urium stood at the entrance looking out over the land. Dark-clad shadows frolicked along the ridges in the distance. An eerie feeling tossed in his stomach, giving him a stomachache. It was symbolic of what was to follow. Urium had never been to Dead Man's Drop before. But he had heard tales from others and they weren't good.

Caboose lay on the ground curled up in a ball, still asleep a few feet behind him. Urium watched him for a moment and wondered what kind of plans The Augur had for him. Whatever it was, it would be the best thing that could ever happen in his life—greater than anyone could imagine. It was that way for everyone. Once a person rejects the broad path in life and ventures down the narrow, he or she finds a life and purpose that surpasses any dream or desire they could have ever possessed. It is then, and only then, that they find the true meaning of life.

Urium walked over, reached down and shook Caboose. "Caboose, we better get started."

Caboose yawned and stretched. "What time is it?"

"Time to get going," said Urium. "We need to reach the Drop before a quarter till noon." Urium collected his things and strapped his sword to his side.

Caboose sat up and shivered slightly. The scent of wet dirt filled the air. "It's cold, has the weather changed?"

"A front moved in last night. It seems to be trapped in the canyon," replied Urium.

During the night, a small Southern gale blew in lowering the temperature several degrees, which was unusual for the valley. It had also created a low-hanging fog that hovered over the entrance to the Drop, making visibility dim.

Urium started down the ledge face. Caboose gave one last sweeping look out across the land and then numbly trailed Urium back down the rocky path. He thought about the story of The Rainmaker, Lucky, and The Scorpion Pass gate. How did all this tie in with why The Augur had formed him with a short leg and his purpose for bringing him to the valley? Urium's stories were beginning to stalk him, like a pestilence in the darkness. He felt caught in a web—a web of deception.

Back on the valley floor a strange looking bug walked in front of him. He stopped and watched it crawl across the path. "Hey Urium, look at this."

Urium stopped and walked back. He bent down to the ground and let the bug crawl up his hand; it edged up his hand and then his arm. Urium laid his other hand on his arm and the colorful creature crawled on to it. "Beautiful isn't it."

"What is it?"

"It's a Click Beetle." Urium lowered his hand. The beetle crawled back to the ground.

"*Click Beetle*," said Caboose, remembering the click he heard right before he fell down the trap door in the Titan. "Why is it called that?"

"It has a small spine on its belly. When in danger it moves it into a special notch and bounces itself to safety making a loud 'clicking' sound."

Click, Click, Click, Click, Click, Click…The beetle disappeared quickly across the rocks. Caboose flinched and moved his neck in all directions. "I don't like."

"You don't like what?"

"The beetle; I don't like it."

Urium laughed and shook his head. "Now why would you say that? It didn't do anything to you."

"I don't care," responded Caboose. "I don't like it."

Dark figures crept back into holes and narrow crags as they walked under the arches and down the path smelling of a pungent cocktail of tang and death. Caboose noticed something strange about the entrance. The wind did not pass through like a normal airstream should. Instead, it pulsed, liked being inhaled and exhaled. Obscuring the horizon, large jagged-tooth overhangs speckled the skyline—long vines checker-boarded their sides coiling down to the ground below. The barbed vines moved back and forth ever so slightly by the raspy gusts causing Caboose to scratch his neck and feel afraid. Deep within the narrows and muffled by the vines, demonic sounds ricocheted off the terraced walls.

Caboose closed the distance between himself and Urium. As he did, he stepped on the back of Urium's foot, causing Urium to trip.

"Is everything alright?" asked Urium.

"Yep. Just fine," responded Caboose, his eyes roaming about.

A sick feeling grumbled in the pit of his stomach and it was not hunger bugs. All he could think of was long hairy arms, teeth, and claws ripping his flesh to pieces. Even the vines seemed to claw and scratch at his head. They wrapped around his throat and strangled him, or so he thought. Jumpy, he whispered, "I don't like this place, it gives me the creeps."

Urium pulled his sword and sliced it through the air and then returned it. Two pieces of something disintegrated instantly.

"What was that?" Caboose jolted his head around at the sound of Urium's sword.

"Nothing," said Urium, jumping and acting like he was going to draw his sword. "Did you hear something?"

Something fluttered behind him again. Caboose spun around. Urium drew his sword and sliced it to the right and to the left. Four more pieces went up in flames. He leaned on his sword resting it against the ground as if nothing had happened. Caboose spun back around and gave him a scorned look. He examined the ground—nothing, nothing but dirt, rocks, and footprints. He made a face and nodded, "So that's how it's 'gonna be?"

Urium turned and smiled. Caboose was literally transforming before his eyes. It made him proud. It made him feel like a father teaching a son lessons about life. He loved the responsibility His Majesty entrusted to him. Serving the people of the circle was a privilege and a command he carried out with great honor. He also knew all celestial beings will be judged by the people they serve. It was in his best interest to serve with great diligence.

High above them, on a ledge covered in thick ivy, a dark creature jumped. It glided through the air and landed behind Caboose making a loud "Crunching" sound in the rocks.

Caboose spun around chopping his arms in all directions yelling—his tail swept Urium right off his feet landing him face first in the dirt.

"Hang on there, big guy. I'm on your side," spoke a soft but robust voice with arms raised to defend against the mighty Kung Fu warrior standing fearlessly before her.

Urium stood up and dusted off his chest and knees. "Frost, I suspected you were in the area. "What are you doing here?" asked Urium.

Caboose didn't move. His hands were still poised ready to attack. Urium walked over and tapped him on the shoulder. "It's alright, she's on our side."

A lengthy sigh came from deep within. He lowered his hands and gave a quivered nod.

"Seven sent me. He said you might need some help in here." She leaned forward close to Caboose's ear and whispered, "This place is infested with crawlers. They're everywhere."

His knees startled to buckle but somehow he found the strength to maintain his composure.

Frost held out her hand. "I'm Cadiamarmegus. But you can call me Frost," she winked, with an icy gaze. "And you must be Caboose."

Caboose reached out and shook her hand. He leaned forward trying to maintain a straight face as her firm handshake crushed every bone in his hand. "Nice t-to meet you." stuttered Caboose. He dropped his hand and stretched it out when she looked away.

"I could've used you days ago," suggested Urium. "We were tracked by trolls in the tunnels, almost eaten by gargoyles in the gorge and then we were attacked by ragooles, howlers, and Magondreas." He scanned the ledges and walked around in a circle.

"You're not the only one in this valley that needs help you know. I've been busy," she responded, turning her back to them. She paced down the path and then looked up. "Besides, what are you doing here? We're not supposed to be here," she whispered, loudly.

Urium unsheathed his sword. "Seven. Seven told me too."

Up ahead the path zigzagged through a maze of stone steeples sagging against a rapid decline. Large boulders rested on jagged terraces as if they had been strategically placed. From deep within, a low gargling breath exhaled thrusting the vines toward the entrance. Frost threw Urium her sword and pulled out a whip, it was a long single cord inset with icy shards that glowed blue.

They backed up and encircled Caboose.

"What is it?" yelled Caboose, as the wind ripped past his ears and small rocks crashed all around.

The ground vibrated.

"They're here," yelled Frost. She vaulted through the air, tucked mid-air and bounced off the ground cutting several crawlers in half. With her elbow, foot, and fist, she smashed, kicked, and uppercutted several others high into the air, splattering them against the walls. She whipped the icy cord over her head several times and then cracked it in the air. The shards broke off and snapped out small wings from their sides before rocketing into the hoard of crawlers pressing in, instantly turning them into ice. With the next crack, the small shards exploded, sending small sonic booms rushing throughout the canyon.

Urium connected the ends of the swords, which glimmered brightly in the dark canyon, and twirled them in front of him. The walls and vines turned black with crawlers oozing out from their holes. They scaled down surrounding him.

Caboose punched, jabbed, and bobbed, dodging long hairy arms and fangs sweeping inches above his head. Urium spread his wings and rose off the ground. With one giant spin, he twirled round and round killing hundreds instantly.

"Urium!" yelled Frost. Urium landed back on the ground, sliced two more in half and kicked another one plunging it into the crowd. He gave a quick glance in her direction.

Frost threw her head up toward the vines.

Urium understood.

"Hold this," he said, handing his swords to Caboose.

Caboose looked down at the bright rods glowing in his hands and twirled them around. The rods rotated around hitting Urium in the back of his head cutting off a chunk of his hair.

"Hey," yelled Urium grabbing his head. "That's my head."

"Sorry," replied Caboose, with a puzzled look plastered across his face.

Frost inhaled deeply. She puckered her lips and, moving her head side-to-side, blew a thick stream of ice crystals into the air. The crystals weaved through the forest of dangling vines forming long icicles overhead. Urium thrust his hands toward the icy daggers, unleashing a force field breaking them off at their base. The icy torpedoes hurtled through the air down the canyon and up the walls piercing hundreds more, toppling the long-legged spiny creatures off the walls and ledges. They fell down crushing hundreds on the floor below.

"Take him to the drop!" yelled Frost. "I'll meet you there." She retired her whip and raised her hands. A blue shock wave pulsed from her feet to her hands and then rippled down the path disintegrating hundreds more. But, their frugal efforts barely put a dent in the thousands that continued to circle them. She ran over and looked down the steep trail winding down the canyon.

She raised her hands again; a massive tidal wave rip-curled down the steep alleyway and hooked around the bend all the way to the bottom, instantly covering the trail in a thick layer of ice.

She looked at Urium. "Well, what are you waiting for?"

Urium grabbed Caboose and dove for the ice.

Struggling to maintain his balance, Caboose slid down the cold steep chute full of rocky obstacles. Raining down from above, large boulders crashed, shattering the ice into hundreds of pieces. Urium raised his hands and disintegrated many of them causing large dust clouds to explode in the air—an onslaught of tiny pebbles pelted them in the aftermath.

They cornered high off the wall coming out of the first turn. Caboose shot into the air, flipped over and ended up face-first on his belly, staring down a large boulder that had fallen in the middle of the trail. Trying desperately to maneuver his body from side to side, at the last second, he used his tail to punch off the side just missing the rock. Urium, tucked safely behind Caboose, didn't see the rock until it was too late. He lowered his head and crashed through the middle. Trying to regain his senses, he spun around dueling with the crawlers skating close behind.

Caboose washed out at the bottom and slid over the cliff.

Urium dug his sword in the ice and kicked right at the last moment.

The crawlers, sliding close behind, spewed webbing trying to catch themselves, but the sticky strings wouldn't hold on the ice: they all tumbled over the cliff and disappeared.

"Caboose!" yelled Urium. He jumped up and slid over to the cliff ledge. Dangling safely a few feet below, lie Caboose on his side, tangled in a trap of smelly grass. He rolled his head and looked up.

Urium grabbed his tail and pulled him up.

The trail ended at a cliff overlooking a dead sea. Caboose stood as far back from the ledge as possible and stretched his neck to its fullest extent. He glanced down over the ledge causing his breath to catch in the back of his throat; the cliff was way too high to see the bottom clearly—his belly turned upside down and his body went limp with dizziness.

"I don't feel so good," he responded holding his head.

"Do you see that ledge way down there? That's Dead Man's Drop."

Caboose stretched his neck again and squinted his eyes. The sea was grey and heaving restlessly. "I don't see anything. I think we'd better turn around."

Frost landed at the bottom and sealed the opening with a thick layer of ice. She walked over and stood off the ledge on the air.

Caboose looked at her with disgust.

"That should hold them for awhile. Nice working with you again Urium, but, if you'll excuse me, I have to go, something is happening on the boarders of Guma."

"Thanks Frost. I owe you big time for this one."

"I know," she wisecracked. "Besides, sharpening my skills on slow deadbeat crawlers is my favorite past-time activity anyway." They looked at each other and laughed.

"Nice meeting you Caboose. Follow Seven's orders and everything should be alright." She spread her wings and disappeared into the clouds leaving a small trail of ice crystals in her wake.

Should, thought Caboose. That's great. That's just great. He shook his head and mumbled, "Should be alright."

Urium held out his hand and pointed again. "Look, do you see the opening to the cave."

Caboose looked and reluctantly replied, "Yeah, I think so, still processing the word 'Should.'"

"Now follow the shore line to the left about five thunder beast tails."

"I see it. Too bad we don't have a rope, looks like we'll have to turn around."

Caboose looked down at Urium's hand slipping into his pocket. Before he could pull it out, Caboose, sarcastically exclaimed, "Let me guess. You just happen to have…some dragon rope in your pocket."

Surprised, Urium answered, "You're good. It's actually dragon intestines. They're a lot lighter to carry and stretch much further than rope."

Oh, well excuse me, thought Caboose. "Great. Say, you don't happen to have my Papa and a secret portal back home in your pocket do you?"

Urium rolled his eyes and shook his head. He reached in and pulled out an old brown cloth and opened it up. He pulled out the intestine, tied it around a rock and threw it over. It fell down about fifty feet and stopped.

Caboose looked over the ledge and smiled. Now they would have to find another way for sure. "It's too short. See, we need to turn around and look for another way down."

"Just grab it with your hands and wrap your tail and one of your legs around it. It will stretch down and drop you off at the ledge."

Caboose didn't say anything. He stood still searching for an excuse.

"I can't swim," he answered, after several seconds.

Urium, fully aware of what was happening responded, "All grunters can swim."

"Well, this grunter can't swim. My short leg, it pulls me under. I can't swim I tell you."

"Seven didn't say anything about swimming."

Caboose snarled and searched for something to comeback with. "I…I—"

"Come on, we have to hurry, we're running out of time."

Urium held Caboose with one hand, looked over the ledge and gave one last encouraging word. "In a few days, you will be at the Sea Throne and will be reunited with your Papa."

Caboose, with eyes closed, reached one leg back and felt for the cliff's face.

"Don't worry Caboose I have…"

"AHHHHHHHHHHHHHHHHHH." Caboose slipped. His hands smoked and burned as he slid down the intestine out of control. Quickly approaching from the bottom, enormous spikes raced upward at him.

Urium dove off the cliff and spread his wings. "Hang on Caboose, don't let go."

Caboose tried not to look down at the rocky spikes reaching up for him. Urium tucked his wings and spiraled off the ledge. The wind ruffled through his wings slicking his hair straight back and making his eyes water. He passed Caboose in mid air and spun his body around upright, parallel to the cliff face. Amazingly Caboose started to slow…slow…slow until finally coming to a complete stop just above the ledge.

"You can step down now Caboose," said Urium, already standing securely on the ledge.

Caboose opened his eyes, looked down and peeled his fingers off the intestine—he looked at Urium secretly wanting to strangle him. Caboose walked over to the edge of the cliff. This time they were about forty feet from the water. Off to his right, being pounded by the waves, was a deep cave covered with seaweed and bones.

"11:35, great. We have ten extra minutes to spare," said Urium.

"What do we do now?" asked Caboose.

"Let me see. Seven said: '*Stand aloof, at Dead Man's Drop,*' check. '*Quarter 'til noon, whistle the tune.*' He tilted his head up at the sky, in exactly seven minutes and 25 seconds I will whistle the tune." '*A ripple, a wave, out of the cave,*' I guess we wait until we see something come out of the cave. '*Count to three, anchors away.*' When you see the wave, count to three and jump."

"Jump! Are you crazy? I'm not jumping…from this ledge… into that water…at whatever is coming out of that cave!"

As Caboose stood sulking, four horns appeared over the water. He looked at Urium and asked, "Do you see that? What are those?"

"The Augur is showing you a sign. The four horns will break down the walls of Thunder Juice Town and scatter its people."

Four craftsmen then appeared standing beside the horns, "Who are they?"

"The horns will scatter Thunder Juice Town so that no one will raise their heads, but the craftsmen will terrify and cast down the horns. The horns are the nations who lift up their horns and come against Thunder Juice Town."

"Get ready its almost time." Urium puckered his lips and whistled the tune. They both eased over the ledge scanning the water and the mouth of the cave.

They waited.

Above them, icing down the bluff, a crawler descended, desperately wanting to appease his ferocious hunger bug pangs. The crawler maneuvered over them and raised his fangs and front legs. Deep within the cave the water rippled. Suddenly, a wave torpedoed through the tunnel and exploded out of the cave into the sea.

Urium counted to three, looked at Caboose and said, "Forgive me."

"For what?"

"For this." Urium knew what he had to do. It was in his nature to carry out orders even if what he was doing didn't make sense. He pushed Caboose over the ledge and shouted, "Anchors away!"

With eyes as big as Mushy Marts, Caboose fell through the air waving his limbs. The wave from his splash plumed up soaking Urium. Caboose had told the truth, he couldn't swim. Yelling Urium's name, he fought to stay afloat but gradually sank beneath the surface. Under water he stopped fighting. Hearing the splash, hundreds of venomous creatures surrounded him from all directions. Caboose boisterously trying to protect himself, stretched out all his limbs in an attempt to appear larger than he really was. The creatures moved closer and closer blocking any means of escape. Petrified with fear, Caboose prepared for the worst. The creatures closed in from every side and then froze in place, their attention averted behind him. In unison, they tucked tail and swam away, disappearing into the shadows.

Flabbergasted, he smiled and gloated, thinking "I showed them who was boss. I'm the man! Don't mess with Mr. C."

Feeling a terrific moment of bliss and forgetting that he was still about to drown, his eyes glimpsed a shadow blanketing him just before the craggy serrated teeth of Leviathan, the fearsome creature of the deep, closed, swallowing him whole. Leviathan jumped out of the water revealing his long terror-gripping body for all to see. His back was like shields tightly sealed together, each so close air couldn't penetrate its seamless contours. His chest was hard like a rock and his snorting threw out flashes of light. His eyes were like the rays of dawn. Firebrands streamed from his mouth and sparks of fire shot out, pouring smoke from his nostrils. He landed on his side igniting a huge tidal wave that overtook the cliff and knocked the crawler into the sea.

The crawler dueled with the creatures of the deep. It swung its legs at the sea creatures shooting out venom and webbing until finally being consumed piece by piece.

Urium shook himself off and watched as Leviathan's shadow disappeared into the deep.

CHAPTER 10

BAMBOOZLED

Although they claimed to be wise, they became fools.

L ike a tree by abundant, fresh-flowing water, The Augur had planted Thunder Juice Town; an orchard of juicy apple, orange, and pear; jujube, cherry, and peach; fig, olive, and plum trees: a variety of every kind of fruit yielding their harvest freely to all. Large leafy green boughs sheltered, shaded, and healed, all supported by thick muscular branches that stretched long and high into the air. Deep roots firmly established in The Redmadafa remained safe and well watered.

Fascinated, yet confused, Old Juicy now sent out its roots toward another great eagle. It stretched out its branches toward him for water from the plot where it was planted. Like cattle being led to slaughter, the exodus began. The Augur, whose hands had formed them by clay, whose truths had established their boundaries and safeguarded their lives, had been replaced by the cunning tongue of The Horn Swoggler.

Lucifer, with great pomp and circumstance, told the people about a lush garden, filled with delicious fruit, juicier than Thunder Juice Town. A garden filled with jewels and a water supply that was far greater than their old but faithful Redmadafa. He told the people that everyone would eat from their own vine, drink cool water from their own cistern, and eat fruit from their own fruit trees. He promised to take them to a land of abundant grain, and thunder juice, a land of bread and vineyards, a land of olive oil and of honey, so that they would live and not die. He eagerly led the way as droves of residents packed and headed for the Promise Land.

Mack and his mother packed for the new land. They were out of money and the eviction notice, swaying in the wind on the door, gave them until the end of the month to be out of the house. This was a blessing from the gods thought Mrs. Davoo, as she packed up the last remaining things. Mack, being the natural born leader that he was, wanted them to be the first ones to enter the garden. He planned to claim his own stake of land and provide for his mother—after all, he was now the man of the house.

Mack needed to do this for his mother and himself. Way down deep inside, he was scared and insecure, and although he would never admit it, and would punch anyone straight in the nose for even thinking it. The loss of his father only made things worse. He used the lixoars to act tough and pick on people, but without them, he wasn't that tough. Moving to a new place and starting over might give him the confidence he had always longed for. For him it was a challenge and he wasn't afraid of a challenge.

Mack longed to get away from Thunder Juice Town, in fact, it was a surprise to many that he hadn't run for the gate years ago. But it really wasn't the town he wanted to get away from. It was his father—Hyben. His father often came in late at night from the tavern and would beat him and his mother for the slightest reason—or no reason at all. He was a man filled with violence and anger, especially after a night of thunder juice indulgence. Hyben had fooled everyone at work with his outgoing personality highlighted by his elaborate jokes. At work he was loved and respected. His knowledge of the mines and many years of experience were looked up to and admired—even though others saw it in his eyes and smelt it in his sweat.

Hyben had been addicted to thunder juice since he was a teenager. He too had grown up in a violent home and turned to the juice to help ease the pain. Thunder juice helped him discover a side of himself that he had never known before, a funny side, a side others liked and liked to be around. At the tavern he was the life of the party, the one everyone circled around. It gave him recognition and a feeling of belonging he had never felt at home. But it was all a lie. It was fueled by liquid courage and its foundations were built upon a delusion. He drank all the time; even his lunch gourd was spiked with it. There wasn't a day that went by that he didn't use the juice to numb the pain of life, guilt, and the shame that stirred inside—the shame that he had followed in his father's footsteps both at work and home.

Mack was embarrassed of his family. His father and mother fought so loudly that neighbors a mile away could hear them screaming. So, he learned to put up a front. His tough-guy act was a mirage, an act, a mask to hide the anger and embarrassment he felt inside. If anyone ever found out, his cover would be blown and the small amount of power he felt by bullying others would come to an end.

He walked outside and approached the cart. He looked it over shaking his head. His mother loaded another basket with many more still waiting at her feet.

"Mom, you can't pack the whole house, we don't have enough room on the cart for all these things." He walked behind the cart and pushed trying to make more room. "Look at this. Do you really need this," he said, holding up a funny looking garment, quickly throwing it aside before someone saw him with it?

"I don't know what we will need when we get there. I hate to leave so much behind," his mother said, feeling abandoned and alone, still mourning the death of her husband.

Mack lifted up a basket and discovered some of his dad's things buried at the bottom. "Mom! We can't take dad's things with us. If you put one more thing on this cart, it will break, and then we won't have anything."

"Ok, ok," she motioned, slipping a few more items on the back—Mack grabbed his head in frustration, "It's useless, I'm talking to a stone wall."

* * * * * *

Rammer, disgusted with his father, slammed the door and fell on his bed. With most of the neighbors fleeing Old Juicy before the serpent and his army arrived, his father didn't think they should leave.

"He never comes to my races. We never go out to eat. We never take vacations, and now that we have a chance to go somewhere new, now he wants to start making the decisions and lead the family. Why me? Why me?" vented Rammer on his bed.

"Rammer, open this door!" shouted his father pounding loudly.

"You never cared before, why start now?"

"You better open this door right now, I mean it!" shouted his father.

Rammer jumped up and opened the door. He ran past his father straight into the living room where his mother sat quietly. "Why are you letting him do this to us? Tell him we're going. Tell him."

"Rammer, sit down, there is something your father needs to say." His mother was not used to this and wasn't sure what to do now that his father seemed interested in their affairs.

Rammer stood puzzled. He didn't understand why his mother wasn't standing up for him. His father, standing in the doorway listening, walked in and sat down.

"Son, please sit down, something happened that I need to tell you about."

In protest, he plopped on the divan with his arms folded, staring intently at the worn-out boards nailed to the floor.

With a jumpy voice he said, "Rammer, I'm sorry." He paused and looked away fighting back the tears.

"I know I haven't been here for you and your mother. There's no excuse, as to why I've acted the way I have. I mean…I don't expect you to understand what I'm saying. I've been working so hard all these years to be recognized by my boss, trying to… be the best at what I do. But, in the process, I've neglected you and your mother and, well, there's no excuse. I didn't tell you, but when the eagle arrived the other day, I remembered what someone told me. I realized that what I was doing and trying to achieve, was wrong."

Rammer wasn't listening. He refused to listen to anything his father had to say.

"Many years ago, I was just like you."

Oh boy, didn't I just hear this lecture from coach the other day. Yeah right, thought Rammer, even though he wasn't listening.

"I was athletic and could race with the best of them. Your grandfather came to almost every race; I think he may have only missed one or two. He pushed me to be the best, to beat everyone at everything I did. He spent hours and hours, training and coaching me, so many that there were days I wished he wasn't there. He was so demanding and tough on me that sometimes I didn't even want him to come. My belly turned in knots knowing if I didn't win, he would find some reason it was my fault…if I would've only listened to him…I would've blown every one away. I said when I grew up I would never treat my son like that. But, I never meant to take it to the other extreme. You want to hear what's strange. Although he's gone, I still hear his voice pushing me, driving me, to beat everyone at work, to be the best. At times, I still think he's controlling my life."

"Then why can't we just leave with everyone else and start over? Everyone is leaving," said Rammer, refusing to look at him.

His dad looked over at his mother and smiled. "Well, a few days ago I would have. I probably would've been the first in line, but your coach came by my work."

Stunned, Rammer answered, "My coach. Why did he do that?"

"I was busy and couldn't see him. I told my assistant to send him away I would talk to him when things slowed down. But, I came out of my office several hours later to go the bathroom and he was still sitting there. I had a few minutes so I let him in. He came in and sat down. I sat down behind my desk and went over a few numbers and said, 'So, what's on your mind. I hear Rammer got tripped at the end of the race the other day…bunch of cheaters, I don't know why he likes racing in that stupid race anyway.'

Your coach didn't say anything he just sat there staring at me. Then he said, "I don't want to take too much of your time but I need to share with you something that happened to me a few years ago."

'Does this have something to do with Rammer?' I asked.

"Yes. As a matter of fact, it does."

He moved to the edge of his seat and said, "A few years back, I enlisted in the military. After training, I tried out for an elite group which called themselves, 'Leather Necks.'"—Apparently they called themselves that because of the thick wide strap of leather they wrapped around their necks to hold their heads up high and protect against saber slashes.

"We trained hard, real hard. I had never been around men so committed to honor and integrity—they were always faithful for the cause. Anyway, about two years in, we took a trip around the circle in a big Tree Floater—number 44. We sailed across the sea and pulled into a port of a unique tribe of people—they too were an elite group that had been chosen to complete a mission—a very special mission.

We left the Tree Floater and went into the desert to train with their army. For weeks we ate, slept, and trained with them in the hot sun learning how to survive in that type of an environment and how to live off the land. We trained so hard and long we didn't even have time to take a bath. When we returned to the floater, I was one of the first ones to strip down, walk across the passageway and take a bath. When I finished cleaning myself, I was one of the first to come back into our berthing area."

'I stopped Coach at this point and asked him what this had to do with you.' "Everything," he replied, and then continued.

"When I walked into the berthing area where we slept, I almost fell down dead because of the stench from our clothes. We hadn't taken a bath for weeks and couldn't smell the dirt and sweat that reeked on our bodies and in our clothes."

I stopped him again at this point and said, 'Coach. I really appreciate you taking the time out of your busy schedule to come see me, but I am really busy and I don't see what this has to do with my son.' Coach stood up and walked over to my desk.

"We couldn't smell how much we stunk until we were clean. This story is not about your son," he said. "It's about you. This room is filled with the stench of a father who has buried himself in his office and is neglecting the most prized possession a man could ever possess—a family. A family that loves him very much…A family that if he doesn't clean himself fast—he will quickly loose."

My head almost exploded from the blood rushing to it. I jumped out of my seat furious and put my nose against his. I was just about to throw him out when he said, 'Rooter, don't you remember me? I used to race against you. I used to watch you and your Dad prepare before each race—I longed to have my father stand by me the way yours stood by you. Rammer needs you. He's changing and fast. He needs you by his side more than ever.'

When he said that, it was like a Magondrea ran right over me. Scales fell off my eyes revealing the truth to what I was really doing. It was then that I realized in my attempt to rebel against my Dad, I had abandoned you and your mother. I don't deserve to be your father. You deserve a whole lot better."

Rammer broke. He fell into his father's arms. "I love you. I'm so sorry for being mad at you."

"And I..." said Rooter, looking down at his head, "Love you, son. I love you and your mother very much."

Still grasping his father and without looking up, Rammer asked, "But I still don't understand. Why can't we leave with everyone else?"

Rooter pulled him away with both arms and gazed straight into his tear-filled eyes. "Before coach left, he told me something else. He told me about The Augur. He told me how The Augur chose this town and its people. How he formed its walls, built the temple and how he was the power behind the split rock from which The Redmadafa flows. Son, all I can tell you is that when I prayed with coach, something happened. Something that, right now is still hard for me to explain. But when I saw the eagle the other day and heard him speak, I knew he was not The Augur. I know I don't have the right to ask you this but I need you to trust me. Something just isn't right. Coach is a good man. I don't think I have to tell you that. If he's staying, we're staying."

* * * * * * *

Brook walked in the house and stood speechless. The luster in her eyes and the smile on her face faded. Baskets lined the hallway. Clothes draped the furniture. Her mother had already packed most of the house and was ready to load the cart. Brook looked completely different. She glowed. She had and extra bounce in her step, joy stretched across her face and her eyes sparkled with delight.

"Mom, what are you doing?" asked Brook, shocked to see her mother packing for the new land.

Her mother emerged from the kitchen and disappeared down the hall. "Hurry and pack your things, we're leaving."

Brook followed. "What do you mean we're leaving? We can't leave Thunder Juice Town."

"Brook, don't argue with me. Your brothers are already packed and it's almost time to assemble at the gate."

Brook grabbed a shirt out of her mother's hand and threw it back in the drawer. "You can't do this. You can't do this. Mom, it's a lie. I knew his voice the moment he spoke. He is the one I told you about. Lucky, the strange man I met at The Scorpion Pass Gate."

"Impossible," replied her mother picking the shirt back up and stuffing it in a basket. "He's an eagle and a beautiful one at that—the most magnificent creature I have ever seen or heard. Didn't you see and hear what he said? The serpent is coming. He is going to destroy Thunder Juice Town and all that stay behind."

"Mother," Brook only said 'mother' when she was really angry or wanted her undivided attention. "You and everyone else have been deceived. He is the serpent."

Brook's mother swung, slapping her in the face. Stunned, they both stood there, staring at each other in disbelief.

Brook grabbed her cheek and cried. "The Augur rescued me from the garden and the falls. What that eagle described the other day is exactly what I was trapped in. I saw who he really was and I saw The Augur, and he is not The Augur!"

"Why are you doing this to me?" cried her mother plopping down on the bed. "I am a single mother Brook, trying to raise three children. We barely get by on what I make. I am so tired of living payday to payday. This is a great opportunity for us and I don't want to miss it."

Brook sat down beside her mother and took hold of her hand. "No matter how good a lie may sound, it is still a lie and no lie comes from the truth. Just stop and think about what is happening. If he is so powerful and strong, and can take us to a new land and protect us from the serpent, then why can't he defend us here?"

Her mother searched her thoughts, running that question over and over through her mind. She began to wonder—What if she's right? What if he *is* the serpent? Why can't he defend us here? She put her hand on top and squeezed but didn't say anything.

"If we don't go, what are we going to do? This sounded so good—maybe…too good to be true."

Through the window Brook saw Tack running down the street. He jumped over the hedge clearing several toys in a single bound and dashed across the yard and onto the porch. Brook jumped up and ran down the hallway opening the door right before he knocked it down. Not anticipating the welcome, he fell face first right on the floor.

"Hey, why did you do that?" he said, gesturing at Brook completely out of breath. "Mom. You won't believe what's happening at the gates and in the square. Everyone's yelling and fighting with the elders from the temple."

"What? Are you sure?" asked Brook.

"Yeah. Rinox said the eagle was the serpent and he wants to lure everyone away from Thunder Juice Town to kill them. He said the new land is a lie and…"

"Hang on there tiger. Slow down, I can hardly understand you," said his mother now standing in the front room.

Tack stood up and wiped himself off. He walked to the ice crate to get something to drink. He opened it and noticed the ice was almost melted. "The temple servants are saying the eagle is the serpent. Rinox called him the 'Father of Lies.' Boy, you should see how mad the people are at him and the other servants of the temple."

"Mom, Rinox was the one who came for me when The Augur left me at The Redmadafa just outside of town. Now do you believe me?"

"Get Timmy."

"Where are we going?"

"I want to hear what Rinox and the others are saying for myself."

* * * * * * *

High thick walls protected Thunder Juice Town. Eight gates ushered people in and out during the day and were tightly shut up at night. Numerous attacks were waged against Old Juicy in the past, but the walls always held. Zion, Dung, Golden, Lion, Flower, North, New, and Jaffa gates where conveniently spread out around the walls allowing people to come and go in every direction. The servants of the temple stood at each gate proclaiming the truth about the eagle, deciphering his lies and unfolding his malicious scheme. Brook and her mother and brothers arrived at Lion's gate just as Rinox shouted:

"That's not what I'm saying. I know you have the right to believe what you want. But, whether or not you want to admit it, this town was created and established on the principles of the ancient scrolls of the temple—Scrolls that were written by those inspired by the Great Spirit of The Augur. It is because of his Word this town has flourished the way it has. If you step outside of those boundaries..."

"We've heard all of this before Rinox. We don't want any more of your visions about what is right. If you would have told us pleasant things, or prophesied illusions, maybe we would've listened to you. But no, it's always, 'Leave this way, get off this path.' Well, we're tired of being confronted with your temple rules," resounded a large distinguished thunder beast from the crowd.

"Yeah! If the Augur loves us so much, then where is he?" echoed another.

"He's abandoned us, that's where. He's probably afraid of the serpent."

Many people turned and started to walk away casting their hands at Rinox, shaking their heads in disbelief.

"The Augur is always at work," said Rinox. "Every human, creature, and beast of this town has ties to The Augur. He flew day and night to save your mothers and fathers, your aunts and uncles, your sisters and brothers, and your great, great, greats. If you leave these walls and The Redmadafa, you will not thrive. You will be uprooted and stripped of everything you've ever known. All your new growth will waste away. It will not take a strong hand or many fingers to pluck up your new roots. Even if you are transplanted, will you bloom? No! You will waste away completely when the East wind strikes you. You will wither away in the furrows where you were planted? Lucifer is a liar. He is the serpent!"

The crowd moved in to seize him. Others picked up stones to stone him. Their anger and frustration were clearly palpable.

"How do we know you're not the serpent, Rinox?"

"You and your teachings are the Serpent."

Rinox had said all he could say. He dusted his feet off and replied, "If that's what you think, then you've...been Bamboozled!"

CHAPTER 11

THE SEA THRONE

*You are a man, not a god, though you
think you are as wise as one.*

Dust stirred in the warm afternoon air outside of Lion's Gate. Golden rays of sunlight streaked the skyline as the excitement of the unknown, the mysterious, the thrill of adventure, twinkled from eye to eye. In town, the sound of chains fettered to cattle and cart, clanged down alleyways and crossroads; stamping hooves and rumbling wheels carried through walls and doors to those sitting inside—those who had decided to stay. Silence hovered inside homes as people listened, wondering if they had made the right decision.

Outside the walls, voices resonated across the open meadow and carried down the trail toward the mountain pass. People from all over town and outlying villages filtered out the gates into the mountains. Light-brown grass-woven baskets, tied shut with long strands of sawgrass, balanced atop heads while others dangled from backs and shoulders as the crowd jostled to get underway pushing and shoving each other with anxious anticipation. Herds of cattle, flocks, beasts, wagons and carts piled high with baskets, trunks and other garments, merged into the mountain paths leaving long grooves cut into them.

Mack and his mother were in the first group that left for the garden. They covered their mouths and looked down at the trail, blindly following through the flurry of dust lingering over the mob.

Large trolls (Serpent slayers, proclaimed Lucifer) dauntlessly led them to their doom. The trolls led them into the mountains over the rolling hills and around the bends. Arriving at the fork days later, talk spread of riches, fame, and fortune and how it would all be divided. The trolls turned right on the broad path and continued until reaching the switchback. They followed it through the canyon and proceeded through the thick black fog, until finally reaching the gate several days later.

Emerging from the fog, eyes raised, hearts pounded and feet danced in anticipation. The garden was amazing—better than the eagle had described. Waterfalls poured purple mountain majesty from high aloft. Jewels hung from the gate and glittered brightly in the sunlight.

Upon entering the gate, a golden mosaic path invited curious spectators to Lucky's caricature carnival, where he waited with arms full of amazing prizes, games and fantastically flavored food. Gog clowns juggled; moogles swung from trapeze; thunder beast rides for little children; ragooles dazzled from the air. Little caricature creatures riding large honey buzzers passed out delicious treats: Blossom Berry cotton candy, Mushy Mart cream pies, Blue Tongue Sickle licky-sticks and Brumpel Melon slushies. Lucky stood in the center with a sea horn to his mouth. Proudly, he announced:

> *"Step right up, to the game of luck;*
> *'Two in wins,' he said with a grin.*
> *Don't worry about the fee, it's all free.*
> *Just a little toss, to collect your dross.*
>
> *Step inside the old oak, to undue his yoke.*
> *Collect your prize, with a spectacular surprise.*
> *Deposit the ransom, for a brand new mansion,*
> *One at a time...no cutting in line."*

He danced and he jumped and he beat his chest, this time he would finally fulfill his soul quest. So he took the children and the little babies, and he bounced them and bounced them on his beastly red knees.

Mack's face looked like a rainbow. Red cotton candy, green melon slushy, yellow mushy mart cream pie and blue tongue sickle covered his face. He handed his mother a bag of cotton candy and with his mouth full said, "Try this, it's good."

She pulled off a handful, "Ummm. That is good."

Mack ran through the garden his mind filled with dreams of riches and wealth. He searched through the trees and rolled in the long green grass. Mack was just like other boys. He longed to do something great. Now that his Dad was gone, he felt responsible for his mother and wanted to show her that he could provide for them and make her proud.

He walked over and got in line. He constantly looked to the side and over shoulders waiting for his turn at the 'Game of Luck.' The girl in front of him walked up to the line, picked up the first bag and landed it dead center. She picked up the next one, squeezed in it her hand and did the same. The clown handed her a shiny silver coin and pointed toward the Titan across the stream.

Mack stepped up and grabbed the first bag. He jiggled it around in his hands a couple of times and then focused before letting it go.

It missed.

His stomach coiled-up in knots.

He took a deep breath before reaching over and grabbing the second bag. He threw it right in the middle of the round crate. He grabbed the last one. He breathed in slowly and then exhaled. He leaned over the line as far as he could and tossed the bag. The bag spun through the air, hit the edge of the crate, seesawed, and then fell in. The clown handed him and his mother a silver coin.

"Son, that's the best right hand I think I ever did see," said the ugliest clown he had ever seen.

With a sigh of relief on his face he turned toward his mom and replied, "Mom, now we can collect our mansion. See, everything's going to be alright. I bet we'll have the biggest one with the biggest yard. Boy, if Dad could only see us now."

They followed the path through the garden and crossed the rock bridge making their way to the Titan. Mack's tongue was bluish green from all the delirious treats. In line, they both dreamt of the new house and life they would now have.

One by one, the clown let them in;
waiting for the knock he heard within.

"Next" he said, as he raised his stick;
listening for the sound of the terrible trick.

Mack eager to provide for his mother, and to prove to himself that he was not afraid, stepped forward and waited for the door to open.

"I'll be right back. Mom, we're finally going to be somebody," he said with confidence. "Everything is going to be okay. Trust me. I know what I'm doing."

The door opened and closed. Inside, hundreds of shiny things filled the walls and ledges—more than were there before. Mack paused, his eyes spellbound by all the glitter. Sitting on top of the stone was a beautiful girl with a long white lace draped over her head; gentle folds of ornate patterns flowed over the stone and ended with red tassels. Their eyes locked as he strutted over and introduced himself.

"Here," she said softly. "Place the ransom here to collect your mansion."

Filled with confidence, he proudly took the silver coin out of his pocket, twirled it through his fingers and flipped it into the air—it spun and spun, and spun and spun, and fell right into the hole—Click!

* * * * * * *

Leviathan descended to the bottom of the sea with Caboose. The Augur had prepared a place in Leviathan's belly especially for the journey. He took the long route and traveled for days until reaching the treacherous shores of The Sea Throne.

High jagged walls protected the island. Watchtowers and terraced battlements overlooked the sea from all directions.

Ragooles patrolled the sky, while gogs and Grike Trolls—riding Magondreas—searched the grounds. In the middle of the Island was a large crystal fortress with hundreds of peaks rising into the clouds—Mageddon's throne. It was surrounded by crawler perimeter defenses. Dark red lava flowed over its sides, hissing into a boiling moat below. Black onyx lined the entrance leading up to The Fire Gate. Pit Trolls stood guard at the gate and gogs kept watch from the towers. Once inside, serpents lined the streets policing captives to the colosseum.

Leviathan made his approach from the West. The waters around it teamed with all kinds of deadly creatures. Although none compared to the gargantuan size of Leviathan, collectively they could destroy him. A cave ran underneath the island all the way to the colosseum; this was where all bodies emptied of souls were loaded for transport back to the valley, to be strewn across its dry floor. Although heavily guarded, Leviathan had the advantage; his body was so large that once inside the cave, nothing else could fit.

A guard atop the Western wall casually threw small pebbles into the water below. He watched small rings ripple and then fade and then noticed a dark shadow slowly rising from the murky depths. Realizing it was the creature his captain had warned him about, he jostled from his position and sounded the alarm, catching most of the guards in a half-hearted slumber. In the water, hundreds of sea monsters rammed him from the side, biting him with iron teeth, but his body armor was thick, impenetrable. He plowed through them like an ox plowing a clay field after the spring rains.

From the towers, gogs launched two harpoons with curved bronze tips. Long cedar logs hummed through the air, cutting the water with a blunted splash. The hooks glided through the water and attached between the scales on his back. Feeling the tension on the rope, the gogs locked the wheels and fettered a thick twisted rope with a rusty hook to a large troll. The troll's body cringed under the massive weight as he walked down the wall slowly towing leviathan from the deep.

Leviathan spun sharply and dove. He flicked his tail stretching the rope to its max. Small cords popped and unfurled. Leviathan flicked his tail again, pulling the troll from its fortified perch, collapsing the tower and spilling several guards into the sea. He swirled back around and headed for the mouth of the cave.

In the cave, and gaining momentum, his body snaked through the tunnel generating a giant wave. Gogs, standing guard at the end, heard a loud rumble right before a wave tsunamied around the corner. They scrambled from their posts, running up the stairs trying to escape, but the wave, which was accompanied by a stream of flames, overtook them drowning and roasting them all. Leviathan spun around, opened his mouth, and vomited Caboose onto the rocks. He then thundered down the tunnel, quickly disappearing back into the depths of the sea.

A large pile of slime, which resembled the afterbirth of a croaker, lie curled up on the rocks. Unsure what had just happened, Caboose opened his eyes. Everything was blurry. He wiped his eyes. Strings of slimy mucus streamed from his fingers. He shook his hands and then wiped his face again. Still traumatized by the whole event, he stood up. Strewn around the cave where dead grike trolls and gogs—the stench from their roasted flesh was unbearable. Not realizing what had happened he walked up the stairs uncertain of his whereabouts.

Long shafts, burrowed in the rock, branched out in many directions. He noticed a flickering light down one of the shafts and followed. Small torches clawed into a long winding tunnel that splintered into numerous tunnels underneath the throne. The light cast an ominous glow on the dirt floor. His eyes scanned in all directions. He turned left and then right and continued straight.

Back at the stairs, two gogs found the bodies and sounded the alarm. Trolls and gogs filled the tunnels searching for anything out of place. Caboose heard footsteps coming his way. He ran back down the tunnel and squeezed into a crag he had past a few yards back.

"Do you smell that succulent stench?" spit a gog walking toward Caboose.

"Yeah, it smells like, rotten fish," said a troll.

"It smells like rotten fish and grunter," answered the gog.

Their eyes leered down the dimly lit passageway. They searched every hole and overhang. The gog stopped. He held his light up and sniffed and then shined it over the hole hiding Caboose.

"Hey take a look at this," said the troll, just before the light revealed Caboose.

"What is it?"

"Tracks; grunter tracks."

Turning to take a look for himself, he tripped over Caboose's tail. The gog fell on his light breaking it and setting himself on fire. He rolled around on ground trying frantically to put it out. Embarrassed, he jumped to his feet.

"What is it?" shouted the troll.

"Nothing! Nothing!" he shouted, embarrassed over what had happened. He turned around to examine the trip hazard, but in the dark, Caboose's tail looked like a rock.

The troll dropped to the ground, sniffed the tracks and then backtracked. They faded into the darkness. With the coast clear, Caboose peeled out of the hole and started to walk away.

"There he is!" cried a small throne slave with his arms full of bloody garments.

Caboose glared at the poor hopeless creature and then darted down the tunnel searching for a way out. He rounded a corner and noticed a door in the distance. He ran around in a circle and then ran down the tunnel to the left for about twenty-five yards. He then tiptoed backwards to the fork and ran headlong for the door.

Hearing voices back at the fork, he burst through the door, slamming and locking it behind him. With his back against the door and eyes closed, he sighed deeply.

"Boys, dinner is served!"

He opened his eyes and froze—he had run into a room full of gogs playing bones.

Without hesitating and tired of being scared, Caboose flung his tail around and smacked two of them off their stools smashing them against the wall. The other one grabbed his battle-axe and hurled it at him. The axe spun end-over-end sticking in the door inches from his left ear. Caboose's eyes cut left and then focused back on the gog. Both of their eyes then cut right at the sword leaning against the wall at the other end of the table. Caboose bellowed a war cry, lowered his head, and charged horn-long, as the gog dove from his stool reaching for the sword.

Caboose charged across the room smashing everything in his path. He rammed the gog in the stomach with his horn crashing them both through the wall into the next room.

Red blood burst through the hole covering Caboose and the gog who was holding his stomach trying to stop his own blood from spilling out onto the ground.

Caboose panicked.

Lying on the floor, he frantically searched his body. He wiped his hand down his leg thinking he had been injured. He sniffed the mysterious fluid dripping through his fingers and then tasted it—Thunder Juice. He had crashed into a room filled with thousands of casks of Thunder Juice. It was everywhere. Pools of it formed on the floor all around him and it had spilled out into the passageway.

Caboose pushed the barrels off of him. He ran down aisle after aisle of wooden casks stacked from floor to ceiling searching for a way out. Finding a door, and without stopping, he scuttled from room to room looking for an exit or a place to hide.

Many of the rooms under the throne were large storage rooms filled with supplies and various objects used around the colosseum. Behind him he could hear gogs and trolls from the tunnels searching the rooms for him, following the scent of aged Thunder Juice left behind by his tracks.

He ran into a room and squeezed behind a mammoth dark-stained trunk with copper handles: The handles looked like ropes twirled together and were attached to two copper plates on both sides of the doors.

The room was dark and cluttered with crates, ropes, pulleys and various sized wheels. Caboose pulled a pile of crates stacked high into the air in front of the crack hiding him and softened his breath.

He listened.

Footsteps stopped outside. The door opens.

Terror caused his heart to beat wildly.

A gog walked in and searched the room. He jabbed his sword into a crate. He threw another one across the room, smashing it against the wall.

He walked over to the crates beside the trunk. He plunged

his sword into the middle and then wiggled it around trying to get it unstuck.

Caboose drew in his stomach. He looked down at the silver blade slightly slashing back and forth inches in front of it.

He let out a short gasp.

The gog freed his sword and walked around to the front. He grabbed the handles and swung the doors open. A thin gaunt man, with sunken eyes, a long scraggly beard, and extremely long fingernails, jumped out of the trunk yelling, "No! I'm not going back! Please don't take me back!" The gog spun out of the way and smashed his face into a crate. He yelled to the others and then dragged the unconscious man from the room.

He paused at the doorway, looked around the room and then shut the door.

Caboose waited several minutes. He moved the crates out of the way and walked over to the door.

He quietly opened it and looked both ways.

Torches lined the walls leading down the hallway. A slight breeze jostled the flames. Hearing footsteps, he entered a cold, dusty room that smelled rancid of flesh and blood; the putrid odor wrenched his stomach causing him to gag.

Barbed hooks hung hauntingly from ceiling planks above his head. The chains clanged against each other as he walked through.

Blood-stained stones screamed out in agony as he walked across their surface—his skin prickled with the thought of what this room was used for. Terrified and feeling sick, he spotted an old weathered door in the back corner. Carved into its wood was a foreboding figure of a serpent with a stinger-forked tail. Without thinking, he opened it and walked around a stone wall and froze—he had just entered the Lair of the Serpent.

Stacked high, in the center of the room, was a pile of bodies. Hundreds of serpents slithered sinisterly in and around the pile gorging themselves on soulless carcasses. His first impulse was to run, but he didn't move. Besides, he didn't know where he was nor did he know where he was going. He edged against the wall trying to make it around to the next door without being noticed, but there was no escape. The long scaly beasts wound tightly around his feet and body with their sinuous coils. Lifting him from the ground, they took him to two gogs standing guard at the death cells.

The gogs smiled.

The dark and dire cells stretched ominously underneath the colosseum and were filled with hundreds of frightened souls awaiting destruction in the pit. As he passed by, prisoners of fantasy scratched frantically at him with dirty hands. The gog slammed its club against the bars driving them back. He swung the door open and bowled Caboose in.

Caboose rolled across the floor and crashed into the people standing in front. He stood up and looked into each battered face searching for his Papa. Each face stared back unable to hide the horror lying within, their eyes filled with tears and hopelessness. The people looked comatose, like they were in some kind of a trance. All their hopes and dreams lost; drowned in a sea of fantasy and delusion. They were scared, real scared, and so was Caboose. Surely his Papa was not in a place like this he thought.

"Papa! Papa! Are you here, Papa?" he shouted, asking people if they had seen his Papa. He yelled at the top of his lungs, "Chesty Puller, can you hear me?" Papa, are you here, Papa?"

From across the cell a head popped up. "Caboose? It can't be." He stood up, "Caboose is that you?"

"Papa, I'm here." They pushed their way through the crowded

cell to each other. Surprised and disappointed, Caboose stopped. "Mack! What are you doing here?"

"I was just about to ask you the same question." Mack didn't say it, but he was sure glad to see a familiar face.

"I'm looking for my Papa. Have you seen him?"

"No." Mack hesitated. "You haven't seen my Mom, have you?"

"Your mother, she's here too?" responded Caboose taken back.

"I don't know. I haven't seen her since I deposited that stupid coin in the tree."

"Oh yeah…me too," said Caboose rolling his eyes.

"Some mansion, uh?"

"Yeah," replied Caboose.

A gog walked by leashed with two howlers. He slammed his club up against the bars and then spit. One of the howlers stuck its head through the bars and snapped at them.

Caboose and Mack made their way to the back of the cell and took a seat. Many questions ran through both of their minds. Both of them had a parent lost somewhere in the valley and neither of them knew what to do about it.

"They're going to kill us, I know it," said Mack, fidgeting with his hands.

"Don't talk like that. Everything is going to be just fine."

"No. I know it—we're all dead. I can smell it in the air. Death lives in these cells." He looked up at the walls. "Whatever you do, don't read the walls."

Caboose looked up at the wall and then back down again. "Why?"

"Just trust me. Where have you been? Everyone at school thought for sure you were dead."

"I've been lost in the valley for months trying to get here. How long were you in the valley?"

"What valley?" replied Mack, with an offended look on his face. "All I remember is putting a coin in a hole in the middle of a tree. A trap door opened up and I fell down a long tube right into a wagon with several other people in a tunnel. The wagons hauled us to a ferry, which sailed across the sea and then I was brought here. Is that what happened to you?"

"Not exactly," responded Caboose, realizing something was definitely wrong.

"I have something I want to tell you," said Mack hesitantly. "Before I die in this place, I want you to know...that...well—"

"What is it?"

"I'm sorry for being so mean to you. I don't know why I acted like that."

"It's alright, a lot has happened since then."

"No...no it's not alright. I want you to know why I did it...I...I was jealous of you."

Caboose was not expecting to hear that. All kinds of reasons raced through his mind, but not that one.

"Jealous, of me? But why?"

"I was jealous of the life you had. You had the perfect family. You guys always went places together and did things as a family. The way you and your Dad spent time together laughing and playing, it made me mad that I didn't have the same."

'Caboose is a goose and he smells like a moose.
Caboo boo is coo coo.
I'm different. I'll never be like everybody else.
But my leg, it's my short leg.'

Voices, excuses ran through his mind. They had become a crutch, a life-line, a way to cope with life, a way to feel sorry for himself. But it was all built on a lie. It wasn't his leg that was hold-ing him back from life. It was his belief that it was.

Caboose didn't know what to say. He thought it was his leg. All these years, he thought it was his short leg. "I…I don't know what to say. Thank you. Thank you for telling me." He reached out and placed his hand on his shoulder. "Can we be friends and put all this behind us?"

Mack's eyes glittered. A smiled cracked across his face. "You mean you want to be my friend after everything I've done and said about you?"

"Any man that can lay aside his pride and say he's sorry, and look another man in the face when he does it, is a pretty good man to me. That's the kind of friends I like to have."

Mack didn't know how to respond. Something was different about Caboose—something good.

A few cells down a burly-looking man looked over and said, "Hey. You. Don't I know you?"

A face looked up, "I don't think so."

"Yeah, you're an elder at the temple. Puller. You're Chesty Puller. I just heard someone calling your name."

"Are you sure?" Chesty couldn't believe his ears. He shoved his way to the front and yelled, "Caboose! Caboose is that you? Son, I'm here. I'm here!"

Caboose jumped up from his seat and pushed hard to the front. He looked down the corridor and there he was. His dirty wrinkled face looked like an angel glowing with the radiance of the sun. They both just stood there in disbelief. Caboose had done it. He had found his Papa.

"Papa, I found you. I found you. Don't worry. I'm going to get you out of here."

"Are you alright? How did you get here?"

"It's a long story. Papa, I'm so sorry for leaving home. I never meant to bring you here. Please forgive me."

"No. I need *you* to forgive *me*." His eyes held him for a moment.

"Papa, it's because of me you are here."

Mack stood there crying. It was the most beautiful thing he had ever seen or heard.

"No son. I should have told you a long time ago but I didn't." He paused and then said, "I've been here before."

Caboose dropped his head, Seven was right. "But how, why did—"

"Son, we all have skeletons in the closet, things that we're ashamed of, things we wish we could go back and change. I'm sorry you had to find out like this."

"But Papa, you're an elder of the temple. It can't be. It can't be true."

"It's hard for many to accept the truth. Judging eyes gawked at me as I walked the streets of Thunder Juice Town, pointing their fingers, whispering lies. With blinded eyes they failed to see the hand of The Augur that rescued me and molded me into what I am today. Today I stand as a prisoner of hope. Hope that they accept the truth—the truth that I am no different than anyone else. I was rescued and blessed only because I called out His Name."

"But Papa, what about the pit? If we die here our souls—"

"I'm fully aware of the pit. Etched into the walls of this cell is a message. It says, 'I will have mercy on whom I will have mercy, and I will have compassion on whom I will have compassion.' Somehow...I think it was written for me."

Caboose stood there transfixed by his Papa's words. Unable to piece together the puzzle before him, he responded, "Don't worry Papa, I'm going to get us out of here. When Urium gets here, he will rescue us."

* * * * * * *

Brook's mother pushed her way through the crowd and made her to Rinox. She stood and listened to the crowd yelling insults and shaking their fists at him. She pondered everything he said and remembered how her father used to rock her to sleep every night, even when she was older and her feet swept the floor. She could still hear his soothing voice telling the story about when The Augur sent one of his servants to rescue him:

"Cotton Top, (everyone called her Cotton Top because of her white blondy hair) have I ever told you the story about when The Augur rescued me when I was a young man?" he would ask while rocking her to sleep. Although she had heard it several times before, she always responded, 'Tell me again Daddy.'

"One day I was listening to a debate at the University between my professor and Pelusium the High Priest of the temple. They were debating the existence of The Augur and where life came from. I did not believe in The Augur, nor did any of my close friends. Pelusium talked about when the sea swallowed the earth and how a man and his family loaded two of every kind of creature and animal into a big Tree Floater. My professor stood up, a very distinguished man, an expert in his field, and said:

'Pelusium, I know you are a respected man of the community and have done a lot of Great Things for the people of Thunder Juice Town. But, with all due respect, do you really expect me to believe and teach this to my students? Do you know how many different kinds of howlers there are in the world? Probably about 300 to 400. There are little ones and big ones and the ones that live here in town with us. And then there are the fierce deadly ones that prowl in the mountains. Do you really expect me to believe that they all came from two howlers on a Tree Floater?'

As I listened to my professor, I was so proud; he supported my views and reaffirmed my beliefs. But when Pelusium answered him, my whole world came crashing down. He said, 'Sir, would you look at what you're teaching your students now. You're teaching them that *all* howlers came from a rock, and that the rock ultimately came from nothing. It takes more faith to believe that all howlers came from a rock that just popped itself into existence than it does to believe that all howlers came from a male and female howler from the big Tree Floater.'

My professor didn't have any more questions after that. It was then that I began to question the things that I was forced to hear at school and the university. I realized when only one side of a story is taught, that that is not considered an education—it's indoctrination. Indoctrination always has a puppet master at the top with a dark hidden agenda.

My story is not like others from the temple who were rescued from some far and distant land holding on to life by a thread. No, sometimes I think it is worse; he rescued me from myself and the deadly poison of the teaching that I came from nothing. Everyone knows that zero times zero equals zero: Nothing can't birth anything."

Brook's mother, viewing what was taking place and hearing what Rinox said, turned around, and picked up Timmy. "Let's go home, we're not going anywhere."

They walked home through the market and passed 'Snails, Tails and Ale,' a local tavern. A large weathered man walked in the door and sat down at the bar.

"Bottle," he grumbled; his eyes ominously surveyed the room, his lips scowled the air.

At the other end of the bar, Babbler, an old regular nodded his head with a short once-over and suggested, "Looks like you're in a hurry, going somewhere?"

Not dropping his defenses, the man responded, "Out of this god forsaken place. Have you seen the streets? It's like a ghost town around here. I'm not sticking to find out if that eagle is right."

He took a drink, motioned for a bowl of soup and continued.

"I had a run-in years ago with a serpent. He gave me this bad leg. No sir, I'm getting as far away from here as I can."

The bartender walked over and plopped a bowl of soup on the counter in front of him. He grabbed a dirty wooden ladle and took a bite. He sloshed it around in his mouth, and with a sour look on his face, spewed noodles all over the floor. He wiped his mouth and choked, "You call this food. It tastes like three-day old squealer slop."

"Honey, God made those vittles," replied the bartender in a sassy tone.

"But the devil made me, Ha, Ha, Ha!" said the cook, stretching his head through a hole in the wall—he had a fat bottom lip that drooped low in the middle.

Two deformed-looking beasts walked over and leaned against the bar to chime in on the conversation. Over in the corner, lit softly by candlelight, a dwarf with floppy green ears played a faded green accordion made from cattle hide and cherry wood from an almugwood tree. Sitting next to him, shoulder to shoulder, sat another dwarf with a baggy hat and a white frothy mug of thunder juice filled to the brim. They swayed back and forth singing:

"If the ocean was thunder juice,
And I was a duck,
I dive to the bottom,
And drink my way up.

It's sparkling red color,
So wonderfully delight,
Appeases the hunger bugs,
In my belly at night.

Rye whiskey, Rye whiskey,
Rye whiskey, my dear,
Rye whiskey, Rye whiskey,
Rye whiskey, my dear."

"Stranger, I don't know where your travels have taken you, but I've been all over this great big circle myself," said Babbler. "Behind these walls is the safest place I know. I'm not going anywhere."

"Then, to each his own," snarled the stranger raising his bottle slightly in the air. Around the room bottles raised high joining the toast. "Besides everyone's leaving; you don't think everyone could be wrong, do you?"

"No, I don't think everyone's wrong. I know they're wrong," said Babbler, picking at the bar.

The strangers face balled up. He downed the bottle. "Old man, I've lived a long time myself. I've done alright by following the crowd."

"I'm no choir boy," said Babbler. "But I do recall a passage from the ancient scroll that says, 'Don't follow the crowd in doing evil.' I may have lost some battles in life son, but one thing I know and that I know for sure—"

"What's that old man, the taste of Thunder Juice?"

The room erupted with laughter.

"I know a snake when I see one. And that old boy that flew in here the other day with his fancy feathers, slippery tongue, and dazzling charm is a snake if I ever did see one." Babbler leaned over and whispered, "Mark my word boy's, that's Old Slew Foot himself."

"Old man, I don't think you could see your hand in front of your face," japed the stranger slamming his bottle on the bar. He motioned with his hand for another one. The bartender reached down and pulled the cork out of a cherry-brown bottle and handed it to him. He slid the bottle down to Babbler and laid two gold coins on the bar as he limped out.

"Come sun-up, and this town will be nothing but a pile of rubble old man."

* * * * * * *

The colosseum was filled to capacity. Beasts traveled from all over the valley and across the dead sea to witness and participate in the slaughter. Mageddon entered the colosseum to the crowd chanting praise. Lucky followed close behind and took his place by his side. Beasts of the worst kind haggled underneath the arena floor outside the dungeons to see who would fight first in the pit. In the middle of the arena was a large silver plate bearing Mageddon's face—it was the door and entrance to the abyss. Mageddon rose signaling the doom of the vanquished.

Back in the cells, the doors unlocked and opened. Bewildered, everyone filtered out into the corridor. Caboose ran out of his cell, pushed his way through the captives and embraced his Papa.

"Papa, what's going on?" he asked, eased by the touch of his Papa's massive hands.

"I don't know, but whatever it is, it can't be good. Look, I don't know what is about to happen so stay close and do exactly what I say."

Their joyful reunion soon faded as the direness of their situation unfurled. An iron door opened at the end of the corridor. Two gogs leashed with howlers entered and funneled everyone down the hallways. The howlers snapped at the heels of those in the back pushing everyone out of the corridors onto the floor of the colosseum.

Upon entering the colosseum, rocks and debris showered down, striking captives in the head. Euphoric laughter erupted across the crowd as the crowd mocked and taunted them.

The gate shut behind them.

Silence fell across the crowd and the captives.

Around the colosseum, sixteen stone columns rose into the sky. Atop the columns, gogs pounded drums signaling two trolls to open the doors on the other side of the arena. Muscles pulsed down long hairy arms as they gripped the chains tightly in their scarred and mangled hands.

The captives looked around unaware of the horrific doom about to befall them. "Click!" reverberated across the arena as the trolls opened two large wooden doors edged in iron.

A human man and a moogle standing in the middle of the

captives ran for the opening. Deep within the dark and drafty tunnel, a thunderous roar resounded. Out of the shadow, erupted a large two-headed magondrea with eyes circling both heads. The beast reached down, its neck prickled with spikes, and grabbed the moogle in its jaws. It whipped the moogle back and forth and then threw it up into the crowd, which barbarically devoured the moogle piece by piece.

The human skidded to a stop and fell back in the dirt—the second head missing him only by inches. He crawled backwards, spun around on his hands and jumped to his feet. He weaved side to side, trying to run back to the captives gathered at the south end. The magondrea swung its tail knocking him into the captives; his lifeless body opened a gap all the way to the wall.

Panic seized everyone. They ran around the arena pleading for their lives, looking for an escape, while Mageddon's beasts spilled from the entrance, and through subterranean trap doors, killing mercilessly.

Chesty moved Caboose behind him, crouched low, and spread open his arms. A giant three-eyed troll rushed through the captives swinging a huge club with protruding spikes. With murderous intent, it knocked captives out of the middle, up against the wall, and into the crowd.

The troll paused, its eyes locked on Chesty. It raised the club above its head, yelled demonically, and stormed forward.

Chesty didn't budge. He fearlessly stood his ground protecting his beloved son.

He waited for the troll to get within striking distance, and before the beast could strike, he lunged forward, striking the beast's hand, plunging the club into the head of a magondrea fighting beside it.

Several Ragooles swooped down raining fire from the sky lighting up the arena with a liquid inferno-of-death. Chesty and Caboose dove behind the dead magondrea using its body as a shield.

From the other side of the magondrea, a howler charged Caboose head on. Caboose spotted it. He lowered his horn launching the howler up in the air, over Chesty, and into the fire still burning from the ragoole's breath.

Chesty, stunned from what he had just witnessed, looked at Caboose in utter disbelief. Where did you learn that?"

Caboose, proud, but nervous, responded, "I've learned a lot in the last few months."

Caboose felt his side and looked up at Chesty. His eyes widened and his voice jumped. "Papa, I forgot I had these," he said, plunging his hand into his pocket.

"What is it?" asked Chesty, moving to get a better look at the battle unfolding around them.

"Dragon claws," replied Caboose. "Dragon claws to be used for friends. I need water Papa."

"Water, for what?" asked Chesty dodging the club of a grike troll.

"You'll see. I need water Papa. Trust me; I know what I'm doing."

Mack ran around the pit overwhelmed with fear and regret. With the death of his father, and his mother lost, he felt alone. Scared, and without hope, he searched for his mother or Caboose or anyone he thought could help. He maneuvered behind a column to wedge himself between the column and the wall. For a moment, he thought he saw Caboose running across the crowd but then lost sight of him through the chaos unfolding all around. He jumped backwards and kicked his back legs, busting the jaw of a troll. He reached up, blocked a crawler's leg and threw it in the dirt, tumbling both of them across the pit floor and out into the open. The crawler landed upside down. It flipped over, shook the dirt off, and then lunged at Mack. Mack jumped out of the way and ran through the crowd. The crawler spewed webbing from its mouth. The fibrous strands latched onto Mack's back leg tripping him face first back into the dirt. With his face in the dirt, he searched for something to anchor him, only to find loose dirt tightly slipping through his fingers.

The crawler winched him closer while Mack searched for something else to hold on to. He skidded past a dead gog and reached for its sword lying slightly out of reach. He stretched further and further finally taking the sword in hand. He turned to his back to cut himself free, but it was too late. The crawler stood right over him, fangs dripping venom. Mack screamed and thrust the sword in its belly just as the crawler sunk its fangs deep in the top of his head, killing them both instantly.

Chesty scouted the arena. Across the pit floor, he spotted a gog mounted on top of a thunder beast standing guard at the entrance next to the doors. Attached to his saddle horn, was a small brown, weathered water pouch. Chesty glanced back at Caboose and shouted, "Follow me!" He lowered his head and let out a deafening grunt that ricocheted out across the pit and up into the crowd. Chesty breathed in deeply, dropped to all fours, clawed the dirt with his front right leg and charged; Caboose scrambled to tuck in behind and keep up.

Chesty bushwhacked through the battle knocking howlers, magondreas, trolls, crawlers and gogs up in the air with his enormous unicorn horn. Clubs, swords and spears rained down from every side cutting, slashing, and piercing his flesh but Chesty's pace could not be broken—he felt no pain; he had no fear.

He cleared the battle-line and quickened his stride right before the gog noticed his approach. The gog pulled back on the reigns raising the thunder beast into the air right before Chesty's horn pierced its side crushing it against the wall.

Chesty, dazed from the impact, scrambled back to his feet and grabbed the water pouch. He tossed it through the air, over several gogs and howlers swinging to catch it, back to Caboose.

Disoriented from the collision, the gog staggered out from under the mangled carcass with a silver blade gripped in his hand. He jumped on Chesty's back and stabbed him several times before Chesty could shake him loose and trample him underneath.

Caboose threw the dragon claws in the dirt and opened the pouch. He poured the water on the claws and blew on them with all his might. He glanced toward the sky and then back at his Papa and bellowed, "Fire! I need fire!"

"What are you doing?" cringed Chesty, bleeding badly from his side and back.

Caboose picked up a spear from the dirt and studied the sky?

"I need one of them to come this way."

"Are you crazy?"

"I need fire, Papa."

Without hesitation Chesty took the spear from his son, pushed him behind the dead thunder beast and threw it into the air. He jumped up on the thunder beast, waved his arms and shouted, "Over here you ugly bush squealer!"

Caboose marveled at his Papa's bravery—he had heard that somewhere before.

The spear joggled back and forth. It grazed a ragoole's wing causing it to spin around midair and focus on Chesty. It dropped low over the top of the colosseum and opened its mouth streaming a line of fire all the way across the pit floor, burning the dragon claws, and scorching the top of the thunder beast which sheltered Caboose—Chesty waited until the last second and jumped out of the way.

The ground around the claws boiled causing the claws to split open, spilling silver all over the ground. The silver formed and grew revealing seven armor-scaled dragons. They joined the battle, killing numerous beasts and creatures, while protecting anyone that called out The Augur's Name.

Mageddon, seeing the commotion happening at the entrance, jumped from his seat and scanned the captives. His beastly eyes stopped and focused on Caboose. Chesty and Caboose slammed a howler, sandwiching it between them. Mageddon pointed at Caboose and yelled, "That one! Kill him now!"

Chesty heard Mageddon's mystical voice shout out from his seat. Mageddon's servants spun around and locked in on Chesty and Caboose. Chesty's eyes followed an invisible line which started at Mageddon's jagged finger and ended at Caboose. Confused and in shock, he spun around to step in front of Caboose, and was stuck in the belly by a grike troll holding a short stubby blood-drenched sword.

Chesty stared straight at his son and uttered, "Caboose."

"No!" cried Caboose, as he watched his father fall to the ground in a plume of dust.

A silver dragon grabbed the troll, bit it in two, and moved over Caboose to protect him. Caboose fell to his knees and lifted Chesty's head off the ground. "Papa! Papa! You can't die in this place. You can't die here. Your soul! Your soul!"

The dragons circled Caboose protecting him and the other captives taking refuge by him.

Mageddon shouted again, "Not that one, that one!" pointing again at Caboose.

"Papa, stay with me. The Augur will come. He will rescue us."

Chesty, with his life-blood spilling out onto the pit floor and shivering in pain, smiled and grunted, "You believe in him; you believe in him now."

"Yes Papa. I believe in him. I believe in The Augur."

With his last breath and struggling to breathe, Chesty turned his head toward the heavens and shouted, "Augur!"

Lucky, hearing 'The Name' jumped from his seat and transformed into Slithler the great serpent. He slid over the wall onto the floor and headed for the silver dragons. He knocked them out of the way and lunged at Caboose.

Caboose rolled underneath a fallen column. Slithler struck at him but Caboose kept rolling from one side of the column to the other. Slithler coiled around and as he did he heard the ruffle of wings. His head cowered right before The Augur grabbed him by the head launching him out of the colosseum into the middle of the sea. One by one, almighty eagles soared in and snatched, from the jaws of death, captives whom had called out his Name. The Augur clutched Caboose in his talons and whisked him to safety over the colosseum walls high into the sky.

"My Papa; we can't leave without my Papa," shouted Caboose, fighting to return to the battle.

CHAPTER 12

THE AUGUR RETURNS

Behold, the precious Lamb of God.

I will also take of the highest branch of the high cedar, and will set it; I will crop off from the top of his young twigs a tender one, and will plant it upon a high mountain and eminent: In the mountain of the height of Israel will I plant it: and it shall bring forth boughs, and bear fruit, and be a goodly cedar: and under it will dwell all fowl of every wing; in the shadow of the branches thereof shall they dwell. And all the trees of the field shall know that I the LORD have brought down the high tree, have exalted the low tree, have dried up the green tree, and have made the dry tree to flourish: I the LORD have spoken and have done it.

(EZEKIEL 17:22-24, KJV)

The galaxy was quiet…too quiet. Giant dusty cocoons, illuminated by coppery leg-like filaments, hovered solemnly in rotary constellations. Massive disks with aqua snowball eyes and ruddy outer rims rotated in the center of millions of white dwarf stars. Sparsely populated and floating abroad in the quietness of deep space, billows of cold gas, topped with broad coalsack necks, towered from interstellar dormitories. Cylindrical shafts of ultra violet bolts jetted from wombs deep within the storehouse of lightning while nurseries of light, incubating in enormous spiral arms, revolved cumbersomely within a huge spherical halo.

Atrokus flew through the outer regions of the Omega galaxy on his way to the Holy Mount. He pulled back on the reigns causing two beastly creatures harnessed at the front of his chariot to spin around and skid to a stop.

He paused.

A Lunar eclipse cast a dark shadow over him, and for a moment, he felt the presence of something, something unnatural…unwelcome…demonic.

A golden elliptical bulge pulsed before his eyes. He unsheathed his sword and waited.

Small particles of luminous dust tranquilly streamed by; the mottled specks of light caught in his hair softly highlighting the contour of his head.

His eyes scanned the area.

The two beastly creatures stomped their feet and slowly backed up snorting firebrands from their nostrils.

Grum, a spy from the Sea Throne, hid in a crater of a dwarf star. He had followed Atrokus for weeks taking note of his route trying to discover the plans of the Southern army.

Atrokus grasped the reigns tight and tilted his head.

He re-sheathed his sword and continued.

He flew over the Holy Mount and landed at the bottom of the beautifully-adorned Steps of Grace. The fiery stones glowed red from the cool breeze of his chariot brushing across their smoldering surface. He wrapped the reigns around a hook on the side of the chariot and dismounted. Two guards ran over and escorted his beastly team off the mount and down a stone road to the stables.

Atrokus walked up the steps and across the veranda to two large emerald doors. The doors opened at his approach ushering him down the wide Corridor of Hope. A faint echo from his footsteps carried down the hallway softly announcing his presence. He wound his way through the Great Hall of Columns, each engraved with the promises of His Majesty and told the story of an eternal son begotten.

He stopped at the King's Fountain to drink of its life-giving waters. The fountain at its base was made from purified gold, as pure as crystal from Sudaveen. Deep sky-blue water rose up a middle column of faces, faces of every beast and creature His Majesty had made. Mounted on top was an eagle with wings spread high and talons raised. Clenched in his talons was a scroll, which no man, celestial being, or beast could open. The water mushroomed over the top splashing back into the pool below.

Leaving the fountain, he approached a Black-Star sapphire door. He opened it and walked into *The White Stone Library*.

The library was gigantic. Breathtaking!

A large semi-circular atrium filled with diamond-cut statues welcomed him. Long crystal rods of different lengths and diameter spiraled from the ceiling above. Different shades of color trickled down the rods from top to bottom lighting the statues in a spectacular array of sparkles. Ten gold plates, engraved with

His Majesty's commands, hung on the walls; five on the left and five on the right.

Thick white marble archways, garland with elaborate designs, mirrored down a central aisle with vaulted tubular ceilings. Quietly nestled behind each arch were dimly-lit rooms filled with tables. Floating above each table where red and white globes burning bright, all fueled by star dust. The globes hovered over angels writing quietly.

At the end of the central aisle, encompassing several square miles was The Grand Hall. It took the eye several minutes just to sweep the vastness of its grandeur and beauty. Thousands of statues and ancient relics stood stationary across its breadth. Floors of trestle archways climbed high around its perimeter. Starry Hosts displayed stunning mosaics along cathedral ceilings, and triangular crystal panes lit by starlight-beamed, bright crimson rays from a dome towering hundreds of stories above.

Centrically aligned on each floor were rows upon rows of dark-cherry solid-oak bookcases. They extended down long narrow corridors that seemed to have no end. Bright Blue beams ran along grooves under each shelf, locking red books of different sizes in place. The books were shut with white stone clasps along their seams and were neatly stacked from floor to ceiling in evenly-sized rectangular compartments. Embossed on the front of each book was a white Titan with branches splayed.

In the middle of the hall, centered under the dome, was a smooth white stone chiseled from a large block of Coral Red Marble; the stone rested in a hand still connected to the base—it was the focal point of the library. The floor around the base was dressed in black with white crawler veins. Sixteen Seraphim's stood guard around the stone. Each Seraph had six wings and was holding swords of fire. Etched into each blade was the inscription "Holy, Holy, Holy." The blades crossed creating a fiery barrier.

The library was filled with activity. Gupa Firewalkers, small creatures with long lime-green wings, black-striped bodies, highly intelligent, and extremely diligent, fluttered up and down the aisles with a book nobly held out in front.

Against the northern wall, stood a massive dark-stained mahogany desk carved in the shape of a crescent moon. Engraved into its panels were twelve gold crowns evenly spaced across its front. Sitting on thrones behind each crown were twelve elders with velvet red cloaks draped over their heads and long, gentle folds streaming down to their feet.

The firewalkers waited patiently in line next to a long hollow tube protruding from the floor underneath a pergola. Every few seconds, a blast of air rushed up the tube, rocketing a light brown container to the top. A firewalker grabbed the container, pulled out a scroll, and then according to the number on the scroll, flew in front of an elder and waited.

When ready, the elder looked down and nodded.

The firewalker flew forward and laid down the scroll. The elder took the scroll, broke the seal and opened it. After vigilant examination, he reached up and touched buttons on a screen floating in front of him. A few seconds later, a small red crystal rose from the top of the desk. The elder resealed the scroll and handed it back to the firewalker along with the crystal.

The firewalker promptly attached the scroll to a latch on its back. Taking hold of the crystal, it proceeded down the corridors searching for the corresponding book. Once found, it inserted the crystal into a hole beneath the book turning the blue beam, red. It then took the book and the scroll to an angel waiting in one of the many rooms down the central aisle.

The angel turned the stone clasp on the seam of the book and opened it. He broke the seal on the scroll and copied the information into the book. Once finished, the angel rolled the scroll back up and inserted it into the globe—the scroll fed into the globe and disintegrated inside. The firewalker then returned the book to its shelf, returned the crystal to a chute in front of the desk, and got back in line by the pergola.

Atrokus walked down the central aisle and ascended a staircase on the West side of the floor. He walked down the hallway past a fountain of four stone horses facing each other. The horses stood on their two hind legs with their front hooves clawing the air. Lava jetted from their mouths and boiled in the fountain below. He climbed another set of stairs several more levels and then circled back down a skywalk that led to a private chamber.

Inside the chamber, a gold table with dragon feet legs stood prominently at the end of a bookcase. Miaphas, with a scroll lying out across the table, and fully expecting Atrokus, in a calm soothing welcome stood up and embraced him.

"Good to see you Atrokus. How are things on earth?"

"I'm not sure. Strange things are happening."

He walked over by three lancet arched windows and looked out over the courtyard below. "They're a lot of new fortifications since the last time I've been here," he said. "Why all the new battlements?"

Miaphas sat back down and finished his last few lines. "Preliminary precautions, that's all."

Miaphas twisted his chair and leaned back. "I received Seven's report several days ago. How's our young grunter doing?"

"Great. The Augur has him and is on his way to Thunder Juice Town. Everything is going as planned."

He walked over and sat down. He folded his fingers together, bounced his leg and looked around the room. "Slithler did just what His Majesty said he would do. The Augur's plans are forthcoming."

He reached back and pulled out a small blade with a beautifully carved black dragon-claw handle. He leaned forward with his elbows on his knees and sharpened one and a half inch long, ash gray, fingernails.

"Where do you need me now?"

"I was just making the last updates. Galamus should be here any moment. When he arrives, I need you to accompany him to Caelum. The final plans are there."

"You know, there is an eerie silence hovering in space. Flying here, it felt different."

Miaphas tilted his head. "What do you mean?"

"I don't know. It was just different. Like something or someone was stalking me."

Galamus walked in a few moments later carrying a small golden triangular object in his hand. He walked across the room and handed it to Miaphas.

"Here it is. What do you want me to do with it?"

Miaphas took the plumb line and held it up. "Do you see this? His Majesty is going to bring disaster on Thunder Juice Town and the ears of everyone who hears of it will tingle. He will stretch this plumb line out from wall to wall, gate to gate. He will forsake the remnant of his inheritance and hand them over to the serpent. They will be looted and plundered because of the evil they have done. But after The Augur's plans are complete, His Majesty will lay a stone in Thunder Juice Town, a tested stone, a precious cornerstone for a sure foundation. All who trusts in it will never be disappointed. He will make justice the measuring line and righteousness the plumb line; hail will sweep away the serpents lies and water will overtake his hiding place. His covenant with death will be disannulled and his agreement with the pit will not stand."

Atrokus, attentively studying Miaphas' face, looked at Galamus with curiosity and asked, "What's going on? What is The Augur going to do on earth?"

"We don't know. But, whatever it is, it's big, nothing like we've seen before. Get ready to leave at once, we must not delay our arrival at Caelum," said Galamus. "When we get there, Zoma will know more."

Galamus turned back toward Miaphas and in a low tone exclaimed, "The war is coming."

* * * * * * *

The Augur flew through the mountain pass and gently landed by The Redmadafa. He placed Caboose at the trunk of the Titan—it was the biggest tree on the circle. Its age was from times past and nothing on the circle compared with its splendor. Its roots ran under Thunder Juice Town sustaining life for all its residents. Its branches were like strong beams of iron bracing the sky from falling. Their leafy boughs spread over the river and meadow providing a lush green canopy that sheltered all who took refuge underneath.

Standing before Caboose was a mighty warrior. An eagle… and not just any eagle, he was the most magnificent creature in all the universe. His wings from tip-to-tip were over 100 feet long. Dark, seamed feathers and a full plumage of varied colors adorned his back and chest. Thick sharp talons dug into the ground. And two golden eyes, crowned with milky white feathers, looked over a long-curled acorn colored beak.

Caboose felt safe and secure just being in his presence. Somehow, he knew everything was going to be all right. As Caboose stared at the eagle, something magnificent happened. Although he saw a powerful almighty warrior eagle, his eyes saw, within the eagle, another form.

Caboose rubbed his eyes and thought for sure they were playing tricks on him. But they weren't. He looked at the eagle and saw seven golden lights and a man standing in the midst of them. The man was dressed in a robe dipped in blood and a golden belt brandished his chest. His head and hair were white like snow, as white as a glacier, and his eyes…his eyes were flaming, like fire, and his feet where fine brass and burned like molten lava in the depths of a magma chamber.

Caboose stumbled backwards against the Titan at the sight of him. He was confused. I must have hit my head hard in the garden, he thought, or…oh no, I must be dreaming. Yes. I must have fallen asleep in the death cells.

"Koby, I heard the prayers of those who love you," spoke the voice from within.

Prayers? Love me? He thought to himself. Why would anyone pray for me? Papa…!

"My Papa loved me and you left him in the pit to die," responded Caboose, with anger in his voice wondering how he knew his real name.

"That is a lie," said the voice, loudly.

Caboose took two steps back. He was puzzled at his voice. It sounded like rushing water from a roaring river. His face glowed like the sun in the brilliance of midday. In his right hand he held seven stars and written on him was a name that only he knew.

The man walked toward Caboose.

As he did, the ground beneath his feet came to life. Grass and flowers sprouted and bloomed. Trees grew to full height around him and draped with fruits, berries, and nuts.

"Koby, be free!"

Caboose fell back on the ground as if he were dead. He stood up and looked around like he didn't know where he was. Something was different, but he didn't know what.

He looked at himself.

He looked at the man.

It was at that moment, that his mind was opened to the truth. In complete awe, Caboose gasp, "You're him! You're him!"

"I am…Justice, but most people around here call me 'The Augur.'"

"You came for me, but why? And why didn't you save my Papa? The scroll says you save all who call out your name. Why didn't you save my Papa? He called out your name. He called out your name."

In a gentle loving tone, The Augur replied, "You're Papa called out my name…for you."

Caboose froze.

A blank gaze bore deep in his eyes.

His face dropped.

"I didn't call out your name. I didn't call out your name."

Caboose looked up.

"Then why? Why did you save me?"

"Love covers over a multitude of sins. You will see your Papa again. Do you trust me?" asked The Augur.

Trust you, thought Caboose. The last time I trusted someone I ended up in a valley of bones and death. Confused, yet calm,

Caboose replied, "Yes, I mean *Yes Sir*. I know I will see him again at the resurrection."

"I am the resurrection. No one comes to His Majesty except by me. You now know the truth and that truth will set you and others free. In a few days things will happen that you will not understand. I need you to trust in me with all your heart. Then and only then will your path be made straight. Do you believe this?"

"Yes sir."

Urium flew through the mountain pass and landed beside Caboose, who was wondering where he had been. He walked over and stood before The Augur.

"Urium guard him when the walls come down. Wait for my signal before you sound the attack."

Urium knelt before him. "Yes, your Majesty. I will await your command."

The Augur opened his wings and with one beat he was gone.

The sun softly dwindled behind the mountains. Silver virga wisps streamed quietly from the clouds. The leaves of the Titan rustled gently in the wind. A facade of burgundy dappled with apricot tenderly rippled down The Redmadafa. Grass, flowers, bushes, and trees continued to carpet the meadow from The Augur's presence. Cattle and wild animals grazing in the meadow jumped energetically with joy; their hooves tickled by the new sprouts jostling underneath. Guards posted around the wall motioned to their friends to see the miracle transposing before them. Guards looked out widows and scaled the stairs while large crowds exited the gates to witness the life germinating across the land.

Travelers along the road stopped. They twisted around, marveled by their new surroundings.

Caboose watched The Augur fly away. His encounter had just changed everything. He had a new purpose, a renewed vision of life and purpose on the circle. His mind was opened to the truth—a truth that transcends understanding; a truth that, though one may walk through the valley of the shadow of death, they need not fear the evil that stalks them.

He gathered his thoughts before speaking.

"Where have you been?" asked Caboose. "A monster swallowed me whole and took me to the bottom of the sea..."

He paused.

"You! You pushed me!"

"I fought gogs and trolls. Serpents attacked me. All kinds of beasts tried to kill me in the arena," he said, throwing his hands up in the air.

He walked over and stood face-to-face with Urium.

"I watched my Papa die in my arms. I thought you were always there. You said you were always there...'Beside me, over me, leading me.' Just when I needed you most, you were gone."

"I couldn't break through the Southern Celestial Forces. There were too many of them. And besides, the Sea Throne is absolutely off limits to us. It is forbidden to intervene. Remember when I said death has a rightful claim on all who enter the valley?"

Caboose listened but didn't respond.

Urium continued. "Well, The Augur is the only one, and I mean the "Only" one, that rescues from the colosseum."

"Urium, my Papa's dead. He died in the colosseum. I saw it with my own eyes. Now his soul will be trapped forever in the pit and the river of fire. Why didn't The Augur save him?"

Urium stood speechless. He carefully searched his thoughts.

"Did he call out his name?"

"Yes, but when The Augur came, he took me instead."

"Did The Augur say why he did this?"

"Yes. Well, he said my Papa called out his name…for me. He also said I would see my Papa again. That's it."

"All I know is there are some strange things going on, things even I don't understand. I know The Augur has something really big planned. We need to wait patiently for him."

Urium placed his hand on Caboose's shoulder.

"Now, why don't you go home and see your mother and sister."

"Home," said Caboose. He looked around. "I'm home? I'm home!"

* * * * * * *

They flew nonstop to the Quazy galaxy. Entering the Caelum Constellation, Galamus and Atrokus arrived at the headquarters of the Western front, which resided inside a billowing tower of gas and dust cloud called the Eagle Nebula. Inside the Nebula, lightning bolt stairs sparked outward and spiraled into a tower camouflaged by a Quasar.

At the top, hallways were packed with thousands of Celestial Guards from all across the solar system. Voices resonated loudly down the stairs making it difficult to hear anything with all the anxious commotion. Angles and delegates scrambled from one room to the other zipping across the hall like prairie grazers crossing a crocodile-infested river.

Atrokus and Galamus reached the top and rounded the corner. They squeezed past a group of delegates debating over what looked like some sort of a map. Atrokus gave a quick once-over and was struck in the left shoulder by someone passing by.

"I'm sorry," he responded, embarrassed by the careless glance.

A medium-sized creature wearing a hooded gray cloak made from leafhopper silk, lowered dark-green bloodshot eyes toward him.

Without looking back, it twisted its chin to its shoulder and nodded.

Atrokus stopped.

He looked back but the creature disappeared in the crowd.

That's strange he thought, sensing the same presence he felt back at the Omega Galaxy.

"Why are so many guards here?" he asked.

"My premonitions must have been right. We only gather like this when war is inevitable," said Galamus, with butterflies mounting in his stomach.

"War. It's been a long time coming."

"Yes…Yes it has," replied Galamus.

They turned another corner and approached the war chamber. They entered and quietly watched from a distance. Galamus observed the crowd gathered around Zoma, which was filled with numerous earth delegations he hadn't seen in years: Rock, tree, water, sky, plant, insect, bird, animal, fish, and beast delegates surrounded Zoma, voicing their concerns.

Zoma stood off to the side talking. He was used to war. Being that he was earth's delegate, he had seen war ravish his planet for centuries. His mind was sharp and his experience highly acclaimed.

A loud, gargled voice spoke from the crowd commanding an abrupt silence in the room.

"Zoma, what about the seas? Shall I maintain their boundaries, the boundaries in which The Augur said '*To this line you may come but no further?*' Or, can I birth upon him, the fury of the storm, breaking forth the womb from which it is chained…

he won't be expecting that," said Hydromus, his tall massive body waving around like a crystal sea even as he stood still.

"No," said Ironwood speaking out, his body full of knobs, twists, and limbs, all giving strength and support to his branches and tender sprig shoots. "Let me march against him. I can ambush him at the mouth of the mountains. I'll have his slimy slithering tongue licking dirt before he knows what hit him. Once we have that winking snake caught in a pickle, Nitrocon can set us ablaze. We will gladly sacrifice ourselves to destroy that traitor."

Nitro's eyes burned in agreement. He shook his head and fired, "Let's do it. Let's do it right now."

"Please, everyone listen," said Zoma reestablishing order. "I know you want your vengeance, especially after what he did to us. The Augur and The Augur alone will execute his punishment."

Galamus and Atrokus slipped through the crowd.

Zoma spotted them and waved them over.

"I trust your journey went well. I was starting to think that you had been diverted. I've received several reports of spies lurking in the outer realm and beyond. Do you have it?"

Galamus pulled out the plumb line and handed it to him. He took it in his hands and signaled for the doors to be closed. He rose off the ground several feet and dropped the plumb; it uncoiled rapidly from a tangled ball in the middle of his hand and then snapped tight causing the plumb to swing back and forth. All eyes focused on the shiny golden sparkle dangling before them and then looked up at Zoma.

"This is the judgment of Thunder Juice Town. The Augur has spoken and it cannot be undone. Every stone will lay in haste. Every tower will bow. Wait for his signal and stand your ground. Protect the remnant!"

He grasped the plumb in his hands and twisted the top, middle, and lower section. The plumb "Clicked" and opened. He reached inside and pulled out a small cream parchment. He looked at the delegates, unrolled the small parchment and read:

"Death to life,
Life from death.
When you see white,
His head, *we shall smite!*"

* * * * * *

The wind from his wings swept across town spinning windmills and weathervanes out of control. Rooftops shook as he soared by bl.owing wooden shingles and straw into the street. Over the university and mill, down the square to the temple, he landed in the outer courtyard. Mushrooms drummed and grasses strummed franticly. The garden bowed in his presence—The Augur had returned.

He knelt down and drank from the cool life-giving waters of The Redmadafa. The water foamed around his beak and then down again. He majestically walked through the garden and up the stairs on his approach to the temple; the doors opened standing at attention, tall and straight for his entrance. He walked down the silent deserted aisles—the ceilings and windows reported what had happened and the blasphemy that took place on the holy altar. He ascended the steps of the altar and turned around. Standing at the entrance, Onuka stood gazing upon his splendor. Onuka ran down the aisle and fell prostrate before him.

"Majesty, your Majesty, you've heard our cries and returned.

I've failed you. I too, was deceived by his beauty. I let him walk right in here..."

"Onuka," interrupted The Augur, "I let him walk in here. But, what he does not realize is that he is walking right into my trap."

Onuka stood up speechless. He was unaware of The Augur's plans and would have never dreamed that it was The Augur who let him walk in and desecrate the temple.

"Your Majesty, the people and even most of the elders, they're gone. They followed him and his cunning tongue."

"Zeal without knowledge is not good, and he that is hasty with his feet will miss the way. My people are destroyed for lack of knowledge. They honored me with their lips only. They removed their hearts from me long ago, Onuka."

"But I don't understand; how could the elders so quickly turn from your teachings of truth to follow hollow deceptive lies?"

"The foolishness of man ruins his life, nonetheless his heart storms against me. A few will return. When they do, they will need you Onuka."

"I fear I can no longer help them, Your Majesty. My heart burns with anger at the mention of their names."

"Wisdom gives a man patience; it is to his credit to forgive a transgression," said The Augur. "Onuka, when the time is right, I need you to stand by them once again."

"I will need your strength, Your Majesty. I will need... your strength."

"And you shall have it."

"What about him? Will he be allowed to get away with this?"

"A false witness will be punished, and he who speaks lies will not escape. Onuka, Chesty's son is back. I want you to visit him. Keep him by your side."

The Augur walked down the aisle and stood over the threshold. He bowed his head and looked through the crystal floor at the cleft in the rock. "Do you see this rock Onuka from which The Redmadafa's headwaters flow? In a few days it will run dry. Not one stone will be standing in the proud walls of this temple. My judgment is at hand."

"Your Majesty," Onuka exclaimed in disbelief. "But how… how will we survive? The trees, plants, the people, what will we do?"

"Do you see the stones of the walls and temple? They will climb down from their lofty towers and kiss the earth once more?"

Onuka didn't say anything he just stood there looking at The Augur in disbelief. The Augur walked down the steps and stood in front of the cleft rock which hovered over him anointing him with glory from on high. A third time The Augur called out to Onuka. "Onuka, do you see these stones, stones which I have made deaf lest they turn to dust and fly away trying to escape my judgment. I am about to wash away the filth of the people; I will cleanse Thunder Juice by a spirit of judgment and a spirit of fire. Then these waters will flow once more and whoever drinks will never thirst again. The water I give will become alive inside of them, a well, springing up to everlasting life."

* * * * * * *

Legion flew over the Sea Throne and through the Fire Gate. He quietly soared through the streets filled with contention and pride and past the colosseum, taking note of the skullduggery happening below. He landed outside the lower chambers of the Sea Throne and proceeded through the bulky dark-tarnished wooden door with large iron handles. Inside, small creatures scurried to get out of his way, as he hurried through the dimly lit hallways. He rounded the corner and quickly closed the gap between him and a four-headed beast with four eyes and four horns on each head standing guard at the throne room door.

The first head was a beautiful woman with crystal-clear eyes, long, wavy locks of green hair and a black tongue. The second head was a man with coal-black hair that brushed his shoulders and curled at the ends. He had black eyes, a large chin, and his ear lobes pointed at the end and covered with diamonds. The third head looked like tree knobs covered with long stripes of rolled sea grass twisted round—its eyes teetered crossways down its face. The last face was the face of death. Skeletal bones outlined a ghostly figure with deep hollow eyes glowing of fire. The beast stood from its slumber as Legion approached, each head greeting him spitefully.

"What come thou Leeeegion?" asked the man in a smug voice.

"Nothing of your concern, Enchanter," answered Legion. "Out of my way," he said, trying to step past the beast.

"Way?" replied the face of death moving to block his way. "We stand not in thy way, Legion."

"To disturb him with the faults of fools would not be wise great Legion," said the woman, as she conceitedly moved her face directly in front of his, trying to persuade him to disclose the purpose of his consult. Her silky-smooth hand adorned with rubies reached up to touch his face. "We stand not in thy way Legion. We are merely graced by thy presence."

Legion grabbed her hand and abruptly threw it back. He slowly lowered his hand and gripped his sword slightly exposing it from its scabbard. "Your pithy charms do not beguile me, nor do they hide the stench from your pestilent tongue which reeks of envy."

Unscathed by his insult, "Envy?" laughed the ghastly face of knobs with a vague smile. "We but pay homage to he who should be," implying that Legion should overthrow Mageddon.

Legion unsheathed his sword in a whirlwind of fury, grabbed the knobby face and pressed the blade firmly against its neck. "What did you use to be?"

Looted eyes looked down for several seconds before looking up. "I was a rich and powerful man with a family and a wife," it replied, glaring feebly into Legion's eyes.

Legion looked long and hard back into its eyes and taunted, "You were an adulterer and a drunkard who gave everything you had for the lie. Treachery you are and treachery will never leave your side," spit Legion, lips almost touching one another."

He released his grip and returned his sword. "Stand in my way again and I'll cut your eyes out and feed them to the ravens.

The beast lowered all four heads in reverence.

Inside the throne room, dark spirits circled. Serpents slithered around the base of the throne and ravens perched on ledges high behind Mageddon.

Legion bowed low upon entering. He drew close to Mageddon's ivory seat sitting high on a pedestal of black marble.

"Where have you been?" asked Mageddon, attended by four beautiful women on each side—two of them transformed into red snakes with a black streak running over their heads and down their backs. They slithered down the steps and around his feet.

"Master, Grum, your spy on the western front, reports that a large army is assembling for war. He believes The Augur is returning to Thunder Juice Town and plans to attack the Scorpion Pass Gate."

A raven transformed into a dark spirit and twirled around Legion before flying out the window.

Furious that this information was just now being disclosed, Mageddon slapped a golden goblet of wine away from his face and yelled, "Must I do everything myself? He assembles his forces right under our nose and I am the last to hear about it! Well, if it's war he wants then war he shall have. Summon Slither and amass my forces. He will not have the chance to attack the gate. I will attack Thunder Juice first and burn it to the ground."

Mageddon met privately in his chamber with Slithler. He placed a crown on his head and gave him charge of all his forces.

"Go now and lay siege to Thunder Juice and all that remain. Break down the walls and destroy the temple. It is time for the Great Serpent to be revealed. Awaken the secret weapon, but keep him concealed until I arrive."

High above the throne room in a long slender turret, a troll sounded the Dragon's Horn. Thousands of servants assembled at the armory. Gathering their weapons, Legion loaded them onto transports and left for the valley.

Lucky stood on the banks watching as the transports crept from the fog arriving below the fall. The transports, long, curved timbers sealed with pitch and adorned with the face of a dragon as its figurehead, mysteriously ascended up the fall. At the top, they maneuvered up stream, unleashing their beastly cargo to the sounds of screams and cackles at the Titan. Blood-thirsty beasts from the Sea Throne united with those of the garden and valley. They made their way through the garden to the Scorpion Pass Gate. Lucky climbed down the gate and mounted the stone scorpion standing guard outside the gate, instantly bringing it to life. He motioned to the mass and proclaimed, "Long ago we lost our place of authority. His Majesty turned on us and cast us to this wretched place. He now plots to come and take the small amount of authority we have left. The Southern army has gathered at the Western front and is on its way to destroy us, and everything we have worked so hard to build:

Trick us once,
Shame on us;
Trick us twice,
And roll the dice."

The army shouted. They beat their chests and shields at the sound of his cunning tongue igniting their wicked murderous hearts.

"The field is ripe," he continued. "We will march to Thunder Juice and trample the harvest. This is the hour that I will kill The Augur. When we reach the wall, we will tear it down and slaughter all who remain. Burn every house and rip the temple down stone-by-stone. After that, we will march on the Holy Mount and destroy His Majesty and take back the fiery stones!"

* * * * * * *

Under the cover of darkness they set out. Large Thunder Beasts pulled battering rams and siege ramps. Trolls carried weapons of mass destruction across their shoulders. They twisted through the mountains thirsty for blood. Up ahead they saw the lights of the temple piercing through the darkness searching for them, but The Shadow of Death covered them, concealing their approach.

The town was quiet. The moon, in full face, looked down on Babbler leaving the tavern headed for home. Shutters closed as dinner tables filled and chimney's smoked with smells of vegetable soups, homemade breads and apple pies. An old surly man with a black hat, a long white beard and a walking stick, walked down the street and stood in the middle of the square. He puckered his lips and whistled a jolly tune, signaling his troops from afar. A soft hum filled the air as lighting bugs swarmed from trees and bushes just outside of town. They flew over the walls and assumed their post in street lamps all across town. A croaker jumped from the banks of The Redmadafa and pushed a wooded plank down into a hole—all the fountains around town and in the temple courtyards stopped flowing.

Brook, lying in bed, sang a song about how The Augur saved her from certain death by his mighty talons. Caboose sat in his room under candle light, reading an ancient scroll. Rooter stood in the bathroom brushing his teeth preparing for bed. He pulled out a bottle of blossom berry gargle and swished it around. His cheeks rolled from side-to-side before he spit it out and wiped his mouth. Silence fell in the bathroom for several minutes. From their beds, Rammer and his brother heard a song—it was a song they had heard many times from their father:

"Stranded…
Stranded on the bathroom hole,
What do you do when you're stranded?
And you can't find a roll.

You can prove you're a man,
If you wipe it with your hand,
Stranded."

Rammer sat quietly in his bed shaking his head at the ridiculous ode. The bathroom door squeaked opened. Rooter walked down the hallway and rounded the corner. He picked up a toy off the floor and placed it in a crate next to the wall. He then walked over and tucked Rammer and Jambles in bed and kissed them goodnight. He had many questions since coming to faith, but he was really starting to come around. He met with Adromus for study during the week and had started going to the temple on Sun Day.

"What is this I see in-between your toes?" he said to Jambles, Rammer's little brother, who didn't say anything, innocently batting his eyes at his Daddy.

Rooter reached between his toes and pulled out a ball of fuzz. "Are you boys going to bed without taking a bath again?"

"Dad," said Rammer, looking over from his bed in the corner. "We took a bath two days ago."

"Two days ago, no wonder it smells funny in here!"

"I don't smell anything," said Jambles, twirling a small stuffed white bear in his hands carved from almugwood.

"Of course you don't, they've probably already crawled up your nose and plugged it up."

"They, who's they?"

"Who's they? They…are the Belly Button Monsters."

"What," said Rammer, knowing his Dad was making it up? "You just made that up."

"You mean you boys have never heard the ghostly ghouly story of the Belly Button Monsters. Gather around boys, but let's be quiet, so they don't hear us."

Rammer jumped out of bed and sat at his father's feet. Rooter held Jambles in his arms and looked around to make sure they didn't see him and then whispered:

<u>The Belly Button Monsters</u>

The Belly Button Monsters,
Are fuzzy wuzzy beasts.
Assembling their forces,
In a lint ball, they keep.

Sounding the alarm,
They drill deep and wide;
Until they break through,
Exposing your insides.

Through your intestines,
They sluggishly creep;
Parading to your heart
For a delicious feast.

So, next time you see,
The fuzzy wuzzy beasts;
Collecting between the toes,
Of your smelly welly feet.

Stop them with soap,
Before they crawl up your legs;
And the Belly Button Monsters,
Eat you: in your cozy wozy beds.

The boys jumped as he shouted, "Eat you!" Smiling ear-to-ear, Rammer in his spooky voice wisecracked, "Jambles, you better go take a bath right now before you wake up and your legs are missing."

Jambles, with a grizzled face, squeezed his father tight. "Daddy, can I sleep with you tonight?"

Rooter smiled. "But, if you sleep with me and Mommy, after they eat you, they will eat Mommy."

"Mommy, Daddy's scaring me."

That night rooter slept on the floor, while a little boy, smelling of soap, slept above his head with Mommy.

* * * * * * *

Morning came early with a red sun quivering on the horizon— it sagged oppressively in the sky as if the mountain pass was clutching its tail. The market opened and slowly came to life. The smell of fresh-baked bread started its early morning door-to-window routine. The blacksmith's hammer echoed down the cool, dew-trodden streets stopping at the square to play in the fountain. Bugler fish tuned their bugles getting ready for their early morning ensemble. Large thunder beast entered town and walked down by The Redmadafa. Their long necks stretched down and drank several thousand gallons before they wandered into the markets.

A soldier dressed in full armor standing guard on the East parameter wall walked down the wall to the end of his post and stopped next to his friend. He rubbed his bloodshot eyes from standing guard all night and then leaned against the wall and looked out at the horizon. "You see that?" he said to his friend standing guard at the next post. "Something bad is about to happen."

"See what?" answered the other guard watching the sun rise over and walk down the black-peaked silhouetted mountains across the plains.

"It's a red sun, that's not good."

"Why's that?" asked his friend. He pulled a small dagger from his side and chipped at the top of the wall.

He looked to the South and then North. "Red sun at night and it's His Majesty's delight. Red sun in the morning…and it's His Majesty's warning," he said.

His friend bristled at the suggestion and clenched his fists. They both stared at each other and then walked opposite back down the wall.

Man and beast grudgingly grabbed their hats and said a prayer before entering the brutal and dangerous mines. Myott, Chesty's brother, unlocked the mill door and opened the shutters. He stretched to wake up, and after a long yawn, he looked out toward the Northern mountain range. A thick dark fog hovered just outside the North Gate. With his mind on the countless jobs he needed to complete, and grossly behind schedule, he turned around, placing his elbows on the desk, and rested his chin in his hands. Abandoned by most of his workers foolishly dreaming of fortunes in the new land, he spun back around.

The pit of his stomach churned vigorously and his spirit leaped within. He vaulted from his seat and ran outside. Oh no, he said to himself in utter disbelief. With Chesty on his mind he scanned the dark fog and grunted, "Little brother, it's my turn now. I won't let you down."

He ran inside and threw open cabinet after cabinet, looking for it. He threw receipts, books and other objects all over the floor. He opened another cabinet door, pushed some old ropes aside and found it. He grabbed the ram's horn and briskly stepped outside. He filled his lungs to full capacity and placed his dry lips to the horn, "AURRRRRRR. AURRRRRRR. AURRRRRRR." He then proceeded down the streets, running at full speed blowing the horn over and over.

Doors and windows sprung open. The people in the market paused. Onuka looked up—he was praying at the altar when he heard the horn. He jumped to his feet and ran down the aisle. He thrust the front doors open and looked around town and then at the North Gate. He spun around and jumped through the temple, swinging from the rafters, down the corridor and through the hallways. Up the Eastern tower stairs he climbed until breaking through the bell room door. His muscular hands grasp the old frayed rope, and pulling with all his might, the bell struck, *Bong! Bong! Bong! Bong! Bong! Bong! Bong!* The alarm sent residents into a frenzy.

The North Gate guards had just finished opening the gate and were securing the ropes and locking the pulley wheel. Two guards patrolling outside the gate heard the temple bells and immediately halted in place.

Koman gazed at Malgog and with a squeamish look on his face said, "It's not Sun Day, why is Onuka sounding the bell?"

"That's strange," replied Malgog. "That was seven bells. Four bells are for Sun Day. Seven bells are rung only if we're under attack."

They looked up. Their eyes scanned the dark fog creeping ominously toward them. "I don't see anything," said Koman.

They drew their swords from leather scabbards and walked nervously into the fog. Visibility was dim, only about five feet. Malgog said, "There isn't anything out here let's go back."

"What was that?" said Koman, his head turning back and forth.

"What?" cried Malgog, jostling his feet backward.

"I thought I saw something."

A dark figure ran by Malgog, catching his eye this time.

Their hearts raced.

They slowly backed up.

A faint thump, thump, thump resounded through the fog just before three arrows struck Koman in the chest knocking him off his feet, plunging him backwards.

Stunned, Malgog yelled, "Shut the gate!"

The guard flipped the lever releasing the pin to close the gate. The ropes smoked, sending tiny rope fibers twirling about into the air as the gate dropped without restraint.

Malgog's claws dug deep into the ground. He wheeled around, throwing dirt high into the air as he ran on all fours trying to reach the gate before it closed, sealing his doom.

"Hurry Malgog, you can make it," shouted the guards, arrows landing all around him.

Malgog, with just a crack left, slipped through the gate as it closed. With a look of horror on his face, he looked up at the tower guards and said, "They're here." He collapsed face-first on the ground revealing the thirteen arrows stuck in his back.

Thunder Juice panicked. Guards scrambled from their homes. They raced to get weapons, while others took up positions along the walls. The Shadow of Death retreated, withdrawing his dark hideous form from the battle line, revealing Lucky and his forces spread out in front of the wall.

Alarms continued to sound all over town spreading from gate-to-gate, house-to-house, and business-to-business. Women and children fled for the temple and the passageways underneath its foundations. Large boulders rained down upon the town. Long black arrows flew over the walls striking the rooftops, igniting homes and businesses.

Lucky advanced from the shadow riding his black yellow-striped scorpion with a blood-red line running down its back. He jumped down from the scorpion and transformed into Slithler *The Great Serpent*. He hissed at the guards melting their spirits, sending fear throughout the ranks. He rose high off the ground and spoke:

"When the sun hits the top tower of the temple, my forces will destroy this wall, this town, and all that remain. Leave your post now. Essscape with your lives while there is ssstill time," he warned.

The clanging of swords resounding up and down the wall. Guards, fearing for their lives, threw down their weapons, hastily abandoning their post.

Hopelessly running down the stairs, they heard the ruffle of his wings. The Augur flew over the town, the wind from his wings extinguishing all fires. He landed atop the North Gate tower and closed his wings. Slithler burned with rage and hate at his sight. He opened his mouth and spit venom at him. He slid back and forth for all to see and hear his lurid proclamation:

"Well, well, well, look who decided to return. Do not think for one moment, he can sssave you. Look at the burden he has placed around your necks all these years. His laws and rules breaking your backs, making you fight your own battles always having to pray to him for help.

He is the one that cursed you. He is the one that makes you work and earn your labor by the ssssweat of your brows. He is the one that increased your wives' pain in childbirth.

What kind of a god would do that? What kind of a god would cast his children from his presence and

THE REDMADAFA

forsake them to this dry and barren land? He is no god. He is a beast just like the rest of us. The sssame fate awaits him as does this town—Death. Open the gate and welcome me in so I can protect you from his judgment.

Oh, I bet he didn't tell you his plans for this town, did he? He wants to destroy everything you have worked ssso hard for. He plans to lay waste this town and every ssstone of the temple. He does not love you. He hates you. Turn from him now and I will ssspare your lives."

Confused eyes cut to The Augur waiting for him to speak, waiting for him to expose the Father of Lies for who he really was. But he didn't. He just stood there. He did not open his mouth or utter a word. He did not defend himself against the serpent's accusations.

"Why does he just stand there?" the crowd asked.

"Why doesn't he say something?" asked a guard.

"It must be true, that's why. He has not come to rescue us. He has come to watch us die. He has come to watch us die. Open the gate, before the sun hits the temple. We must save ourselves," yelled another guard standing atop the adjacent tower.

CHAPTER 13

THE REDMADAFA

The River of Life.

The temple burst to life with the outer courts preparing for battle. Trees broke off their branches and formed them into wooden spears, bows and arrows. Rocks sharpened against each other, like iron sharpening iron, formed themselves into arrowheads to be used for the tip of the spears. Grasses wound tightly together forming string for the bows and ropes for the catapults. Mushrooms secreted a toxic poison into the cisterns to lace the arrowheads.

The Redmadafa surged readying itself for the fires of doom that lay outside the walls waiting to burn the town and temple to the ground. Its calm waters swelled to small rapids, tossing quick cross-diagonal water in all directions foaming against the rocks at water's edge. Toby swam up-stream while Tyku swam down, warning all Bugler fish and creatures that teemed in the waters of The Redmadafa about the terror to come.

Inside the temple, the aisles overflowed with activity. Hundreds of women and children rushed into the sanctuary, seeking shelter. Beyond the town walls, in the crags of the mountain, flat lands and gullies, Slithler's army positioned themselves readying for war. Hordes of deadly beasts erected battering rams, catapults, and towers of doom that reached high into the sky to breach the outer walls' defenses.

Along the wall, soldiers stockpiled shields, spears, swords, and bows and arrows, reinforcing their positions. All able-bodied men and boys drew armor from the armory and fastened tightly-braided mesh underneath. Shields bearing an Almighty Eagle with protruding talons shined around the wall as steady eyes peered through helmets with long, steel black-pitted nose guards. Others prepared large caldrons of burning tar to pour down upon anyone or anything that tried to scale the gates or walls.

Down below, young boys shuffled cattle-drawn carts from the mines bearing medium- sized rocks and boulders for the catapults. Moogles drew the ropes down fastening them to rusty hooks. Others loaded them with rocks and stood by waiting further commands.

Down by The Redmadafa, numerous croakers emerged from the water and removed several boards from pipes leading to town. The boards where used to shut off the flow of water to different areas of town to control the amount of pressure to each location. By removing all the boards from certain pipes, maximum pressure built up behind the giant nozzles atop the guard towers, which stood ready to blast enemy forces trying to penetrate the perimeter walls and to extinguish fires along the walls and in town.

Myott arrived at Caboose's house just as they were getting ready to leave for the temple. He could see the worry in their eyes and hear it in their voices. Myott was a good man, a faithful and humble man who worked hard providing a living for his family. Although he was a large unidor like his little brother, he was exceedingly gentle and caring.

Myott grew up in Thunder Juice Town and never left. He worked for his father from a young age and inherited the mill after his death. He had several employees that worked for him and he felt personally responsible for them and their families. Myott had never told anyone before, but he respected Chesty for his adventurous heart. He longed to venture out and see the world like Chesty had when he was young, and he longed to do something *Great*. But up until now, he had only seen Thunder Juice Town and served the people of the mill.

"Penoba, is everyone alright?" he asked Mrs. Puller walking through the door. He embraced each of them in his large gentle arms.

Mrs. Puller took one look into his eyes and lost control of her emotions. Myott and Chesty had the same slanted bluish-gray eyes. She fell into his arms sobbing.

"I'm so sorry I couldn't come earlier but things are chaotic in town. The streets are crowded with people making their way to the temple, and others closest to the walls are deserted and barricaded." He bent down toward Pepper and grabbed her up in his arms, "Your Papa would be so proud of you."

Tears streamed down her face and her chest jumped as she breathed in. Pepper loved her uncle very much. She spent many nights at his house on the weekends playing with her cousins and having fun. She spent hours in his backyard participating in games and swinging from the huge rope swing he built which hung high in a mature oak tree, back by the fence. Myott pushed her and her cousins for hours way up in the sky, so high that their feet kicked the branches hanging down from above. He read them bedtime stories at night making funny noises with his mouth as he read the adventures he dreamed himself of taking.

Myott sat down and listened to Pepper talk about missing her Papa. She went on-and-on about what Caboose had told her and how brave her Papa was. Mrs. Puller made him brumpel melon juice and brought it to him to drink. She looked tired, really tired—he could see it on her face. But, being around Myott brought her renewed strength and hope. With everyone present in the room, Myott lowered his head and confessed something that had been on his heart for a long time.

"I don't know what is going to happen in the next few days, but there is something that I feel I need to share with you. There was a time in my younger years when your Papa and I didn't get along...but it wasn't his fault. When he was young, he asked our father for his inheritance and when father gave it to him, he abruptly left town. He was gone for a number of years scouring the circle, living out his childhood fantasies of wild adventures into the great unknown. For a long time, we didn't know where he was or if he was even alive. But then late one day, in the evening, just as the sun lowered below the horizon, he came strolling along the trail like he didn't have a care in the world, having lost all of his inheritance.

At first, I was glad to see him. I wanted to hear where he had been and what he had been up to. But, to my surprise, when our father saw him, instead of scolding him and bringing the rod of correction to his back like I thought he should, he did something I will never forget—he ran and embraced a son he thought was lost and dead, and wept uncontrollably. He ordered his servants to fetch his robe and ring, and he lavished them on him. He then held a large feast and invited all his friends throughout the land. My heart seized inside me. I was mad and pushed him away. I thought my father had acted foolishly and showed contempt for his irresponsible behavior.

For years I held that against them both but it was to my own demise. Your grandfather knew exactly what he was doing. Chesty had already learned a tough lesson and deeply regretted not listening to our father in the first place. The only thing left to complete his journey in becoming a man, with a good new name ready to face the next chapter of his life, was to be embraced by a loving father and receive his forgiveness.

Years later after our father died, your father came to work for me at the mill. I assigned him the worst jobs and tried to get him to quit, but the more I pushed, the harder he worked to please me. He worked so hard to gain my trust and confidence that I soon couldn't imagine work and life without him—it didn't take him long, either, to know and run the business better than I could. He was so funny. I loved having him by my side and there was no one I trusted more to help me run the business. I can honestly say that today, without any reserve, that I loved him greatly and I will miss him more than you will ever know."

Caboose sat quietly with tears running down his face. His Papa did have some skeletons in his closet but they were good ones. Ones that had shaped his life in a positive way and made him appreciate life and the love of others that cared deeply for him. His uncle Myott also had some skeletons that he was finally getting rid of.

"Uncle Myott," said Caboose.

Myott lifted his head.

"I was there when he died. You would have been proud. He charged through the middle of the colosseum tossing all kinds of beasts up in the air, gouging them with his horn. He protected me and countless others from certain death, even with his body was cut and bleeding. He gave his life so that we could live."

"Proud," responded Myott, smiling. "It will forever be an honor to be known as the brother of 'Chesty Puller.'" Mrs. Puller turned her head and wiped her face. She walked into the kitchen and sat down. Myott had just closed a door to a wound that she bore with her husband for many years. A calming peace swept over her as she heard Myott speak again from the front.

"You kids get your things. I'll make sure you make it to the temple."

Onuka and the remaining elders escorted everyone in and tried to keep them calm. People were everywhere. They lined the aisles and hallways, and packed into the outer rooms and corridors. Rinox took several temple servants with him to help move the ancient scrolls into the secret passageways and hide them, lest the wall be penetrated and any harm befall the temple. They carefully packed them into baskets and loaded them into the tunnels. Other servants passed out water and food and helped direct traffic in the outer courts and gardens.

Myott and his family, with Penoba, Pepper and Caboose, hurried down the cowardice streets, empty and quiet. Baskets and clothes rummaged the alleys, and market tables were bare, picked clean by fleeing oddities; little creeptails high-footed along, scraping every unclaimed morsel into their bulging, rubbery cheeks.

Small pets wandered the streets, left behind by their owners. Many doors and windows remained open, unsecured.

Caboose wasn't afraid. He had survived the valley and knew the tricks of Lucky. With the temple in view, he felt at peace—a peace that many others could use at the moment. Pepper on the other hand, was extremely scared. She had never seen the town in such an uproar. She stopped and cast an abandoned peek at him, and in a kind act of brotherly love, something he had not displayed before, Caboose picked her up, kissed her on the forehead and carried her the rest of the way.

Inside the temple, Myott made his way to Onuka, whose tired figure stood at the front, directing traffic and giving orders. No one was allowed in the underground passageways yet. No army had ever broken through the walls. No need to panic. No need to excite the people any more than necessary.

Myott walked over and listened to Onuka giving instructions to bring water and help to the elderly and sick. Not wanting to impede, he motioned to Onuka, "Onuka, can I speak with you for a moment?"

Onuka finished his instructions and walked over. "Myott, I'm so sorry to hear about your brother. Chesty was a close friend and a faithful servant to me and the members of this temple."

"Thanks. I know he thought the world of you. He was always rambling on about your messages." He stopped and thought about what he said, "In a good way of course."

Onuka smiled, missing his old friend dearly.

"I brought his family here, where can I put them?"

"Caboose is here?" responded Onuka, anxiously wanting to see him.

"Yes, he's right over there." Myott pointed through the crowd.

"You know, there is something different about that young grunter. He has matured well beyond his years."

"Bring him to my chamber." He watched Caboose help people find a seat. "The Augur has special plans for him. Great Things planned for him."

Myott made his way back through the crowd to Caboose. Caboose helped his mother and sister find a seat and then proceeded to talk to several people around them. Myott placed his hand on his shoulder from behind. "Can I speak with you for a moment?"

Caboose turned around, "Sure. Is everything alright?"

He led Caboose to the front doors, the doors over the cleft rock, and out onto the steps. The outer courts teamed with activity. People shuttled into the yards, others moved into outer buildings and covered shelters. "Onuka wants to see you in his chambers. He said you can take the back way around the temple...up the stairs."

"The High Priest wants to see me in his chambers?" asked Caboose. "Did he say what this was about?"

"No. Just that The Augur has something for you to do."

Caboose stood gritting his teeth for a moment. The Augur, what would he want with me? And what would he possible want me to do? He walked down the steps, carefully making his way through the people—he felt like he was back in the valley stepping over gargoyles—people were everywhere. He walked around the side of the temple, down a long corridor, and turned into a large, arched opening. Proceeding through the door, he walked down the hallway filled with people, looking into each eye, each face, noting the fear and helplessness and then walked up a narrow stairway leading to Onuka's chamber.

He rounded the corner and stopped outside a slightly-open door. He looked inside before softly knocking. He waiting for a brief moment and then pushed the door open and entered. Large vanilla-colored candles flickered silently throughout the room. Scrolls and books lined shelves; others lay open on beautifully carved wooden tables. Priestly garments hung on a pedestal near the door and a washbasin, with a decorative pitcher beside it, in the corner. He walked over and looked at an open scroll on one of the tables.

Onuka emerged from the back room. "Ezekiel." Caboose looked up. Onuka pointed at the scroll. "That was written by Ezekiel, a powerful seer, about 600 years ago. His prophecy in chapter seventeen seems to point to what is happening now. I've been studying it for weeks. I don't understand what he means when he says, '*His Majesty will plant a tree on a high mountain and birds of every kind will nest in it and find shelter.*' I'm sure there's a mystery behind it that I have yet to discover. Please have a seat."

Caboose thought it strange that the High Priest would want to talk to him, especially with everything going on outside. He took a seat at the table and unraveled the scroll. He picked up a breastplate with twelve colored stones lined across its front—three across and four down. He rubbed his fingers across its surface—it reminded him of the Scorpion Pass Gate and its cool jagged surface. He placed it back on the table and looked around the room.

"Your father was a good friend. He was a sounding board for me on many occasions." Onuka walked over and pulled two books off the shelf and laid them on the table. "I can't begin to understand how you must feel, nor do I know what you endured in the valley. It saddens me that he isn't here with us now."

Onuka opened a closet and took out a brightly-colored garment and laid it next to the books. "I don't know what will happen in the next few days but there is something I must tell you.

Caboose listened but didn't respond.

"The Augur spoke with me the other day about you. He wants you to stay by my side, no matter what happens. He has something special planned for you. So, I need you to stay close to me and keep yourself alert. Stay courageous no matter what you see taking place around us and at the temple. Stay loyal to what he wants you to do and obedient to his teachings. This is a time to be honest with yourself and courteous to those who are fearful." Onuka stopped what he was doing and walked in front of Caboose. "What's happening outside these walls is not a battle of the flesh. It's a spiritual battle. Make sure that when the time is right, you will look beyond what your eyes see and peer into the spirit world."

Caboose didn't say anything. He just shook his head. He was not expecting to hear that, especially after everything he had endured in the valley.

"I watched my Papa die in my arms. I saw the Sea Throne and the garden. I heard and believed the lies from his cunning tongue. When The Augur rescued me instead of my Dad, I was angry. But I know he is God. His touch, it changed my life forever. If he chooses to use me now, with the strength of his body, I will be ready for anything. I am no longer afraid of death."

Onuka smiled. "Young grunter, my heart is filled with joy. Whatever I can do to help you, you just let me know. My door is always open."

* * * * * * *

The guard standing below him reached over and placed his hand on the release leaver. The commander of the guard placed his hand over the guard's hand, "Wait."

"For what? Didn't you hear him? If we open the gate, he will let us live."

The commander looked up at The Augur. "Aren't you going to say something? Should we save ourselves and let him have Thunder Juice?"

The Augur didn't reply. He stared at Slithler watching his every move.

The commander leaned over the tower wall and shouted, "If we open the gate and surrender now, will you let us and our families leave in peace?"

Slithler, feeling confident and proud, stood tall and hissed, "The sun is about to strike the temple. Raise the gate now and I will let you passssss without harm."

The commander looked up at The Augur—nothing, he didn't acknowledge him.

"Commander, raise the gate, you can save our lives, raise the gate," echoed a voice down the wall.

He tapped his fingers on his bloodless sword knowing he shouldn't. Forgetting his past and trusting the advice of fools he regrettably said, "Release the pin, raise the gate."

"Sir," he said with an uncertain voice. "Are you sure?"

"Just do it."

Click! When the commander heard the click, his stomach convulsed. That sound, I've heard that sound before, he said to himself. He knew he had just made the biggest mistake of his life.

The rope smoked, chains chattered, dust flew, fibers darted. The gate skyrocketed open, slamming against the top, echoing back at the guards. Slithler smiled and yelled, "Attack!"

A gog raised the battle horn to his mouth. "AURRRRRRRRR," cackled the horn instilling fear in the guards. Slithler dashed toward the gate. The Augur dropped down, knocking him to the ground. Slithler coiled, flinging The Augur away from the door while trolls stormed the gate.

"Fire!" shouted Miaphas. Spears hummed through the air gouging the huge trolls, pinning them three-deep to each other. A company from the Southern Celestial Guard surprised the stampede and drove them back, with Miaphas leading the charge. The wall guards couldn't see the protective curtain stretching up into the sky prohibiting Slithler and his army from flying over. Miaphas and the others struggled to close the gate as all eyes focused on The Augur and Slithler.

Slithler circled The Augur, whipping his stinger-forked tail repeatedly at him. The Augur lifted out of the way and hit him with his wing, sending him crashing into a catapult, knocking it over, smashing a crawler underneath. Slithler transformed into an eagle and ascended into the air after him.

The Augur circled and tucked his wings.

Slithler spun to his back and locked talons spinning them into a cliff-face adjacent the Southern North Gate tower. They rolled down the rocky face, Slithler's talons ripping plumage from The Augur's face.

At the bottom, The Augur grabbed Slithler and hurtled him over the wall, through the invisible curtain, toward The Redmadafa. Slithler's army ran up the mountainside to watch the battle ensuing over the river.

The air turned black as Slithler flew over the outer courts. Tracking his every move, trees launched spears with toxic arrowheads affixed, into the air. The spears shot straight, while others shot cross-diagonally, minimizing his escape. The spears plunged into his feathers causing him to bank hard right and open his wings like a parachute. The trees heaved, pulling the grass ropes affixed to the spears, wrenching him down to the river to drown him. Slithler ruffled his feathers, shaking the spears off.

Ironwood, the Celestial Tree Commander, yelled, "Come back around again, traitor! I have more where that came from!"

The Augur flew over the wall and collided with him over The Redmadafa. Slithler dug his thorny talons deep into the top of his head, shaking him violently. The Augur countered and grabbed his belly, pulling him loose; Slithler transformed his lower body and struck him with his tail, relinquishing his grip.

Upset at the commander of the gate, Miaphas climbed the tower and allowed the commander to see him. "Don't open this gate again, no matter what happens. Do you understand me, commander?"

Bewildered, he looked at Miaphas, the Imperial Commander of the Celestial Guard, richly adorned in his battle armor, "Ah, Yes…Sir," he said, looking him over from top to bottom, not knowing what to think or say—the commander had never seen anyone like him before. Slithler dove through town, knocking shingles and chimneys down, fleecing the streets below. Around the university, over the market, and into the mines he flew setting his trap.

The Augur followed close behind, disappearing into the long, dark tunnel. Slithler smashed the lights and transformed back into a serpent, blending-in with the black walls.

The Augur ebbed cautiously down the cold, dark, wet tunnels. Water dripped from the ceiling landing in small muddy pools below. Wind ripped through the tunnel and into the lower shafts before rebounding in a backdraft.

The Augur scanned the darkness and moved further into the tunnel.

He stopped.

His breath highlighted the darkness as he turned his head.

He proceeded into a large subterranean room filled with mine equipment. The walls rumbled, speaking out to The Augur, exposing Slithler's hiding place. He stopped and listened, his ears grasping every sound, his eyes searching the darkness.

Slithler slid along the ceiling, quietly rappelling over him.

The Augur, fully aware of his evil presence, rolled onto to his back and kicked, impaling him into the support timbers overhead. Wood and rocks disintegrated while dust filled the room.

The remaining timbers waned to support the ceiling, as large cracks raced across the ceiling and down the walls. Large rocks broke from the ceiling and pummeled the floor, barely missing The Augur.

Slithler recovered and slid around the room. He chucked large wooden beams and rocks with his tail at The Augur, shredding his feathers and smashing him up-against the wall. The Augur jumped to his feet and bobbed and weaved through the shower. He pressed forward and tackled Slithler, driving him out of the mines and into the rock quarry outside.

The rocks swallowed them, digging at Slithler, cutting him with jagged teeth. A dust cloud masked the fight as Slithler transformed and took to the air. The Augur spun and scanned the dust cloud for any sign of him. Slithler climbed high into the sky and then twisted back. He dropped quietly with his eyes closed and hammered The Augur into the ground, creating a large crater. A dust cloud mushroomed into the air covering the hillside. Clutching his back, Slithler ripped it to shreds with his sharp talons, spraying feathers and flesh into the air. The Augur winced, flipped over and locked talons with him. They both bit viciously at each other, ripping plumage and tearing flesh.

From atop the mountainside outside the North Gate, Legion watched the battle with his arm raised. "Wait, wait," he said, waiting for the signal. Slithler threw The Augur across town and over the walls, indenting him atop a small hill just outside of town. The Augur crashed into the hill that bore the resemblance of a skull, and tried to stand but his frail battered body collapsed back to the ground unable to hold his massive weight. Slithler glided to victory and landed beside him boldly casting his shadow over his mangled disfigured body.

This was the moment he had waited for. All his tricks, all his widespread trading and control of the markets and all his evil alliances had been for this sole moment. With victory in his grasp, he stood strong and gloated, "Bow before me now and I will kill you quickly."

The Augur lay on the ground helpless and defenseless, his broken and bruised body writhing with pain. He struggled to stand. Unable to stand by his own power, he used his wings to help push off the ground. Staring long and deep into Slithler's eyes he whispered, "**The God in me…Will never bow…To the coward…In you.**"

Slithler raised his talons and locked them around The Augur. He screeched out giving the signal. Legion dropped his hand with a curt nod.

Click!

A large pulley launched a long rusty iron spear across the sky. Miaphas and the Southern army watched it climb high into the sky. Locked in on The Augur, the spear honed in on the battle. Slithler peered back into his eyes, spun him around and said, "Time to pay the fee!"

The spear pierced The Augur. It ran all the way through, gushing blood and water from his side. The dirt turned dark red as it soaked up his life-blood.

The Augur took to the sky flying high to escape. Shocked and paralyzed, everyone stopped and watched. The Augur, with only seconds left and darkness closing in yelled out, "Your Majesty!" and then whispered, "It is finished." He spun, round and round, and round and round, and crashed into The Redmadafa, sinking beneath its surface.

Galamus, in disbelief, searched his mind for an explanation. Unable to find one, he looked at Miaphas, "It can't be. This can't be happening." They flew over town and landed on the bank waiting for him to rise. Slithler landed on the bank opposite them and peered into the water. The Augur lay on the bottom, motionless. Toby, Tyku, and numerous creatures swam to his aid lifting his body back to the surface but it was too late. He was dead. His lifeless body drifted back to the bottom. A dark, red line streamed from his side to the surface and flowed down the river, turning The Redmadafa blood-red.

Slithler was stunned. He stood in disbelief waiting for him to burst forth any second. "He's dead. He's really dead. I've done it. I've killed him. I've killed The Augur." He changed back into the great serpent and lifted his head to the sky, "Vengeance is mine!"

He confidently looked at Miaphas, lowered his head and drew his eyes, "You're next."

The invisible curtain protecting Thunder Juice ripped, opening the skies above town. Slithler's evil eye, glimpsing the opportunity, shouted, "The curtain has fallen. Kill them." He turned and hissed at the temple. "Kill them all!"

* * * * * *

You could see it in their eyes; you could read it on their faces; their silence speaking louder than ten thousand Bugler fish blowing triumphantly at morning's dawn. Minds raced. Hearts constricted. Stomachs churned. Hope? It sank to the bottom, forever lost in the muddy blood-red water of The Redmadafa. The rock, the cleft rock from which the headwaters flowed, closed its mouth. The river stopped flowing. The wind stopped blowing. Trees and plants in the outer courts and all throughout the land withered in the plots where they had been planted. The sun and moon turned to blood and darkness descended upon the land. The hum of death filled the air.

Onuka and Caboose watched the battle from atop the East tower. Stumbling down the stairs, they trudged their way to the main sanctuary. Onuka searched his mind. Surely there had to be something in the scrolls; something overlooked. They emerged out onto the front. All eyes looked at him waiting for him to speak.

He stood, speechless.

"Onuka, is it over? Did The Augur crush the serpent?" came a heavily accented voice from the crowd."

He tried to respond, but confusion gripped his tongue, stammering his words. He didn't understand what had happened. He didn't know what would become of them.

"Onuka, what's going on? Is it over?"

He examined each face. He noted each weary eye. He gasped, shaking his head, "He's dead. He's dead."

A young human boy sitting at the front with a blue shirt stood up and yelled, "The serpent is dead, the serpent is dead!"

The crowd cheered and embraced each other. Others danced around.

"No! No! yelled Onuka. The Augur…is dead."

"What. What did he say?" said an elderly woman from the middle. "Did he say The Augur is dead?"

Whispers flooded the sanctuary. Heads shook in disbelief.

"Onuka, please say it isn't so. The Augur...he can't be dead."

Onuka didn't reply. Everything he had ever believed in was lying at the bottom of The Redmadafa. Caboose, looked at Onuka, swallowed a massive blossom berry of fear and nervously addressed the crowd:

"I...you....many of you don't know me but my Papa was an elder of this temple. Several months ago I ran away from home and found myself outside *The Scorpion Pass Gate*. I met a man named Lucy, *Lucky Lucy* he called himself. I was deceived by his splendor. I entered the gate and found myself trapped in the valley of the shadow of death. Bones; millions and millions of bones covered the valley floor. Tormented souls cried out to me from the pit, begging for rest, begging for one drop of living water from The Redmadafa.

In the colosseum, I met another man, or...creature. His name was Slithler. He sounded like Lucky. His eyes looked like Lucky. His tongue spoke with the same cunning and deception, as Lucky. Slithler and Lucky are one and the same. He is a master of disguise and the Father of Lies—I now know that Lucy was short for Lucifer.

I don't know what is going on. But when I was in the colosseum, staring Slithler right in the face, moments from death myself, The Augur came and rescued me. Before he did though, in that split moment, I looked into Lucifer's eyes and I saw fear, a fear like I've never seen before. His body cringed. His eyes groveled. He was scared—really scared.

The Augur brought me back to Thunder Juice Town. Before he left, he told me to not trust in my own understanding. He said things were going to happen that were impossible to understand, and that if I would trust him, my path would be made straight.

My Papa died in the colosseum. He gave his life so I could live. A life I am unworthy to experience. A life where I can serve others and tell of The Augur's amazing love for this great big circle we live on. He promised me I would see my Papa again. He promised me he would never leave me nor forsake me.

I am going to stand upon those promises. This is not the time to fall apart and abandon the faith you know to be true. Will you stand with me? Will you stand up now? The Redmadafa will flow; when you see *The White Wooly*, it will flow once again."

Onuka, remembering what the ancient scroll foretold, smiled and with confidence shouted:

"*Who can save themselves from the slimy pit? Who can approach His Majesty without a bloodstain?*

Surely he has taken up our griefs and carried away our sorrows. His Majesty has laid on Him the punishment of us all. It was the will of His Majesty to crush him, to make his life the bloodstain.

The Augur will see His seed. He will see the light of life once

*again. He will divide the spoil with the strong, because He
poured out his soul unto death so that we may have life.*

*He will arise and smite the serpent. He will arise and crush
the shadow of death. He will arise and take back what is
rightfully his!"*

* * * * * * *

Legion, hearing Slithler's command, surveyed the wall and yelled,
"Arsonon!" Arsonon stepped forward, his body flaming, ready to
unleash destruction upon the town.

"Fly over the wall and unleash your fury."

"But, what about the shield?"

"Didn't you hear Slithler? It's down!"

Arsonon hesitated, to fly into the shield meant certain death.
Legion, angry that his orders were being questioned, and not carried out in a timely manner, picked Arsonon up and threw him
over the wall. He flew through the air and sideswiped the corner
of the tower, splashing into the outpost barracks instantly disintegrating, engulfing the barracks in dark yellow and red flames.

Arsonon hauntingly rose from the fire gaining strength and
power. "Yes…Yes…Time to burn!"

Legion, without saying a word, raised his arms and dropped
them rapidly. Arrows of fire, boulders and spears shot over the
wall, exploding houses, killing guards and igniting an inferno
that spread rapidly house-to-house, building-to-building.

Slithler's dark celestial guards took to the skies and punched
over the wall. Galamus and several others from the Southern
Guard dispersed, and with swords flaming, clashed in mid-air,
dripping sparks down over the town—they were allowed to

protect key individuals, but that was all, no further involvement until the signal was given.

Legion stayed directing fire upon the wall to bring it down. Six large magondreas with a dragon-carved battering ram charged the gate, ramming it over and over. Overhead, four soldiers rolled a large black caldron filled with pitch and tar to the edge of the wall and heaved. The tar dumped down on the magondreas covering them in a black sticky slime, soaking their heads, necks, and backs. The magondreas looked up and watched a torch spin through the air toward them—it dropped inches from their feet. One of them reached over and spit on the fire, and then roared loudly at the miss. A Ragoole swooped out of the clouds eager to join the battle and spewed fire down the wall, setting ablaze the magondreas.

Fire burned from their head all the way down to the end of their tails. The magondreas dropped the battering ram and ran toward the river. In the water, the bugler fish remained steadfast as they made their approach. The magondreas jumped in the water and splashed around trying to extinguish the fire. The fish ascended from bloody waters ambushing them in great numbers. Holding long strings of vines in their teeth, they wrapped them around their legs and pulled them into the depths of The Redmadafa, drowning them. Their lifeless bodies surfaced downstream and disappeared out of sight.

Rammer and his father tried to exit down stairs but the fire spread fast. Running back up the stairs, they jumped through a window onto the roof and headed for the temple—they had gone back to retrieve a few things, never expecting the breech. A Ragoole spotted them, cocked its wings, and dove, raining fire across the rooftops. Rammer and his Dad jumped roof-to-roof evading the fiery onslaught. Rammer jumped onto a clay-tiled roof held together with clumps of mud and grass, and slipped. The tiles fell off the roof, shattering on the ground below.

"Rammer, grab my hand," cried his father, reaching for him before he fell over the side. He reached to maintain a grip, but slid down the steep angle, over the ledge and crashed right on top of the Ragoole. Desperately trying to hang on, he dug his claws deep into its back.

The Ragoole spun over trying to shake him loose. Hanging upside down, one of Rammer's claws caught between the Ragoole's wing sockets, keeping him securely anchored. It dove in and out, around buildings and trees, and then through an old barn, crashing through its doors trying to knock Rammer off. Scared, he hung on for dear life. Rammer reached for a hay hook, stuck it in its wing, hitching a ride from the barn. Stretching for the hook, he lost his grip and slid down its back, his left claw catching its tail; he whipped around behind the beast like a flag caught in a storm.

The Ragoole reached back and snapped repeatedly at Rammer wildly swinging off-sync with its tail. Rammer frantically climbed up its tail and back onto its back. He grabbed the hook and, not thinking through what he was about to do, jumped for its ear, hooking it. The Ragoole made a hard right and dropped rapidly out of the sky, crashing head-first into the University's Research Center.

Fire exploded through the windows and door ejecting Rammer from the building. He rolled across the ground and jumped back to his feet, dazed but fully alert. The Ragoole lunged from the building and spotted him running for the fountain. Rammer, uncertain about what to do or where to go, jumped over the fountain like it was Meteor Rock in *The Little Round*

About and headed toward the market. Unable to climb due to an injured wing, the evil beast swooped over the yard and crashed into the fountain, toppling it over, spewing water into the sky. Water poured out of the fountain and raced down the hill, overtaking Rammer, sweeping him through the streets in its torrent. Rammer whipped down the street, around corners, and through the alleys, riding a wave of excitement. He crashed into several poles and storefronts before finally washing-out in the market square.

Dizzy from the wild ride, he pulled himself up. Feeling a strange heat beating against his back, he spun around and found himself eyeball-to-eyeball with the deadly beast. It drew back and opened its mouth. Rammer, frozen with fright, looked deep into its throat as the pilot light kindled. Fire raced up its elongated throat, into its mouth, and across its barbed, slimy tongue.

Rooter, jumped off the roof with a wooden fence post raised over his head, and bounced its head off the ground, flattening it like a fly.

"Nobody messes with my son. Nobody!" he said, smacking the post in his dirty cut hand. A puff of smoke smoldered out of its mouth, as if begging for mercy, as the ragoole lifted its mangled head and looked at Rooter.

Rooter, with a new vision for life and family, swung the post, delivering the final deathblow. "Sweet dreams, beautiful."

CHAPTER 14

THE WHITE WOOLY

Seven horns: Seven eyes. They fell down and worshipped him.

"What was that?"

"What was what, I didn't hear anything?"

"I thought I heard something in the gully," said a gog patrolling outside the western wall. "Come on, we'd better check it out."

Traegor traveled for days through the mountains and across the flat lands. He witnessed the destruction of Guma and heard about the siege forming around Thunder Juice Town. He pushed his body to the limit to make it back in time knowing Onuka would need his experience in battle.

He crept up the gully, slipping quietly beneath a pile of brown teeth. His heart raced seeing the gogs jump down into the gully, making their way toward him. The gully was a wash-out full of green spikes and brown teeth. He had slipped past the perimeter guards and wasn't far from the outer West wall.

"Look," said the gog, bending down to the ground moving the dirt with his finger. "Tracks: fresh tracks." He looked up and whispered, "Someone is here and close."

The other guard dropped to the ground and sniffed. "Howler—I'd know that stench anywhere."

Traegor tried to control his breathing but his back rose moving the pile on top of him. His eyes glowered through the cracks, scanning the gully floor. He could hear a faint whisper and the sound of rocks crushing beneath their feet but couldn't see them. They followed the tracks to a corner in the gully where a large pile of brown teeth was trapped by the crooked bend. Their eyes looked down into the pile. They nodded at each other and slowly unsheathed their swords and raised the blood-stained blades over their heads.

Whispering softly, they counted, "One, two, three."

Red and silver marked the sky as their blades plunged into the pile. Traegor lunged forward hitting one of the gogs in the stomach knocking him to the ground.

"Spy! It's a spy!" yelled the other guard. "Get him before he reaches the wall."

One by one gogs and grike trolls rose from their sleep and scanned the area for any sign of him.

"There he is," yelled an ugly lop-sided troll emerging from behind a boulder.

Spears and arrows pierced the dirt all around Traegor as he

ran up the gully toward the wall. From the wall, a guard noticed the commotion and signaled his commander, pointing at Traegor.

"Sir, he's one of us. What do you want us to do?"

"Protect him. Protect him now!"

The tower guard looked down the wall, "Fire!" he shouted.

A barrage of faint thuds reverberated as spears and arrows hurtled down all around Traegor taking out gogs and trolls. With a suppressive fire-support showering down from the wall, Traegor made his escape up the gully and through the bodies piling up along the trail.

Spotting the unruly commotion from above, a fire breathing ragoole flew into the gully, igniting the sandy turf behind Traegor with a stream of flames. With only a few yards left before reaching the wall, Traegor jumped over a gog trying to block his way, and dug his claws deep into the cracks quickly ascending its rough, rocky face. The Ragoole spiraled out of the gully and up the wall after him.

"Behind you!" yelled a soldier at the top of the wall pointing downward.

Traegor spun, kicked off the wall, and landed on the head of the ragoole who was opening its mouth to cook him alive. He wrapped his two front paws around its mouth and squeezed, buttoning its mouth shut. The ragoole crested the top of the western wall. Traegor waited patiently and then stepped off at the top like he had been riding a rope ladder carrying supplies to the towers. Friend and foe cheered at his spectacular display of military skill and agility. He bowed momentarily and then disappeared down the other side.

The tunnels filled quickly with the sick and elderly. Dust leaked from the ceiling, joggled loose by the constant pounding from above. A stale, damp smell penetrated the air. Caboose walked up and down the tunnels comforting fearful eyes and dim faces, learning about life with every step. Little children darted and dashed around people playing hide-and-seek, oblivious to the danger lurking outside. Rooter and Rammer filtered down the tunnel, finally finding his wife and Jambles.

"Dad, what took so long," asked Jambles, happy to see them both. "Did you have to wrestle a big ragoole out of the sky while jumping across the rooftops to save Rammer from the claws-of-death?"

Their eyes winced toward each other. Rooter smiled, "That's exactly what happened Jambles. Only there were twenty of them."

Jambles shook his head, not believing a word, "And I bet the Belly Button Monsters were riding them with swords and shields in hand."

They all looked at each other and busted up laughing. Jambles grabbed his Daddy's hands and asked, "No really, how did you get all cut up?"

Rooter slipped his arms around Jambles' head putting him in a headlock and kissed him over-and-over on the top of his head. He winked at Rammer and laughed, "What am I going to do with your little brother?"

Onuka and the temple servants gathered in the outer courts and laid-out battle plans in case the walls were breeched. Rinox spotted Traegor moving down the Western corridor. "Traegor is here. We can use his battle experience and mind."

Traegor's large body emerged around a portico and approached Rinox and Onuka. The drumming of catapults abruptly caught his attention just before Onuka greeted him.

"Traegor, so good to see you my old friend," said Onuka.

"You look exhausted." He motioned to a temple servant, "Get him something to eat, we will need his mind sharp and alert."

"Thank you Onuka. I came as soon as I heard. I was two days journey from here, speaking to the last remains of Guma, when it was over-ran by gogs and beasts from the valley. They ravaged and burned the villages and set ablaze the forest. We held them off as long as we could, but there were too many of them. Many have already reached the outer walls and are heavily armed."

"Traegor, take command of the outer courts. Secure them as you see fit. We must protect the temple."

Traegor was no stranger to the temple and its members. His life stood as a beacon of hope to all who were trapped by the lie's of Slithler. It was a testimony of how The Augur could take a life lost in the valley, a life that had murdered, stole, and pillaged, and could completely change it, turning it around to be used for a greater purpose.

Traegor lost his life to The Augur and found a life that he could have never imagined. He traveled day and night all over the circle speaking of the wondrous love and forgiveness he found at the mercy of The Augur. Many lives were changed, homes and relationships mended, as purpose was restored to countless lives.

* * * * * * *

Arsonon vaulted from rooftop-to-rooftop, annihilating everything in his path. Residents fled for their lives, looking for a safe haven, a rock to shelter them from the destruction that rained down overhead. Hydromus, with the strength of The Redmadafa behind him, launched a barrage of spears, bucketing large columns of water on Arsonon and the fires. Showering each other in a furious rage, the battle soaked the town in a gloomy tribulation of elements.

Legion, frustrated that his attempts to break through the wall, fell contentiously before him, signaled to Arsonon and the rest of the southern guard to return. They landed on the hill above him, and waited with great anticipation of what was coming next. Legion bent over and drew a large sigil in the dirt, summoning the secret weapon—*Viper.*

The ground shook violently, toppling mountain ranges, causing avalanches and rock slides in the pass. A deafening roar crippled the town, reaching all the way down to those hiding in the tunnels under the temple. Lava atomically exploded into the sky as everyone watched in horror. A large orange flaming beast emerged from Mount Viper. Each step crushed mountains, imprinting the ground with large craters.

The temple vibrated intensely.

Traegor and the outer courts melted at his sight. The outer walls emptied with men and beasts running like yellow-bellies.

"Traegor, what is that? What do you want us to do?" asked Stumpy, the Mushroom King.

"There's nothing we can do against that."

He wheeled around and climbed up a statue. "Gather everyone left in the tunnels and seal them up. The walls are going to fall. When the army comes through, we will rise-up and smite him with everything we have. Until the last breath!" he shouted.

Fearful, but courageous, they turned to each other and in perfect unity shouted, "Until the last breath!"

"Miaphas, what is that?" asked Atrokus.

"Evil; evil of the worst kind."

Miaphas called for Galamus. Galamus flew over and landed beside him. "Assemble the earth delegations together. Have them muster their forces from every sector and region from across the land, sea, sky and universe." Distressed, he looked at the beast with eyes of contemplation. "Do it quickly Galamus. Do it quickly before we all die."

Celestial delegates flew over the walls and past the enemy army, summoning help. Slithler glided over and landed by Legion. "When the walls fall, send the pawns first. Something's not right, this is too easy."

"What could they possibly be withholding that our spies have not already uncovered?"

"I don't know. But I don't want to be surprised by anything this time. When it falls, I will kill Miaphas. Once you have destroyed the temple, reassemble the forces. His Majesty will be waiting for us. I don't want to disappoint."

"Yes, master. We will move quickly. We will trample the fiery stones under our feet with the blood of all who remain loyal to him."

* * * * * * *

"Man, I wish we could be there right now. I would give the next three souls, just to see the look on their faces when the walls come down," said a gog standing post in the watchtower above the Scorpion Pass Gate, overlooking the valley of bones.

"Yeah, I bet they all turn to stone, petrified with fear," said another guard.

"Slithler really outdid himself this time. Opening the gate and letting them just waltz right in like they own the place. He's a genius."

"You should've seen their faces when they deposited the dross. I've never laughed so hard in my whole, miserable life. You know what's funny about the whole thing?"

"What?" said a grike troll tearing a piece of flesh from a thunder beast bone.

He stared out across the valley shaking his head, "Most of them had heard the truth. They knew what they were doing was wrong but they went ahead and did it anyway. Why does everyone think there is a better way?"

"You're starting to sound like that voice calling out in the desert."

Startled, he unhooked the looking rock hanging from the notched post beside him and looked out. He moved it in and out trying to bring it into focus.

"What is it? You see something?"

"I don't believe it."

"What is it?" he said pawing for the looking rock.

"It can't be. It just can't be. We killed all of those years ago."

"What is it?" He couldn't stand it any longer. He grabbed the looking rock out of his hands. "Give me that!" His eyes throbbed, scanning the valley. "It can't be. It can't be! What are we going to do?"

"Send the trolls at the bottom. We must kill him fast and pray Slithler never finds out about it."

He opened up a small copper tube that ran all the way down the 15,000-foot drop, and rang the outpost command on the valley floor at the base of the cliff. Three gogs looked at each other and then one finally stood up and walked over.

"Yeah, what is it?" answered a gog in the middle of a game of bones.

He listened, "Yeah, yeah, yeah, what? Impossible! We killed all of those years ago."

He slammed the tube shut, grabbed up the bones and tossed them across the table. He studied the bones and picked up three.

Another gog picked up a mug of thunder juice and guzzled it down. He wiped his face and burped loud and long. A muscled gog with a big, shiny metal helmet and armor covering his body, entered the room and walked behind the table.

"What was that about?" asked the gog, commander of the valley guard.

"Oh, nothing." He pointed upward and said, "That idiot said he thought he saw a wooly in the valley."

The table looked at each other and erupted with laughter. They fell backwards in their chairs, kicking their feet in the air.

"What did you say?" barked the commander, grabbing him up by the throat and thrusting him against the wall.

With a somber look in his eyes he choked, "He…said he saw a wo…wooly."

The commander threw him against the adjacent wall, knocking his helmet off—it rolled all the way across the room and stopped at the feet of his companions. He walked outside and glowered over the valley, the dark valley, the valley controlled by the shadow of death—the valley where sunlight had not shone for hundreds of years. Suddenly it lit up, blinding the battalion of trolls and thousands of Slithler's servants guarding the South gate entrance.

He ran down the steps and mounted his Magondrea. He pulled back on the reins, lifting the beast off its two front feet. "Form ranks and follow me. Something's not right!" he shouted. Gogs ran inside the armory and handed out shields, swords and spears. Others saddled Magondreas and prepared for battle. Hundreds of gogs and trolls filtered out of the caves along the base of the cliff and mounted Magondreas, crawlers and thunder beasts. Others walked behind, all dressed in heavy armor ready for war.

The battalion, tired of no action, beat their shields and roared. They marched out across the valley toward the light, looking for a fight. All eyes squinted to see through the immense light piercing through the darkness, exposing their hideous forms. Anxious hands tapped swords, eager at the chance to use them on a massive army approaching from an unknown or distant land.

"Commander, do you see anything?" rang a voice from the ranks.

The commander continued to stare blindly into the light. He dismounted and took several steps toward the light and then abruptly stopped.

A small white wooly with seven horns and seven eyes walked out of the light, looking as if it had been slain. It looked at the beasts gathered for battle, as laughter and disappointment filled the valley.

A large troll japed loudly, "Commander, do you need us to protect you from the savage beast? You better sound the retreat before he kills us all."

Laughter dynamited up and down the ranks again.

His face remained steadfast. "Hold your tongues, before I cut every last one of them out and eat them myself!" fumed the commander, knowing Slithler would find out about this and have his head.

The large loudmouth troll walked toward the wooly and drew his sword. "Here commander, let me protect you from his deadly sharp hoofs before he rises up and beats you to death with them," he said.

As he approached the wooly, his heart raced. He felt something. Something sharp and smooth moved quickly across his belly. He looked down and watched his legs fall one direction and his upper body fall the other.

Mouths zipped across the line.

A sharp, double-edged tongue came from the wooly's mouth, so fast the naked eye could only glimpse a glimmer of its shiny silver blade of judgment.

The wooly walked toward the commander and stopped a few feet from him. The commander raised his blade as the wooly spoke to the bones scattered across the valley floor.

"Rise; rise my children. Show yourselves now and believe in me. Comfort and mercy from your afflictions—*I give you life!*"

Bones rattled all across the ground. A massive earthquake struck The Sea Throne dislodging its foundations and sinking it into the sea. Towers broke off and torpedoed into the sides opening large holes that poured lava inside, melting floors and ceilings. Serpents and beasts ran, trying to escape the falling debris and lava. Mageddon rose from his seat and flew for the window. Pieces of ceiling and columns beat upon his back as he weaved through the hailstorm, making his escape.

The colosseum vibrated. Seats crumbled and statues fell as columns broke off and spiked into the dirt below. On the floor, the silver door, imprinted with the face of Mageddon, rattled over the pit, stretching the lock.

Mageddon flew over the colosseum and yelled, "Secure the door! Secure the door!"

Hundreds of servants dove through the air, piling on top of the door. The door bent up, sucked back in and then burst open, launching Mageddon's servants out of the colosseum and into the sea. A large column of millions and millions of souls poured out of the hole. The column climbed high into the sky and headed straight for the valley of bones.

With the battalion looking on, bones flew in every direction. Phalanges connected to tarsal's; tarsal's to tibia's; tibia's to femur's; femur's to pelvis's; pelvis's to vertebrae's; vertebrae's to ribs; phalanges to ulna's; ulna's to humerus'; humerus' to clavicles; clavicles to skulls. Cells molecularized; tendons and tissue formed; blood cells and veins threaded; muscle, skin and hair grew. The column of souls reached the valley and poured down into the lifeless bodies.

With the breath of life in its lungs, the wooly opened his mouth and blew across the valley causing the bodies to open their eyes. They looked at the wooly and came to attention. The wooly rose up on its hind legs and proclaimed, "I am the resurrection and the life: He that believes in me, though he were dead, yet shall he live: And whosoever lives and believes in me will never die. Do you believe?"

The bodies, numbering in the millions, shouted, "We believe! We believe!"

The white wooly dropped back to all fours, turned around and looked at the battalion of trolls and yelled, "Attack!"

* * * * * * *

The Southern Celestial Guard watched Viper, the lava beast, drawing nigh. They formed ranks and awaited Miaphas' orders.

"Miaphas," yelled Atrokus, "What do you want us to do?"

"Fall back, and wait for the signal."

"Fall back?" questioned Oxymus. "We must attack now, before he destroys everyone and flattens Thunder Juice."

"The Plumb Line approaches," said Miaphas, secure in his command. "We will obey His Majesty's orders and wait for the signal. Fall back to the temple. We must protect the remnant."

Hearts bellowed, bodies protested, minds rampaged, pushing beyond the limits of faith. Man, creature and beast rabid with fear, ran through town, disoriented and confused. The Shadow of Death moved across the wall, concealing Thunder Juice Town in darkness.

Viper stopped outside the wall. A foreboding look shot up from Slithler, "Break them. Tear down their proud walls, return everything to ash, crush the temple—leave no survivors." Viper looked at the temple and roared.

Temple servants climbed the towers, and lit the liberty torches. Chestnut rays beamed through the Shadow of Death, lancing his grip on the temple. Viper tore open the wall, unleashing Slithler's dark army upon the town. Thousands of crawlers, howlers, magondreas, moogles, trolls and gogs charged through the opening, spilling into the town.

Viper flattened everything in his path in his procession to the temple. Screams reverberated down the streets from the worshippers of Ra that had stayed in their houses hopelessly praying to a blind, deaf, and mute god. They were cut down in their hiding places and their houses burned.

Traegor and the outer courts glared in disbelief watching Viper and the army approach. "Draw swords; ready the archers; steady the catapults!" he shouted, staring evil in the face.

Viper spewed lava on the wall surrounding the temple, opening a large gap in its side. Miaphas and his army waited for the signal. Ready to attack, they stood patiently in obedience to The Augur. Traegor, unaware of Miaphas and his army, for they had not shown themselves to him, stared motionless at the evil descending upon the temple. The front line watched lava trickle down the stone wall exposing them to the evil outside. Traegor ran to the front line and yelled, "*Until the last breath!*" as the sky flooded with arrows, spears, and rocks. Hundreds jolted back, struck by courage, courage unknown to Slithler's forces, as servants clashed with the enemy rushing through the breached wall.

Vines weaved through the battle and wrapped around their legs, pulling them into The Redmadafa, as Bugler fish and other river creatures torpedoed out of the water slamming them from every direction.

"Traegor, the line is giving way. There's too many of them," yelled Oka, the Plant King.

"Hold the line Oka, we must hold the line."

Mushrooms piled into baskets and catapulted over the wall. They sacrificed themselves by releasing a toxic cloud of poison in the air, inflaming throats and choking others.

Viper broke through the wall, crushing both armies mercilessly under his feet. He crossed the courtyards and punched the temple over and over, breaking off numerous towers.

Urium flew into the temple, through the chapel, down the hallway, and up the stairs searching for Caboose. Rounding the corner he found him standing in Onuka's chamber, helping him gathering the rest of his things. The room shook violently each time Viper struck the temple.

"Caboose, you must get in the tunnels now." Traegor can't hold them back much longer. The line is falling."

Caboose reached into his pocket and fished around for something. He searched all over…

"What are you looking for," asked Urium?

"The dragon claws. They'll help Traegor and the others," he said, still searching his pockets. "I can't find them Urium, do you have them?"

With a puzzled look on his face, Urium replied, "Dragon claws? I don't know what you're talking about."

"What do you mean you don't know what I'm talking about?

The dragon claws you gave me. You know, '*pull them out, cast them about!*'"

"Caboose, I don't know what you're talking about. I never gave you any dragon claws."

Confused Caboose grabbed him, "Of course you did. You gave me dragon scales to heal my wounds. You gave me dragon intestines to scale down Dead Man's Drop. You gave me dragon's blood to renew my strength and Seven gave me dragon claws to help fight for my friends."

Urium looked at Caboose and shook his head, "Caboose, I never gave you any of those things."

"But… I used them in the colosseum. What's going on? Urium, what's going on?"

Urium, realizing what had happened, smiled and affirmed, "What you experienced was not of this world. It was not by might, nor by power that The Augur helped you in the valley, it was by His Great Spirit. It was His power that delivered you from death. It was His power that renewed your strength. It was His power that gave you the courage to scale down the cliff at Dead Man's Drop. And it was His mighty hands that fought for you in the colosseum."

"His Spirit? I don't understand?"

"You will," said Urium. "After all of this is over and The Augur pours Him out, you will."

The ceiling above them cracked and buckled in the middle. Onuka and Caboose ran out of the room as it caved-in and they raced down the hallway, dodging falling debris. Stairs crumbled beneath their feet as they headed for the tunnels, causing Onuka to fall to the ground, pinning him underneath a wood beam.

"Keep going," said Onuka, "You have to make it."

Caboose, didn't listen. He grabbed the beam and lifted with all his might but it was too heavy. He looked for something to give him leverage, but found nothing.

Rinox appeared at the top of the stairs, which was collapsing, and jumped. He landed on the stairs, which had partially collapsed behind Caboose, and swayed back, about to fall into the gap that had opened up. Rinox teetered back just as Caboose grabbed his arm pulling him to safety.

"You must get into the tunnels. The wall has fallen and crawlers and trolls have already entered the sanctuary."

Rinox and Caboose lifted the beam off of Onuka and turned to run, just as a troll dropped down on Rinox thrusting him to the ground. Rinox' stood up and stabbed it in the side with his horn. The troll jumped back on Rinox and pinned him to the ground again. Caboose jumped on its back rolling it off Rinox and down the stairs—Caboose rolled out of the way just as the troll slammed against the door, blocking their route. Rinox followed suit and rammed it again before it could get up, stabbing it in the stomach. He moved the large troll out of the way with his powerful neck muscles leaving a crack large enough for them to squeeze through.

Crawlers oozed down the sides, scampering to join the fight. They spewed webs from their mouths but missed, as Rinox, Caboose, and Onuka squeezed through the crack and ran down the hallway to the hidden door leading to the tunnels. Onuka counted the torches on the wall as he ran by and then reached up and pulled a torch holder that looked like the talons of an eagle. He twisted it around to the right once and then to the left twice.

"Were not going to make it!" yelled Caboose, waiting for the door to open.

"Go," said Rinox, "I'll hold them off." He wheeled around and charged the crawlers ramming them against the wall. Their hairy legs beat against his back as they spit webbing all over him trying to free themselves. Trapped, he looked back at Caboose and yelled, "Close the door! Close the door now!"

Caboose hesitated at the door. "You can make it Rinox. You can make it." Onuka pulled him in and closed the door as Rinox said, "You're the one Caboose—*until the last breath.*"

The door closed. Rinox backed up, roared, and slammed the sides of the walls as hard as he could. The crawlers turned to escape his fury, but it was too late. The ceiling caved crushing all of them beneath the rubble.

Outside, Viper blasted the temple. He hit it over and over, spewing lava from his mouth, melting the walls, caving-in the sides. The temple crumbled under his blows and struggled to maintain its foundations.

Over the horizon, the earth delegations approached the outer walls of Thunder Juice Town. Rocks, trees, plants, beasts, creatures and humans marched through the holes in the walls and raced through the Eastern streets to the temple valiantly fighting along the way. Arsonon broke from the fight and found Legion standing outside the temple wall, observing the destruction inside.

"Reinforcements have arrived from the East. What should we do?"

"Take the second battalion and strike them head-on. Divide the third, and flank them from both sides. Don't let them reach the temple."

Atrokus and the rest of the Northern celestial guard remained hidden over the temple, covered in a protective invisible shield keeping their presence unknown. Atrokus left the shield and flew over to Miaphas who was in the middle of the garden protecting key individuals His Majesty had ordered to stay alive. "Miaphas, they've arrived," said Atrokus. "Look, Zoma is leading the charge."

Stumpy, perched high in a tree given orders to those on the ground, yelled down at Traegor, "Traegor, look; our friends, they fight for us. They fight for us!"

"It's too late. They'll never make it to us in time. Have everyone climb the trees."

Stumpy looked at him awkwardly.

"Just do it, and hurry Stumpy. We're running out of time."

Traegor broke from the fight and ran through the outer courts. He jumped over dead bodies and ran up and over a magondrea and then under a crawler slicing its belly with his claws. He jumped on top of a gog and broke its neck with his paws. Dozens of howlers pursued him trying to reclaim his life. Traegor ran into the middle of The Redmadafa, spun around and called out:

> "*Mighty river*
> *Cumber and red,*
> *Rise from your slumber,*
> *Protect us from the dead!*"

Spikes rippled across the water. Rumbles filled the air, shaking the temple mount and all of Thunder Juice Town, as The Redmadafa erupted high into the sky. A tidal wave ripped into the outer courts flooding it, drowning Slithler's army instantly. Others struggled to stay afloat as wave after wave pummeled them.

Leviathan lunged around the bend and entered the outer courts plucking beasts out of the water like mushy marts being gobbled up by younglings.

A large column of water, shaped like a hand, thrust from the river and punched Viper knocking him off his feet and into the temple. Viper stood up and spewed lava but The Redmadafa was too powerful. It punched him again, sending Viper crashing back into the temple mount—or what was left of it.

In the middle of the river, a whirlpool opened. Viper fought violently, punching at the water and clawing at the temple, but the more he struggled the further he sank beneath its torrent. Viper disappeared beneath the majestic, red waters, extinguishing his flames, quenching his fury.

The water receded from the outer courts, revealing the aftermath. Traegor and the remaining temple servants looked around in disbelieve. Slithler's army had been swept away by Leviathan and the waters of The Redmadafa, but the war was far from over. The temple lay in shambles—its massive walls left unsecure and gapped. The beautiful botanical gardens, sculptures, porticos and cisterns all destroyed, ruined by the pride and disobedience of man.

Stumpy and the remaining army climbed down from the trees.

"Secure the wall. Hurry before they attack again," ordered Traegor.

The courtyard came to life again with trees, plants, and rocks using their bodies for supports to close and seal up the gaps in the walls. The remaining delegates from earth assembled inside the walls and laid out new battle plans.

Legion, turned to Slithler and snarled, "What now Master?"

"Unleash the Shadow of Death. They have foolishly played all their cards. Finish them off; don't leave any survivors."

Legion pulled out a dragon's horn and blew. His army gathered around the temple walls and waited.

* * * * * * *

Inside the tunnels, the people were puzzled. They did not know what had happened outside. The sudden quietness, which should have brought a sense of calm and subtle peace, turned deathly peculiar. The noise outside had stopped. Ears twitched and listened, wondering if it was over. Speculation filtered through the tunnel, was it over? Were they safe? Conclusions were dim, dangling faith by a thread.

Caboose walked down the tunnels, attending the sick, looking for his mother and sister.

"Young grunter, did you just come from outside?" asked an old frail voice sheeplessly tucked away in a corner.

Caboose stopped and acknowledged the elderly woman, comforting her, reassuring her everything would be alright. By the time he had finished talking, another voice reached out to him.

"Koby?" This time a young human girl addressed him. "Is that you?"

He focused on her face—her voice unfamiliar.

"It's me, Brook."

Her face looked different—better—alive. "Wow, you look different. Good. I mean, you look *really* good." I didn't think she knew me especially my real name, he thought.

Brook began to cry. She stood up and wrapped her arms around him. "It *is* you. It's so good to see you." She stepped back from him for a moment and looked him over and then hugged him again. "You're alive. You're alive."

Caboose was at a loss for words. He hugged her back and smiled. "Are you ok? I mean, is everything alright?"

"It is now. Your Papa, have you seen your Papa?"

Caboose drew his face, puzzled that she was asking such a strange question. "Yes, I have seen him. How…"

She interrupted him, "How is he? Is he ok?"

Puzzled he asked, "You know my Papa?"

Brook dropped her eyes and straightened her shirt. "I…left home several months ago and found this gate."

His chest heaved.

"I was in the middle of this tree about to drop my last silver coin into a stone when your Papa came busting through the door, knocking the coin out of my hand, yelling at me to never touch it again. At first, I thought he was crazy. He explained to me that he had been there before, and how it was all a lie. Anyway, long story short, He saved my life. How is he?"

Caboose stood in shock. He didn't know how to tell her his father was dead. He searched his thoughts and rubbed his hands. "Brook, my Papa is…dead. He gave his life, protecting me in the pit."

She froze. Tears welled up in her eyes and rolled down her rosy red cheeks, full of color and life. "I'm sorry. I'm so sorry." She thought for a moment and then replied, "A rainbow. Your Papa was a rainbow of many colors."

Caboose never expected to hear his Papa described so, colorfully.

"He was a great man. He changed my life and the life of my family forever."

Brook, remembering what Chesty said about a song coming from the heart, stood up and to ease the tension in the tunnels, sang:

Yellow is a golden crown
Of precious jewels placed all around,
That someday I will lay at his feet.

Green is the breath of life
Carried by the wind,
Whispering his name for all the earth to hear.

Purple adorns His Majesty
The proof that he made all things,
I am now a child of the King of Kings.

I thank you Lord, for blessing me abundantly;

I can see the many colors
The colors of the rainbow
Shining brightly way up in the sky.
Red, blue, yellow, purple and green

A promise made for eternity,
A promise that we can all be free
A promise that, I was made to do Great Things.

Blue is an ocean
Waving in the distance,
Guiding me through the storms of life.

Red is the crimson flow
That reminds me of my savior,
And the blood that he shed for you and me.

I thank you Lord, for blessing me abundantly;

I can see the many colors
The colors of the rainbow
Shining brightly way up in the sky
Red, blue, yellow, purple and green
A promise made for eternity,
A promise that we can all be free,
A promise that, I was made to do Great Things.

Outside, atop one of the broken statues, a small mushroom began to drum vigorously. He jumped down and ran through the ranks, pushing his way to Traegor. Climbing up his leg and across his spiky back, he whispered in his ear. Traegor whirled around and climbed back up a tree. His formidable eyes scanned the eastern mouth of the mountains. His heart bubbled and his tongue rejoiced, his body tingling with joy. With a strength that transcends understanding he shouted:

"Behold, The White Wooly! The precious Lamb of God!"

CHAPTER 15

THE SHADOW OF DEATH

Death, where is thy sting? Grave, where is thy victory?

AURRRRRRRRRRRRRRRRRRRR!!!!!!!!!!!! The Redmadafa vibrated, its waters rippled with thousands of Bugler Fish sounding their trumpets, rupturing the eardrums of Slithler's cryptic army. Trees snapped, water clapped and rocks tapped. Mushrooms drummed, flowers hummed and grasses strummed. Glory shone, praise rejoiced, jubilee danced, and victory shouted!

The Southern Celestial guard stood at attention, their hearts and minds backwashing with memories of times past, waiting for justice to smite its evil enemy. Miaphas' eyes glossed with the sight of White; he had waited faithfully for the signal. With victory in his voice and triumph filling the air, he towered into the sky, and as the invisible shield fell revealing the Southern celestial guard, he prophetically proclaimed:

> *"A trick for the trickster,*
> *A cross for the dross.*
> *His death has brought life,*
> *Now your head he shall smite!"*

Weakness turned to strength; despair to hope. Temple servants climbed anything still standing, to see The White Wooly. Around the mountain ridge, glory and honor appeared, leading captives in his train—an army too numerous to count: the souls of those that had died in the valley, now free, paid for by an *Eternal Fee*.

"Traegor, what do you want us to do?" asked the mushroom clinging atop his shoulder."

He searched his thoughts and replied, "This is a new story. The old is gone and the new unfolds. With The White Wooly for us, how can anyone stand against us?" He turned and scowled at the enemy, while giving his final orders with a raised voice. "We wait. The White Wooly is not what you think it is."

Slithler's blood shot to the top of his head. "Impossible!" he shouted, screaming at Legion. "I thought you killed all of them!"

Legion stood speechless. He moved away from Slithler fearing his wrath. "Secure the East Gate. Man the walls. Don't let him step one foot back into this town!"

Slithler's army panicked. Swords turned on each other, cutting and slashing anything around them. Beasts, delirious at his site, tore through town fighting and destroying themselves. Slithler ascended into the air, trying to gain control of his forces. Confused, he flew to the East Gate and landed in front of The

White Wooly. Legion sounded the dragon's horn, stopping the frenzy and re-establishing order. They quickly maneuvered through the streets and scattered across the wall. Both man and beast, watched and listened.

Slithler kept his distance. Years of injustice, debts, pain and sorrow swept before him. A small bloodstain soaked The Wooly's side. A voice…a voice that sounded like the rushing of a mighty river, resounded from his sharp double-edged tongue:

"It is finished, the fee has been paid." He looked straight into Slithler's eyes and with full authority he triumphantly said, "You are trespassing on my land. You are standing on Holy Ground. Remove thy self at once or you and all your forces will suffer the full extent of my wrath."

"Legion!" shouted Slithler. "Cut to pieces anyone that leaves his post. The fee has not been paid. It will never be paid until I am standing atop the fiery stones, with the head of His Majesty in my hands."

Slithler shook violently, his serpent skin boiled and bubbled, collapsing-in on itself until only a pile of ashes remained, while his army gaped and hissed. From the ashes, a small red creature stretched and grew. Growing and growing, the puppet master emerged revealing his true identity. Mageddon, the seven-headed red dragon, formed from the black ash.

"I am the heir to His Majesty's throne. I was anointed and ordained to sit on the fiery stones. You! You cast me from his presence. You blocked my way and took away my place of authority."

His heads twisted toward the wall and the Northern Celestial Guard, "The Augur stands before you. Kill him! Kill him now! Take back what is rightfully ours."

All seven heads erupted, bathing The White Wooly in a molten flame of fire. Mageddon's forces attacked. Thousands of them flew over the wall toward The Augur. Miaphas raised the ram's horn to his lips and blew, signaling Atrokus, who was waiting with the Southern Celestial Guard in the broken remains of the temple. He flanked Mageddon and his army.

Gogs, thunder beasts, crawlers, trolls and every dark beast of Mageddon's army pleaded for their lives, running blindly for the mountains, groveling back to the murky holes from which they had crawled. The White Wooly's seven horns reached through the fire and grabbed each of Mageddon's heads rendering him powerless. Galamus, Atrokus and the rest of the Southern army surrounded his remaining forces, blocking all means of escape. Surrounded with nowhere to run or hide, the battle belonged to The Augur.

The White Wooly walked toward Mageddon, and as he did, his wool peeled off, revealing an Almighty Warrior Eagle. Miaphas landed beside The Augur, and taking a large silver chain, silver made from the dross of every coin that had ever been deposited in the stone, he bound Mageddon.

With all authority in heaven and on earth, The Augur exclaimed, "I am the way, the truth, and the life: no one comes to His Majesty, but by me. If you would have known me, you would have known His Majesty: For, *I Am His Majesty!*"

Mageddon's army cowered before His Majesty begging for mercy. "Miaphas," said His Majesty, "Take Mageddon and his army and cast them into the Abyss."

"Yes your Majesty."

"Seal it and place Cherub and a flaming sword over it. Justice has returned and filled his cup. My peace will inhabit this land once again.

* * * * * * *

Traegor, still atop the tree, watched the battle from afar. Behind him, the temple lay in ruin. Majestic towers that once reached into the sky, sparkling light and filled with splendor, now lay in shambles, destroyed by pride, bowing with the weight of disbelief. Mounds of rubble covered the sanctuary, trapping the temple members in the tunnels below.

Underneath the ruins, dusty eyes and eager ears opened, listening for any sounds of hope. Onuka, with the strength of others, pushed with all their might to open the tunnel door, but it wouldn't budge. Broken windows and ceiling, cried out beneath the rubble echoing up and down the tunnels.

"Mommy, are we going to die in here?" asked a little round face with long eye lashes filled with dust."

Her mother, scared and uncertain, brushed her battered fingers through her hair and squeezed her tight, "I don't know sweetheart. I don't know."

Caboose was exhausted. He sat by his mother and sister, too tired to think. Too tired to worry about what was going to happen. Frail whispers bounced from side-to-side. A small howler peaked out from a blanket, secure in a calm quietness that seemed to sooth hearts and minds. Faint sounds muffled outside. Stone's shattered and broke against each other. Traegor and all the others dug through the night trying to clear the massive mound of debris. But, their efforts were to no end. There was too much. The crumbled temple remains smothered the tunnels, holding the people hostage. Even with the help of the men and equipment from the mines, they were only able to clear a small amount of the mountain before them.

At dawn, a dark crimson, scarlet rose, candy apple, ruby red sun peaked over the eastern mountain-tops and slowly danced across the town. The stars dimmed as soft puffy clouds, floating just above the mountain ridge, lit-up in various shades of Purple Mountain Majesty. Brilliant shiny rays of life dawned upon long, drawn faces covered in black-soot and mud. At the temple, shovels, picks, and movers paused, thankful to be alive, thankful to have witnessed the redemption of the circle and to have fought on the side of justice.

Off in the distance, cutting through the clouds, a small figure appeared in the sky. An Almighty Warrior Eagle with powerful wings, long feathers and a full plumage of varied colors soared on the wings of justice. He circled the town along with the scattered remains of the temple, and then gently landed in the outer courts. Everyone bowed in his presence and worshipped him. He walked out into The Redmadafa at the base of the temple where the stairs once circled. Mangled stones and timbers covered the cleft rock from which headwaters had once flowed. He looked at the people and said:

> "Whoever drinks of this water, will never thirst; it will be in them a well of water springing up into everlasting life. Unless a kernel of wheat falls into the ground and dies, it remains alone: but if it dies, it brings forth much fruit. He that loves his life will lose it; and he that hates his life in this world will keep it for all eternity."

After he finished, he blew a mighty breath across the temple. Stone and timber, glass and marble all brushed away leaving the cleft and the altar. The cleft opened pouring living water down The Redmadafa, bringing life and hope once more. Traegor ran across the slab, past the altar and down the stairs to the tunnel.

Inside, they heard the commotion. Men and beast drew their swords ready for battle. Onuka, concerned it was Slithler's army, pushed everyone further into the tunnels. The door swung open as silver blades greeted Traegor with trembles of delight.

"It's me, don't be alarmed," said Traegor noticing the fear in their eyes. "It's over; it's all over." Onuka looked back and joyfully shouted down the tunnels. It's over. We've won!"

Shouts of praise and thanksgiving permeated throughout the tunnels. Little children whirled in the air, spun by their parents, who quickly pulled them in their arms squeezing them tight.

"It's over. The hand of The Augur has delivered us. He's defeated the great serpent," said Rooter, tossing Jambles up in the air.

"Come. Come quickly. For your redemption is near. He awaits you now," said Traegor greeting every face that emerged from the door.

Weary, war-torn faces filtered from the tunnel and up the steps to the altar. Sprightly eyes squinted as heads swept the town. Fires still lingered across town. Small, dark plumes of smoke drifted up from the ashes of several businesses and homes. Onuka lifted his head in disbelief. Where was everything? Where was the temple? he wondered. He walked across the altar and collapsed at his feet. The Augur stood atop the altar, counting each face, calling out each name. One-by-one the people came and bowed before him, marveling at his majestic splendor. With a still, calm voice he said:

"I am the true vine and His Majesty is the gardener. Every branch that does not bear fruit will be cut: and every branch that bears fruit he will prune, so it will produce an abundance. I am the vine, you are the branches: He that remains in me will do Great Things.

You are now clean. For without me you can do nothing. If you remain in me and I in you, ask what you will, and it will be done. As His Majesty has loved me, so have I loved you; continue to love one another. These things I have spoken, that my joy might remain in you, and be full."

Onuka listened, quietly observing the crowd. He rose from the ground. "Your Majesty, we will build it back, brick for brick, stone for stone."

The Augur pointed to the stone—the cleft stone standing in the mist of the outer court:

"The stone that the builders rejected has now become the chief corner stone. I will no longer dwell in buildings built by the hands of men. My Spirit will now enter your hearts and will write my commandments within. For creation itself, bears witness of my glory and my children will forever sing my praise. Ask of me and I will give the nations on your behalf. For wherever two or three are gathered together, there will I be."

After he finished, he breathed on the crowd.

Pepper clutched her mother's hand, her eyes beholding a wondrous site. Standing beside the wall, looking over the crowd, Chesty, her Papa, searched for them. Pepper stood up and with tears streaming down her face cried out, "Papa! It's Papa!"

Mrs. Puller stood in shock as Pepper pushed her way through the crowd overcome with a flood of emotion and thanksgiving.

She ran and fell into his arms. One-by-one, shouts rung out from the crowd as loved ones returned to their families, saved by the sacrifice of The Augur—The Augur wept.

Caboose walked across the stones of the remaining foundation to the altar and bowed before The Augur. He had many questions, many unanswered puzzles still floating around in his mind, but now he had a peace that strengthened him, allowing him to trust in a divine power far greater than anything he had ever known before.

"Forgive me your Majesty. I was mad at you for making me different. I didn't understand that that was your plan for my life; your plan to help me find the truth and finally solve the False Triad. I didn't realize that your love is greater than my pain and your wisdom beyond my understanding."

The Augur laughed. "My strength is made perfect in weakness, young grunter." With Onuka standing beside Caboose, The Augur reached out and touched Caboose. In front of the whole assembly, he proclaimed:

"That which is short will now be the same;
you wise grunter will no longer live in shame.
For from this day forth, 'Petra' they will exhale;
And upon this rock I will build my church,
And the gates of hell will not prevail."

Caboose felt a strange tingle flush through his body; it ran from his head all the way down to his feet, stretching his leg, healing him completely. Caboose jumped from side-to-side and then ran around the altar shouting, "I'm healed. I've been healed!" He ran and tackled Onuka who was standing beside the altar with tears of joy streaming down his broad, black face. Caboose knelt down on the ground and with his arms raised up to the sky he shouted, "Hallelujah! Hallelujah!" to the Ancient of Days.

The Ancient of Days:

When darkness comes, I shall not fear,
Because I know that he is near.
He's waiting for me to proclaim,
That name which is above all other names.

Because in that moment and in that hour,
He shall deliver me by his power;
And forever will I give him praise,
The One: The Only: The Ancient of Days.

The crowd, with one voice and as one people, raised their voice and sang, "Hallelujah, Hallelujah. Hallelujah, Hallelujah. Hallelujah, Hallelujah. Hallelujah, Hallelujah."

The remnant watched The Augur ascend into the sky—his plumage in full color: his wings brushing the horizon. Caboose stood confused. He did not understand what The Augur meant. Onuka walked over to him, and with a face smiling bigger than a rainbow, despite the destruction of his beautiful temple, he rested his arm on his shoulder—which stood a little taller.

Caboose looked at Onuka and then turned his head back high. He watched The Augur fade into the big blue sky and asked, "What just happened, Onuka? What did that mean?"

Onuka, with great excitement in his voice replied, "From this day forth, your name will no longer be Koby or 'Caboose.' You will now be known as 'Petra,' and you will take my place as High

Priest and lead this remnant into its future. Generation upon generation will look back to you, Petra, as the founding Father of a new covenant. A covenant bought and paid for by the blood of The Augur."

Petra stood speechless. He didn't know how to respond. He couldn't believe The Augur would choose him to carry his Word to all nations. "Does this mean my dreams of becoming a racer and winning 'The Little Round About,' are over?"

Onuka, lifted his eyes toward the sky and said, "Can you see where the blue ends?"

Petra looked into the air and into the beyond. "It's impossible to see that far," he answered.

"So are his plans for you Petra. There are no limits to what he has planned for you."

Onuka turned toward Petra and took him by the hands, "I am here to help you in any way I can. All that I have," he paused and looked around at the crumbled remains and laughed, "Or did have, is now yours. The ancient scrolls, the sacred objects, all of them are now in your charge. Great Things you will now go and do."

Chesty stood behind them listening. He dropped to his knees and with tears trickling down his face, he said, "Thank you Great Augur. Thank you for allowing me to see this day. I love you. I… love…you."

Petra, recognizing his Papa's voice, spun around and fell into his arms. They embraced each other, while Chesty kissed him over and over and over on his head.

Later that night, Petra walked into the front room. His Papa sat beside Pepper watching her draw a picture of The Augur while his mother quietly cleaned around the house. Petra looked at his

Papa and then walked back to his room and sat down on his bed. Chesty rose from the floor and rounded the corner. Petra looked up from his bed. "The Augur told me I would see you again."

Chesty didn't say anything. He just smiled.

"What happened to you in the colosseum? Did he save you before they could throw your soul into the pit?"

Chesty stepped inside and shut the door. He sat down by Petra and scooted to the edge. "I felt the blade pierce my back. I felt death clawing through my body, waging war against the life within. I remember seeing your face and hearing your cry after I called out His Name but The Shadow of Death moved over me quickly. I tried to run and hide; we all tried to run, but he was powerful—I was scared. But, down deep inside, I knew some-how, someway, The Augur would not abandon me to the pit.

After the battle, the door to the pit swung open. Thousands, upon thousands, millions upon millions of screams shot up, cry-ing for one drop of water to quench their thirst. They cried and begged for mercy but there was no one to help."

Chesty paused.

"All were down there; rich and poor, king and queen; women and men; beast and creature. All who had never called upon The Augur or believed in His Name. The Shadow of Death knew me. Right before he threw me in, he raised me to his face. I looked into his eyes,"

Chesty paused again. His voice struggled... "Eyes of death... eyes of despair...eyes of murder, strife and envy—Eyes of..." Chesty looked up, "Unforgiveness."

He laughed a vulgar haunting laugh and spit into my face. He cast me through the hole and slammed the door shut. Below me, a river of fire stretched so far my eyes could scarcely hold it.

Millions of hands reached out and grabbed at me, grabbed at all of us. They tried to pull us into the fire.

We ran.

We hid behind rocks.

We climbed the ceiling and tried to open the door.

We ran through caves looking for a slight glimmer of hope.

But there was no escape. There was no hope. All was lost.

Dark Demons chased us through the tunnels. They hunted us down through long dark shafts laden with thorny spikes. They threw us against the walls and floors, impaling our souls over and over on the spikes. They beat and tormented us night after night. I heard my name."

Chesty started to cry. He put his hands over his ears and continued.

"People from Thunder Juice Town; people I knew but had never told them about The Augur. They cursed me, over and over—they attacked me. 'Why didn't you tell us? Why didn't you tell us the truth…*Elder*?' The demons mocked me; they mocked us all. And the thirst—I was thirsty, so thirsty."

Petra watched each subtle expression of his Papa's face. He could see the agony deep within as he retold the story. But he was proud—proud to be his son and proud to be a "Puller."

But, then the ground began to shake. A bright light passed through the pit door and descended into the depths of the abyss forcefully landing in the middle of the river, splitting it in two. Blood dripped from his side into the river releasing our souls. A White Wooly stood in the middle of the river and said:

'I am the way, the truth, and the life. No one comes to His Majesty except through Me!"

The door of the pit shook violently. It burst open just as he said:

"Follow me and I will give you living water. Drink of it and you will never thirst again!"

Petra listened carefully, his ears soaked up every word, every emotion—he couldn't get enough. "Well, what happened?" he asked.

Chesty looked at him with a sharp uncertain look on his face, "What do you think happened? That place cleared out like darkness escaping from morning's light. We got out of there as fast as we could!"

Petra sat there running visions of that moment through his mind. He knew there must be a reason why his Papa was sharing this with him.

"Wow. Papa, wherever He takes me, wherever I go, I will make sure this great big circle knows the truth: The truth that there is no other way to His Majesty except through the sacrifice of his son—The Augur.

Petra stood up, walked over to his desk and took out a writing pad. He thought for a moment and then wrote:

"Blessed be His Majesty, Father of The Augur. According to his great mercy he has given us new birth into a lively hope by the resurrection of The Augur from the dead, and into an incorruptible and undefiled inheritance that cannot fade away, kept in heaven for you, who are kept by the power of His Majesty's through faith unto salvation ready to be revealed in the last time."

* * * * * * *

He marched through the mountains and turned at the fork. With a flicker in his eye, he scoured the switchback. Down the gorge he moved with stealth, before splintering into the draws, melting the fog. Up the jagged walls he climbed with fame; today was his day, the valley was about to change forever. Over the shattered remains of Mount Viper he sprang his trap, soaring across the valley, with victory on his face. No longer would his glorious light be kept at bay. Over fingers and under cliffs; in ravines and through the tunnels he searched. He even dove to the bottom of the Dead Sea—he gawked, he gazed, he asserted himself.

"Come out, come out, wherever you are," he tantalized, standing outside Gravers cave.

Deep down in the cold dark cave his hideous form hid. Afraid and perplexed, he heard the echo, "Come out, come out, wherever you are." It followed every crevice; it searched every shaft. It hid under rocks, but it was all in vain.

"Shadow of death, reveal yourself cowered! I challenge thee; come, let us make war and display our power."

A monstrous growl roared exploding a hurricane-force wind from the mouth of the cave instantly freezing Sun, encasing him in a glacial tomb of ice. The Shadow of Death burst from his hiding place and collided with Sun, knocking him across the valley into the side of Mount Viper.

Deep underneath the mountain, in the smoldering remains of lava and caved tunnels, in a heavily fortified secret chamber, a dark red crystal standing in the middle of the room cracked from the impact. Inside the crystal tomb, behind the transparent rock, yellow eyes opened. The crystal rattled and shook. Rocks bounced off the ground and collided into each other. The crystal shattered into thousands of tiny pieces, covering the floor with a dark, rosy-red shine.

Beelzebub, the prince of demons, emerged from the tomb. He rose up, spread his wings, and shook off the remaining debris. He screeched out a blood curdling roar which shattered the outside wall, bursting sunlight into his dark chamber. With the sun beating down on his black red-striped face, he smiled, exposing ivory fangs that sparkled bright.

Mageddon had entombed him there hundreds of years earlier for insubordination and mutiny. Beelzebub had tried to overthrow Mageddon with several other fallen angels after King Ichabod sold his soul and the kings of the earth handed their land over to Mageddon. Grum, Mageddon's spy, had caught wind of the mutiny and alerted Mageddon of his plans. Mageddon ambushed him before his plot could unfold and entombed him in the depths of Mount Viper, where Viper kept watch over him, day and night. The rest of his followers were cast into the pit. They became the demons of the abyss and the tormentors of souls.

Sun shattered the ice around his body sending ice daggers shooting across the valley. He crushed Mount Viper with his heel and shouted, "Is that all you got, Shadow? You hit like fog in an early morning rain, retreating at my first rays."

He doubled his fist and swung his cyclopean arm of fire across the valley, striking Shadow up into the universe, smashing his dark form against the planet Milkxy, fragmenting it into trillions and trillions of pieces, creating the Milky Way Galaxy. Dazed, he recovered and hurtled large boulders from the explosion at Sun. Swallowing them with his body, Sun grew in strength and power.

Shadow spiraled into a black hole, concealing his body in its dark, bottomless chasm. Sun entered the black hollow fluxing slowly into its vortex. Shadow circled around him like a serpent coiling around its prey. He looped rapidly around Sun and then thrust out of the hole, launching Sun through the galaxy—his body scorched Mercury and Venus and disintegrated millions of stars.

Sun recovered. He shot around Jupiter and Saturn knocking Shadow into Uranus toppling it on its side. He pursued Shadow around the Milky Way spinning it around and around and around.

Shadow pressed into Orion's Arm and spun around, bombarding Sun with star clusters, meteors, and asteroids. Unfazed, Sun doused the barrage with rainbow beams exploding the massive boulders into tiny fragments that floated throughout the cosmos; each fragment sparkled with beautiful red, blue, yellow, purple, and green rays of light.

Sun clutched The Shadow of Death by his throat and pulled him close. "Your reign has come to an end Shadow. You will no longer suck the life from the ground nor will your darkness torment the inhabitants of the earth."

Shadow constricted his coils around Sun again, but Sun's light was too powerful; it pierced the darkness, chaining his body with thick bolts of lightning.

"This is not over Sun. The battle for earth may be lost, but the War of Souls is coming. When my power has been restored, we will meet again."

Hundreds of Cherubs and Seraphs circled around Shadow. They escorted his tightly bound body to the constellation of Musca, which lies South of the Southern Cross, and imprisoned him.

Sun slowly made his way back through the solar system and took his place back in its center. The earth, watching from afar, rotated, and for the first time in, a time, times and half a time, Sun rose over the valley displaying his merciful rays of life and hope upon its dry and parched surface. Defeated and his power locked away, The Shadow of Death could only watch with his evil eye in the center of Musca's nebula as Sun lit up the valley revealing a rainbow of a thousand colors.

The valley was no longer a valley of death and despair. It wondrously transformed into a valley of hope, teaming with an abundance of life. The land grew lush and green, vibrantly feeding and sustaining life for all its new inhabitants. Rain nourished the land from above. Magnificent clusters of flowers, bushes, trees and grass sprung from rich organic soil. Streams flowed down parched and dry riverbeds, ushering in cool life-giving water; Bugler fish followed in suit, as if leading a grand parade. They played harmonious hymns of praise up and down the banks, all of which spilled into an abundant fresh-water lake.

Beasts, from Mageddon's remaining army, crawled from hiding and regained their sanity. They drank from the water and ate from the abundance of the land. They lost their hatred of men and became one with the land, as harmony filled the valley once again. Peace sprouted, covering the land in spectacular green foliage, so thick and tall that thunder beasts could lie in shade under the lotus plant. Flowers of every kind bloomed, blanketing the valley with every color known to man. Trees, with their roots firmly secure under *The Redmadafa,* swayed in the wind. Grasses strummed their tunes to the beat of Mushrooms dancing merrily 'round-and-round' with Blossom Berries. Life was restored. Hope renewed. And Justice…well, He was just getting started.

* * * * * * *

From deep within the black Abyss, below the river of fire, a voice echoed brokenly:

> *I am happy, I am free,*
> *I'm in charge of my destiny.*
> *No more hurting, no more sob,*
> *Pass through me gate and become like God!*

I will have my vengeance! I will trample the fiery stones! I will return! I will return!

ECKELBESH!!!!!!!!!!!!!!!!!!!!!!!!!!!!!!

EPILOGUE

The Big Round About

*Lay aside everything that hinders and
run with patience
the race set before you.*

Junction Point filled with race huts, vendors, competitors and spectators—they spread out across the land like ants coming in from the savanna to devour a mushy mart cream pie. There was room for everyone. It didn't matter if you walked upright or on all four. It didn't matter if you swam, hopped, ran, walked, crawled, hobbled or soared; everyone was welcome—after all, it was the biggest race of the century.

The Wind Whistler swept through the valley with a cool breeze. The cold refreshing gust cooled the valley, causing small peaks to ripple across the arms of spectators all along the trail and up into the newly-built wooden stands held together by bamboo poles and twisted vines. Along the trail, freshly-bloomed red roses mixed with sharp shades of indigo. Each folded cup swayed gently in the cool breeze, which bore the fresh scent of spring. Fruit trees bloomed all across town and for miles along the banks of The Redmadafa. Women plucked off the lovely blooms and slid them behind their ears. Others made necklaces and placed them around necks as people exited the gates and ventured up the trail.

Thunder beasts, harnessed with chains around their necks, pulled logs up and down the trail next to the finish line making it smooth and level. Large trelaby's flew amongst the crowd, selling delicious rainbow treats of every color and flavor. Race officials returned from inspecting the trail and reported to Mike and Johnny. There was still one report missing—the report from Skull Tunnel. The race official was seen entering the tunnel but hadn't been seen since.

Off in the distance, through the race huts and colorful pennants flapping in the wind, a strange medium-sized figure bobbed up and down. Petra was so excited about being in the race that he floated through the air like a butterfly. He had thoughtfully put together a pre-race warm-up routine that he was certain would propel him past the other racers. But what he didn't realize was that it made him look like he was doing the funky chicken instead up warming up for a race; his head, shoulders, arms, feet, and legs swiveled around like a fall leaf being tossed around by the wind. He then proceeded to add jumping up and down, and swinging his arms like a mad man to his routine. Oka and Chesty remained inside the hut looking over the race map trying to calm their own nerves.

Brook and Rachael walked through the huts and spotted

Petra—in fact everyone had spotted Petra—he was hard to miss. In the last few weeks they had been joined at the hip—BFF's. Rachael had several sleepovers and Brook never missed a service at the Temple.

"Hey Petra…looking good. You ready for your big day?" said Brook, holding a large bag of blossom berry cotton candy in her hand. She twirled off a big blue piece and stuffed it in her mouth.

Rachael, sipping on a brumpel melon slushy, quietly waved. "Nice headband you got there."

"Thanks. You like you?" Petra had tried to make a rainbow headband but the colors all faded leaving it tie-dyed.

They both nodded their heads. "Oh yeah…It's…groovy."

They observed Petra for a moment and then several other competitors. "What are you doing?" asked Brook, with a strange look on her face.

Continuing his routine, Petra added in bending over and touching his hands to his feet. "I'm warming up. I need to get loose and stay loose."

Brook considered her words wisely. She reached up over her head and picked a couple of flowers off the tree and stuck them behind her ear and Rachael's. "That's quite a routine you've got there. Did you get that from the other competitors?" (implying that maybe he should watch the others and learn from them since this was all new to him) and the race officials had bent the rules to let him in—they were going to let him run in the race even though he hadn't qualified.

"Nope. I made it up myself. I call it, 'TDS 90,' short for 'The Dragon Strike.'" He struck a Kung Fu pose and raised his left brow.

"Oh…neat. That's creative," said Rachael, thinking it looked more like the 'TDF 90,' short for 'The Dragon Flop.' How's that working for you?"

Petra stopped and grabbed his back. He bent his head way back and pushed his lower back forward and sighed, "Not good. Maybe I need to do more spring thrusts." He squatted down crossing his arms and then jumped up uncrossing them.

Brook's eyes widened and her head tilted back. Trying not to laugh she said, "Now that's a good one…an original."

"You think so?" answered Petra breathing hard. "This is my secret move." He spun his head to the left and then to the right. "You don't see anyone looking, do you? I wouldn't want them to steal it."

"Steal it. No, I think you're good." Brook and Rachael looked at each other. "We have to go get a seat now. We'll see you later."

"Good luck…see you at the finish line!" waved Rachael.

He didn't say anything. He just waved and nodded his head— he was in 'The Zone!'

Mike and Johnny floated above the starting line in their leaf hut, carried by four flying trelaby hummers. Mike looked out over the field of contestants, his heart filled with compassion. Johnny looked over and gently placed his arm around him.

"Moving."

"What?" responded Mike, looking back at him with tears in his eyes.

"It's moving…so many, so happy, so…free. We are blessed to have witnessed what happened here.

"The Augur did a Great Thing," said Mike.

"He sure did. He sure did."

Johnny leaned over and grabbed the sea shell. "Beasts, creatures, and humans welcome to the 50th 'Big Round About.' Competitors from all over the circle have come to watch Trax

"The Cat" Louise defend his title against some the strongest, fastest runners on the circle."

"Johnny, I've never seen a more fit and even field before in all my life."

"You can say that again, Mike. This will be the biggest race ever. If you're not in this race, then nothing else will ever matter."

"Johnny, there's a lot of new faces out there. I think we're in for an upset."

"Mike, in this race, the odds are in favor of the long shot. I'm going to keep my eyes on the no names, those we know nothing about."

"Yeah, like that kid from Jasmine Crossing. I hear his family lost everything in a fire and had to rebuild from scratch."

"Absolutely Mike."

"Or, what about the new girl who gave up her young'un?"

"Mike, I heard she got help from the temple servants and has started over. I heard a smile has returned to her face and that she's been helping out on Sun Day with the little ones."

"Johnny, with so much hope and love spreading across the circle, how could anyone stay discouraged?"

Coach was so excited he didn't know what to do. He scrambled through his bag and then ran over to Rammer. He pulled out a long piece of white, sticky fabric and wrapped it around his left ankle.

"There how's that?"

Rammer stood up. He walked around and then jumped up and down shaking his legs out.

"Great." Rammer looked at coach's hands—they shook wildly. "Are you alright? I thought I was the one that was supposed to be nervous."

"Nervous." Coach held out his hands—they vibrated. "Just excited, that's all. Just excited…Now remember, in Crooked Creek Pass there's a lot of loose gravel. As you approach the turn, keep to the left inside corner; it will keep you in-line coming out of the turn and keep you from going over the edge. Watch the loose gravel in the turns and—"

"Coach, I remember, you told me this last year."

"I'm just making sure. Rammer, you can beat him, but you must believe that you can beat him."

"Coach, I've already beat him. I've already beat them all."

Coach looked at him with a puzzled look as he tossed the white fabric back in the bag.

Rammer pointed into the crowd. "Do you see him? There, in the red shirt."

Coach looked into the crowd and there, standing on the front row, was Rooter. "I see him. Your Dad is here."

"Yeah." With confidence in his voice and a smile longer than the rainbow shining up above, Rammer boasted, "Like I said coach, I've already won. Trax doesn't stand a chance. Do you think that's cheating? I could have him move back a few rows."

Coached laughed and grabbed Rammer in his arms. "If it was anyone else, I would say no. But in your case, I think I'll need to check the rule book." He rubbed him on the head and pushed him out the door. "Now, get out there and show'em kid."

The front line moved as close to the line as they could get. Heads bobbed up and down in the middle and at the rear.

"Ok, whipper snappers, shut your yappers, and open your flappers," said the old shellback hobbling out in front of the starting line.

"You are standing on the start and the finish line. This is a one-lap event. You must obey the rules and keep in-step with the Great Spirit. If you get off the trail for any reason, you will be disqualified. But don't lose heart, there's still time to re-qualify. Now, get ready, it's going to be a bumpy race. So, put on the belt of Truth. Slip on your Breastplate of Righteousness and put on your shoes, ready to deliver the Gospel of Peace. Take up your Shields of Faith and the Helmet of Salvation. And most importantly, under no circumstances, *and I mean it*, are you to do anything without first praying in the Spirit. Are there any questions?"

"I have..." said a creature standing in the middle.

"Good, then:

"Let's get ready to Thunder...!"

Trax looked over at Rammer, Rammer looked over at Tank, and Tank looked over at Petra. He raised his eyebrows a couple of times and smiled. Petra looked back to the front waiting for the horn. He raised his eyes a couple of times and wondered if that was something you were supposed to do before the race. If it was, he sure didn't feel any different. Oh well, he thought. He looked over to the guy standing next to him. He raised his eyes two times and smiled. The beast, which was smiling, dropped his smile and snarled back. Petra swallowed and looked back to the front.

"Hey preacher boy," spoke a voice from behind.

Petra rolled his eyes to the rear but didn't look back.

"The first shall be last," whispered Mumba in one wattle, a creature with three heads and four legs, and "The last shall be first," he whispered in the other. He raised all six eyes two times, each face smiling grimly. He nudged the crawler standing next to him and laughed.

Petra looked back to the front. He figured he better just concentrate on the race before him.

The old shellback stretched his head out of his shell and raised it high into the air. He signaled the small dragonfly and pointed at Petra. The dragon fly flew over with a small stick in his hand and smacked his feet. Petra jumped back across the line—he wanted to take that stick and... bless him with it... yes... bless him with it.

The dragonfly turned around to fly back. Tank reached his right front leg up and slapped it down the line. It spun around and gawked at Petra. Tank pointed at Petra and snickered under his breath. The dragonfly flew back beside the shellback and spun around—his eyes burned a steady hole right through Petra. He took two fingers and pointed them at his eyes and then pointed them at Petra. Maybe this wasn't the place for him after all, he thought. The race hadn't even started and already three people were out to get him.

"On your mark..."

Everyone leaned forward across the line.

"Get set..."

Mumba stepped on Petra's tail.

AURRRRRRR, the sea horn sounded.

The front line took off. Petra fell flat on his face as Mumba stepped on his head and the crawler ran him over. He popped up from the ground only to be trampled by the rest of the field.

"Bunch of no good, double-crossing, lying, cheating..." what am I saying he thought? He picked himself up and took off, completely disoriented as to what had just happened—"Forgive them Father, for they know not what they do."

The pack closed in around Trax trying to contain him and slow him down. He bounced around in the middle from everyone pushing and shoving him, jockeying for position. Tank ran Trax into the howler twins who returned the favor and knocked him into the lixoars. Rammer, who had been sandwiched at the start, had somehow found himself at the rear with Petra. He looked for an opportunity to pass but couldn't make it pass the tails that swung rowdily in the back.

The pack jumped up and over the first set of jumps. Mumba slammed Tank with one of his heads in mid-air causing him to lose balance and land on his side, tripping several others. Petra cleared the jump and landed right on Tank who was starting to stand up. "I'm sorry, are you ok?" He stopped and helped him back up and then took off.

Tank looked at the others, "Who is that guy? How did he get in this race?" They all shrugged and took off.

The pack cleared the other jumps and approached meteor rock. One of the howler twins jumped on the back of a large thunder beast and ran up its body. He jumped off its head clearing meteor rock, taking the lead. The other twin paced abreast Rammer keeping him close.

Rammer and Trax cleared the rock and started to navigate their way through the pack.

Dust and small pebbles shot high into the air as the pack closed in on Skull Tunnel. The trail was so dry and thick with dirt that it covered the competitors in a dust cloud hiding them from view. Petra maneuvered through the dust cloud, stepping on tails and tripping the lixoars as he passed by. The lixoars rolled along the edge of the trail and quickly recovered. They focused on the howler twins, convinced they had tripped them. Petra was oblivious to his surroundings. He was so happy to be in the race, that he just smiled and waved as he passed several others.

The crawler entered the tunnel and took to the ceiling. Three new members of the lixoar gang waited around the corner and up in an overhang. Mumba entered the tunnel next to the large thunder beast. Spotting a split ahead, he shoved with flank and shoulder running the beast and the rest of the pack down the left side tunnel, while he and those in the rear cut down the right.

The large thunder beast ran into the left-side wall of the tunnel breaking off numerous stalagmites, which littered the tunnel floor peppering the face of the other racers. Three other competitors spilt-off down another tunnel, which wrapped around and then shot them back out with the rest of the pack. Waiting at the merge was the lixoar gang. They pulled a large rope tripping the front two, rolling them back into the pack creating a mass pile up. Rammer and Trax jumped over the fallen debris and shot around the pile.

Mumba, Tank and the lixoars ran through the short-cut tunnel. They rounded the corner and ran into a large web attached from floor to ceiling. They shook hard in the webbing trying to free themselves. Tank tried to free himself but all four limbs where stuck in different directions. Petra rounded the corner, tripped on a rock, and plowed right through the webbing, freeing all captives. Tank hit the ground and landed face to face with Petra. He looked at Petra with disgust. "Why me? Why me?" he yelled, looking upward. He shoved Petra's face in the dirt and then took off.

The crawler emerged first out of the tunnel followed by the howler twins and then by the rest of the pack. They ran down the trail and got in single-file as they approached Shifting Sand Bridge. At the bridge, the crawler spread its legs and crossed in record time. The howler twins jumped from spot to spot carefully recognizing the packed and unpacked soil. Mumba plunged face first into the first sinkhole—Tank ran right over him but then sunk waist-deep in the middle. Mumba grabbed the side and pulled out. He used one leg to test the ground while the others crawled around the sink holes. The large thunder beast thought he was a ragoole. He jumped in the air like he was going to fly across. He landed about a quarter of the way across and fell—his head and tail covered the entire bridge. The rest of the competitors ran across him and the bridge with ease.

Once across the bridge, the pack formed back together. The lixoars, seizing the opportunity, singled out a howler twin for payback from the tripping earlier—which was accidental by Petra in the dust cloud. They waited for the curve and then hit him from the side. The howler skidded off the trail and down the side of the mountain into a patch of green spikes. Mumba, sensing the opportunity, rammed the lixoars trying to send them off the trail as well, but they collided into Tank and regained their balance. They moved behind Mumba who was fast approaching Lava Pit.

The crawler, still in the lead, didn't bother with the rope. About twenty feet back it shot a web of rope to the top beam. Not missing a stride, it swung over Lava Pit and disappeared down the trail. Mumba zoned-in on the rope and jumped. As he did, a lixoars shot from behind and snatched the rope out of mid-air, right before his hand reached it. Mumba planted all fours in the dark red lava mud and struggled to climb out. Rammer reached the rope right before Trax and swung across, jumping off one of Mumba's heads. His other two heads snapped ferociously at Rammer but were sideswiped by Trax.

Petra jumped for the rope and missed. He landed on Mumba's back who was just climbing out of the pit, causing them both to fall back into the mud. Mumba kicked him in the ribs and shot out of the pit. Petra's head popped up out of the pit just as Tank jumped across. His head clipped Tank's feet causing him to tumble over and land on his head on the other side. With his mouth filled with dirt, he shot his eyes back at Petra.

He jumped up, looked at Petra and yelled, "I'm gonna kill you. When this is over, I'm gonna kill you."

Petra innocently shrugged his shoulders and asked, "What? I didn't do anything."

The lixoars reached Rolling Timber Jam just ahead of the howler. When they arrived, the crawler was wobbling all over the place. Its legs couldn't grab on to the rolling logs spinning wildly out of control. Blocked by the crawler, one of the lixoars grabbed a long stick and knocked the crawler off its feet. It rolled upside down off the logs and off the trail. The howler ambushed the lixoars from behind and knocked one of them off the trail and into the crawler, still on its back swinging frantically. The crawler looked over and covered the lixoar in a barrage of webbing, entombing it instantly.

Rammer and Trax reached the jam together. Rammer lowered his body and prepared for his special move, only to discover the logs were rolling in a different direction this year—he struggled to pull out just in time. Trax jumped across the logs using a side-to-side, jump-and-stop motion. Rammer observed and then followed suit. Petra passed the pack and steadied himself for the jam. He stopped at the first log and got ready to jump. Tank, eager for revenge, rammed him from behind, catapulting him up and over the jam. He landed next to Trax and Rammer, raised his eyes twice and smiled. He then jumped in front of them and sped up—he was in second and loving it.

The pack cleared the jam and set their sights on Rammer and

Trax. Rammer and Trax went up and over several hills and then started the descent into Crooked Creek Pass. Up ahead the lixoar and the howler rammed each other in the side. They both entered the turn extremely fast and on the outside edge. The howler knocked the lixoar back inside. The lixoar shot back and hit the howler out of the turn, sending them both tumbling over the side and out of sight.

Petra was now in the lead with Rammer and Trax closing fast. Petra hugged the inside wall but slipped in the turn on the loose gravel. He slid across the path and ran alongside the edge. Rammer and Trax, both hugging the wall, came out of the turn with miner slippage. They caught Petra who was still tiptoeing down the edge, trying not to fall. An apparent gust of wind— Urium—pushed him back on the trail. He fell in behind them and waited to make his move.

People were lined up a mile long down the trail. They roared loudly at the sight of the racers emerging over the first hill. Arms and heads waved back and forth, others jumped up and down. Rammer, Trax, Petra, Tank, Mumba and several others raced up the trail and entered the crowd. Trax pulled ahead as they entered. Petra moved from behind Rammer and took the lead. Tank, gaining momentum in the straightaway, passed them all and shot to the front. Mumba's three heads moved back and forth like a logger sawing a log, he was in the lead and then he wasn't.

It was the closest race in history. Every face in the stands jumped up and shouted at the top of their lungs. Wind from the racers whipped by and twirled people around. Trax jumped back in the lead, then Rammer. Mumba stretched his heads forward for a moment and then Tank cut in front. They could see the finish line.

From the crowd, wearing a bright red shirt and with a deep voice, came a long drawn-out shout. "You've got'em Rammer. You've got'em!" shouted Rooter.

Rammer's heart exploded. Adrenaline rushed through his body propelling him instantly to the front. Rooter threw Jambles up in the air spilling Brumpel Melon slushy and Blossom Berry cotton candy all over the crowd as he yelled, "Drop the hammer, Rammer!"

Rammer raced for the line and was overtaken by Trax who was then overtaken by Tank. Petra slipped passed them all and regained the lead. Petra reached his head out to clip the long red ribbon that stretched across the finish line vigorously rippling in the wind. Tank's horns inched passed his head and Trax' mane inched passed his horns. Rammer's nose inched passed Trax. It was Trax; it was Tank; it was Petra; it was Rammer; the winner is…

And so goes the race of life. I hope you enjoyed *The Redmadafa* and its message of hope, love, and salvation. Although this book does not follow the timelines of the Bible accurately, nor do its characters, its central message of hope, forgiveness, and salvation do. I believe God has a divine purpose for every person on the face of the planet. He created every one of us in his image and he has plans for us to prosper and plans to give us a future so we can all go on to accomplish Great Things.

This is contrary to what many of you were taught in public schools. The theory of evolution—and that is exactly what it is, 'A Theory,'—is now being taught as, 'Fact,' when there is absolutely no proof to any of its claims. The theory of evolution is another lie straight from the mouth of Lucifer himself. He wants you to think you came from nothing, that you are nothing, and will never accomplish anything. Just like the river of fire is opposite of the river of life, so is the theory of evolution, the opposite of what the Bible says about the life God has planned for you.

I am the oldest in my family. I have a sister, a half-brother and a half-sister. My mom was sixteen and my dad seventeen when I was born. They both came from broken homes, homes filled with violence and abuse. They tried to provide for my sister and I but they were young, and were still dealing with their own pain and childhood struggles—after all, they were still children themselves. My parents turned to alcohol (Thunder Juice), as many do at a young age, and things got a lot worse from there.

If you haven't figured it out by now, the character of 'Rammer' tells my story. Rammer is me when I was young and the character of 'Coach' is me now. When I was young, there were many nights that my house was filled with violence. When I turned twenty, my parents divorced and I left home and joined the United States Marine Corps—it was the best decision I ever made. It got me out of an abusive environment and helped me to grow into a man filled with honor, integrity, justice and courage.

At the age of nine I met The Augur—Jesus. At the age of eleven he called me to the ministry. His calling on my life was hard to accept for many years. How could the son of an alcoholic and a drug addict preach a message of hope and love, when I was filled with so much hate and anger? Four years in the Marine Corps and time on my own, allowed God—His Majesty, to slowly take away the bad and wisely usher in the good. He brought people into my life, people like Sharon Reichle, Reverend Thomas and Bonnie Block, people who took me in as a young man and loved on me and showed me the love of Christ that surpasses all understanding. People like Nancy Sheppard, the character of 'Aunt Nanny,' helped me realize that God would never make me love him, he can't; that is the one thing he cannot do. God loved me so much that he gave me the freedom to chose him or reject him—Christians call this *Free Will.*

There have been many others along the way that have influenced me, taught me and loved me even when I did not deserve it. But that is the beauty of love. It keeps no record of wrongs. It does not boast; it is not proud. It always trusts, hopes and perseveres. It truly never fails.

The Redmadafa is taken straight from Ezekiel chapter 17. The year was 1992. I was a young Marine in Camp Lejuene, NC. I was attending a small church and they asked me to be the youth leader. My first Friday night service was a few weeks away and I needed to prepare a topic to speak about. I had never spoken in front of a crowd before and deeply regretted that I agreed to being the youth leader. I struggled for weeks thinking about what I was going to say. It was Wednesday night, two days from my first service, and I had no idea what I was going to speak on. I couldn't sleep, so I began to pray. As I did, I heard his still small voice say, "Get up and I'll show you."

I got up and turned to Ezekiel chapter 15 and read it, along with chapter 16. Nothing. I mean absolutely nothing. I scratched my head and laid back down. I heard him again, "Get up and I'll show you." Reluctantly, I crawled out of bed and opened the Bible back up, this time to chapter 17. As soon as I finished reading it, I grabbed my small notebook and a pen and wrote *The Redmadafa.* It was only five pages then, but I couldn't believe it—he even gave me the name that night. I preached it that Friday night and everyone loved it. I preached it for several years after that, but then put it away and went on with life and ministry.

God called me back to the military in 2005 to serve as a chaplain. In 2010, my family moved to San Diego, California for our next duty station, where we attended City View Assembly of God. Craig Cruz, the Men's Ministry director and Royal Ranger Leader, asked me to be the guest speaker at an upcoming Pow Wow for Royal Rangers, a church adventure club for boys—similar to Boy Scouts but with a spiritual influence. I would be speaking over three days, so I began to study and think about what I would teach. *The Redmadafa* called out to me. I pulled it out, dusted it off and rewrote it; it completely transformed before my eyes.

After that service, I heard His still, small voice once again say, 'It is time." I always knew the day would come when I would write the book. It was a few months later that I sat down and began to write *The Redmadafa*. And do you know what happened, as I began to write the third addition of the story? It completely transformed again. Its central message and passage of scripture stayed the same, but everything else changed. Why?

In 1992, when I first received the story, I was not ready to write a novel. I was still filled with too much hate and anger. I had a small view of myself, life, this world, and God. But over the next 18 years, God transformed me. He took away my hate and anger, and replaced it with love and forgiveness. I sat and listened to hundreds of people in my office, talking about life and the struggles they faced. I saw victory and I saw failure. I saw people trapped in sin, and I saw people climb out of those sins and go on with life and do Great Things. With God's help and the help of His body—The Temple, the Church, I began to understand that life was not all about *me*!

I give all glory and honor to His Majesty for never giving up on me. And that is why I wrote this book. To give you hope. To let you know, that if God can take this old country boy, from the back woods of Des Arc, Arkansas, the son of an alcoholic and drug addict, and use me to the glory of his kingdom to do Great Things, then he can use you too. I've done many things that I am ashamed of. There are a lot of skeletons in my closet. Things I wish I could go back and change, but you know what? If I did, I wouldn't be me. I wouldn't be able to relate to the men and women He sends to my office on a daily basis and help them the way I do.

So, I write to *you* now. Please give him a chance. Please don't think you have to change before you come to him and ask him into your life. His plans for your life far exceed anything you could ever dream or imagine. Come to him now before time comes to an end.

Let me leave you with this: I hear all the time from people that the reason they do not go to church or except Jesus as their personal Lord and Savior, is because the church is full of hypocrites. Yet they go to football games, basketball games, movies, etc… They go everywhere else that is full of them, but they won't go to church. I hope the church is full of hypocrites, because the church is a place for the lost, hurting and imperfect. I'm there and I am far from perfect. Don't listen to that lie, don't pass through that gate. Lucifer is the Father of Lies and the last place he wants you is in church, doing your part for the Kingdom of Christ.

Find a church that believes the Bible is the inerrant (without error) Word of God. Ask Jesus to forgive you of your sins and to come into your life. Get plugged-in, into the Truth, and go out in the world and do Great Things:

GREAT THINGS

At the end of history,
When the Book is closed,
His Majesty will I behold.

And gaze upon His glorious face,
Safe and secure from this dreadful race.

For time recedes, the end has come;
It's time to choose a side—the second Adam.
Look to the East, it's the compass,
Look to the rainbow, it's his promise.

Great Things, I have done,
Through the sacrifice of his Son.
Great Things, even greater,
Yes, you too, said the creator.

Now you've been told what to do,
Now you know his Word is true.
So rise up and take his strong hand,
Let His Spirit lead you, to the promise land.

* * * * * * *

Are you still here? Still wondering who won the race? It was the long shot. He came from out of nowhere at the end and clipped the ribbon beating Trax, Petra, and Rammer in a single bound. It was the long shot. The one everyone had given up on. The Winner…was…is—YOU!

God Bless and go Des Arc. Home of the Mighty Eagles!

CPSIA information can be obtained
at www.ICGtesting.com
Printed in the USA
LVHW081102091118
595692LV00002BA/4/P